Here's What Readers Are Saying about the Christy Miller series...

"I wish I could find the words to tell you what a blessing your books have been! I've learned a lot from Christy's character, and Todd makes me want to wait for a hero! ☺ Please keep writing!"

"Before I finished the first chapter of *Summer Promise* I was hooked. I had always called myself a Christian, but it wasn't until your books that I really knew what it meant to lay down my life to Jesus Christ. You would not believe what a difference God has made in my life already. Thank you!"

"If people ever tell me that being a Christian is boring, I tell them to go read your books! They helped me to start living for God and to look to my Bible for answers to everything."

"I read the Christy Miller books during a really stressful time, and they were like a calm in the storm. I have learned so much from them, too! When Doug told Christy that godliness is beautiful, it was an entirely new concept to me! I will not hesitate in saying these books changed my life."

"My best friend and I have been reading your books since we were twelve years old. We love them! They have brought us closer to the Lord, and we treasure this more than anything in the world."

"I had to read a book for school, and I chose *Summer Promise*. I never knew it would change my life. I've read the series at least six times. I now have a personal relationship with Christ. Thank you for being obedient to God."

"When I was in sixth grade, my mom gave me the first Christy Miller book. These books changed my life! Please don't stop writing until your hand falls off!"

"I'm thirteen years old, and I love your books! All my friends are reading your books, too. We wish they were movies."

"I absolutely love your books. You are my favorite author. After I read the first one, I immediately became a Christian and turned my life over to God. I have struggled some, but your books helped me to stay on track. I thank you from the bottom of my heart for writing them."

"I wanted to thank you for all the books you have written. They have been my joy when things are hard. Every book has been amazing."

Christy Miller

COLLECTION

●●●●● VOLUME 2

SURPRISE ENDINGS

ISLAND DREAMER

A HEART FULL OF HOPE

ROBIN JONES GUNN

Multnomah Books

THE CHRISTY MILLER COLLECTION, VOLUME 2
published by Multnomah Books
A division of Random House, Inc.

© 2006 by Robin's Ink, LLC
International Standard Book Number: 1-59052-585-X

Cover photo by PixelWorks Studios, www.shootpw.com

Compilation of:
Surprise Endings
© 1991, 1998 by Robin's Ink, LLC
Island Dreamer
© 1992, 1999 by Robin's Ink, LLC
A Heart Full of Hope
© 1992, 1999 by Robin's Ink, LLC

"An Apple-Gathering" and "Twice" used in *A Heart Full of Hope* are by Christina Rossetti taken from *The Complete Poems of Christina Rossetti*, volume 1 (Baton Rouge & London: Louisiana State University Press, 1979).

Unless otherwise indicated, Scripture quotations are from:
New American Standard Bible (NASB)
© 1960, 1977 by the Lockman Foundation

Multnomah and its mountain colophon are registered trademarks of Random House Inc.

Printed in the United States of America

For information:
MULTNOMAH BOOKS
12265 ORACLE BOULEVARD, SUITE 200
COLORADO SPRINGS, CO 80921

Library of Congress Cataloging-in-Publication Data
Gunn, Robin Jones, 1955-
  The Christy Miller collection.
    v. cm.
  ISBN 1-59052-585-X
  [1. Friendship--Fiction. 2. Christian life--Fiction.] I. Title.
PZ7.G972Chr 2006
[Fic]--dc22

2005025580

08 09 10—10 9 8 7 6 5

TEEN NOVELS BY ROBIN JONES GUNN

THE CHRISTY MILLER SERIES

Volume 1
Book 1: *Summer Promise*
Book 2: *A Whisper and a Wish*
Book 3: *Yours Forever*

Volume 2
Book 4: *Surprise Endings*
Book 5: *Island Dreamer*
Book 6: *A Heart Full of Hope*

Volume 3
Book 7: *True Friends*
Book 8: *Starry Night*
Book 9: *Seventeen Wishes*

Volume 4
Book 10: *A Time to Cherish*
Book 11: *Sweet Dreams*
Book 12: *A Promise Is Forever*

THE SIERRA JENSEN SERIES

Volume 1
Book 1: *Only You, Sierra*
Book 2: *In Your Dreams*
Book 3: *Don't You Wish*

Volume 2
Book 4: *Close Your Eyes*
Book 5: *Without a Doubt*
Book 6: *With This Ring*

Volume 3
Book 7: *Open Your Heart*
Book 8: *Time Will Tell*
Book 9: *Now Picture This*

Volume 4
Book 10: *Hold On Tight*
Book 11: *Closer Than Ever*
Book 12: *Take My Hand*

BOOK FOUR

surprise Endings

To my parents,
Travis and Barbara Jones,
who encouraged me to be
only what God made me to be—
nothing more, and certainly nothing less.

Dreams for a Price

Oh yeah! We've got the spirit
Oh yeah! That cougar spirit
Say, hey! Get outta our way
Cougars are on the prowl TODAY!

Christy Miller ended the cheer with a long, leggy leap. The other girls watched her land just slightly off balance.

"Good, but try to keep your arms straighter next time," the cheerleading adviser said.

Christy nodded at Mrs. James and tried not to feel self-conscious, even though so many girls were standing around watching her.

"And be sure you stretch out after practice today." Mrs. James turned her attention to the next girl in line.

Stepping away from the critical stares of the varsity cheerleaders, Christy took a deep breath and silently mouthed the cheer. Keeping her arms straight, she began going through the motions again.

It seemed to Christy that the first few days of practice hadn't been very hard or very competitive. Now that it was getting closer to tryouts, fewer girls were showing up every day. And the ones who did show up were, in Christy's opinion, all much better at jumps than she'd ever be.

"Give it a rest, Miller!" one of the varsity girls said, coming in her direction. It was Renee, a junior with short dark hair and eyes like a raven.

Christy tried to ignore Renee and finished the cheer with a solid jump.

"Give it up. You're not cheerleader material, and you know it. Besides, you're only a sophomore."

"Sophomores can try out like anyone else," Christy said quietly, lifting her damp nutmeg brown hair off the nape of her neck. She shaded her blue-green eyes from the afternoon sun and tilted her head. "Tryouts are only two weeks away, Renee. And I'm not going to drop out."

Christy meant the statement to sound firm and threatening, but it affected Renee as much as a harmless kitten batting at a thread.

"You only made it this far because of Rick Doyle." Renee flung the words at Christy. Two of her friends now stood beside her. "So don't look so innocent. We know what's going on between you and Rick."

"Between me and Rick?" Christy couldn't stand the way the three girls were staring at her. She wasn't sure what Renee was trying to prove. "Rick and I are just friends."

"Oh, right. Friends. Buddies. That explains why the most popular guy in school hangs out with a little sophomore who thinks she's going to be next year's star cheerleader."

Christy felt her heart pounding and her throat swelling. *Why is Renee all over me like this?*

"Come on, Renee," said one of the other girls, who

walked over toward Christy. "Leave her alone. It's not Christy's fault Rick turned you down."

Renee spun around. "Who asked for your opinion, Teresa?"

"It's Teri. Only my grandmother calls me Teresa. 'Teresa Angelina Raquel Moreno,'" Teri mimicked in a high-pitched voice with a heavy Spanish accent. "But you're not my grandmother, Renee. So you can call me Teri, like the rest of my friends."

Christy admired Teri's friendly spunk. She obviously wasn't threatened by Renee. Christy wished she could appear as confident as Teri. But then Teri was a junior like Renee, so that had to count for something.

Renee turned to glare at Christy with a hard, pinched expression. "You're not good enough, Miller. Okay? You're not good enough to be a cheerleader, and you're definitely not good enough for Rick Doyle." Renee turned with a flashy cheerleading swish and marched off the field with her two friends beside her.

"What was that all about?" Christy asked Teri. Her hands were shaking. "What did I ever do to her?"

"It's not you." Teri wrapped her long, wavy brown hair up in a knot and tried to secure it with a scrunchie. "She's mad at Rick, and she's just taking it out on you. Don't let her get to you. You're doing great, Christy. By the time try-outs get here, you'll be ready. Don't worry."

But Christy did worry. She worried all the way home. As soon as she was in the front door, the first thing she did was call her closest friend, Katie, to tell her about the incident.

"Oh come on, Christy," Katie said in her bubbly, self-assured voice. "You know what Renee's problem is. It's

Rick. She likes Rick. Didn't you know that? Everybody knows that."

"Katie, almost all the girls at Kelley High like Rick. He and I are good friends. You know that."

"Sure I do. But Renee doesn't. She thinks he's taking you to the prom."

"The prom? Why in the world would she think that? My parents would never let me go to the prom. You know how strict they are."

"Well, get this," Katie said. "I heard that Renee asked Rick to the prom, and he turned her down."

"You're kidding! Why?"

"That's what she's so upset about. He didn't give her a reason, but from what she heard from one of his friends, Renee thought he was taking you."

"No way! He'd never ask me. He could choose from a dozen girls, all seniors. Besides, I think a senior guy should take a senior girl. I mean, it's their last year of high school and everything."

"Christy, get a clue! He wants to take you. The problem is, he thinks you won't go with him since you're not supposed to date until you're sixteen."

Christy twisted the phone cord around her finger. "But Katie, I'm the kind of girl Rick teases and calls when he's bored. I'm not the popular rah-rah type he'd take to the prom. He's probably waiting to find out who's got the best chance of winning prom queen. That's who he'll take."

"Wake up, girl! Don't you see what's happening? Rick is turning you into the rah-rah prom-queen type. You're like putty in his hands. He's making you into the perfect girl-friend."

"Katie, that has to be the most ridiculous thing you've ever said!"

"Ridiculous or not, it's the truth."

A frustrating silence hung between them.

"I didn't mean to hurt your feelings," Katie said, all the fire doused from her voice. "But if you don't think I'm right, then just ask yourself to honestly answer one question." Katie paused.

"Yes?" Christy knew that although Katie often went overboard with her exuberance, she also could be right sometimes.

"Ask yourself, *Would I have tried out for cheerleading if Rick hadn't talked me into it and gone with me to practice the first day?*"

"Yes," Christy answered immediately. "I would've gone on my own."

"Don't answer me. Answer yourself. Honestly. And if you're honest, I think you'll see what I'm saying. Rick has more control in your life than you realize."

For at least twenty minutes after they hung up, Christy remained sitting on the hallway floor with her back against one wall and her stocking feet against the other, searching her heart for an honest answer to Katie's question.

The tricky part was, Christy had always wanted to be a cheerleader. She had thought about it a lot when tryouts were announced. But maybe Katie had a point. Deep down, Christy wasn't sure if she ever would have worked up the nerve to try out if Rick hadn't coaxed her into going to the first practice.

However, Todd had a lot to do with it too. If Katie wanted to talk about Todd's influence on Christy, well, that was another story. She would gladly admit that Todd had a unique way of challenging her and directing her decisions. He had ever since the day they met on the beach last summer. She remembered looking up into the screaming silver-blue eyes of this tall, blond surfer and thinking how he fit her description of the perfect guy. Then she got to know him, and Todd became an important part of her life. He strongly influenced her when it came to things that mattered in her heart.

Even though Todd lived two hours away, when it came right down to it, if she had to define their relationship, she would consider Todd much closer to one day being her boyfriend than Rick. Christy and Todd saw each other only a couple times a month, but Todd was in her heart. Forever. Nothing could ever change that. And what mattered to Todd mattered deeply to Christy.

She tugged at her socks, cuffing them and uncuffing them, remembering when she had scrunched in the hallway last week, the night before the first cheerleading practice, and talked on the phone with Todd for an hour. Christy had told him all about how she was thinking of going out for cheerleading and eagerly waited for his opinion and encouragement.

But all Todd had said was, "I think if you're going to do it, you should do it for the Lord."

"You mean I should pray about it?" Christy asked.

"That's part of it. But you need to think about how you can take some risks on your campus. If you become a cheerleader, you'll have an audience."

"An audience?"

"There will be lots of people who suddenly know who you are, and they'll watch your life a lot more closely. You

can't just blend in with the crowd anymore. Being a cheerleader might put you in a good position to let people know
who you really are and what your life is all about."

"I hadn't thought about that."

"Being up front can be good. It kind of forces you to
take a stand for what you believe."

Christy had taken Todd's words to heart, and that night
she had written in her diary:

> *God, I want to do this cheerleading thing for You. I know Todd's
> right. If I become a cheerleader, people will look up to me and
> respect me. That will give me a better chance to tell them that I'm a
> Christian and maybe to invite them to church with me or something.
> I just want whatever is best, and I want to be a good example to
> others.*

In thinking through the whole situation now, Christy
felt certain that even if Rick hadn't walked her to practice
that first day, she still would have gone. Her heart was set on
doing this, and just as Todd had advised, she would do it for
all the right reasons.

"Christy," her mom called from the kitchen, "are you
off the phone yet? Dinner is ready. You need to come set
the table."

"Coming!" Christy left her cheerleading thoughts
huddled in the hallway as she went into the kitchen. Her mom
had made stew, which wasn't her favorite dinner. Mom's stew
generally consisted of whatever leftovers had been in the
refrigerator long enough to be unappealing if eaten by themselves. They were all dumped into the Crock-Pot in the
morning and left to simmer all day until they became "stew."

Venturing a sniff of the concoction, Christy had to admit it smelled good. She teased her mom, saying, "Spices are your friends, aren't they?"

"What?"

"You know how to put in just the right seasonings to make even leftovers smell as though you started fresh."

Mom gave Christy a puzzled look.

"Never mind." She realized what she was saying was not exactly a compliment and would be better left unexplained.

Her mother stepped in to make a familiar point. "We need to be thankful we have food on the table, Christy. It may not be fancy, but we've never gone hungry, and we should be grateful for that."

"I know," Christy said quietly. She pulled the silverware from the drawer and began setting four places at the kitchen table. The last thing she wanted to be reminded of tonight was how tight money had been since her family moved to California from Wisconsin. Or how all of them needed to work harder to stay on their budget.

At dinner, Christy's nine-year-old brother, David, monopolized the conversation. Christy and her mom and dad all listened patiently as David reenacted, with considerable exaggeration, his teacher's facial expression when she found gum on her shoe.

He was kind of funny, for a little brother. But Christy would never tell him that. It would only encourage his goofiness.

As soon as David excused himself from the table, Mom leaned over, and a sweet smile spread over her lips. Christy knew that look. Her mother was trying to create an encouraging environment. Christy also knew that her mother was about to say something Christy probably wouldn't be glad to hear.

"Dad and I have gone over the paper you brought home from the cheerleading adviser, and we've decided that the only way for this to work is if you find a way to come up with half of the money."

"Half!" Christy squawked. "That's more than three hundred dollars!"

"Well," Dad said slowly in his deep, authoritative voice, "is this something you want to do? Are you willing to commit yourself to the practices and the games?"

"Yes." Christy tried hard to hold back the tears that pressed against the corners of her eyelids.

"Your mother and I think it's a worthwhile goal. It's also a big commitment. And an expensive one. We feel you should share a part of that responsibility by participating in the financial responsibility."

Christy wanted to say, "But you don't understand! There's more to this than me fulfilling my goal. Can't you see that? This is something I need to do so I can take a stand on my campus." But as usual, Christy couldn't make the really powerful words come out, and all she said was, "How am I going to come up with that much money?"

"You have to understand, Christy, that this expense isn't in our budget. But we're willing to find a way for it to work out for you if you're willing to come up with your half. You could babysit this summer," Mom suggested.

"Get a position during the weekdays with someone who has small children. Perhaps you could advertise in the toddler Sunday school class you've been helping out with the last few weeks. You could let some of the parents know you're available."

"Babysit? This summer?" This wasn't a good time to mention to her parents that she had been planning to stay in Newport Beach all summer with Uncle Bob and Aunt Marti, just like last summer. Christy already had a long list of plans for things she and Todd would do. She hadn't even considered the possibility of staying home in Escondido all summer—especially to babysit.

"You decide how you want to come up with the money," Dad said. "If you're serious about cheerleading, we're with you 100 percent, and we'll find a way to come up with half the cost. But you've got to put in your share too. It's time you learned there are no free rides."

"I definitely want to do it. I mean, I want to at least try out and see what happens," Christy said.

Mom sat back in her chair. "Before you give such a firm answer, why don't you think about it some more. In the meantime, do you have much homework tonight?"

"Tons."

"I'll do the dishes, then," her mom said. "You can do them tomorrow night. You'd better get at your homework."

In the sanctuary of her room, Christy found it impossible to concentrate on her "tons" of homework. She went over to her dresser and picked up the San Francisco music box her aunt had bought her on their trip there last summer.

Winding the brass key on the bottom, Christy set it back on the dresser and watched the ceramic cable car move up the little hill as it played "I Left My Heart in San Francisco."

Wish I knew where I left my heart. It certainly doesn't seem to be where it's supposed to be tonight, Christy thought. *I feel pulled in so many directions.*

She was convinced that becoming a cheerleader ranked as an important dream at this point in her life. It was a worthy goal. Weren't adults always telling her to set goals? She believed being a cheerleader would be something she could always look back on and say, "I did it! I worked hard, and I accomplished my goal." Plus, she would be able to take a stand for what she believed, as Todd had said.

But she never dreamed she would have to come up with half the money. And babysitting all summer was practically the last thing Christy wanted to do with her precious free time.

It seemed there were so many obstacles to her trying out for cheerleading. The incident with Renee had been discouraging enough. Now she had the money part of it to struggle with too. She never guessed it would be so hard.

Do I want to be a cheerleader badly enough to really work for it? With a determined twist of the knob, Christy wound up the music box once more. Effortlessly, the little cable car took its free ride to the top of the glassy hill.

2

Rah-Rah Girls
Don't Quit

Decision-making had never been Christy's strong point, and she knew it. For three days now, she had wavered on whether to try out for cheerleading. Her legs ached from all the jumps at practice, and Renee had continued to take every opportunity to remind her that she was "lower" than the rest of the group.

Every day Christy told herself it wasn't worth it and she should skip practice. Yet every day she went, halfheartedly hanging in there, anxious for a good enough reason to stay, willing to accept a respectable reason to give up.

At lunch on Thursday she looked for Rick. He had been a great encouragement when he walked her to practice that first day. Then he'd done one of his famous disappearing acts and ignored Christy. Or maybe he was avoiding her. Whatever it was, she decided it was time to get his opinion.

When she found him clustered with his usual batch of senior friends, Christy boldly approached the group. Rick spotted her, smiled, and called out, "Hey, Rah-Rah!"

Christy gave him a look she hoped communicated that he was embarrassing her and she wanted him to leave the group to talk to her. Rick read her expression amazingly well and stepped away from the group.

"Don't tell me," he said, towering over Christy, warming her with his chocolate brown eyes and teasing her with his half smile. "You flunked your algebra quiz."

"No," Christy said softly, "the quiz is tomorrow. It's something else."

"It's your parents, right? They want to move to Romania because housing is cheaper."

Christy let out a puff of a laugh. "No, Rick. It's something I'm trying to decide."

Swarms of students passed them on both sides, making it a noisy, confusing spot to carry on a conversation.

"Well, the answer is red."

"What?"

"If you're trying to decide what your best color is, it's red. You look great in red."

Christy stared up at him without responding. *This is pointless. Why did I think he would be serious long enough to offer any help in this situation?*

"Never mind," she said and started to walk away.

Just then the bell rang.

"Wait a minute!" Rick caught up to her and grabbed her by the elbow.

Christy looked at him, but she couldn't decide what to say. She wasn't mad at him, just confused, and his joking had made her dilemma seem trivial. She tried to think of a way to phrase her question: *Rick, do you really, truly think I should try out for cheerleading?* It sounded stupid and phony. She couldn't think of how to rephrase it so that it sounded like a real problem.

"I'll meet you here after school, okay?" Rick let go of her arm and waited for an answer.

"It's really nothing."

"Just be here." Rick walked backward and pointed to the spot where they had been standing. "After school." Then he turned and sprinted toward the science building.

Christy turned abruptly. She ran into a guy who was heading for the garbage can with a handful of trash.

"Whoa, look out!" he said.

Too late. A carton of fruit punch splattered across Christy's arm, staining her white T-shirt with a huge red splotch.

"Sorry," the guy said, then hurried on.

Christy felt like crying when she realized she'd have to go to the restroom to clean herself up, and then she'd be late for class. As if things weren't bad enough, Christy heard Renee's snippy voice behind her saying, "It's your color, Christy. You look great in red."

Christy turned to face Renee, but Renee kept walking, her back to Christy, as if she hadn't said anything.

The tears came, hot and fast, streaming down Christy's cheeks. *That's it! That does it! I can't take any more of Renee. I'm not going to try out. Not now, not ever. Never! It's not worth it.*

That was exactly what she would tell Rick too. He wouldn't have to help her make a decision because she'd just made it once and for all.

Christy's blazing emotions stayed red hot until after school. With her jaw set, her walk brisk, Christy plowed through the maze of picnic tables, ready to give Rick the news. He stood there waiting for her—cool, tall, confident, oblivious to all the turmoil Christy had suffered that afternoon.

"How's my favorite Rah-Rah?" he called out.

"I am not a Rah-Rah, and I wish you wouldn't call me that!"

"You're going to be." Rick smoothed back his wavy brown hair and shifted his books to his other arm. "Legs like yours, you can't miss."

Christy gave him her best disgusted look and slugged him in the arm. Rick started to laugh.

"What's so funny?" she asked defensively.

"You. You crack me up!"

That was it! With as much determination in her steps as she'd had when she first approached Rick, Christy bolted in the opposite direction.

"Wait a minute. Stop!" Rick hollered, coming after her.

Christy didn't stop.

Rick did. He stood still and said loudly and firmly, "I thought we weren't playing this game anymore. You know, the one where you run away and I chase after you?"

Christy stopped, but she didn't turn around.

"Come here." Rick came alongside her and pulled her over to a low brick wall. He put his books down, took Christy's books and put them down, then waited for her to sit on the wall.

Rick sat next to her and in a deep voice said, "Now, will you tell me what's going on?"

"It's nothing. Really." She felt so immature. *Why am I so emotional about all this? Why did I start to run away from him again like that?*

"Christy, come on! Don't you remember how weird things were between us after Christmas vacation?"

Christy nodded.

"And remember that long talk we had? The one where

we decided 'no more games'? That's what you said. 'No more hiding and running away.' So what's going on?" Rick folded his arms across his broad chest.

Christy looked down, blinking to hold back the tears. "I'm sorry, Rick. It's this whole cheerleading thing."

"And…" Rick prodded.

"Renee's right. I'm not cheerleading material. I'm not going to try out."

"Yeah you are," Rick said firmly.

Christy didn't look up. "Even if I made it, my parents say I have to come up with half the money. How am I going to do that?"

"You'll find a way."

"It's not worth it."

"Yes, it is."

They sat silently for a minute while Christy blinked back a runaway tear.

Rick's voice turned smooth and persuasive. "If there's one thing I know about you, Christy Miller, you're not a quitter. You're better than any of those girls, and you know it. You can't let Renee get to you; she's trying to make you mad enough to quit. Don't let her. You have to give it your best shot. You have to try. Promise me you'll try."

Christy looked up, clear-eyed, her mouth easing into a promising smile. "All right, Rick. I'll try."

"Oh man," he said, shaking his head at her. "If you only knew how you did that!"

"Did what?"

"It's your eyes. You have killer eyes, Christy. You have this way of looking at a guy with those killer eyes of yours, and you don't have any idea what you do to him."

Christy felt the blood rushing up her neck and racing to her cheeks. Then with a little more boldness than she usually had with Rick, she said softly, "Well, you have a way of using just the right words and making a girl feel like Play-Doh."

"Like Play-Doh?"

"You know. All soft and mushy."

"Well, Killer-Eyes, that's exactly what you do to a guy when you give him that innocence-and-bliss look."

Christy playfully batted her eyelashes and in a Scarlett O'Hara voice said, "You mean like this, Rick?"

"Nope." Rick's expression remained serious. "That's what makes it a killer. You don't even know how you do it. It's just you. It's your innocence. Not many girls at this school still have that."

They looked at each other, and Christy felt warmed, energetic, and more encouraged than she had in days.

"You'd better get going," Rick said. "You're going to be late for practice."

"Thanks, Rick," Christy said, impulsively swinging her arm around his neck and giving him a buddy hug. Rick looped his arm around her shoulders and returned the gesture.

Christy spotted Renee a few feet away, glaring at them. So Christy purposely held on to Rick even after he began to let go.

He then put both his arms around Christy and, just to be funny, acted as though he were going to tip her off the wall. But he held on to her and pulled her back up. They both laughed, and Christy noticed out of the corner of her eye that Renee was gone.

At practice, Christy gave it all she had, her enthusiasm making up for her lack of experience. Every time she glanced at Renee, she received flaming, snarly glares. If their adviser hadn't been there, it looked like Renee might have charged Christy and scratched out her eyes.

It didn't matter. She was going to give it her best shot. She wasn't a quitter. She had made her decision, and there was no turning back now.

3

Hopeful Romantics

Christy could barely read her two chapters of history homework. Her mind was flooded with cheerleading thoughts. Mentally she ran through all the moves of the routine she planned to do for tryouts next Friday. She pictured herself in the blue and gold skirt and sweater the school had promised to all the girls who tried out. The adviser said all the girls should be dressed the same so the judges wouldn't be influenced by appearances.

Christy put down her history book and cleared a space on her bedroom floor. Facing the mirror on her closet door, she quietly went through the routine, making sure her smile was its biggest and brightest.

She had told herself a dozen times before and now coached herself again to give it her best. What she lacked in coordination she could make up for with enthusiasm. After all, she had killer eyes, right?

With one hand on her hip and the other arm jutting up into the air, her fist tight, Christy froze her position before the mirror and critically examined her eyes, her smile, her stance. She liked what she saw. Taking one more vibrant leap into the air, she imagined she was jumping for the judges.

"Christy?" Her mom tapped on the bedroom door then opened it slowly. "Are you still bouncing around? It's after ten o'clock, and your father is already asleep."

"Sorry," Christy said softly.

"Did you finish your homework?"

"Not exactly."

"Christy, you've had plenty of time to do it. I don't like the way this cheerleading is taking you away from your studies. If your grades suffer, you'll not be allowed to go out for cheerleading. Do you understand?"

"Yes."

"All right, then. Get ready for bed, and I'll wake you up when Dad leaves for the dairy in the morning. You can finish your homework then."

Being awakened at five-thirty in the morning to read history should be some kind of punishment for criminals Christy decided the next morning. She could barely keep her eyes open at the kitchen table. The textbook lay beside her bowl of cereal like a dried-up old mummy.

"History is so boring," she moaned to her mom, who poured a cup of coffee and joined her.

"It wasn't to the people who lived it," Mom said.

"Why do we have to study it now? What does it matter?"

Mom's round face looked fully awake, and Christy thought it must be from all the years they had lived on the farm and her mom got up before dawn. She was definitely a morning person.

"The thing about history," Mom said, "is that we should try to learn from other people's choices, good and bad.

Then we as a nation and as a people should try to make bet-ter choices, based on what we know."

"Huh?"

"I don't think you're awake yet, are you, Christy?"

With a huge yawn, she said, "I want to go back to bed."

"Why don't you shower and get dressed? Then you'll be more alert. Have you done all your algebra?"

"Almost."

"I'm serious when I say your grades mustn't suffer because of this cheerleading business."

"I know, I know. I'm going to take a shower. Is my red sweater clean?"

"Your red sweater? It's going to be warm like yesterday," Mom predicted. "It'll be too hot for a sweater."

Christy rose and ambled from the table. "Do I have anything else that's red?"

"Why?"

"Oh, never mind. I'll find something to wear."

It took twenty minutes, but Christy finally decided on a dress she hadn't worn in a long time. It was a summery cot-ton dress that badly needed ironing after being scrunched up in the closet for so long.

If her mom proved right and it was another warm May day, Christy thought she would look fresh and stylish, like the rich girls at her school. They seldom wore the same thing twice and had a variety of accessories to match every-thing in their wardrobes.

Christy pulled her hair back and worked at brushing her teeth an extra long time. With a wide cheesy grin in the mirror, she examined her work and thought her teeth looked okay. Her hair looked pretty good today too.

Amazing! How often does this happen?

"Christy?" called Mom from the hallway.

Christy was working to apply mascara on her bottom lashes without leaving skid marks.

"You need to leave in about five minutes."

"Five minutes?!" Christy jammed the mascara wand back into its holder. "I didn't finish my homework!"

"What have you been doing all this time?"

"I took a shower and did my hair, and then I had to iron my dress..." She opened the bathroom door, displaying the finished product.

"Goodness!" Mom exclaimed. "You look as though you're going to church or something."

Just then the phone rang, and David answered it. Christy could hear him say, "Hey, dude! When are you going to take me skateboarding again? Huh? Yeah, she's still here."

Christy dashed to the phone. She knew it had to be Todd. Snatching the receiver away from David, her voice came out as light and pretty as she felt. "Good morning!"

"Hey, how's it going?" Todd's easygoing voice made her feel as it always did: full of anticipation for when she would see him again.

"Do you have to work this weekend?" Christy asked.

"Tomorrow I do. I thought I'd come down to see you tonight, if that's okay with you and your family."

"Of course! You know you're always welcome. What time do you think you'll get here? I'm sure you can have dinner with us."

"Five-thirty okay?"

"Sure."

"Cool. I'll see you then. Later."

"Bye, Todd. Have a wonderful day!"

But Todd had already hung up. He always hung up first. And Christy would always hold the phone, listening to the dial tone, letting her imagination fill in the blanks, since Todd's phone conversations were usually short and to the point.

Christy's parents adored Todd. Her brother idolized him. Once when Todd had come down on a Saturday, he had spent several hours skateboarding with David and then helped Dad paint the living room. After dinner when he started to wash dishes, Christy picked up a dish towel and joined him, realizing this might be the only time she would get to spend alone with him.

That's when she realized that with Todd, there would probably never be such a thing as the two of them "going out." Their time together would be with her family and with their friends, and it would be just as much fun as if the two of them went somewhere alone. It felt so natural to Christy that she was amazed when one of her friends at school had said that she and her boyfriend had been going out for three months and he hadn't met her parents yet.

"Mom," Christy called out, "Todd's coming for dinner tonight, all right?"

"He is? What time?"

"Five-thirty. Is that okay?"

"All right!" shouted David. "Is he bringing his skateboard?"

"I didn't ask him, but David, don't beg him to spend all his time with you when he gets here, okay?"

David smirked and marched past Christy, snatching his lunch sack off the table.

"Mo-om!" Christy groaned. "Would you tell David not to bug Todd like he always does?"

"I do not!"

"Yes, you do!"

"All right, that's enough." Mom stepped between them. "You're both going to be late for school."

"Mom?" Christy asked, oblivious to her need to get going. "I was wondering something." She paused. "If, well, do you think Dad would let me go to the prom with Todd, I mean, if he asked me? Since this is his senior year and everything?"

"Oh, Christy! How can you ask me something like that when you're supposed to be walking out the door?"

"Do you think Dad might make an exception if it was Todd?"

"I'm not even going to try to answer that. We'll have to talk about it. Now get going, both of you!"

During first-period history, Christy thought about going to the prom with Todd. Getting a new dress. Having her hair done. It made her feel like Cinderella.

The more she thought about it, the more it seemed like a practical dream—one that needed to come true. After all, this was Todd's senior year, and she was about the closest thing he'd ever had to a girlfriend.

She laid her right arm across her open history book and moved her wrist back and forth slightly. Her gold ID bracelet caught little slivers of light, shimmering with promise. Christy ran her finger over the engraved word *Forever*. She had felt it many, many times since Todd had given it to her last New Year's Eve, and she knew its touch by heart.

You don't realize how good you have it, Christy told herself. She had Rick as a good buddy at school and church. And she had Todd. She would always have Todd. She just knew it.

We have to go to the prom! It's one of those "forever" memories that a couple like us should have, she thought.

The bell rang and history was over, with an assignment of two more chapters to read over the weekend. Christy grabbed her books and hurried to meet Katie at her locker, their usual meeting place.

"Cute outfit!" Katie said, her bright green eyes scanning Christy's outfit. "What's the big occasion?"

"Katie, do I look like a girl who is about to be asked to the prom?"

"Oh, I get it. You figure if you look the part, your fairy godmother will be able to spot you in the vast sea of us hopeful romantics, all wishing to be asked to the prom," Katie said with a dramatic twist of her wrist in the air and a swish of her copper-colored hair. "She'll pick you out of the lot of us and make your wish come true because you look as though you deserve it."

Christy laughed quietly and looked around, hoping nobody had seen Katie's performance. "A girl can dream, can't she?"

"What about the minor detail of your parents?"

"That's the part I'm being extra hopeful about. I asked my mom this morning, and she didn't exactly say no. I mean, I know he would have to ask me first, but I told her since it's his senior year and everything—"

The shrill bell interrupted Christy, so she finished with, "It doesn't hurt to set high goals, now does it?"

Katie laughed and bubbled with her usual enthusiasm.

"Wouldn't that be great! If your mom didn't say no, then she's probably getting ready to say yes. That's how my parents are. I'm sure your mom will say yes. And when she does, I'll ask Lance to go with me."

Christy looked wide-eyed at her friend. "Do you think he'd go with you? What am I saying? Of course Lance would go with you. Do it, Katie! Ask him!"

"First you find out if you're going," Katie said.

The halls began to clear.

"Yikes!" Katie squeaked. "We're going to be late. I'll call you after school. I hope you do great on the algebra quiz!"

Oh no! I forgot all about the quiz! Christy thought in a panic.

All during her next class, Christy crammed for algebra. But it was no use. Her mind was too full of prom dreams to let anything else in. The quiz was impossible, and she knew she missed at least half the problems.

Christy tried to ignore the sour feeling in her stomach as she recalled her mom saying, "Your grades mustn't suffer because of this cheerleading business!"

4

Under the Flower Trellis

"Next Friday," Mrs. James, the cheerleading adviser, said, "you need to be here right after school to dress for tryouts. Tryouts will be in the gym beginning at three-thirty. Any questions?"

"Yes." Renee stepped close to Christy and mumbled under her breath, "What do we have to do to keep Christy from coming?"

"What was that?" Mrs. James asked.

"Oh, I just was saying how fast tryouts are coming," Renee said.

Christy clenched her teeth and swallowed hard. This daily harassment was eating a hole inside her. *What have I ever done to you, Renee? Why are you so mean to me? It's not fair, and I won't let you treat me like this any longer!*

Christy determined that she would beat Renee in the tryouts. She would show her and the others that she had the strength and ability to beat them all. It was the only way she could think of that would allow her to get back at Renee.

The girls ran through the routines with mechanical precision, and Christy gave it all she had. By next Friday she would be cheerleading material, and she would prove to Renee that she deserved to be on the squad.

Christy began to take on the same determination about the prom. She would find a way to talk her dad into letting her go. If she tried hard enough, she could find a way—she just knew it.

That anticipation and determination made Christy feel more excited than usual about seeing Todd that night. Her heart brimmed with expectations. She directed some of her nervous energy into showering and fixing her hair and makeup with extra attention.

Her mom had been right about the weather; it had been a warm spring day. Christy carefully scrutinized her wardrobe. She had only five minutes before Todd was supposed to arrive, not that he was ever on time.

He tended to be pretty casual about everything. He usually wore shorts—even in the winter. He would probably have shorts on tonight.

Christy decided on capri pants with her favorite red knit sweater.

Rick thinks I look good in red. Does Todd think the same thing?

She pushed up the sleeves and took one last look at herself in her bedroom mirror before scooping up her ID bracelet from the dresser and fastening it securely.

"You smell good," Mom said as Christy cheerfully set the table for five. "What is that perfume?"

"Midnight Gardenia. Remember, I got it for Christmas? I'm almost out." Then she thought but didn't add, *I've been saving the last few squirts for when I see Todd. He told me once when I had it on that I smelled exotic.*

"Do you think Todd likes lasagna?" Mom asked. "I've never served it when he was here."

"I'm sure he does. You know how he always says the worst part about living with his dad is that he lives on microwave dinners. Besides, Todd likes whatever you make."

Christy thought it funny that even her mom wanted to please Todd. He had a way of making people feel like doing nice things for him.

As an only child whose divorced dad traveled all the time, Todd impressed adults as being more responsible and independent than most seventeen-year-olds. Without trying to, he also seemed to make adults want to lend him a helping hand, just because he was such a "nice young man," as Aunt Marti would say.

"Oh, someone called while you were in the shower. David took the message." Mom slipped on a pot holder and slid a cookie sheet full of garlic bread into the oven.

"Who was it?"

"I don't know. Ask David. He's out front."

Christy stepped out onto the front porch and yelled for her brother, who was nowhere in sight. She caught a whiff of tiny white jasmine blossoms climbing up the trellis by the porch and remembered how awful this rental house had looked when they moved in last September. The only thing on its barren porch then had been a smashed clay pot. Mom had done amazing things with hanging and potted plants, and Dad had built a trellis archway at the front steps.

The jasmine seemed to be twisting its way up the trellis a few inches more each day. She thought of how romantic it would be one starry night this summer for Todd to escort her up those steps and kiss her good night under the fragrant canopy.

"David!" she called. What if it was Todd calling to say he would be late? "David!"

"What?" He appeared from around the side of the house with one of the neighborhood kittens in his arms.

"Who called? Mom said you took a message."

"It was that guy."

"What guy?" Christy asked impatiently.

David dangled a long blade of grass above the kitten as it eagerly batted at it. "I wish Dad would let me keep this one."

"David! Who called? Todd?"

"No, that other guy."

"Rick?"

"I guess."

"David! What did he say?"

"I'd call her Boots if I could keep her, 'cause see?—she has white on her feet."

In one swift motion, Christy glared into her brother's face, grabbed him by the shoulders, and in a stern, controlled voice said, "What did Rick say?"

"I dunno. I told him you couldn't talk because you were grounded."

"I was grounded!" She dug her fingers into his shoulder. "Why did you tell him that?"

"Oww!" David jerked away from her grip and edged a few steps back, holding the kitten in tight defense. "What was I supposed to tell him? That you were in the shower? That's gross!"

Christy stared at her brother in disbelief. Sucking in a deep breath to compose herself, she stated, "Why don't you try telling the truth next time? Honesty is the best policy. Don't they teach kids these things in third grade anymore?"

David scrunched up his face in his hamster look as his glasses slid down his nose. Her comments seemed to be beyond his understanding.

Feeling pleased with her self-control, Christy calmly said, "Okay? Do you understand? Next time, you tell the truth. Got it?"

Whether David "got it" or not didn't matter at the moment. The kitten decided to make a fast getaway and scratched David's arm in its exit.

"Come back, Boots!" David yelped, running after the tiny flash of fur.

Christy stayed out front on the porch a few more minutes, enjoying the evening breeze and watching for Todd's familiar VW bus. Plucking a jasmine blossom from the vine, she twirled it between her thumb and forefinger, drawing in its wild, sweet fragrance.

Should I call Rick back? she thought idly. *He probably wanted to make sure I went to practice after his pep talk. I don't want to be on the phone with Rick when Todd comes though. Tonight belongs to Todd. Todd, where are you?*

Todd, unpredictable Todd, arrived more than a half hour late. The family had given up waiting for him and sat down to dried-out garlic bread and mushy lasagna. Then they all recognized the familiar sound of Gus the Bus chugging to a halt in front of the house.

"I told you if we started to eat he would show up," David said proudly, jumping out of his chair and opening the screen door wide in an eager welcome. "Did you bring your skateboard?"

"Not this time, dude."

It happened again. It always happened. Whenever Christy heard Todd's easygoing deep voice, something inside her stirred. The sensation was the same feeling she had on a hot summer day when she dove into a sparkling pool and felt that immediate, exhilarating splash of cool water. It took her breath away.

"Smells great in here! Italian?" Todd's six-foot frame entered the room, his sandy-blond hair windblown, his silver-blue eyes scanning the dinner table. He had on shorts, as Christy had predicted, and a white T-shirt with a volleyball logo on the pocket. In his arms he held a bright yellow produce box.

"What's in there?" David strained to see into the flat box.

"Strawberries. You know that fruit stand off Highway 76? They were closing up for the day, but I talked them into selling me their last flat."

Christy could believe it. Todd could talk anybody into anything.

"Check 'em out." He held up a strawberry as large as a small plum. "Vista is the only place I know where the strawberries grow like this. Sweet too. Try one, dude."

David willingly shoved the entire strawberry into his mouth and gave a muffled "Mmmm-mmm!"

"How thoughtful of you, Todd." Mom rose and took the flat from him. "Please sit down. I'm sorry we started without you."

"Hey, no problem. I'm just glad David saved some for me." Todd grinned at David, who returned a huge beaming smile of admiration to his hero.

Todd sat next to Christy, and she asked him, "Why did you go through Vista?"

"Tried to beat some of the traffic. I picked the wrong time of day to head south on the 5 freeway. How are you, sir?" Todd stretched out his hand to greet Christy's dad with a handshake.

"Fine. You'd better dig in there and get yourself some dinner."

Dig in he did. Christy had never seen anyone eat so much at one sitting. More than once Todd said, "You're a great cook, Mrs. Miller. This lasagna is incredible!"

Mom loved the compliments, of course, and it made Christy feel even more secure about how much her parents liked Todd. She knew for certain that things would work out and she and Todd would go to his prom. There was no way her dad would say no.

Mom rinsed off several baskets of strawberries and served the fruit in bowls with puffs of whipped cream from the dairy where Dad worked. As Todd promised, the straw-berries tasted sweet and fresh; they seemed to vanish in minutes.

Whenever Todd joined in one of their family meals, it always made the conversation more lively, and they always sat around the table longer. It didn't matter what they were talking about. Sometimes Todd had stories about what had happened during the week. Sometimes David tried to be the center of attention, and everyone let him because Todd didn't seem to be bugged by David at all.

A few times Christy had held all of their gazes as she told about her week. Each time she did, her mom would say, "I didn't know that," or, "You didn't tell me. When did that happen?" It always made Christy feel as though she'd hurt her mom's feelings for not confiding these bits of information the moment they occurred. It was as if she'd been holding out or trying to keep a secret from her parents. And she wasn't.

The truth was, most of the time the incidents weren't that important or that memorable. It was just that when Todd started talking around the table, it always made her think of other things to talk about.

Tonight Todd was giving a rundown of how Gus the Bus had sprung a leak in one of his hoses earlier in the week and how complicated it had been to find the right size replacement hose.

They chatted until David got bored with talk of car repair and excused himself from the table. Christy got up and began to clear the table. As much as she enjoyed sitting around talking like this, she was eager to be alone with Todd so they could talk about a few certain topics that were more interesting than leaky hoses.

Todd stood to help her clear the dishes, as he often did, and suddenly he said, "I was wondering, Mr. and Mrs. Miller, if you would mind if I took Christy someplace."

Christy stopped midstep into the kitchen and held her breath. *He's going to ask me to the prom like this? In front of everyone, with my hands full of dirty dishes? Todd!*

Mom flashed a look at her husband and then back at Todd. "What did you have in mind?"

"I wondered if we could go out for some ice cream or something. It's a great night for a walk. Is there any place close?"

Christy released her breath and lowered the dishes into

the sink. *How romantic! He's going to take me out for a walk and ask me to the prom. Under the jasmine! I'll get him to ask me under the jasmine.* Her mind raced ahead, her hopes soaring.

"I'm going too!" David jumped up from the couch in the living room.

"No, you're not!" Christy snapped. "I mean, you proba-bly should stay home. Shouldn't he, Mom?"

Everyone looked at her. Christy realized she'd overre-acted. There was no doubt from anyone in this room that she wanted to be alone with Todd. She felt like they had all read her deepest, most secret wishes as easily as if they had been written on her face in fluorescent letters. Mom looked at Dad. He paused.

"Please?" David pleaded. "Can I go too?"

"It's all right with me," Todd offered, standing between the kitchen and the table like a net over which passed a vol-ley of looks between Christy and her mom, Christy and her dad, David and Dad. Todd held the empty lasagna pan in his hands, and in that moment Christy wanted to rub his face in the smeared tomato sauce.

How can you say it's okay for David to come with us? she thought angrily. *Todd, work with me here. I'm trying to get some time for just us.*

"I think," Dad said slowly, "that you need to stay around here, David."

"Aw—" David began in protest. Before he could say any-thing else, Dad gave him a look that silenced his complaining.

Now Christy was afraid that her dad was going to say no to her as well and that she'd have to try to be more mature than David and hide her disappointment in front of her dad and especially in front of Todd.

But Christy's dad surprised her. "Christy, you and Todd can go over to Swenson's at the Vineyard, but I'd like you home before dark. Nine o'clock at the latest."

"Thanks, Dad." Christy tried not to sound too exuberant. She was sure her face showed her relief and delight, so she turned away from Todd so he wouldn't see her cheeks turn rosy.

Usually when Todd came to see her, they did stuff around the house. Todd seemed more like one of the family. This was good though. Very good. If Christy's dad didn't mind their going for a walk and for ice cream, then he probably wouldn't object to their going to the prom. Perhaps her dad realized something of which Christy was becoming more and more sure: She and Todd were ready to move forward in their relationship.

Todd stepped over to the sink and began to rinse off the dishes.

"I'll do those," Mom insisted. "You two get going. You only have an hour or so."

"Great dinner." Todd gave her a broad smile. "Thanks."

"You're welcome, Todd. You're always welcome. You know that. And thank you for the strawberries."

"Hey, dude," Todd called to David, who had flopped back on the couch, arms folded across his chest, glasses falling down, pouting like an expert. "You and I can do something together next time."

"When?" David stuck his lower lip out even farther.

"Next time I come down."

"Can you come next weekend?" David looked up hopefully. "Can you come on Saturday? And can you come for the whole day?"

"Naw, can't come next Saturday."

"Why not?"

"It's my school prom that night."

David resumed his pouting, but Christy's heart stopped. *There, he said it! The prom is next Saturday. He's going to ask me tonight, I just know it!* But then Christy's thoughts swung sharply to the other side. *Next Saturday? That doesn't give me much time! Tryouts are Friday! When am I going to have time to get a dress and everything? Why didn't he ask me sooner?*

"Ready?" Todd broke into Christy's teeter-totter thoughts.

"Oh yeah. Sure."

For the first time that night, Todd's gaze fully met hers. He kept looking at her a bit longer than necessary, and Christy wondered, *Am I doing it? Am I giving Todd a killer-eyes look like Rick said? Does he feel for me what I feel for him?*

"We'll be back by eight-thirty or nine," Todd called over his shoulder as he held the door open for Christy. "Later, dude!"

The screen door slammed behind them, and they heard David whine, "It's not fair!"

Todd and Christy smiled at each other and headed down the front steps and under the arch of climbing jasmine.

An Enchanted Evening

Some spring evenings can be enchanted. Especially when the birds sing a little longer, and the colors of the sky pale into ethereal shades. When the wind snatches fresh blossoms from the trees, festively tossing them into the air like confetti, it's clear that it's a night for celebrating. Tonight was such an evening.

Not enchanted in a magical way, but in Christy's awareness that everything around her breathed with evidence of a living God. A God who thought up daffodils and the scent of grass and transparent rainbows in lawn sprinklers. A God who knew and cared about the hidden, treasured dreams of a young woman's heart.

Adding to the enchantment was the comfortable silence between Christy and Todd as they walked the first block. It was usually this way with Todd. He would often be quiet for a long while and then say something deep and wonderful. His conversations tended to be thought-out and deliberate. Christy could talk on and on when she wanted to, but by nature she was more reserved and quiet too.

One of the things she'd always liked about Todd was that he never made her feel uncomfortable because of her quietness during moments like this. Christy wondered now what he was thinking. Should she reach over and take his hand? She let her arm dangle close to his, hoping he would notice and mesh his fingers with hers.

"Did I tell you that I'm being discipled?" Todd said. "By a guy at church."

"What do you mean by *discipled?*" Christy asked, moving a smidgen closer as they walked on.

"Well, we meet once a week and study the Bible together and help each other memorize verses," Todd explained. "You want to hear my verses?" He looked eager and excited, like a little boy who had something to recite for class.

"Sure."

"It's 1 Corinthians 13. It's called the love chapter," Todd said.

Then without Christy's expecting it, he reached over and took her hand. She closed her eyes for just a moment, determined to mark this moment in her memory very clearly so she could write about it in her diary that night. She couldn't imagine anything more romantic in the whole world than holding hands with Todd on an enchanted spring evening, listening to him recite what God had to say about love.

Todd began. "'If I speak with the tongues of men and of angels, but do not have love, I have become a noisy gong or a clanging cymbal. And if I have the gift of prophecy, and know all mysteries and all knowledge; and if I have all faith, so as to remove mountains, but do not have love, I am nothing. And if I give all my possessions to feed the poor, and if I deliver my body to be burned, but do not have love, it profits me nothing.'"

He paused and Christy thought, *This doesn't sound very romantic.*

Todd went on. "'Love is patient, love is kind, and is not jealous; love does not brag and is not arrogant, does not act unbecomingly; it does not seek its own, is not provoked, does not take into account a wrong suffered, does not rejoice in unrighteousness, but rejoices with the truth; bears all things, believes all things, hopes all things, endures all things.'"

He paused again and said, "That's all I know so far, but there are more verses."

Now it was Christy's turn to ponder her words before responding. The verses weren't anything like she thought they would be. The only part she really caught on to was at the end about "hopes all things" and "endures all things." Those were qualities she felt she had become well acquainted with lately in cheerleading.

"Did it take you long to memorize all that?" Christy finally asked.

"We've been working on it a few weeks now. I'm not a very fast memorizer."

"I'm not a very good memorizer either."

"It helps me to write it out on cards and carry them around with me," Todd explained. "I worked on it while I was driving down here. That's probably why it's still pretty fresh on my mind."

"You did a really good job." Christy liked praising him. She loved being beside him like this.

Todd squeezed her hand. "Hey, do you know where we're going?"

"We turn down the next street, and it's about three blocks after that."

"What a great night!" Todd said, filling his lungs with the evening air. "Smells almost…tropical, exotic."

"Could be my perfume." She lifted up her wrist to his nose so he could smell it.

"Yeah! What is that?"

Christy told him, and he said, "Reminds me of Hawaii. You ever been there?"

She felt like saying, "Oh, sure! When would I have ever gone to Hawaii?" but she settled for, "No, but I'd love to go someday."

"My dad and I lived there for a couple years."

"You're kidding! I never knew that."

"Yeah, I went to King Kamehameha III Elementary School in Lahaina."

"Where?" Christy laughed at the mouthful of names.

"It's on Maui. I loved walking to school because of all the plumeria trees. They smell like your perfume. I'm going back there this summer."

Christy stopped walking. Their arms went taut in the sudden space between them. "You are? This summer?"

Todd smiled at her reaction. "Yeah, or next summer. I'm not totally sure yet."

They resumed their walk, and Christy fired a string of questions at him. "What are you going to do there? What about school in the fall? Where are you going to college? Don't you need to work this summer?" Her mind added, *And what about me?*

"Man," Todd said playfully, "you sound like my mother. Are you sure you don't want to ask if I put on clean socks this morning?"

"I'm sorry. I'm surprised, that's all," Christy said with a

smile pressing the surprise out of her expression. "I just thought you'd be at the beach all summer, you know, like last year."

Todd shrugged. "Might be. I don't know yet."

Christy held his hand a little tighter and kept her feelings to herself the rest of the way to Swenson's. The deep-down truth surfaced over and over again: *He's not yours to hold on to.*

She deliberately ignored the thought. Enchanted evenings are to be enjoyed, not analyzed. Besides, there had been plenty of other times when she and Todd had been alone and Christy had spent the whole time brooding and missed the adventure of being with him. Tonight she was determined not to let her mood overwhelm her and take her deep inside herself, away from Todd.

To keep the conversation going, Christy said, "So, tell me about Hawaii. What did you like about it? Where did you live?"

Todd talked about the simple life he and his dad experienced living on Maui and how the two of them were together all the time. He almost made it sound like an ideal childhood, which surprised Christy, since she'd often felt sorry for Todd because his parents divorced when he was very young and he didn't have any brothers or sisters. Todd didn't seem to have any regrets.

Christy loved listening to him tell about his childhood and was a little disappointed when they arrived at the ice cream parlor. When he let go of her hand to open the door and then didn't take it again once they were inside, Christy was really disappointed that their walk had come to an end.

"Know what you want?" Todd asked, reviewing the list of flavors above the ice cream counter.

Her instant mental response was, *Yes! You! I want you to be my boyfriend and take me to your prom. And spend the summer with me on the beach. That's what I want!*

"Umm, I'd like a scoop of Swiss Orange Chip in a bowl, not a cone."

The girl behind the counter went to Christy's school, but Christy didn't know her name.

Todd smiled at her and gave his usual greeting, "Hey, how's it going?"

The girl responded with straightforward flirting. Christy couldn't believe it. As if Christy wasn't even there, this girl started asking Todd his name and why she hadn't seen him before. She suggested that if he came back at closing time, she would give him free ice cream.

Todd stood like a rock, seemingly unaffected by this pushy girl.

Christy swelled with jealousy. *How dare she act like that? Can't she see Todd is with me? Who does she think she is?*

"Hey, thanks," Todd said when she handed him his change.

The girl grabbed Todd's hand. "Remember, next time come at closing, and you won't have to pay for it."

Christy couldn't stand the sight of that girl's hand touching the strong hand that had warmed Christy's only moments earlier. She wanted to leave—to get out of here and go back to their walk, hand in hand. She wanted to have Todd all to herself, even if for only an hour.

But Todd wanted to stay. He directed Christy over to an open booth against the back wall. They ate in silence for a few minutes, Christy scooping up tiny spoonfuls and slowly letting them dissolve in her mouth. Todd had a shake, and when she had calmed down enough to focus on him, it reminded her of their very first "date" at an ice cream parlor in Newport Beach.

"Do you remember the first time we had ice cream together?" Christy asked in a soft voice.

"When was that?" Todd said.

Christy felt her emotions scrambling to be strong and secure. How could it be such a strong memory for her and something he needed to be reminded of? "Remember? Last summer after Shawn's party."

Todd's face clouded, and she realized Todd was being overwhelmed with another more powerful memory. That was the night his friend Shawn died.

"Oh yeah," Todd said slowly.

Now Christy was the one who had brought a somber mood to their time together, and she knew Todd might retreat deep into himself the way she sometimes did. She quickly changed the subject. "So, how's the end of your senior year going? Are you getting excited about graduation and everything?"

The "everything" meant the prom, but Christy didn't want to come right out and say it.

"I've got only a few more weeks left. My mom called the other night and said she would fly out for my graduation, so that's pretty cool."

"That's great," Christy answered brightly. "I imagine it will be nice for you to spend some time with your mom."

Todd nodded.

Out of the corner of her eye, Christy saw the door open, and the familiar bouncy blur of Katie entered. Katie spotted Christy and zipped over to their booth, immediately sliding in next to her without even noticing Todd.

"I can't believe you're here! This is so perfect! You'll never guess what happened? He said yes, Christy! Can you believe it? Lance said he'd go with me! You should have heard my mom. You'd think I'd won a gold medal or something!"

Christy looked at Todd and then at Katie and said quickly, "That's great! Katie, this is Todd; Todd, this is Katie."

"Oh!" Katie noticed Todd for the first time, and her eyebrows rose. "Oh! Todd? *That* Todd. The Todd! Hi! I thought you were David. I mean, not that you were David, but that Christy had come here with her brother because who else would she come with? I mean, besides you?"

Todd responded with his typical chin-up nod and said, "How's it going?"

"Katie goes to my school," Christy said, feeling a little embarrassed at her friend's loud enthusiasm. "We go to church together too. I've told you about Katie."

Todd nodded.

"And she's told me a lot about you, Todd," Katie said, wide-eyed. "But what are you doing here tonight?"

"Katie!" Christy laughed nervously at her friend's lack of tact. "I told you Todd was coming tonight for dinner."

"No, you didn't." Katie seemed to catch a look in Christy's expression that caused her to take her voice down a notch.

With a big smile at Todd, Katie said, "Nice to meet you, Todd. Really. I kind of feel as though I already sort of know you because of all the stuff Christy has, you know, told me about you guys. Not that she's told me any of the really private, personal stuff. But you know, all the good stuff about you, and I think you're really great. I mean, according to what Christy has told me."

Katie caught her breath, then turning to Christy she flashed her green eyes and said between her teeth, "I thought you were grounded."

Christy's expression asked, *What?*

Katie moved closer to Christy. She casually put her hand to her cheek in order to hide her mouth and spoke in a strained whisper. "That's what Rick said. Everyone went to the movies, and he said—"

"Excuse me," Todd said, getting out of the booth. "I'm going to get some water. You two want anything?"

"No." Katie turned to face Todd with a bright smile.

"No thanks," Christy responded calmly, but everything inside her felt like exploding.

They both smiled pasted-on smiles and waited until Todd walked out of earshot. Then as if a starting gun had fired, they took off talking, fast and furious.

"My dumb brother told Rick I was grounded when he called today. But it's not true."

"That's Todd?"

"Yes."

"Christy! He's…"

"I know. He is."

"But he can't be here now. You guys have to leave."

"Why?" Christy asked, checking over Katie's head to see if the flirty girl at the counter was trying to capture Todd's attention again.

"Rick thinks you're going to ask him to the prom!"

"Rick? Why?"

"Because I told him you were."

"Katie!"

"This morning you said you were."

"I did not!"

"Yes, you did! At the lockers. You said you asked your mom since it was his senior year and everything…"

Christy squeezed her eyes shut and let her head fall forward.

"Katie!" It came out like a muffled scream. "I was talking about Todd. Todd's prom at his school. Not going to our school prom with Rick."

"Uh-oh." Katie moaned, leaning back in the booth. "I told Rick you were going to ask him, and that's why I asked Lance, so the four of us could go together."

Christy lifted her head and stared at her friend in disbelief.

Katie ignored Christy's glare and perked up as if a brilliant scheme had just hatched over her head. "Wait! It'll work! You can go to both proms! With both of them. You could even wear the same dress. Nobody would know!"

"Katie, they're on the same night. And my parents would never go for that. You know that. If I had a choice of even going to a prom—any prom—I'd go with Todd."

"I don't blame you. I mean, you told me he was cute, but *cute* isn't the word. He's, well…he's…"

"I know," Christy said, calm returning to her voice. "He's not like any other guy you've ever met, right?"

"Exactly." Suddenly, Katie's expression went starkly sober. "Oh noooooo!"

Christy followed Katie's line of sight, and her heart stopped. Through the glass door, she spotted a group from her school, ready to enter the ice cream shop. And leading the group was Rick Doyle.

6

Inside, Outside

The small ice cream parlor exploded with male laughter as the guys pushed the door open. Christy and Katie watched silently, frozen next to each other like two ice cream bars in the take-home case.

Rick faced the guys behind him, keeping them laughing with his nonstop jokes. Rick didn't even see Todd right in front of him, balancing a cup of water in his hand.

Christy clenched her teeth and watched the whole fiasco as if it were a well-rehearsed act. Rick's arm barely tagged Todd's cup, but on impact Rick spun with trained reflexes and used his right arm to block whatever it was that had just touched him. Todd, perfectly balanced as if standing on his surfboard, took the toppling of his water cup without flinching, then curved his back and tucked in his chin just in time to avoid contact with Rick's reflex-driven arm.

Katie gasped, and Christy grabbed her arm.

"Oh, man!" Katie wheezed. "Did you see that?"

Christy couldn't talk. This couldn't be happening.

"Whoa! Sorry!" Rick said, but he didn't sound as if he was. He sounded more like he was embarrassed.

The other guys walked past Rick and Todd, and one of

them laughed and said, "Surf's up, dude!"

Todd good-naturedly gave him a chin-up, it's-cool gesture.

Rick snorted an embarrassed laugh then brushed past Todd. He quickly scanned the room, probably concerned to see who had noticed. Immediately he spotted Katie and Christy. A strange, almost angry look spread over his face, and Rick plowed right over to their table.

"Thought you were on restriction," he said, as though he had a right to be mad at Christy for being there.

"No, I...it...my little brother lied. I'm not."

Rick nodded slowly, like he was trying to decide if he believed her or not. "I called you tonight."

"That's what I found out." Christy's gaze went past Rick to Todd, where he stood at the counter getting another cup of water.

The girl behind the counter had dashed to the other side to bring Todd a towel. She eagerly helped Todd dry off his shirt. Christy couldn't hear what she was saying, but she could clearly see Todd's face, so calm, so willing to let this pushy girl make a fuss over him. *How dare she! How could he?*

"Katie, would you mind letting me talk to Christy alone for a minute?" Rick said.

Katie looked to Christy for an answer, but Christy gave her a blank response. She still couldn't believe this was all happening.

"Sure," Katie said slowly, sliding out of the booth.

Christy felt like grabbing her and saying, "Don't leave me, Katie! Not now! Get back here!"

Rick's long legs bumped the table as he seated himself next to Christy. "So." He turned to her and gave her his usual half smile. "Katie tells me your parents agreed to release you from the rule that you have to be sixteen before you can date."

"Well, um...ah..." Christy could hardly think. The most awkward thing in the world was just about to happen. Todd was coming back to the booth.

"Katie explained it to me," Rick said confidently, one arm across the top of the booth, the other arm resting on the table. He moved closer to Christy. "Since it's the prom and my senior year and all...and Lance said his dad would pay for a limo for the four of us."

Christy wanted to disappear. She wanted to absolutely vanish.

Todd now stood before them. His expression was a mixture of questioning and confidence, with a pinch of hurt puppy around the eyes. Christy knew that if she gave Todd only the slightest shake of her head, he would walk away and let her have a private conversation with this guy he didn't know who had just made himself at home in their booth.

But Christy didn't want Todd to leave her alone. And she certainly didn't want him to go back and strike up another conversation with Little Miss Overly Helpful at the counter.

With her gaze held steady on Todd, Christy tried to find some kind of calming smile deep inside. She pulled it out, pasted it on her still-numb face, and quickly said, "Hi, Todd. This is Rick. Rick, this is Todd."

Rick abruptly turned and looked at Todd. "Yeah, we met. Bumped into each other earlier."

"Hey, how's it going?" Todd casually slid into the seat across from Rick and Christy, apparently certain that he wasn't interrupting anything important.

Rick stared at Todd, as if expecting him to leave them alone. When Todd didn't move, Christy could see by Rick's expression that he slowly was realizing that Todd and Christy were together and that he was the outsider. Rick pushed himself out of the booth with the same strong, swift motion an athlete would use to do calisthenics.

"I'll see you at church Sunday," Christy said. It was all she could think of at that moment, since Rick's awkward invitation to the prom had been cut off. She hoped with all her might that he wouldn't say anything more about it here or now. Her noncommittal sentence would say something to both guys. To Rick it would say, "I want to talk to you some more." To Todd it would say, "This is just a guy from church. No big deal."

The two guys exchanged a few "cool" phrases, and Rick walked away. He didn't look back at Christy or acknowledge her statement about church on Sunday. The way he was act- ing it would never appear to Todd that he had been sitting there, trying to invite Christy to the prom. She decided that was good because it wouldn't make things uneasy now with Todd.

Yet it also made her wonder if Rick would just as soon forget the invitation as well. Last Christmas, Christy and Rick had hit an uncomfortable bump in their newly grow- ing relationship. He kissed her in the church parking lot—twice—and Christy had pulled away. The rest of that night Rick ignored her. It was several weeks before they started talking again, and when they did it was like they were starting all over again, like nothing had happened. Neither Rick nor Christy had mentioned the kiss, nor had they kissed again. It was one of those memories Christy buried deep inside since she didn't know what to do with it.

Now the memory was back, sparked by the way Rick was once again ignoring her. He strode across the room and blended in with his group of buddies, pulling a chair up to their table.

Christy still felt as though her heart hadn't begun to beat again.

"I'll call you tomorrow, Christy," Katie said, instantly appearing at their table, giving her a look that said a whole lot more than the five words that came out of her lips. "It was really great to meet you, Todd!" Katie patted him on the shoulder. "I hope to see you again sometime."

Todd smiled and said something about Katie coming up to Newport Beach with Christy someday. She didn't hear the exact words.

She was trying to casually glance over her shoulder. To her surprise, she caught Rick staring at her. He wasn't ignoring her as she'd expected, and he didn't look away when she looked at him.

Neither did she.

Rick gave her a strange look. Was he furious or hurt or jealous? Maybe he was trying to express with his face how deeply he cared about Christy. She couldn't tell. She had never seen that look on him before. And the strangest part was that he wasn't ignoring her as he had in the past. It was all very unsettling.

And what is my face telling him right now? Does he still think I have killer eyes?

Katie gently punched Christy in the arm and said, "And don't forget our little angels in the nursery Sunday." She explained to Todd, "Christy talked me into volunteering to help with the toddler Sunday school class."

"Wait a minute," Christy said, trying hard to pull her full attention back to their booth before either Katie or Todd noticed she'd been staring at Rick. "If I remember correctly, you were the one who talked *me* into it."

"Whatever," Katie said.

"I'll be there. Don't worry." Christy tried to flash a confident smile at Katie, but she could tell that her friend was reading her like a billboard.

"I'm going," Katie said. "I'll call you tomorrow."

Christy nodded. It was nice to have a friend who could recognize the agony she was in at this moment. Katie exited, saying good-bye to the people from school who'd entered with Rick. They all knew her and waved as she left.

"I guess we probably should get going too," Todd said.

Christy wished there was a way to get out without having to go past Rick. But there was only one door, and Rick and his friends were between them and that door.

Todd led the way, winding through the thin trail between the tables and heading for the door. Christy purposely tugged on the bottom of her sweater and smoothed the back of her capris. Anything to appear preoccupied so she wouldn't have to make eye contact with Rick. She could almost feel him watching her leave with Todd.

What must Rick be thinking right now?

Todd opened the door for Christy. An overly eager high-pitched voice from behind the counter called out, "Good-bye, Todd. Don't forget!"

Todd turned slightly to give a chin-up to the girl behind the counter.

"Don't forget what?" Christy asked. The question gave her the opportunity to look back at Todd and then glance over his shoulder at Rick.

Rick was talking with the guys at his table, leaning over as if telling them a secret. He wasn't watching Christy at all. For some crazy reason, that made her mad. Never mind the fact that she'd been doing the same thing and ignoring him. It just didn't seem right for a guy to ask her to the prom and then ten minutes later ignore her.

"She was reminding me about the free ice cream." Todd seemed so casual about the whole encounter with that irritating girl.

They were only a half a block from the ice cream shop when Christy decided to speak her mind. "Don't guys hate it when girls throw themselves all over them like that?"

"I guess," Todd said with a shrug. He had his hands in his pockets and didn't appear ready to hold hands with Christy at all.

"Todd, she's such a flirt!"

"Some girls are."

"But Todd," Christy argued, picking up steam, "she was so obnoxious in there. And did you see how much makeup she had on? What a cake-face."

Todd abruptly stopped walking. They were standing in front of a Mexican restaurant. Pulling his hands from his pockets, he lifted Christy's chin with his right hand and shot his piercing silver-blue gaze into her eyes. In a voice that shook her and melted her at the same time, he said, "Chris, I want to tell you something, and I don't want you ever to forget it."

His touch on her upturned chin felt gentle yet firm and

decisive. All her confused thoughts began to drain through invisible holes in the bottoms of her feet. All that mattered at this moment was Todd and what he was about to say to her.

"God made her face."

Christy blinked and tried to take in the meaning.

"God made her, Chris. God made her face. It hurts me when someone makes fun of something God made."

He let go, but Christy remained frozen in place, trying to put his words together with a returning rush of her emotions.

Then as if adding a PS to his statement, he said, "Don't you see? People look on the outside, but God looks at the heart."

It shook her. All the way to her core, it shook her. *How does Todd do that to me? Is he mad at me for what I said?*

They started to walk again, side by side, without any words between them. Once they were out of the shopping center and on the quiet tree-lined street, Christy bravely reached over and looped her arm in his.

"I'm sorry," she whispered.

Todd took her hand and squeezed it. She felt warm and secure, and all the eager anticipation of this being an enchanted evening returned. It wasn't over yet. They could still stand beneath the jasmine. He could still ask her to the prom.

"Don't ever get too proud to say that to somebody, Christy."

"That I'm sorry?"

"Yeah. Only people with soft hearts say they're sorry. And soft hearts are the only kind of hearts that God can hold in His hand and mold."

"Todd..." Christy drew herself closer to him. She spoke in a delicate, sincere voice. "I honestly don't know what I'd be like if God hadn't brought you into my life. You are like nobody else I've ever known. You will never know how much you mean to me."

Then something she hadn't planned on happened. Her eyes welled with tears that couldn't be held back, and without warning a throaty gasp escaped.

Todd stopped walking and put his arm around her. Gladly burying her face into his chest, Christy sobbed a few more tears then started to laugh. Pulling away, she looked up at a startled Todd.

"Your shirt's already wet, mister." She wiped her damp cheek. "There's no room for my tears."

They both laughed as Christy dried her eyes. Hand in hand, they continued the walk home.

What a stupid little outburst! Why am I so emotional tonight? What is it with all these feelings for Todd and all the confusing feelings I still have for Rick? Am I losing my sanity, or is it normal to be so easily overwhelmed when it comes to guys? Especially guys that I really care about. And how do I know how either of these guys really feels about me? I mean, do their thoughts and feelings about me change as quickly?

Then a reassuring thought overtook her: *Todd is just as comfortable with my tears as he is with my laughter.*

She wanted to tell him that, to try again to somehow express her deepest feelings for him. But if she tried, she felt certain she would start to cry all over again.

"I like holding your hand." Christy hadn't planned to say it, but it seemed the most natural comment at the moment. Everything inside her could go on feeling like a broken-up jigsaw puzzle as long as Todd kept his strong, warm hand wrapped around hers. She could work on putting the puzzle together later, when she was alone. Right now she wanted to be with Todd and not off in the Land of If Only, with all her perplexing thoughts.

"You know what?" Todd said. "I like holding your hand too. I was just thinking what soft hands you have."

Christy gave Todd's hand a squeeze, and they walked on in silence, the pastel sky giving way to dusk.

7

Jasmine and Other Poisonous Flowers

About a block from Christy's house, Todd said, "I need to be at work by six-thirty tomorrow morning. I should leave as soon as we get back to your house. Hope it's okay if I don't come in."

"Sure. Thanks for the ice cream, and sorry about the tears and everything."

"No need to apologize for your tears, Christy. You know that." He smiled an easygoing Todd smile, and Christy smiled back.

Inside, Christy was beginning to feel a rising wave of nervousness now that they were almost to her front door. If he was going to ask her to his prom, it would be in the next few minutes. That's when she noticed that Todd's hand felt suddenly moist and clammy. *Could he be nervous about asking me to the prom? It's not like him to be nervous, but I guess there's always a first time.*

Then Christy wondered if maybe it was really *her* hand that had turned sweaty when she started thinking about the prom again. She willed her emotions to remain calm—to hang in there just a few more minutes. The last thing she wanted to do was go into another one of her emotional outbursts in their last few minutes together.

They were in front of her house, slowly shuffling up the sidewalk together, when Christy stopped precisely under the arched trellis. She picked off a white blossom of the night-blooming jasmine and twirled it beneath her nose.

"Mmmmm. You must love jasmine too," Christy said.

"What?" Todd snapped, looking shocked.

She had never seen him look so startled. Christy laughed at his reaction.

"The jasmine," she said, waving the tiny flower in front of him. "It has a sweet, tropical smell, like those trees you said you liked that grow in Hawaii. By the school you went to."

"Oh, right! The plumeria trees. Yeah, this smells good too. I like the way it's climbing up this thing," he said, admiring the trellis. "It'll be cool when it's covered with..." He paused and said the word as though it were enchanted: "jasmine."

"I know," Christy said dreamily. "Won't it be gorgeous?"

Todd let go of Christy's hand and sat on the top step. He cleared his throat. "You know how I told David that next Saturday is prom night?"

"Yes." *This is it! He's going to ask me. Here under the trellis, exactly as I dreamed! This is so perfect!*

"I wanted to talk to you about it, but funny thing is, I wasn't sure how to say it." Todd leaned back on his elbows and looked up at Christy.

She felt giddy but tried to look calm as she seated herself next to him on the step. "Just say it, Todd."

"Okay."

Christy waited. She smiled sweetly at Todd, encouraging him to open his heart to her and say the words she was waiting to hear.

"I'm taking a girl from school."

Christy immediately bit the inside of her mouth on both sides to keep from screaming. Her smile remained exactly the way it was before Todd had said the words that shattered her whole world.

"I knew you'd understand and everything, but, I don't know... I guess sometimes girls get their feelings hurt over nothing." Todd tilted his head and waited for her to respond.

She had drawn blood inside her mouth. She could taste it. Quickly swallowing, Christy exercised all the control she could find and asked the first thing that came to mind. "Is it anyone I know?"

"No. I just met her a few weeks ago."

A few weeks ago? And you picked her over me? I can't believe this!

"You'd like her a lot. She's been a Christian longer than I have, and she's unbelievably strong in her walk with the Lord."

Inside, Christy felt as if she'd been shattered into a million pieces, the way a fine china plate would shatter if someone smashed it with a sledgehammer. But she kept smiling.

"It's pretty incredible that she's so tight with God after all she's been through. She was in a car accident last summer. Spent three months in the hospital. She's in a wheelchair. Probably will be the rest of her life."

Pity and envy collided inside Christy. Envy was the stronger of the two. *So what? Am I supposed to feel sorry for her? Is that what you feel, Todd? Pity? Or does she mean more to you than I do? How could you possibly want to take someone in a wheelchair to a dance? Why, oh why, do you want to take her instead of me?*

With her last pinch of stability, she ventured another question to hide her pain. "What's her name?"

Absolutely the most horrible, devastating moment of Christy's evening arrived when Todd's lips curled into a contented smile, his dimple showing on the right cheek. With a faraway look in his eyes, he answered, "Jasmine. Her name is Jasmine."

Christy jumped to her feet, ready to fight. But who was she fighting? She felt as if an invisible monster had punched her in the stomach, forcing all the air from her. No words came. Her frozen arms didn't know which way to return a swinging punch.

Todd stood too. "I knew you'd understand. Hey, let me know how your cheerleading tryouts go on Friday. I'll be praying for you." He gave her a brotherly hug and a quick kiss on the cheek.

Don't pray for me! Don't do anything for me! Leave me alone, Todd. Get out of my life and don't ever come back! Christy felt like her heart might explode.

Todd waved and then hopped into the front seat of his van. As Christy stood alone under the jasmine-covered trellis, Todd took off down the street in noisy old Gus.

Numbly, Christy made her way through the front door and past her parents, managing to mutter a few sentences about being tired. At last she stepped into her room and pressed the door closed, sealing herself in her private tomb.

She fell on the bed, grabbed Winnie the Pooh, and silently sobbed into his furry yellow body. When she came up for air, she realized that this was the stuffed animal Todd had bought her last summer at Disneyland. With a ferocious throw, Christy catapulted poor Pooh across her room, where he landed on a mound of dirty clothes.

Sitting up, still trembling and sniffling, Christy grabbed her pillow and hugged it close, wiping her tears on the pink-flowered pillowcase.

"He doesn't care about me. He never has. It's all a big lie, and I believed it," she told her soggy pillow. "He doesn't care about what's important to me or what really matters! No matter how much I want him to, it won't change anything. He doesn't love me at all!"

Bubbling to the top of her emotions' cauldron came an ugly truth. Christy didn't know if she was talking about God or Todd. Which one didn't care? Which one had stopped loving her? Both? Either? The two had been so closely intertwined in her life up to this point that it seemed difficult to think of one without thinking of the other.

"Okay," she coached herself calmly, "figure this out. You can do it. Come on. It's going to be okay. It's going to work out. It always does."

A wild burst of anguish pushed its way out of her throat, and she quickly pressed her mouth into the pillow and sobbed.

When the tremor passed, Christy decided not to think about it anymore. She would go to bed, and she would choose to let all her feelings die. It was the only way for them to stop controlling her like this.

First she needed to do one thing. Still wobbly, she rose and slowly stepped over to her dresser. Lifting a Folgers coffee can from the corner of the dresser, she popped off the plastic lid and prepared to dump its contents into the trash can. Those dozen dried-up carnations, the very bouquet Todd had handed her last summer before kissing her for the first time, were as dead as she wanted her feelings to be. They were brown and withered and there was nothing lovely about them anymore. In fact, they were ugly—sad and ugly— and they needed to be thrown away.

She couldn't do it.

Instead, she removed the *Forever* ID bracelet from her wrist and buried it deep in the mound of stale carnation petals. With a snap, the plastic lid fit over the tomb of her dreams, and ceremoniously Christy tucked it into the deepest corner of her closet. She placed Pooh Bear on top to stand guard and stated solemnly, "Never again will I give my heart away so easily."

The next morning she felt exactly the same. Nothing had mellowed during her fitful night of half-sleep, half-senseless dreams.

Part of her felt stronger, though. The determination part. During the night she had pictured herself in her cheerleading outfit with Todd, Rick, and Renee watching her spring into the air and land with perfect precision. The ultimate cheerleader, that's what she was.

She would show all of them: Todd, Rick, Renee, her parents, Katie. She would prove that she was important and desirable.

For more than an hour, she lay in bed and let her searing thoughts burn into her emotions. She refused to feel sorry for this Jasmine girl. She refused to ever, ever get her hopes up with Todd again. He was a friend. Nothing more.

The longer she lingered in bed, the more time she had

to form a plan. She needed to do something to make the hurting go away. It occurred to Christy that all wasn't lost with Rick. She hadn't said yes or no at the ice cream shop. She had, of course, been thinking no the whole time he was there, but Rick didn't know that.

Going to the prom with Rick was a good plan. It would certainly help the hurt she was feeling over Todd, and it probably wasn't too late to make it happen, if she went to work on it quickly.

That resolved, Christy allowed herself to make plans about cheerleading. Staring at the ceiling, she drew in a deep breath and determined she would make the cheerleading squad—period.

As far as her hopes in God and the way she had promised Him her whole heart last summer, well, she didn't want to think about that. It would be easier to figure out where God fit in her life after next weekend, when the tryouts and the prom were behind her. First things first.

Christy's mom knocked on her door and entered. "Do you realize what time it is?"

Christy glanced at her clock. "I was just going to get up."

"Do you want to go to the mall with us? I'm taking David to get a new pair of shoes. Dad ran over to the dairy for a few hours."

"No. I'll stay here. I've got a lot to do."

"Just don't waste the whole morning away, okay? And can you unload the dishwasher and put the towels in the dryer for me? They should be done in the washer in about ten minutes."

"Sure."

"Oh, and Katie called about eight o'clock. I told her

you were still asleep and that you'd call her back later. She said something about not being surprised that you were still asleep after last night. What do you suppose she meant by that?"

Christy sat up in bed and stretched. "Todd and I saw her last night when we went for ice cream." Christy considered giving more details of why it was an exhausting experience, like mentioning that Rick was there as well, but she wasn't sure. It would be too complicated to explain. And since she wanted everything to be set up perfectly before she asked her parents about going to the prom with Rick, this wouldn't be a good time to launch a discussion that might end up needing a lot of explaining.

"Oh, well don't forget about the towels."

"I won't," Christy said as her mom exited, closing the door behind her.

As soon as her mom and David left, Christy called Katie. She told Katie, rather calmly, that Todd was taking another girl to his prom, so she was ready to move on and arrange things so she could go with Rick. They talked on the phone for almost two and a half hours, making elaborate prom plans—everything from how to smooth things over with Rick and present the idea to her parents to what she and Katie would wear and when they would do each other's nails.

With their plan of attack settled, Katie returned to a topic Christy had so cleverly skimmed over in the beginning of their conversation. "Are you going to write Todd a 'Dear John' letter or what?"

"No. What would I say? 'You're a jerk because you'd rather take this Jasmine girl to your prom instead of me'?

Or, 'Sorry I'm not a very strong Christian, and Jasmine is. I suppose you spiritual giants need to stick together'?"

"You know what I can't figure out? How are they going to dance?"

"You got me. Maybe he's going to sit on her lap, and she'll wheel him around the floor. Or being such a gentleman, maybe he'll push her chair around in circles until she gets so dizzy that she sprays punch out her nostrils."

"Christy!" Katie acted shocked, but she laughed loudly. "That is so rude! What if you were her? Wouldn't you love it if a guy like Todd came into your life and took you to the prom?"

"Of course," Christy mumbled. "And I would have loved it if Todd had invited me. But he didn't. He invited her. And he seemed real happy about it. You should have seen his face, Katie, when he said her name—" Christy stopped midsentence when a thought came to her. "Oh, no. I can't believe it."

"What?"

"I just remembered something I said." Christy felt herself sink into an unwelcome depression.

"Well, what?"

"When we got back to my house, we were standing under the trellis, and I picked a flower and said, 'I bet you love jasmine too.' I meant the flower, the one I was holding for him to smell. But you should have seen his face! I can't believe I said that!"

"You didn't know her name was Jasmine."

"He's in love with her, Katie. I know he is."

"Oh, stop it. You know who you remind me of?" Katie went on before Christy had a chance to answer. "You sound like Renee in English last week when she was moaning over how Rick turned down her invitation to the prom. Only she was moaning over you being the 'other woman'!"

"She was?" Christy felt a strange sense of exhilaration.

"Don't let it go to your head. You have a better relationship with Rick than any other girl I know. I don't think you should mess that up. My advice is give Todd a rest, and tomorrow at church we'll work out all the prom plans with Rick and Lance. You'll see. Everything will be fine." Then Katie added exuberantly, "This week is going to be a week to remember."

Oh great! Christy thought. *Just what I need—a week to remember.*

Then, because Christy heard her mom's car pull up in the driveway, she said, "I've got to go, Katie. My mom and David just got home."

"I'll see you tomorrow in the toddler Sunday school class. Don't forget."

"I won't. Why do you keep reminding me?"

"Because I know you, and when you get too much on your mind, you tend to forget some of the more obvious things in life."

"I do not," Christy protested.

Just then Mom walked in the front door with two shopping bags in her arms. She took one look at Christy lounging on the couch, still wearing her pajamas, and said, "Did you put the towels in the dryer?"

Christy closed her eyes and made a pained expression to demonstrate she'd forgotten. One of her mom's major pet peeves was towels that smelled mildewy because they'd sat too long in the washing machine out in the garage.

"How can you deny that?" Katie continued, apparently

unaware of the moment of truth between Christy and her mom. "You know you forget things, Christy. Admit it."

"Okay, okay! You're right. I admit it. I've gotta go now, Katie. Bye." She hung up the phone and sprang from the couch. "I'll do it right now, Mom."

"Don't bother." Mom put down the shopping bags and hustled toward the garage. "I'm going to run them through a second rinse." She was shaking her head as she walked away. At the door that led into the garage, Mom stopped, and turning with her hand on her hip, said, "I don't understand, Christina Juliet Miller, how you can manage to have such a selective memory."

Before Christy could defend herself, her mom said, "Would you please get yourself dressed now and empty the dishwasher?"

"Okay." Christy couldn't stand moments like this when her parents were disappointed with her. As a child she rarely disobeyed them outwardly. But she knew she often disappointed them, like now. And this feeling in the pit of her empty stomach was worse than any punishment she ever could have received for disobedience.

The worst part of her realization was that this was not a good step in paving the way with her parents before convincing them that she should go to the prom.

Hurrying to her room, Christy dressed, made her bed, picked up her dirty clothes, and then unloaded the dishwasher. She also made peanut butter sandwiches for herself, her mom, and David without being asked. Then she folded the towels after they'd finally tumbled dry.

Even though Christy knew her mom wasn't expecting her to do all these things to make up for forgetting earlier, it was the least she could do. Her mom worked part time at a real estate office, and that made the weekends anything but restful for her because so many household chores had to wait until Saturday to be done.

One lesson her parents had tried to get across to her over and over was that if she wanted more privileges and freedom as she got older, it was up to her to show them that she was responsible. She knew that was part of their tactic in making her pay for half of her cheerleading expenses. And she had every reason to believe it would be a huge factor in their decision about letting her go to the prom with Rick. She had to do everything she could to prove to her parents that she was responsible.

Katie called again that afternoon, but Christy told her she couldn't talk because she was about to mop the kitchen floor.

"Mop the kitchen floor?"

"Yes," Christy said firmly, "mop the kitchen floor. I'll talk to you tomorrow."

When Christy met Katie in the toddler Sunday school class the next morning, Katie was ready to put their prom plan into action.

"Did it work?" Katie asked, her green eyes full of sparkles. "Did you mop your way to a yes from your parents?"

Christy opened her mouth to answer, but before any words came out, they were interrupted by a circumstance that happened to have the feeling of a miracle about it. However, since Christy wasn't exactly on speaking terms with God at the moment, she refused to acknowledge it as such.

Mrs. Johnson, one of the mothers, stepped up to Christy with her three-year-old daughter, Ashley, in her arms.

"My daughter has talked about you all week long," Mrs. Johnson said.

Ashley played shy on her mommy's shoulder. Christy gave her a grin and reached out for her. Ashley gladly hopped into Christy's open arms.

"Look," the little cutie said, holding up a Band-Aid-wrapped finger. "I got an owie."

"She stuck her finger in her brother's pencil sharpener," Mrs. Johnson said.

"Aw." Christy kissed it. "All better?"

Ashley nodded, her blond ponytail bobbing up and down.

"I was wondering, Christy, if you'd be available to babysit for me sometime?" Mrs. Johnson asked.

"Sure."

"Oh, good. We can talk about it some more later, but I'm going to need a full-time babysitter during the summer. If that might work out for you, let me know. Ashley adores you."

Mrs. Johnson left, and Ashley scooted down to make herself at home with two little boys in the play kitchen.

Had to be a coincidence, Christy thought. *Or maybe my mom knows her and told her I needed a job to pay for cheerleading.*

The next hour and a half zoomed by with little-kid activities scurrying all around Christy. The room full of toddlers demanded her complete attention, and she and Katie barely talked to each other.

One little boy sat by himself most of the morning. He wore glasses strapped over ears that were too big for the rest of his head. The combination of his ears, the glasses, and the strap made him look peculiar.

He finally joined the other kids toward the end of class, when paper and crayons were passed out.

"You made a funny picture," another boy said when the little guy in glasses held up his work.

"I did not!"

"Yes, you did! It's funny."

The boy burst into tears and, poor thing, couldn't get to his eyes because of the strapped-on glasses.

Christy and Katie both went immediately to the scene since the teacher had her hands full with a wildly kicking toddler in the corner.

"What's the problem here?" Katie asked firmly.

"He made fun of what I made," the wounded boy cried.

Sober-faced and appearing innocent, the other child explained, "I only said it was funny because it is."

"But you made fun of what he worked hard to make." Katie lifted the crying boy while Christy went for a tissue. "Tell him you're sorry."

"No."

"You need to tell him you're sorry."

The boy froze, defiant and determined not to say the words.

Katie forced the issue by using a stern voice and an angry look. "You say you're sorry. Now!"

"Sorry." A peep from a chick would have come out louder.

Katie seemed satisfied that justice was served, and she left the coloring table because the first parents were arriving to pick up their children.

Christy, about to walk away, heard the defiant apologizer say in a low voice, "You have funny ears and a funny face!"

The memory of Friday night with Todd rushed upon her. Christy spun around and looked sternly at the child. In a quiet, firm voice, she said, "Don't you ever make fun of what God made. Do you understand me? God made that little boy. Don't you dare make fun of him!"

The boy sat perfectly still, his head down. Christy realized her words had frozen the little guy. She had used the same words Todd had, but the way Todd said it had melted, not paralyzed, her.

Christy wanted to walk away from it all. It felt awful quoting Todd, especially when she wanted to still be angry at him. She didn't want Todd to be right about anything, and she detested the way she had imitated his spirituality.

She busied herself by sorting toys, cleaning them, and placing them in the appropriate boxes. This gave her time to calm down and sort through her feelings, putting them back into their appropriate boxes.

She didn't see the little guy with the big ears sneak up behind her. He tugged on her skirt. Christy turned and looked into what could have been the face of an angel—his expression shone. His smile, so wide and so sincere, overshadowed the glasses and large ears. He looked up at her as if her reprimand to the bully had changed his life.

"Bye, Teacher," he said in a squeaky voice. Then he galloped over to the door, where his father stood waiting.

People look on the outside. God looks on the heart. As much as she hated her thoughts and the way they forced more of Todd's words to the front of her mind, she let them linger a brief moment, remembering the little boy's smiling face.

8

Prom Plans

Katie got Christy's attention and motioned from the door to the classroom. "Come on. Let's go."

The two girls slipped out of the toddler room and into the bathroom to check their hair before beginning step one of their prom plan.

"Okay," Katie began, "it's by the book now, Christy. Just as we planned yesterday. Lance is going to be waiting for us, and you let me take it from there."

"But Katie—"

"I don't want to hear it. This is no time to turn faint-hearted on me. Come on. Exactly as we planned. Follow my lead."

They stepped out of the bathroom, and there was Lance, waiting for them as Katie had predicted. Lance was a unique guy. He dressed wildly—always. And his hair changed week to week, not only the style but usually the color as well. One thing could be said for Lance: Everyone at school knew him, and most people knew he was supposed to be a Christian. At least he was really involved in the youth group.

"There you are," he said dramatically, offering Katie his arm. "May I escort you to church?"

Katie played along with the dramatics, which Christy thought looked kind of cute for those two.

"Have you seen Rick?" Katie asked, giving Christy a glance over her shoulder. "We need to check and make sure everything is all clear with him, you know, about making it a foursome on Saturday."

"He's around here someplace. Let's go find him." Lance spoke like some kind of cartoon character. Then he did a little hop and walked off like Charlie Chaplin.

The church hallways filled with people moving to and from classrooms and the sanctuary. The three friends stayed together and found Rick talking to a group of girls out front.

When Rick saw them, he kept talking, indicating that the group he now entertained carried more importance than the threesome approaching him. Christy started to feel more nervous than she thought she would. This whole thing wasn't settling well inside of her.

Katie took over as only Katie could. "Yo, Doyle! Get your brown eyes over here. We have plans to discuss."

Suddenly, Christy lost all nerve. Going after guys like this had never been her style. She wished she had never agreed to Katie's prom plan.

Too late now. Rick sauntered over, cool, calm, and confident. Christy thought about how great Rick would be for a deodorant commercial. He had a nothing-can-faze-me look on his face. Christy, on the other hand, felt like a perspiring mess. Rick gave Katie and Lance a smile but deliberately did not make eye contact with Christy as they talked.

Is he mad about Friday night and Todd? Or is it my killer eyes? Is he afraid to look at me because he might read something deep and desperate in my

*eyes? Is that what I am? Desperate? I must be. At least I'm desperate enough
to let my friend run my dating life for me, such as it is. Oh, this is really getting
pathetic. I wish...*

Before Christy could complete her "wish," Katie had
sewn up the prom plans—and in less than three minutes. All
that needed to be decided was what time the limo would
come by to pick them up. It had to be a world record in
persuasive speech. Katie even told Rick to get flowers that
would go with a red dress, since she had heard he liked
Christy in red.

*Why did Katie blurt that out? How embarrassing! And where am I going
to come up with a red dress by Saturday?*

Rick's glance finally fell on Christy, and he jokingly
said, "Not going to cause waves with Moondoggie, am I?"

"Who?" Christy scanned her memory until she remembered that Moondoggie was the name of a surfer in an old
beach movie. She forced a laugh with the others and shook
her head. "No."

"Believe me," Katie said, "there's no chance of that
relationship surviving. 'Moondoggie' is long gone."

Rick's gaze shot directly to Christy's wrist, where the ID
bracelet she had worn since New Year's was now conspicu-
ously absent. She never knew Rick had noticed it before.
Only her girlfriends knew Todd had given it to her.

"Is that right?" Rick's charming smile showered Christy
with his approval. He wrapped his arm around her and
pulled her to his side. "Good," he said in a low voice,
"really good."

So it was decided. They were a foursome for the prom,
and to make it official, they all walked into church together
and sat where everyone could see them.

Christy didn't hear a word of the service. At this moment she knew of nothing she wanted to hear from or say to God.

By the time church let out, Christy had convinced herself that all of this scheming and forcing together of the pieces was fine. So what if she didn't have Todd and those dreams; she could make this prom plan work! She would go with Rick and be beautiful and have a wonderful time, and everyone would be happy for her. Everyone except one person whom she forgot to include in the prom plan.

Her dad.

"No, Christy. Absolutely not," he said at the kitchen table after their Sunday meal. "You are not going to any prom. It's completely out of the question."

Christy went on as if she hadn't heard him. "But Dad, it's not really a date because four of us are going together, and see, they're counting on me. Lance's dad already rented a limo for us."

"A limousine?" Mom blurted out. "I don't understand you, Christina! Did you think for one minute that your father and I would ever approve of your going to a prom? And in a limousine?"

"Well, I thought maybe you'd make an exception because I'm going with my friends from church, and like I said, it's not really a date."

Mom and Dad looked at each other as if silently urging the other to go first. Christy still felt she could persuade them, so with polite persistence she asked, "Could you just explain to me why I can't go?"

"For starters, you're not allowed to date until you're sixteen," Mom said.

"And," Dad cut in, looking upset, "we don't approve of proms and dances."

"But why?" Christy asked.

"The music—"

Mom cut in. "We don't let you listen to that kind of music at home. Why would we let you go to a dance and listen to it all night?"

Dad pressed on with his list. "And the atmosphere, the way the girls dress, and the..." He cleared his throat. "...The suggestive dancing. The answer is no, Christy. You're not going."

"What if I went, but I promised not to dance?" Christy turned to her mom, hoping for support. But Mom's gentle face had a firm, set expression.

"That's not the whole issue, Christy. Other parents from church may let their kids go, but your father and I don't want you to go. You will have to tell this boy that you can't go."

"I can't." Christy's voice came out as more of a whine than she had intended.

"Of course you can. You simply tell him, 'Thanks for asking me, but I can't go,'" Mom coached.

"But he didn't exactly ask me. I, well, I kind of asked him."

Mom stared at Christy. "You did what?"

"I kind of asked him. Actually, Katie asked him for me, because she wanted to ask Lance. And she did, and so now we all have to go together."

Her father rose from the table, pressing his knuckles against the tabletop. "You handle this, Margaret. If I do, I'll regret it later."

He pushed away from the table, leaving Christy with a mother who looked flame-broiled.

"What's this boy's name?"

"Rick. Rick Doyle. You know him, don't you? He's really nice, Mom."

"Do you have his phone number?"

"Yes."

Mom pressed her lips together. "I want you to call Rick right now and tell him you're sorry, but it was a big mistake and you're not going to the prom."

"I can't, Mom."

"Yes, you can." The words came out evenly spaced and with quiet intensity.

Christy swallowed a lump of tears and pride. How could she possibly tell Rick she was sorry, but the plans were off?

It would be best to get it over with. The scariest moment of her life had to be the moment Rick answered the phone.

With her mother standing next to her, Christy forced out, "Rick? Hi, it's Christy."

"Hi, Killer. What's up?"

"Rick…" She couldn't do it. She couldn't tell him the plans were off.

"Yeah?"

Mom moved closer and said firmly, "Would you like me to talk to him?"

Christy shook her head and turned away slightly. Mom stepped back and waited.

"Um, Rick, something has come up, and well…I can't go to the prom."

Silence.

"I…I'm sorry."

Click. Dial tone.

Christy turned to her mom, holding out the buzzing receiver like a dead mouse. "He hung up!" She burst into tears.

Mom replaced the receiver and did her best to comfort Christy.

As she had been doing a lot lately, Christy swallowed back the onslaught of tears and tried her best to cover up her feelings. As much as her mom was trying to console her, it wasn't helping. Christy was anxious to be alone in her room.

Her mom let her go, saying, "I know it's hard, honey. I know it's hard."

Then why did you make me do it? What's so awful about going to one stupid little dance in my life? Why do you treat me like such a baby? You don't care about what's really important to me! You just don't care.

Christy flopped onto her bed, ready for a long cry. But her dad tapped on the closed door and let himself in. Christy wasn't sure if she should hide her feelings and turn off the tears, or go ahead and make a real scene. There was a wild, random flit of hope that if she threw a tantrum, he might change his mind. Not that he ever did change his mind once he had made his decision known.

She gave him a strange combination of the two options, turning an expressionless face to him. A face that said, *You can't hurt me. I won't let you.* The only problem was, the tears refused to turn off and cascaded down her cheeks.

Dad lowered himself to the edge of her bed, and the whole side sloped downward. Rubbing his hands on his lap, he began to string his words together.

Christy lay motionless, inwardly pleading, *Don't yell at me.*

Please don't tell me what a stupid mistake I made getting all wrapped up in this prom thing. Don't lecture me. Just hold me. Couldn't you just hold me and let me cry my heart out?

He ran his big fingers through his thick reddish-brown hair. "You know, things are different now from when your mother and I were your age."

She knew that.

"And some things are different here in California from Wisconsin."

She knew that too.

"You need to understand that guys are different from girls."

She *definitely* knew that!

"I know what guys think about when they dance, especially nowadays with the suggestive words in songs—"

"Dad—" Christy tried to interrupt, but he had more to say. He held up his hand to silence her.

"I know how it is, Christy, and I don't want some guy thinking about my daughter that way. And I especially don't want my daughter trying to make herself fit into that kind of a...a...into that kind of environment."

Christy sniffed. The tears kept flowing.

"Your mother and I want you to be what you are and not try to be something you aren't. You're fifteen, not sixteen. And you're the daughter of a dairyman, not some movie star who rides around in limousines."

The way he said it sounded so absurd that a spontaneous cough-laugh popped out of Christy's throat. Her dad's face softened. His eyebrows relaxed, so they weren't as scrunched together.

"You're going to have to trust your mother and me,

Christy. You may not like the decisions we make, but we're doing the best we know how."

"I know," Christy said softly, her heart turning a little bit tender. "I'm sorry. I got kind of wrapped up in my dreams. You know. It's important to a girl like me to be able to dream of getting all dressed up and feeling, well, really special. I need to feel that I'm special, Dad."

The statement surprised her. She hadn't realized it until she said it. It was the most deep-core, honest thing she had said to him in months. Maybe years.

"Nothing wrong with dreams," he said, still trying to look stern but not succeeding. "We all need to have dreams. The question is, does the dream control you, or do you control the dream?"

Christy nodded her understanding, blinking the final tears off her eyelashes. This felt good—talking to her dad almost like they were both adults. And he hadn't even yelled at her. At least not yet.

Christy felt ready for a final tender moment with her father. Maybe she should try to explain to him the crazy thought she had just now. The thought that if he would make her feel more special, then maybe it wouldn't be quite so important to her that she got that kind of attention from other guys.

She didn't know how to tell him. But she knew what she wanted. She wanted him to hold her moist face in those huge, rough hands of his and kiss her on the forehead the way he did when she was little and he tucked her in at night.

But just then David knocked on the bedroom door. "Christy, phone."

"Who is it?"

"Some girl."

Christy made a face at her dad that said, "Little brothers!"

He smiled.

"What's her name?"

"I dunno. I told her you were crying your eyes out in your room 'cause you were getting yelled at for not having a boyfriend."

"David!" Christy yelped and sprang from the bed then shot a glance at her father. "Is it okay if I go see who it is?"

He nodded, and she was out the door, grabbing David by the shoulders. "Why did you say that?"

David trembled—a mocking kind of "Help, I'm scared!" tremble. His words matched his comic actions. "You told me to always tell the truth on the phone."

Christy brushed past the little clown and retrieved the dangling receiver. "Hello?"

"Christy?"

"Yes, this is Christy."

"Hello! How are you? This is Alissa!"

"Alissa? You're kidding!" Christy had met Alissa on the beach last summer. They had written a few times but never called because Alissa lived in Boston.

"How are you doing, Christy?"

"Fine! How are you?"

"We're doing wonderful."

"We?" Christy ventured. "You mean you had the...I mean, you had your baby?"

"Last week. It's a girl."

"Really? That's great, Alissa."

"I named her Shawna Christy after you and, well, after

Shawn. She's beautiful, but she doesn't have any hair yet."

Christy giggled along with Alissa. "You're doing all right, then?"

"Besides being twenty pounds overweight, yes. I'm probably doing better than ever before in my life, thanks to you."

"What did I do?"

"Christy, if you hadn't written me and encouraged me and told me that God cared about me and everything, well, when I found out I was pregnant, I probably would have killed myself or had an abortion or I don't know what. I never would have gone to the Crisis Pregnancy Center. The only reason I went was because you kept telling me to go to church and meet some Christians. I knew I couldn't just walk into some church, pregnant and everything, and expect people to accept me."

Todd's words flashed before Christy, and to get rid of them, she used them in her reply. "You know, Alissa, people look on the outside, but God looks on the heart."

"I know that now. That's what my counselor, Frances, tells me. She has a support group for expectant and new mothers at her home. I've been going every week. They talk about God a lot, and I'm starting to understand some of the things you told me in your letters about trusting God enough to give Him your heart."

The words stung. Right now Christy felt like she and God were having a tug-of-war with her heart, and she was winning. Apparently, Alissa and God were having the same struggle—only God appeared to be winning with Alissa. "Well, have you?"

"Have I what?" Alissa asked.

"Have you done that yet? Given God your heart?"

"Not exactly. Frances has explained it all to me: how I need to be sorry for what I've done to hurt God and ask Him for forgiveness and then surrender my life to Him. I just haven't done all that yet. It's always been hard for me to say I'm sorry, and I have an even harder time trusting someone to take control over my life, or however Frances explained it."

Christy felt disappointed. Ever since last summer she had wished Alissa would surrender her life to the Lord and become a Christian. She seemed so close to making the decision.

"How's Todd? Are you two still together?" Alissa asked, changing the subject.

"Not exactly."

"What's going on? Your brother said you were in trouble for not having a date or something."

"He got it all mixed up." Christy hesitated then decided to tell all to this faraway friend who had been so transparent with her. She concluded the whole saga by adding, "And things with Todd are not very great. He's taking some girl named Jasmine to his prom next Saturday, and since she's in a wheelchair, he seems to think I should feel sorry for her, like he does."

"She's in a wheelchair?"

"Yes, from a car accident. She's probably got long blond hair like yours, and I wouldn't be surprised if she's elected prom queen."

"Really?"

"Well, I don't know, but he's crazy about her, so I figure there must be more going on than he's telling me. I've put him on my list of 'just friends.'" Besides, he might not even be around this summer."

"Where's he going?"

"Hawaii. Don't you feel sorry for him?" It came out as sarcastically as she meant it.

"I loved Hawaii when we lived there. My dad and I used to walk on the beach every night."

Christy knew Alissa's dad had died a year ago. She wondered if she should venture a question about Alissa's alcoholic mom.

"Are you still living with your grandmother?"

"No, she kicked me out a couple months ago because I embarrassed her in front of all her proper Bostonian friends. She hasn't seen Shawna yet. Neither has my mom."

"How is your mom?"

"The same. She's been in and out of the same treatment program twice."

"So, where are you living?"

"With Frances's daughter. She's married to a really nice guy, and they have two little girls, so Shawna has built-in playmates."

"That's great! I'm so glad things are better for you."

"I think about you a lot, Christy, and how you said that God knows and cares about everything in my life. It's hard for me to believe, but I think about it a lot.

"Would you tell Todd hi for me? That is, when you start speaking to him again. Did I tell you he wrote me the most incredible letter a couple of months ago? Five pages long. I think I've read it a hundred times. I'm going to save it forever and let Shawna read it when she's old enough."

Todd wrote her a five-page letter? He's never written to me!

"I really need to go. And don't worry, Christy. Things with you and Todd will work out. They always do. But when you do talk to him, tell him I think he should have taken you to the prom."

"Right, I'll tell him." She said good-bye to Alissa, hung up, and added silently, *That is, if I ever speak with him again in my life.*

9

Jealous Love

On her way up the front steps of the school building Monday morning, a girl Christy barely knew came up to her. "Are you the girl who dumped Rick Doyle?"

"Excuse me?"

"I heard you gave Rick a taste of what he's always dishing out. Good for you!"

Christy ignored the girl's comments and entered the building. Out of the corner of her eye, she thought she saw Rick coming in her direction. She got up the nerve to look at him, but when she looked, he wasn't there. She didn't know if he'd turned and gone the other way in the crowded hallways or if it hadn't really been Rick to begin with, but she just expected to see him.

Someone bumped hard into Christy's shoulder as they passed in the hallway. She turned and recognized the girl as one of Renee's friends.

"What is going on?" Christy muttered to herself. She hurried to meet Katie at their lockers as usual.

Katie gave her a cool look. "I don't know if I'm speaking to you or not."

"You too? Take a number. Or better yet, why don't you

call me and when I answer you can hang up on me."

"What is that supposed to mean?" Katie said, giving Christy a disgusted look.

"I mean, I'm sorry. I know I messed everything up. I tried to tell you Sunday before the toddler class that I hadn't asked my parents yet, but then everything got going so fast..."

"You're trying to say this is my fault?"

Christy leaned against her locker and looked her friend in the face. "No, I'm not trying to say that at all. This whole mess is my doing. And I'm sorry it didn't work out the way we planned. I was hoping it would work out, Katie. I was dreaming big things. But my parents absolutely won't let me go."

"Are you sure?"

"Yes, I'm positively sure."

Katie seemed to soften. "You could have called me, Christy. It's pretty awful hearing it from one of Rick's friends."

"I'm sorry."

"What's worse is when I tell Rick's friend he doesn't have the story straight because I know what's going on and he doesn't, and then Rick walks up and says I'm wrong."

"Katie..."

"I don't know if I want you to apologize. You see, Rick's never been stood up before. I'd probably be more mad at you, except I think it was time he got some of his own medicine, and you were just the one to give it to him."

"I wasn't trying to—"

"Lance and I will have a miserable time without you, you know."

"No, you won't! You two will have a wonderful time. Besides, isn't Rick going anyway?"

"How would I know? He's playing it so cool. Nobody knows what he's going to do. Besides, why would he still want to go with me and Lance? He's not exactly friends with either of us."

The bell rang, and Katie gave Christy a playful slug in the arm. "Don't look so depressed. You've got to come up with a few smiles for cheerleading tryouts this Friday, you know. Wouldn't hurt to start practicing now."

Christy forced a pathetic grin.

"Never mind. Go ahead and be depressed all day today and get it over with. I'll check on your smile again tomorrow morning."

Christy shuffled to class. The luxury of being depressed all day didn't sound so bad.

"How was your weekend?" Liane, a girl in her algebra class, asked.

"It was interesting," Christy answered cautiously. She wondered who else knew about Rick. Liane didn't usually talk to her. Had her life become an open book at Kelley High School?

"Oh really? What was so interesting about it?" the girl probed.

"It was a hard weekend, that's all."

"Well then, I sure hope your week turns out better than your weekend!" Christy couldn't tell if the girl was being serious or sarcastic.

Class started and Christy thought, *This week has to get better. Everyone is watching me! I have to work hard at tryouts, and on Friday I have to make the squad. It won't make up for the prom and Todd and Rick, but it'll show everyone that I did it. And I did it on my own.*

The algebra teacher passed out the corrected quizzes from Friday. He handed Christy hers first. A huge, red F had been circled on the top of the page. She had never received an F before. Ds and Incompletes, but never an F. In horror Christy discovered she had missed every problem. This was not the way to begin a week that was supposed to turn out better than her weekend.

"One-third of the class failed this exam. Those of you who did will need to take a makeup test," the teacher announced. "I'm giving the makeup tomorrow after school."

Oh, great! How am I going to be in two places at once? I need to be at practice, but if I don't make up this quiz, I'm in deep trouble. And when am I going to find time to study?

Her troubles didn't get any easier at practice. Renee huddled with her friends gossiping, and all three turned to look Christy over as she came on the field.

When Christy got close enough to hear, Renee said, "Well, at least my mommy and daddy are letting me go to the prom, not like some people we know, who are still too young to play with the big boys."

The girls giggled. Christy ignored them, doing her stretching exercises by herself.

"Watch, she's going to admit she's too young to be a cheerleader too. Just wait. Yoo-hoo," Renee mocked, "change your diaper before practice? We wouldn't want any accidents, you know."

Christy closed it all out, pounding a single sentence through her mind over and over: *Ignore her. Ignore her.* Then she added, *I can do this. I can do this.*

As the rest of the girls gathered, it became obvious that the hopefuls had dwindled down to the determined. Eight girls remained. On Friday the judges would select seven cheerleaders. That meant all but one of them would be chosen.

The girls were highly motivated now, each trying to prove that she deserved to be one of the chosen seven. As they ran through the cheer a few more times, Christy concentrated on making her arms the straightest, her moves the sharpest, her voice the loudest.

We're on our way
Straight to the top
We'll never give up
We just won't stop!

"Okay," Mrs. James reminded them after practice, "those of you who are here today know that it's between you eight. We might have one or two more who just couldn't come today. The next three practices are crucial. Please be here for all three; otherwise, I'm sure it will affect how you do on Friday. Any questions?"

Christy waited until the other girls had left before asking about Tuesday. "I need to take a makeup test in algebra tomorrow, and that's the only time he's giving it."

"It's up to you," Mrs. James said. "These last three practices are the most critical. You're doing well, Christy, but I think you need the practice. You'll have to decide which is the most important to you."

"I could help you," Teri said. She had stood up to Renee last week, and now she was being nice to Christy again. It was wonderfully refreshing after the way the rest of her day had gone. "If you take the test and then come late to practice, I could stay after and show you what you missed during the first part."

"Are you sure?"

Teri nodded, her brown eyes showing her sincerity.

"Is that okay, Mrs. James?" Christy asked, still amazed at Teri's generous offer.

"It's up to you, girls. I'll be here until four-thirty. After that, you're on your own."

"Thanks, Teri," Christy said.

"Sure. See you tomorrow."

That night Christy spent at least two and a half hours on her algebra. She decided not to tell her parents about the F. Why get them all upset when the teacher would be recording the makeup grade?

She busied herself with her homework until ten o'clock, trying hard to concentrate. Wanting to get her homework done was only part of the reason for plunging in so diligently. The other reason attacked her as soon as she climbed into bed.

It was her thoughts. And her feelings, which she had so carefully guarded in her heart. Churning around like sneakers in a dryer, her thoughts and feelings now bumped into each other in the darkness: Todd, Jasmine, Rick, Katie, Renee, and all the pressure she had put on herself to make the squad. All the issues in her life spun around in her subconscious through the night.

She didn't pray. She hadn't since Friday. She knew she would feel better if she did, but her stubbornness kept her from yielding. Instead she chose to stay motivated by anxiety and jealousy.

Katie noticed at lunch on Tuesday that Christy wasn't wearing her *Forever* ID bracelet. Christy told Katie that she would keep it as a memory, but it didn't really mean anything anymore.

"What are you saying?" Katie questioned. "That you've dismissed Todd from your life? I find that hard to believe. I thought you said once that he would be in your heart forever."

"Did I?"

"Yes, of course you did. You want to know what I think?"

"No." Christy bit into her peanut butter and honey sandwich, knowing that Katie would disregard her reply.

"I think you really, truly love Todd deep down, but you're afraid to get hurt because your relationship is so up and down."

"No, Todd's only a fantasy. I've wanted him to care as much about me as I care about him, but he's always been off in his own dimension. We're not good for each other. I'm too jealous."

Christy didn't even realize she felt these things. It amazed her to hear what was coming out of her mouth. "Did I just say that?"

"What, that you're jealous?"

"Yes."

"That's what you said. But do you want to know what I think? I think jealousy is normal when you love someone, and it's a good way to tell how much you care about him. The more jealous you get, the more you care."

Christy questioned whether that was true. After all, Katie had no experience in love. How would she know what's normal? Plus, when Todd quoted those verses on love, he had said that love was not jealous. She remembered that part.

"I don't know, Katie. All I know is that this Jasmine girl obviously means more to Todd than I do, and I must be pretty worthless if my competition is a girl in a wheelchair."

"Oh, low, Christy, low!" Katie cringed. "I can't believe you said that. I don't think you're looking at this the right way. I mean, even if Todd had asked you, do you honestly think your parents would have let you go?"

"I don't know. Maybe. They treat him as if he's a long-lost nephew or something."

"I don't blame them! I'd treat Todd that way too. He seems like the perfect guy."

"Yeah, well maybe he's a little too perfect—a little too spiritual. He's always trying to see things from God's point of view, and it's too hard for me to catch up. I just don't think the way Todd does or see things the way he does. Besides, weren't you the one who was telling me only a few days ago to let Todd go and to move on since Rick wanted to go to the prom with me?"

Katie wadded up her lunch bag, aimed, and made the shot into the trash can. She shook her head, her straight red hair swinging like tassels.

"I don't know what I said then. But if you want my opinion now, I think Todd's worth trying to catch up to. I mean, wouldn't you rather be with a guy who's a few steps ahead of you emotionally or spiritually or whatever? Seems as though the few guys in my life have only been ahead of me physically, if you know what I mean."

Christy smiled and nodded. She knew exactly what Katie meant.

"You do know, don't you," Katie leaned over and spoke in a hushed voice, "that a bunch of couples have rented hotel rooms at the Coronado for, you know, after the dance."

"Are you kidding? People from our school?" As soon as she said it, Christy realized she was being awfully naive. Of course, other students at her school were doing stuff like that. She just never thought of who was doing what. She tended to think all her friends were innocent in the same way she was—except Alissa. And she certainly hadn't caught on until much later how intimately involved Alissa had been with her boyfriends.

"I heard that last year after the prom six of the guys on the football team and their dates were arrested for having a party in a hotel room. They were drunk and loud and smashed a bunch of furniture. The hotel security kicked them out."

"That's disgusting," Christy said. "Why can't it be a nice, sweet, innocent dance like, well, in the movies?"

"I know," Katie said as the bell signaled the end of lunch. "I really hope another couple goes with us because, to be honest, I don't exactly know what Lance's idea of a good time is."

Christy hurried to Spanish class, but Katie's final comment stayed with her. Would Lance really have a different idea from Katie's of what prom night should be? He did lean toward the dramatic, as the limo already represented. And Christy had learned enough to know that just because a guy said he was a Christian didn't mean he was operating out of the same value system that a deeply committed Christian would live by.

In a strange way, for the first time Christy felt relieved that she wasn't going to the prom with Rick. Cheerleading tryouts presented enough pressure for one week, not to mention the algebra quiz.

The makeup quiz turned out to be harder than the first test. Christy handed it in and left class with a terrible headache. The last thing she wanted was to face Renee and be behind the rest of the girls who were trying out. If it hadn't been for Teri's offer to stay after and help, Christy probably would have given up the whole dream then and there.

"What are you doing here?" Renee said through clenched teeth as Christy slid into place as a routine ended.

Teri turned to Renee. "You know what, Renee? The rest of us are getting sick of your comments. We're supposed to be building a team here. If you're so set on slamming somebody, why don't you slam me for being Hispanic?"

"I would never do that, Teri!" Renee looked indignant. Her friends gathered around her, and Renee went on defending herself. "I'm not prejudiced against Mexicans or anybody!"

"Oh really? Then why are you against Christy just because she's a sophomore and the rest of us are juniors? It's the same thing as slamming me because the color of my skin is different from yours. I can't change my skin. Christy can't change her age. You're the only one who can change, Renee. You can change your attitude."

Mrs. James stepped in and told the girls to sit down. They complied but spaced themselves out and took turns glancing at Renee, who sat with her arms crossed in front of her.

"I should have said something earlier," Mrs. James said with a concerned look. "I don't know what has gone on over the last few weeks of practice, but I can tell you what will go on during the next few days of practice and then once the team is formed. We will be a team: working together, looking out for each other, helping each other. Each of you will have equal value to me and to each other. Understand?"

The girls quietly nodded.

"There will be absolutely no more of these bad attitudes or cruel remarks. I don't know what all has been said, and I don't want to know, but I think now is the time for apologies. If any of you need to apologize to anyone else here, I'll wait and let you do that before we go into the next practice set."

No one moved. Christy searched her mind for something she could apologize for, but she saw herself as the victim who should be apologized to.

"Sorry," Teri said to the group. "I shouldn't have blown up like that. I apologize if I came on too strong, Renee."

Renee neither acknowledged Teri's apology nor offered hers to anyone.

"Okay," Mrs. James said, breaking the tension. "I can't make you apologize, but I will form this group into a team. Let's get going, and remember, I want you to work together on this."

They practiced the next routine for twenty minutes; then Mrs. James dismissed them. No one had much to say to anyone else. Christy stayed on the field with Teri, and they went right into the moves Christy had missed at the beginning of practice.

"Thanks for what you said, Teri. I really appreciate it."

Teri batted her long braid of dark hair off her shoulder and shook her head. "I didn't say it very nicely."

"But you got the point across."

"Maybe. But if I didn't do it with love, it counts for nothing."

Christy froze. She had heard that phrase before. From Todd? "Is that in the Bible?"

"Yes, in I Corinthians."

"The love chapter," Christy added excitedly. "My boy— I mean, this guy I know said it to me last week. He's memorizing it. The whole chapter."

"Then he's a Christian?" Teri asked.

"Slightly! I mean, yes. So am I! Are you?"

"Yes!" Teri said, nodding enthusiastically.

The two gave each other a hug as if they had just found out they were related. Then chattering quickly, Teri filled Christy in on the details of how she went to a church in which only Spanish was spoken and her dad was one of the pastors. With all the eager sharing between the two girls, they failed to get much practice in but decided to stay after on Wednesday and Thursday to help each other.

On her way home, Christy thought of how differently this day had ended than it had begun. She started by nearly losing Katie as her friend, and she ended with a new friend, Teri.

10

A Hollow Victory

Wednesday and Thursday flew by, and Christy improved a lot as Teri coached her. But Christy realized that Teri was the better of the two of them. She had a certain grace and a vibrant smile that could be spotted halfway up the bleachers.

Christy's plan to beat out all the other girls had fueled her with angry energy for more than a week now. But getting so close to Teri made it hard, because she wouldn't want to make the team if Teri was the one who didn't.

It wasn't much of a prayer, but the only scrawny bit of communication Christy had with God on the day of tryouts was, *Please let us both make it. Together we could be a much better witness for You*.

She added the last part, thinking God might be more apt to do what she wanted if there was something in it for Him. Even as she thought the scrawny prayer, she realized how far she'd come from her original plan of honoring God by being on the cheerleading squad and being recognized on her campus as a God-lover. Right now she wasn't much of a vibrant testimony. She wasn't much of a vibrant anything.

The only thing she was being recognized for on her campus was as the girl who turned down Rick Doyle. Or, more accurately, the girl who invited Rick to the prom and then turned around and canceled on him. It was awful to have so many people watching her and judging her by her actions.

Originally that was what she thought would be the advantage of holding a position as a cheerleader. Now she detested the way people she didn't know came up to her and made strange comments about Rick. Many of them assumed she was a snob or at least extremely vengeful for what she had done to him. She didn't like the spotlight at all and determined that when she did make cheerleading, she'd be a quiet witness—a very quiet witness. That way people wouldn't expect so much from her.

The few times during the week that she had seen Rick, he had turned away or ignored her. She couldn't stand this tension and wished he would say something and get it over with. Christy wanted to say something and break the ice, if only she had an idea of what to say. Lately, it seemed that everything she'd done or said had soured. She didn't dare risk goofing things up with Rick even more than she had already.

Scholastically, Friday was a waste for Christy. She couldn't sit still or pay attention in any of her classes. She even moved her legs through the steps of her tryout routine under the desk in Spanish class. She couldn't eat a bite at lunch, so she searched the lunch area until she found Teri. Together they went to a quiet corner in the gym and went through the motions of their cheers, generously encouraging each other.

At last, three o'clock came. Christy was the first one in the gym and the first one to put on her tryout uniform. She stood in front of the locker room mirror to admire the way the blue and gold stripes made each swish, each move, look sharper and more defined.

The other seven contestants filtered in soon after. By 3:15, Christy felt a current of electrical excitement crackling through the room as the girls briskly cuffed their socks and adjusted the ribbons they had been instructed to wear in their hair.

"Here, Christy," Teri offered. "Try tucking your ribbon under your ponytail holder before tying it. Wait, I'll do it for you. That way it won't slip off while you're doing your routine."

"My hair never stays back on the sides," Christy nervously complained as Teri calmly tied the royal blue ribbon.

"Use more spray." Teri's own hair looked perfect, curled tightly on the ends and held securely with a gold ribbon. "Here. Close your eyes. I'll do it."

Teri sprayed and tucked and fussed with Christy's hair before announcing, "There. It looks perfect, and believe me, it'll stay in place now."

Christy opened her eyes and saw how much better her hair looked after Teri's loving touch. She also saw Renee. Renee's dark hair was set off by both a gold and a blue ribbon.

"Why are you helping her?" Renee asked Teri.

Teri didn't look up. She calmly tucked her brush and hair spray back into her bag. "You don't want to know."

"What do you mean, I don't want to know? I asked, didn't I? Why are you helping her?"

Christy was amazed at Teri's strength and confidence and the way she held her ground with Renee.

"I'll tell you why, but you won't want to hear it."

"Why?" Renee challenged, her hand on her hip.

"Because it's the same reason I told you last year after tryouts when you asked if I was mad that you made it and I didn't."

"Oh." Renee looked bothered. "You mean that stuff about being a church girl."

Christy watched the two girls' reflections in the mirror as they faced each other. Teri's face looked soft and kind, while Renee's looked hard and angry.

"It's not that I'm a church girl, Renee. It's that I love God. And His Word says that if I love Him, I'm supposed to love my neighbor as much as I love myself."

Renee had no answer. Only a slight flinching look on her face. Then snapping out of their conversation, she shouted to all the girls, "Let's go! We're supposed to be on the floor at three-thirty exactly. That's right now!"

With a few last glances into the mirror, the girls lined up and filed as calmly as possible into the gym. Mrs. James handed each of them a small numbered paper circle to pin on the front of their uniforms and pointed to the eight chairs before them, each with corresponding numbers.

As Christy found her chair, number four, she took a quick survey of the partially filled bleachers. In an instant, she spotted her mom. She flashed her mother a forced, nervous smile. It was nice of her to come. Christy hadn't expected it. It meant her mom was taking time off work to be here for her. That knowledge made Christy feel special.

Still smiling, trying to look energetic and confident, Christy scanned the row of judges. None of them smiled back.

"Number one," a judge called, and the first contestant stood.

Wouldn't you know it would be Renee? Christy thought.

When the signal was given, Renee rallied out to the center of the gym, giving it all she had. She was good. On the outside she had exactly what it took to be a great cheerleader.

Number two was called, and Christy felt her stomach doing cartwheels. *What if I forget everything? What if I fall flat on my face? What if—*

Her thoughts were interrupted by a tap on her shoulder. Someone she didn't know handed her a slip of paper and then hurried away. She glanced down at the note: "Go for it, Killer. I'm with you all the way."

Rick?

She looked around but didn't see him. She had managed to avoid contact with him all week and wasn't sure that even if she did spot him at this moment, she would want to make eye contact.

What does this mean? That he's not mad about the prom anymore?

The judge called, "Number three," and Christy thought, *Actually, he has been supportive of me all through this cheerleading thing. We did agree to be friends no matter what. He must understand about my parents' rules and everything. I feel so relieved!*

It was a good thing she felt so relieved, because suddenly number four was called. With gusto and a bright enthusiasm that made her stand out from the others, Christy rushed to the center of the floor.

Stand back, watch out
You're up against the best
Cougars, uh–huh, a step above the rest!
You'd better back off
We're hot on your trail
The KHS Cougars will never fail!

Breathing hard and shivering with excitement, Christy jogged back to her seat. She felt like every nerve inside her was quivering. *I did it! I did it!*

It took every bit of composure to settle calmly into her seat and stay there. She had done her best. She was cheerleading material. After that performance, there couldn't be any doubt from anyone. Not from her own opinion of herself. Not from Rick. Not even from Renee. She'd proved herself to all of them, just as she'd planned.

Christy scanned the bleacher rows for Rick. Her mom caught her eye and waved, offering Christy a big smile. After returning the smile, Christy kept searching for Rick.

Where is he?

Leaning back slightly in her chair, she tried to see if he was behind her. Instead, her gaze met Teri's. What an energetic, encouraging smile!

Teri mouthed the word *perfect,* and Christy felt showered with the warmth of her friend's praise.

Teri really knows how to show people that she loves them. I'd like to be more like that.

Christy gave up trying to find Rick. She focused her concentration on numbers five and six. Inwardly, she began to cheer for Teri. *Come on, Teri. I know you can do it.*

The next two girls did very well, and then came one of

Renee's friends. Christy didn't think much of her routine, but then she didn't think much of the girl either. Only one eight-count into the cheer, the girl messed up and had to ask the judges if she could start over.

Christy tried to feel sympathy for Renee's friend, but she actually felt glad to see her lose points. That gave Teri an advantage, and she needed it. Poor Teri had number eight, the worst slot to have, the last contestant.

At last number eight was called, and Teri sprang onto the floor.

Come on, Teri!

Christy knew Teri would be the best of all of them. Not just because she knew the routine so well, but because Christy had seen how Teri stood up to Renee and wasn't afraid to tell people about her relationship with God. Of course God would let Teri become a cheerleader—especially since she didn't make it last year. She'd be the vibrant living testimony Christy had once thought she could be for their whole school.

Teri did a toe touch, something she did better than anyone else. But somehow she came down off balance and fell awkwardly. She sprawled on the gym floor as the spectators gasped. Managing to pull herself up, she finished the routine as best she could, but it turned out weak and sloppy and minus two important jumps. Not Teri's usual style at all.

The observers clapped the loudest for Teri as she awkwardly hobbled back to her chair. Christy could see tears streaming down her cheeks. With dignity, Teri lowered herself to her chair and waited with the others, even though it was obvious that she was in pain.

Christy wanted to rush over and do something. The

adviser quietly spoke to Teri and handed her a bag of ice, which Teri calmly placed against her ankle and waited for the next part of the tryouts.

The judges finished their scoring and then called the contestants back out to the center of the gym floor. The final part of tryouts was the easiest. The girls had to perform a short cheer together so the judges could see how they worked as a squad.

Springing from their seats, clapping, cheering, their skirts swishing, the girls rushed into formation. Christy ran with the others, clapping and smiling. That's when she noticed that Teri was missing. She hadn't come out on the floor with them.

Christy glanced over at Teri, sitting alone holding the ice on her ankle, the tears still glistening on her cheeks.

That was it. The decision had been made. They all knew it. Since Teri didn't compete in this event, she wouldn't qualify, and the seven girls who now stood on the gym floor would be next year's cheerleaders.

They ran back to their seats after the routine, giving each other looks of triumph, knowing the cut had been made, and it wasn't one of them. They couldn't let their assumptions be known because they'd been instructed to control their responses.

Christy wondered why the judges didn't go ahead and say something. It was an unusual year in that never before had so few tried out for the squad. Usually a dozen girls competed. The only reason Christy could imagine the judges remaining silent about the winners was that Kelley High had an old tradition that the announcement of who made the squad wasn't posted or made public to the school until at least a week after tryouts. It was the same way with other sports teams as well.

Mrs. James had once said the reason was to allow the teachers to agree on the involvement of the students in the sport or activity and make sure there was no conflict with conduct or grades. This year the big announcement would be no surprise. All the students and parents who had come to tryouts knew they were looking at the chosen seven.

Christy couldn't stop smiling. She was going to be a cheerleader! Why, oh why, didn't they break their tradition for this year only and announce the names of the winners right now? What good was it to know and be so excited when you couldn't let out a squeal of delight?

With tryouts officially over, the girls were dismissed. Noisy feet stampeded down the bleachers. Christy ran off the floor and into the locker room, looking for Teri. She found her in the coach's office, her foot covered with a large bag of ice and propped up on a chair. The tears had smeared her makeup, and Teri looked pitiful.

"You okay?" Christy asked softly, her emotions leaping every time she thought of her victory then instantly crashing when she thought of Teri. It was a terrible combination of feelings to have to endure in the same moment.

"No, but I will be." Teri's voice quivered. Then with a strength and dignity that Christy knew she never could have at such a moment, Teri said, "Congratulations, Christy! I'm so glad you made the squad."

Christy could tell that she really meant it too.

"I feel awful," Christy began.

"Don't! You should be very proud of yourself. You did a great job. The best I've ever seen you do!"

"I wouldn't have if you hadn't helped me. I hope you know that. I just feel so bad for you, Teri."

Christy's mom walked in at that moment and looked at Teri. "Are you all right, dear?"

Teri nodded.

Turning to Christy, Mom said, "Christy, I must say, I didn't even know you were my own daughter out there. You did an excellent job!"

"Thanks, Mom." Christy smiled weakly. This is what she had wanted all along: the recognition, the praise, and the affirmation from her friends and family. But hearing it in front of Teri turned the victory into a hollow pleasure. How could she enjoy her dream when the one who helped make it come true had just lost hers?

"Do you want to go home with me now, or spend some time with all your friends back in the gym?"

"I'd rather go now. Bye, Teri." Christy gave her a gentle hug. "I'll see you Monday. Take care of your foot, okay?"

Teri forced a smile. "I will. Thanks."

Christy and her mom stepped out of the office and nearly ran into a giddy, flying Renee. Even the sight of Christy didn't diminish her enthusiasm.

"Oh, hi!" she squeaked. "I guess you're officially one of us now, huh? Well, congratulations, and I'm sure you'll be a great addition to our team."

Is it because my mom's right here that she's being this sweet? Is it because of what Mrs. James has been saying all week about being a team? Or is it because the pressure is off and she knows she made the squad so there's no doubt that she'll be head cheerleader?

"Thanks," Christy returned cordially but not as sweetly. "And congratulations to you too, Renee."

Her face looked bright and zingy as she cheerfully retorted, "Was there any doubt that I'd make it?"

Christy excused herself so she could change out of the uniform and leave with her mom before Renee decided to continue gushing all over them.

"Let's stop and get some ice cream to celebrate," Mom suggested on the way home. "Your dad will be so proud of you. I wish he could have seen you. Why, Christy, I never would have guessed that you had this side of you! You were very, very good out there."

Christy should have been excited and ready to celebrate, but inside she felt dismal and small. *You'd be surprised, Mom, how much you don't know about the real me. Nobody does. Except maybe God. But what kind of a God would let Teri hurt her foot knowing how much I need her to be on the squad with me?*

Heavy questions weighed Christy down all weekend. On the outside, she responded the way everyone wanted her to: happy and excited and proud that she had made the squad. Aunt Marti and Uncle Bob even called Friday night and promised to come see her at as many games as they could. Marti insisted on paying for Christy's entire outfit, no matter how much it cost. That relief of the financial pressure alone should have sent Christy's emotions soaring. However, on the inside she had never felt so lonely.

Saturday night, prom night, Christy talked her mom into renting a movie, and the two of them sat on the couch watching *The Man from Snowy River*. Mom cried during some parts; Christy cried all the way through. The piano music that Jessica, the girl in the movie, played when she brooded over her boyfriend haunted Christy.

She couldn't fall asleep that night. *I wonder if Katie is having the time of her life? I wonder if the dress she borrowed worked out okay? Who did Rick go with? Did he think of me at all? Why didn't he call me after he sent that note to me at tryouts? Was he even there? I never saw him. I wish I knew what he was thinking.*

Then because she couldn't help her thoughts from taking her to the next turn in the winding path of her remorse, Christy wondered about Todd. *He's probably not thinking of me at all now that he has Jasmine. I wonder if he's going to kiss her tonight. Has he kissed her before? The kisses he's given me can't be all that special if he's also kissing other girls.*

Then a sharp, painful realization hit Christy deep in her heart. *I've kissed another guy. I've kissed Rick. Todd doesn't know. If he did, would he think the times I kissed him were less special? I wish I'd never kissed Rick, or more accurately, I wish I'd never let Rick kiss me. And I wish I'd never kissed Todd. I wish I'd never kissed either of them!*

Christy felt tears coming to her eyes in the darkness of her bedroom and in the darkness of her heart. *No, I don't mean that. I don't wish I'd never kissed Todd. I only wish it didn't hurt so much now. I wish I didn't care about him so much. I have to stop these feelings from growing. Bury them even deeper. It won't hurt so much if I don't care so much. Come on. I managed to hide my frustration with Renee. I can hide these feelings too.*

Christy was exhausted by Sunday morning, having wrestled all night with herself. She turned especially moody when she arrived at the toddler class and found out Katie wasn't there.

Christy couldn't believe how heavily this sadness hung on her shoulders. It didn't matter one bit that she had made the cheerleading squad. She still felt empty and all alone. And that bothered her. Christy assumed that once she became a cheerleader, all those stressful feelings would go away and she would feel good and satisfied and energetic all the time.

Not so.

And she couldn't bury all her feelings about Todd. Nor could she hide the depression she felt over the fact that Katie went to the prom without her. She felt melancholy as she passed out Play-Doh to the toddlers.

"Here you go." She handed Ashley a lump of the dough.

"Make something fo' me, Cwissy," Ashley said, her blue button eyes looking up expectantly.

"Okay." Christy pulled up a low chair next to Ashley. "What do you want me to make?"

"I dunno."

"Here," Christy quickly rolled out a long line, then held it up for Ashley. "It's a snake!"

"Eeeee!" Ashley squealed. "I don't want a snake."

"Look, Teacher," one boy said. "I made a snake too." He dangled it in front of Ashley, and she appropriately squealed again.

"Okay, okay." Christy squashed the green gushy stuff in the palm of her hand so that it squeezed out through her fingers. "We can make anything you want, Ashley. Here, you squash some too."

A waterfall of thoughts cascaded through Christy's mind as she pressed the warmed clay into her hand. She had told Rick once that he made her feel like Play-Doh. Was he, like Katie said, still interested in trying to make her into what he wanted her to be, like a pliable plaything?

And then another Todd thought crashed over the rocky places of her mind: *"Soft hearts are the only kind of hearts that God can hold in His hand and mold."*

"Story time!" the teacher called, and some of the children scrambled over to the rug while a few slowpokes tried to finish up their projects. Christy helped scoot them along and then got the snack ready, half listening to the story.

The teacher had begun to tell about Jonathan and David when a little girl interrupted her. "My friend has twin brothers, and their names are Jonathan and David."

"This is a different Jonathan and David," the teacher explained with a smile. "These boys lived a long, long time ago, in Bible times. They were very good friends, and they both loved God. Jonathan's father was the king."

"My friend has a dog named King," a little boy said.

"Let's listen to the story now," the teacher continued patiently.

I could never teach a bunch of interrupters like these kids, Christy thought. *I'd never have the patience.*

"Now, Jonathan deserved to be the next king because he was the king's son. But do you know what? God wanted David to be king, and Jonathan knew it. Did Jonathan fight with David and say, 'I deserve to be king. Get out of my way!'?"

All the toddlers shook their heads and said, "Noooo."

"That's right. Jonathan loved David and he helped him become the next king because Jonathan knew that God wanted David to be king and not him. Do you know what the Bible says love is?"

Christy stood perfectly still, waiting for what the teacher would say, not for the toddlers' benefit but for hers.

From memory the teacher quoted part of the love chapter. "Love is patient, love is kind and is not jealous…"

Christy shut it all out. Not those verses again! She didn't need another reminder of Todd. Not now. Quietly humming the piano music from the movie the night before, she ignored the rest of the story.

11

I Can Wait

Christy walked alone into the church service. None of her friends had showed up; they were probably all too tired from the prom. The loneliness she had felt for several days now throbbed within her. She found her parents and sat with them, which felt safe and comforting.

She tried to put a lot into the service, singing and following along with her Bible during the sermon. She even underlined a verse or two.

Oddly, the thought that kept pounding to the front of her mind was a line from the teacher's story to the toddlers. "God wanted David to be king, and Jonathan knew it." She didn't know what to make of this thought that refused to go away.

That afternoon, while everyone at her house took a nap, Christy reread a letter that came the day before from her friend Paula. Paula and Christy had been best friends since they were toddlers, but Paula still lived in their hometown in Wisconsin.

Paula's correspondence tended to be short and written with large curvy letters with tiny hearts instead of dots over the i's. She wrote about guys. Several guys. Guys Christy had never met. It all seemed so far away. Like another lifetime.

Paula wrote at least once a month, and in every letter she talked about how she was saving money to come see Christy that summer. At first she wanted nothing more than to have Paula come and be part of her new life in California. Yet as the year wore on, Paula seemed more and more like a stranger.

Christy knew she should write Paula back and tell her about the cheerleading victory and all. But after ten minutes of doodling on a piece of notebook paper, Christy gave up and called Katie instead.

She was actually a little mad at Katie for not calling her first and giving her all the details about prom. Christy punched in Katie's phone number and tried to coach herself to sound positive when Katie answered the phone.

"Well? Tell me everything. Did you have fun?"

Katie paused before saying, "I guess. It was all right."

"All right! That's all you can say? It was all right?"

"Yeah, it was all right. I don't think you missed much."

"Katie, what happened?"

"Nothing. That's just it. Here I had this big dream about what the prom would be like, but it wasn't like I thought it would be at all."

"You mean you didn't have fun being with Lance? He's usually the life of the party."

"Exactly! And that's why it turned out the way it did. Mr. Life of the Party took off and ignored me the whole time. We danced only once, for half a dance, and that was because I made him. The rest of the time I just sat there, watching everybody else."

Christy didn't know what to say. She searched for some

possible positive points. "Well, did he give you flowers?"

"Yeah." Katie laughed, but it wasn't a happy remembrance kind of laugh. "He gave me a corsage. A huge corsage that didn't match my dress at all. I told him my dress was blue. He said he forgot. The flowers were green. Green, Christy! You know how they spray-paint white carnations? Well, these were painted green and looked like some leftover bargain from St. Patrick's Day."

Christy laughed and sympathized at the same time. "How awful!"

"Oh, that's not the worst of it," Katie said, warming up. "You know my dress? The one I borrowed from Janelle? Well, you never saw it, but there's no place to pin a corsage. Especially when my corsage was a head of lettuce."

They both laughed.

"I carried it around all night. In the box. I felt like I was carrying around a cafeteria tray! Oh, and the food—oh man, we're talking major mystery meat. They poured some creamy mushroom sauce over it, but nobody ate it. I ate some of my salad, and that's all. I hadn't eaten anything all day, and I was starving!"

"Sounds like you could have nibbled on your corsage if you got real hungry," Christy teased.

"I thought about it, believe me!"

"So what else happened? Did you go with Rick and his date?"

"No. Rick didn't go. I didn't see him there at all. Nobody said anything. I don't know what's going on with him."

"That's strange. I wonder why he didn't go," Christy said.

"Who knows. Oh, you want to hear more? After my

mom got all excited about my going, she decided I had to be home by midnight. Can you believe it? We had this big fight about my curfew right before Lance came. Then he got there, and my mom took all these stupid pictures. I didn't smile in any of them."

"Katie!"

"I was so mad. It didn't help when Lance came in wearing, get this, a white tux with tails, a black top hat and—are you ready?—orange high tops!"

"No!"

"Yes!"

"What a nerd!"

"Not Lance. He turned out to be the life of the party, like I said. He must have danced with half the girls there, and he had his picture taken with at least a dozen of them. They all wanted the nice formal picture with their dates, then a wild and crazy one with Lance."

"That's incredible. I can't believe this happened to you!" Christy tried to sound sympathetic, yet she couldn't help feeling relieved that she hadn't gone through the same embarrassing experience.

"I haven't even told you the worst part. When I told Lance I had to be home at midnight, I was totally humiliated. Then, when it was eleven-thirty, I had to interrupt him while he was dancing with Renee."

"Oh, of all people! She'll never let you forget it either."

"So, get this. Lance walks me to the limo and tells the driver to take me home and then come back for him."

"No!" Christy tried to muffle her scream so she wouldn't wake her napping family. "That's awful!"

"Tell me about it!"

"What did you do?"

"I ate half the food in the refrigerator and watched TV."

"You mean when you got home?"

"No, in the limo. They had a refrigerator and TV in the limo."

"You're kidding!"

"Nope. It was the only highlight of my pathetic evening, believe me."

"What a riot!" Christy said.

"I'm glad you think so. That was one evening I hope I never have to repeat. And since I asked him to the prom, I was the one who paid for the tickets! What a joke, huh? I don't want to go to school tomorrow. I don't think I can show my face around that crowd ever again."

"Oh Katie, it won't be that bad. Renee has been torturing me for a couple of weeks now, and I've survived. You'll bounce back. You always do."

"I don't know. I just wish you could have gone. You and I would have had fun together, even if both our dates turned out to be jerks."

Christy wondered if Rick would have turned out to be such a jerk, spending the whole time flirting with all the other girls. She told Katie about the note she got at tryouts.

"If you want my opinion, I think Rick has it set in his mind that one day he's going to marry you."

"Oh, come on, Katie! Why would you even say that?"

"His parents are pretty strict. Did you know that? I think he likes you because you're so young, sweet, innocent, and all that. He flirts with all the wild girls at church and school, but he probably figures that you're the kind of girl his parents would approve of."

As usual, Katie's comments gave Christy something to think about. After hanging up, she went outside and sat on the front step. It was a cool afternoon with thin clouds veiling the blue sky. The fragrance of the jasmine was faint under the trellis. The neighborhood was quiet except for the sound of a lawn mower in the distance.

For a while Christy hummed the piano music from the movie and thought about Katie, Lance, Rick, and Todd. For some strange reason, the time she spent sympathizing with Katie on the phone had helped to soften the hurts she'd been feeling. At least she had some good things to look forward to when she went back to school tomorrow. She would be identified as a cheerleader even though the announcement wasn't yet official. Still, everyone would know. And they would look at her differently.

Then all of a sudden the line from Sunday school pushed all the other thoughts aside and marched boldly before her: "God wanted David to be king, and Jonathan knew it." It was beginning to bug her. That one line was like a line from a commercial that kept coming back even when she tried hard to forget it.

"Was does that mean? Why do I keep thinking of that one line?" As she spoke the words, she realized she was talking to God the way she used to—openly and easily.

Christy knew the time had come to stop ignoring God and to get everything out in the open. She didn't like being cut off and isolated from Him the way she'd been. It was like a bumper sticker she once saw that said, "If you feel far from God, guess who moved?"

It wasn't hard to admit that she'd been the one who'd moved away from God. She was the one ignoring Him, and it had only made her feel lonely and miserable.

I'm sorry, Lord. I've been doing everything without You. I can tell, because even though I got what I wanted, the cheerleading and all, well, I feel so lonely. I know it's because I haven't spent any time with You. I'm sorry.

She felt relieved. Not as though all her burdens had been lifted or anything like that. All her problems were still there. But now she didn't feel that she was all alone in trying to figure things out.

What am I supposed to do with my relationship with Todd? There was no answer—only the calm afternoon breeze dancing through the jasmine, sending the flowers' perfume into the air.

Love is patient, Christy found herself thinking. She took it into her heart and held it a moment before telling herself, "You need to be more patient. The relationship isn't over yet. You're the one who tried to bury it, not Todd. You need to wait and see what happens, Christy."

Not exactly a settling conclusion, but one she could live with. She knew deep down that she needed to be fair with Todd and let go of the jealousy that had eaten a hole in her pride.

After all, I've been able to be friends with Rick, but it's not in the same way that I'm friends with Todd. So why can't Todd be good friends with Jasmine and still be close to me?

Then she thought about Rick. *What am I supposed to do about him?* No answer came on the wind. No clear thought paraded through her mind.

Something still nagged her. It wasn't Todd or Rick. Something else, but she couldn't figure out what.

Am I doing something wrong, God? I really want to do what's right. I want to make You happy.

The only thing she could think of was cheerleading. But what was wrong with that? She had made the squad, she had gotten past the point where Renee seriously bothered her, and she had made a good friend.

Teri. I wish she had made the squad. She's better than I am, and I know it. She's a stronger Christian too. And it's going to be her senior year next year. I wish there was some way Teri could be on the squad.

Christy pulled a flower from the trellis and plucked its petals. She still wasn't certain what was bothering her. She would try to get it out by writing in her diary.

Going back to her room and stretching out on her bed, Christy found a fresh page to write on. She opened up to her last entry from almost two weeks ago and read about her desire to become a cheerleader for God, but above all, to pursue her cheerleading dream in such a way that she would be a good example of a Christian.

"I didn't really do it for You, did I?" Christy whispered into the stillness. "I did it for myself, and it didn't make me a whole lot more like You. It kind of made me more like Renee and the others."

Now with devout determination, she penned:

I'm going to do it for You now, Lord. I'm going to let all the girls on the squad know that I'm a Christian. I'm going to be a good example of You to them and the whole school.

Such a sincere vow should have eased Christy's heart considerably. It didn't. She still felt a strange nagging. It persisted all evening, so before she went to bed she knelt beside her bed. "I still feel as though something is wrong between us, God, but I don't know what it is." She paused.

"Will You please show me what it is and what I should do to make it right, whatever it is that's bugging me? Thanks, Father. Good night."

Christy wondered if she was trying to make things right with God the way she'd tried to make things right with her mom when she forgot to put the towels in the dryer. Even though she knew that wasn't the way God wanted her to approach her relationship with Him, it still seemed it would help smooth things over for the way she'd ignored Him for so long.

When she got up at seven, Christy felt as if she hadn't slept at all, which made her even more exhausted than she'd been the day before.

She bustled around her room, getting ready, and bumped into her dresser, giving herself a huge black and blue mark on her hip.

Katie said her morning had gone about the same when the girls met at their lockers. They decided to be miserable together all day.

That proved difficult for Christy. She kept receiving congratulations from people she didn't even know, and then at lunch Rick came looking for her. She could tell he was looking for her by the way he walked toward her with his eyes set in her direction.

"Killer!" he called while still a few yards away. A couple of people looked to see who Rick was talking to. Christy could almost hear their whispered answers: "Oh, look! That's the new cheerleader."

Christy stared at her half-eaten orange. This wasn't her. She didn't like the attention. She didn't want people watching her, breaking through her invisible wall of privacy.

"Hey, Killer," Rick said again, now standing right behind her, his hand on her shoulder. He squatted down to be more on eye level with her.

She turned around to look at him, fully aware that they had an audience.

"Come here," he said, motioning with his head. "I reserved a place for two over there."

Gathering her things, Christy followed him. She felt like a puppy on a leash. She knew people were talking about them. Rick led her over to "their" wall, where they had sat when he gave her the pep talk about hanging in there with the cheerleading tryouts. Rick planted himself on the wall. Christy remained standing, hugging her notebook in front of her like a shield. She had no reason to fear Rick; yet she felt insecure and timid.

"So, how's my favorite Rah-Rah? Didn't I tell you you would make it? You were perfect. Absolutely perfect. I looked for you afterward to tell you, but you had disappeared. Did you get my note?" He smiled at her, his deep brown eyes melting her.

"Yes. Thanks for all your encouragement. I probably wouldn't have made it without you."

"I told you you'd make it! I would have been really disappointed in you if you had quit. You deserved to make it. You know, I feel like you and I are more on the same level now."

Christy wasn't sure how to take that. "You mean I wasn't good enough for you before?"

Rick smiled his half smile. "Let's just say that now you're more my kind of girl."

The way he said it she couldn't tell if he was teasing or

serious. In any case she felt uncomfortable. The thought of being "good enough" for Rick disgusted her.

What a shallow value system you must have. All on the outside for show. What about the real me on the inside? Doesn't that matter to you? Katie was right. You are just trying to shape me into the perfect girlfriend.

"So," Rick said, changing the subject, "Katie said you canceled going to the prom with me because of your parents."

Christy paused a moment, debating how to best respond. Honesty was always the best way. At least that's what she'd tried to tell her little brother. Maybe she needed to take her own advice. "Well, to be honest with you, my parents never said I could go in the first place. I just hoped they would, and so I went ahead and made plans. But then they said no. Actually, they said it a lot stronger than that because they're not at all in favor of dances or proms or any of that. So that's why I had to cancel on you."

Christy remembered the hurt she felt when Rick hung up on her. She wanted him to apologize and hinted by saying, "I'm sorry things worked out the way they did. As I told you on the phone that day, I'm really sorry."

"Don't worry about it," Rick said, without apologizing for his part of the hurt. "I still have first take on your birthday. I even wrote it on my calendar. July 27. It will be a night you'll never forget."

First take! Who do you think I am that you can push me into any shape you want? Maybe I don't want to go out with you ever! And why couldn't you apologize for hanging up on me? You're too proud to say you're sorry. That's your problem, Rick Doyle!

Months ago, when Rick had asked if he could take her out on her sixteenth birthday, she had blushed and felt honored. Now she wanted to push him off the wall for his cockiness. *Oh, if only I had the nerve to say those things to him!* She swallowed all of it and said absolutely nothing.

Rick swung his legs back and forth, kicking his heels against the bricks. "Did you hear much about the prom? From what I hear, we didn't miss much."

"Why didn't you go?" Christy blurted out. It came out like an accusation.

Rick looked surprised. "What was the point if I couldn't go with you?"

Christy gave him her best let's-get-real look. "Why don't you just tell me the truth?"

He fumbled around with a few meaningless words before looking over his shoulder and saying, "Okay, I can tell you, Christy. Actually, you're the one I should be telling." He rounded his shoulders and said quietly, "My parents didn't want me to go."

"There's nothing shameful about that. If you remember, that's why I didn't go either."

"I know. But there's more," Rick continued. "Mine said they weren't in favor of it, but if I was determined to go, they didn't want me to go behind their backs. They said I could go only with a Christian girl, preferably someone from church. And I had to pay for it myself."

"So, why didn't you go with one of the girls at church?"

He looked at her as if she had asked a stupid question. "Because none of them are my kind of girl. You know, the rah-rah type. And besides, do you know how much it costs? By the time I rented a tux and bought flowers and everything, it would have been half my life savings. For that kind of money, I wouldn't show up with some girl who would be off with her friends all night."

It all made sense. Rick's personality became transparent to Christy as he spoke. Katie had been so right. He did want to make Christy into "his kind of girl"—someone who had all the right qualifications on the outside, a girl who would give him undivided attention and follow him around, shy and quiet, letting him be the star.

"You know, Rick..." Christy felt her heart thumping as she spoke up. "I'm not so sure I am your kind of girl."

"Sure you are! Or at least you're going to be. You've come a long way, Christy. I can wait until you get it all together."

"Okay, then let me rephrase that. I'm not so sure that you're my kind of guy. You see, I want someone who's patient and kind and not jealous. A guy who knows that what's on the inside is more important than what's on the outside. And I just don't see you being that kind of guy."

Rick looked shocked at her truthful words. "You don't see me as that kind of guy?"

"No," Christy said bravely, "but you could be." And then for flair she added, "And I can wait."

Christy turned and walked off fast and strong, with her heart pounding wildly.

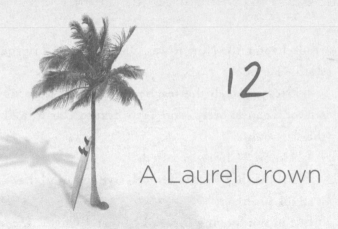

12

A Laurel Crown

"That's on Friday afternoon, as in tomorrow, not next week," added Christy's history teacher while reading the announcement. "An all-school assembly will be held in the auditorium at two o'clock. Next year's football team will be presented, and next year's cheerleaders will be announced."

"As if we don't already know who the cheerleaders are," said a girl in the front row.

Christy could feel the gaze of her classmates on her. She kept looking straight ahead.

"Open your books to chapter 17, and since I'm sure you all read this last night as I asked you to, I'd like you to spend the rest of class answering the review questions at the end of this section."

The usual groans and shuffling of books ensued, and Christy hurried to get going on the assignment. She already had plenty of homework and didn't want any more. Unfortunately, she made it through only half the questions before the teacher announced that whatever they didn't finish in class would be due tomorrow, and they also needed to read chapter 18. Now it was Christy's turn to groan and shuffle her books.

"Seems like all the teachers are piling it on now that school is almost over," said a guy next to Christy as they left the classroom.

"I know," Christy groaned.

"I think they want to cram everything in so they can put it all on our finals."

"I'm not looking forward to that." Christy inched her way down the crowded hall with the guy. She didn't even know his name, and he hadn't spoken to her all year. It seemed a little odd that he'd suddenly turned so friendly. Just then Christy spotted Teri standing by her locker.

"Excuse me," she said. "I want to see how Teri is doing."

"Yeah," the guy said quickly, "too bad about her foot. Glad you made cheerleading, though. Congratulations!"

So that's it! He's suddenly paying attention to me because I'm going to be a cheerleader. How shallow can people be?

"No crutches?" she asked Teri, coming alongside her.

"No, I hobbled around this weekend, but it's fine now."

"That's good news," Christy said.

"Yes, well, the real good news is going to be tomorrow," Teri said without a hint of jealousy. "I know how much you wanted to be a cheerleader, Christy, and I'm really glad you made it."

"It hasn't been announced yet, Teri."

"No, but everybody knows who got it. It's not going to be a surprise this year. I mean it's obvious, don't you think?"

"Aren't you even upset about it? You worked so hard, and you're so good, and it's going to be your senior year and everything. Aren't you even a little hurt or angry?"

Teri smiled her dazzling smile. "Kind of. You know, I really thought that's what God wanted me to do—be a cheerleader next year. But I guess I was wrong."

The bell clanged loudly above their heads. Teri squeezed Christy's arm before slipping into her classroom. "I'm going to be in the front row tomorrow, cheering my heart out for you, Christy."

At that instant, it was as if a loud bell went off inside Christy's heart, and suddenly she knew what she had to do. It was completely clear.

Katie came looking for Christy after school at her locker. "Where were you at lunch?"

"Oh, I had to talk to somebody."

"Who? Rick?" Katie prodded.

"No, Mrs. James. About some cheerleading stuff."

"Are you getting excited about the assembly tomorrow?"

"I guess." Christy shrugged and tried to smile at Katie.

"Well, this is your first year here, so maybe you don't realize what a big deal they make of this at Kelley High. The athlete of the year calls the girls' names, and they run onto the stage and line up in front of the football players. They always start crying. It's a big deal. Better wear waterproof mascara tomorrow."

"Okay," Christy said.

"Did I tell you who made mascot for next year? It's supposed to be a secret until they announce it at the assembly tomorrow, but of course they told me because they wanted to know if my cougar mascot outfit from last year would fit him."

"Him?"

"Clifford Weed! Can you believe it?"

"I don't think I know him."

"He's huge! He'll make a great cougar. But they'll have to come up with a new cougar suit."

"Are you kind of sad that your year as mascot is already over?"

"Not really." Then Katie quickly added, "Well, kind of, I guess. It's funny how it always ends up being different from what you think it's going to be."

"Like the prom?" Christy ventured.

"Don't go there, Christy."

Christy pulled her algebra book from her locker and crammed it into her already full backpack.

"Do you want to come over this afternoon?" Katie asked.

"I've got so much homework," Christy said. "I need to get going on it. I want to get it all done during the week because my mom said Todd called last night after I'd already gone to sleep, and he's coming down this weekend."

"So you guys are back together?"

"Oh, I don't know."

"What? Aren't you anxious to see him?"

"Yes and no. I want to see him and spend time with him and get things settled and back to normal with our relationship, but I'm not ready to hear about his prom and Jasmine and all that."

"Well, if you ask me, after going to the prom with Lance, I can sincerely tell you that whatever it takes to hold on to a guy like Todd, well, honey, JDI."

"What?"

"You know, JDI—Just do it. You've got to give it your best shot and don't ever give up! There are too many Lances in this world and not enough Todds."

"You know what amazes me, Katie?"

"What?"

"Sometimes you are so right!"

"Only sometimes?"

They both laughed, and Christy said, "Yes, only sometimes. And that's because you change your opinions faster than anyone I know. First you say I should go for Rick; then you say I should hold on to Todd. Make up your mind!"

Katie tilted her head. "Make up my mind? Why? It ultimately doesn't matter what I think, does it? I mean, aren't you the one who should make up your mind and stick to what you believe and what you want?"

Even though Katie's words were offered lightheartedly, they stung. Christy knew she had a problem with making decisions. It made her wonder if some of the decisions she'd made the last few days were ones she'd regret later.

"As I said, Katie, sometimes you are so right. I do need to get better at making my own decisions and sticking with them no matter what."

"But Christy..." Katie's voice and expression turned soft and understanding. "Don't you think you've done about the best you could lately with all the stuff that's been thrown at you?"

"I don't know."

"Well, if you want my opinion—and remember, this is only my opinion—you have to decide this for yourself. But I think you've done just fine. Look how everything turned out. You made the cheerleading squad, you made your point with Rick so he doesn't think he can run your life, and you're going to see Todd and pick up where you left off with him. I think for all that's happened you've done just fine."

Christy gave her pal an appreciative hug. "Do you know what the best thing is about going to school every day?"

"No, I have no idea what could be the best thing about going to school. Believe me." Katie's eyes were full of mischief.

"It's that I always know you're going to be here for me."

Katie smiled. "Thank you. I feel the same way. I know you'll always be there for me too."

"Even when I goof up on prom plans?" Christy said.

"Oh hey, that's what keeps life interesting. Think how boring life would be if everything always went the way we planned it. Believe me, I've learned that sometimes the best answers to prayers are the ones God doesn't answer."

"What?"

"You think about that for a while. Think about how often we change our minds. If God gave us everything we asked for, we'd be in chaos."

Christy nodded. "Once again, you are so right."

"Hey, I'd better get going," Katie said. "I'm going to miss my ride."

"Would you save me a seat at the assembly tomorrow if you get there before me? Sit in the front row if there's room."

"Front row? Why? You want to be up close so you don't have far to run onto the stage when they call your name?"

"Something like that."

That evening Christy overheard her mom talking to

Aunt Marti on the phone. "I tell you, she's a natural. I didn't even know it was my own daughter out there when she tried out. I'm so proud of her."

Christy listened quietly in the background as her mother went on about how wonderful everything was going for their family and how blessed and happy they were. Her final comment surprised Christy. "I have to admit, Marti, you and Bob were right about talking us into moving out here to California. Norm is content at Hollandale Dairy, David's reading has improved tremendously, and Christy, well, all I can say is that we are so proud of how she's turning out."

After Mom hung up, she began to fix dinner. Christy followed her into the kitchen.

"Mom," she began without really thinking through how to phrase her thoughts, "would you love me as much if I wasn't a cheerleader? I mean, if I didn't get good grades or if I didn't make cheerleading, would you and Dad still be proud of me?"

"How can you even ask such a thing? You know we love you and are proud of you no matter what the circumstances."

"Yes, but I messed up on that whole prom thing."

"It worked out, Christy, and you learned from the situation. That's what matters."

"But what about cheerleading? I heard you talking to Aunt Marti about it and, well, what if I wasn't a cheerleader?"

Mom leaned against the counter and put down the can of green beans she was about to open. A gentle look settled on her face. "All your father and I want is for you to become what God wants you to be. If that means becoming a cheerleader or a soccer player or president of the math club…"

Christy made a face. "Math club?"

"Okay, maybe not the math club. The point is, it doesn't matter to us. As long as you're obedient to what God wants you to be."

Those were intense words coming from Christy's mom. She had never before said anything like that. Especially the part about being obedient to God.

"Why do you ask, Christy?"

She almost told her mom all that was on her heart, but the right words didn't come. "I don't know. I was just wondering."

Mom sunk the can opener into the can of green beans. "Would you make the salad for me please? There are two heads of lettuce in the refrigerator. Make sure you use up the littlest one first."

Christy pulled out the smaller head of lettuce and giggled to herself, remembering Katie's description of her corsage. Christy told her mom about it as they worked together preparing dinner. They didn't have too many open, fun times like this, so it made tonight even more special. During moments like this, Christy felt more like an adult. It was as if the two of them were getting to be more on the same level and were becoming friends.

Christy thought about how much she liked these few times of open spaces in their relationship, when her mom spoke to her as though she were a friend rather than a child. Christy wondered if her mother treasured these times too.

The next morning Christy and her mom had another

"becoming friends" moment when Mom offered to fix Christy's hair.

At first Christy said, "No, that's okay." Then she saw a look of disappointment on her mom's face and quickly said, "Well, okay. Sure."

Inwardly, she figured if it didn't turn out, she could always change it at school. It had been years since her mother had "fixed" Christy's hair, and it seemed strange that she wanted to do it today.

Mom set to work. Christy examined her hair in the mirror. "This is exactly what I saw in a magazine, and I couldn't figure out how to do it. I thought it was a brand-new style."

Mom laughed. "Funny how all the old styles come back around eventually."

Five minutes later Christy admired the results in the mirror. She carefully sprayed her hair, feeling thrilled with the way it had turned out and confident that she looked good.

"I'm coming to your assembly today," Mom said. "I'm only going to slip into the back, so you don't have to worry about looking for me or anything."

"That's okay, Mom. You don't have to come."

"I've worked everything out so I can be there. This is a big day for you. I'd like to be there to enjoy the moment of glory with you." Mom smiled into the mirror at her daughter. "I feel as if I've just placed a laurel wreath on your head."

"A what?" Christy returned the gaze, fastening tiny pearl earrings on her ears.

"Oh, I know I'm being silly. I was referring to ancient Greece at the Olympics when the winners received a crown made out of leaves as their reward."

"Oh. Guess we haven't come to that yet in our history class."

"I'll go see if David's ready." Mom looked cheery and pleased with life. "You need to leave in about five minutes." She began to walk away.

"Um, Mom?"

She turned, her face looking soft and gentle—completely approachable.

"Remember what you said last night about how I should obey God?"

"Yes."

"Well, I just want to say that if sometimes it seems that I've done something that doesn't make sense to anybody else, well…maybe I've done the right thing, even if it seems weird."

Mom looked confused.

Christy tried to rephrase her statement. "I guess all I'm trying to say is that I want to obey God, and I want to do what He wants me to do, and well, I guess sometimes if I truly obey God, it will only make sense to me and not to other people. Does that make sense?"

"Sort of. Your heart is open to God, and that's what matters. Now get going. You don't want to be late."

Christy checked her appearance in the mirror and then knelt and probed through a mound of dirty clothes in the back of her closet. Her hand touched the cold Folgers coffee tin, and Pooh toppled off his guard post.

"Hi, Pooh. Sorry I left you in there so long."

Christy placed Pooh on her bed and popped the lid off the coffee can.

"Christy," her mom called, "time to go."

"Coming."

Being careful not to crush any of the precious carnation buds, Christy fished through the dry petals and retrieved her *Forever* bracelet.

Then scooping up her books, she rushed out the front door and bounded down the steps, under the jasmine trellis, ready for everything this bright spring day would hold.

13

Surprise!

The auditorium began to fill with students for the two o'clock assembly. Christy looked for Katie among the few people already sitting in the front rows, but she wasn't there. Slipping into the second row, Christy quietly waited.

Deep in her heart, she whispered a prayer. *Father God, I want to become the person You want me to be. I want You to be pleased with me. You are—*

Her prayer was interrupted by a familiar voice. "Hey, how's it going?"

"Todd? Todd!" Christy jumped up and impulsively gave him a hug. "What are you doing here?"

"Heard this was a big day for you." He looked excited, with his wide grin and clear eyes.

Suddenly aware that people were watching them, Christy motioned for Todd to sit next to her. He stretched his arm across the back of her chair and sat looking at her, still smiling. He clearly was proud of her.

"I like your hair," he said. "You look like an angel with a halo."

Christy felt thrilled and uncomfortable and confused

all at the same time. "Thanks. But how did you know about the assembly today?"

"I was at your aunt and uncle's last night when Marti was talking to your mom. Thought I'd surprise you. Did I?" He looked almost silly he was so pleased with himself.

"Yes! I still can't believe you're here. But Todd, there's something I should tell you about the cheerleading announcement—"

This time Katie's voice interrupted her. "Christy! Todd?" Katie's face reflected her surprise.

"I know!" Christy laughed. "Kind of a surprise, huh? Do you want to sit by us?"

Katie inched her way into the empty seat on the other side of Christy as Todd pulled an envelope from his back pocket. "You want see my pictures from prom night?"

Christy's emotions plummeted. How could she say no? Especially with Katie leaning toward Todd and saying, "I want to see them. Pass 'em this way."

"Jasmine's mom took these at their apartment before the prom dinner." Todd lifted a photo out of the envelope as if it were a rare treasure and handed it to Katie.

Christy closed her eyes for an instant, then opened them and looked at the photo Katie now held in front of her. All of her jealousy fled. Christy's first thought sped to her lips, but she held back from speaking it. *That's Jasmine?*

The picture showed Todd standing, tall and dashing in his tux with a teal blue bow tie and matching cummerbund. He looked finer than any knight in shining armor. Jasmine wore a long blue satin gown with straight long sleeves. The skirt covered the bottom part of her wheelchair, and in her lap lay one long-stemmed white rose with a blue ribbon.

Jasmine didn't have the long, flowing blond hair of a prom queen, as Christy had imagined. Instead, her dark hair was cropped short. Her hands lay useless in her lap, with fingers frozen in a twisted grip. And although she wore makeup, she still had a plain, simple-looking face.

But her smile! Her heart shone from her face as she smiled.

"Isn't she beautiful?" Todd asked.

Katie pulled her head back so Todd couldn't see her and gave Christy a doubtful look.

Christy knew exactly what Todd meant, so she sincerely answered, "Yes, she is. She's beautiful."

Jasmine deserved to have a special prom night, and she deserved to have it with Todd.

"So," Christy asked bravely, "did you have a good time at the prom?"

"We didn't go to the dance. Just out to dinner," Todd said. "I'm not big on dressing up and stuff like that. But I heard some of Jasmine's friends say they were all going to dinner in Laguna Beach before the prom. I thought taking Jasmine would be the best present I could give her—something no one else would think about giving. That's my favorite kind of gift."

Christy felt the cool metal of her *Forever* bracelet and realized how carefully Todd planned the gifts he gave. Her bracelet meant more to her at that moment than it ever had before. She was so glad she'd run back that morning and fished it from the coffee can.

"You didn't go to the prom, then?" Christy realized that neither she nor Rick nor Todd had gone. She had ridden a colossal emotional roller coaster for nothing. "You guys didn't go to the dance part of the prom?"

Todd looked at Christy as if he didn't understand her question. "No. Dances aren't exactly my idea of a good time."

"Tell me about it," Katie muttered.

"Jasmine and I had a great time with her friends at dinner, and that's the part that really mattered to both of us."

Christy remembered when she and Todd and the rest of her beach friends had gone ice-skating last Christmas, and Todd had turned out to be a klutz on the ice. She wondered if maybe he wasn't really comfortable with dances for some of the same coordination reasons. The thought made her smile. There were so many things she didn't know about Todd. She was glad things were back to normal so she could keep getting to know this one-of-a-kind guy.

Todd slipped Jasmine's treasured photo back into the envelope. "I can't wait for you to meet Jasmine," he told Christy. "I told her that you and I would fix breakfast on the beach for her one morning. Only this time the birds wouldn't get to the food. I told Jasmine her job would be to keep the seagulls away."

"You told her about our breakfast on the beach last Christmas?" Christy asked.

"Of course. She said she's anxious to meet you. You know, she asked if you were upset that I took her to the prom dinner instead of you, and I told her you weren't like other girls."

Christy felt awful. She was about to argue the point and tell Todd that she really failed more than succeeded and that she'd worked herself into a jealous rage over his taking Jasmine to the prom when the curtain began to go up in the noisy, packed auditorium.

A girl slid into the seat directly in front of Christy and turned around. "Hi! Hope you didn't think I was going to miss this!" It was Teri.

"Hi!" Christy greeted her and quickly introduced Todd.

The football coach began to introduce next year's lineup, and soon the stage bulged with proud young men roaring with school spirit and slapping each other on the back.

"And now," the coach bellowed into the microphone, "Kelley High's best all-around athlete from this year will introduce next year's cheerleaders! I present to you Rick Doyle!"

Rick jogged onto the stage in his letterman's jacket, his half grin showing how much he loved the wild applause that filled the auditorium.

Will Rick see me sitting here with Todd? Will he even notice? Do I even care? Then Christy began to feel nervous. Up until then she had been fine. In the garden of her heart, she knew the right seeds had been planted, but now that the moment had come for everyone to see the harvest, she felt her stomach jumble. *What will everyone think of me? And do I even care?*

Rick stepped up to the microphone, seemingly quite at home in front of an audience, and waved his hands for the applause to die down. It reminded Christy of when Rick had announced her name as *Christina* in front of the youth group the first Sunday she visited his church with Katie.

That time he had embarrassed her and made her feel nervous to be noticed by him. Now she felt strong and unafraid of him. And not just because Todd was beside her. It was because she knew that she was becoming who she was meant to be, as her mom had said. And she could rest in that confidence. Not Rick or anyone else could shake the strange confidence she felt in the midst of her nervousness.

"Okay! I have the list here." Rick held up an envelope. "As I announce the cheerleaders by name, come on up and stand in front of these men that you're going to be cheering on to victory next fall."

Rick tore open the envelope and scanned the list before saying, "Renee Duvalt."

Renee sprang from her seat and, with mock surprise, swished onto stage, giving Rick a perky little hug. With a halfhearted response to Renee, Rick kept looking at the list. Christy saw him turn it over and check the back.

Rick called the rest of the names loudly and clearly. Then he paused on the very last name.

Katie reached over, squeezed Christy's arm, and whispered, "Get ready! This is it!"

"And our final cheerleader is...Teri Moreno!"

Christy felt like the whole world was looking at her, gasping its surprise.

"Teri!" Katie snapped.

Teri turned around, stunned.

"But Christy..." she stammered.

"Go on, Teri! They called your name."

"But why?" Teri slowly rose from her chair, searching Christy's face for the answer.

"Because God wanted you to be a cheerleader, and I knew it."

Teri, dazed and overjoyed at the same time, gave Christy a big hug. Then she ran—leaped—onto the stage as the other girls whispered among themselves and clapped for her. She gave a mighty jump and eagerly received the astonished congratulations from the other girls. Then, facing the audience, Teri turned on her electric smile, shooting a current of absolute joy right at Christy.

Christy kept applauding until her hands hurt, ignoring Katie's nonstop questions.

Todd leaned over. "You did that, didn't you? You gave up the spot you earned so she could be on the squad?"

Christy nodded and blinked back the tears of happiness.

Rick's voice boomed over the microphone as he said, "I'd like to say something here. Please sit back down. I think it's important to say that some people give to our school in ways that no one else sees. Those people, and they know who they are..." Rick paused and looked directly at Christy. "Those people rarely get the thanks they deserve."

The auditorium had begun to quiet down.

"For those people who never quit giving of themselves, this is what I think of you." Rick crumpled the list and stuffed it into his pocket. Before a hushed audience, he slowly, dramatically, with deliberate strokes, stepped back and pounded the palms of his hands together in applause, his gaze glued on Christy.

Katie sprang to her feet and, facing Christy, joined in the applause. In a breath, the whole student body stood, clapping and cheering. Christy instinctively stood too, surprised that the applause was for her.

Todd put his arm around her and spoke so she could hear above the roar, "They're clapping for you, Chris. They know a real God-lover when they see one." He leaned closer and added, "Or should I say, they know real love when they see it."

Christy felt the warmth of Todd's breath on her neck. She looked at him. "Are you sure?"

Todd laughed and held her tightly. "Am I sure? Just look up on the stage."

Christy saw the cheerleaders all lined up, smiling their approval at her and clapping. Even Renee, with a soft expression on her face, stood there clapping—clapping for Christy. Rick also stood there applauding and looking like a guy who indeed was willing to wait.

And then Christy looked at Teri and knew for certain she'd made the right decision. Tears danced down Teri's cheeks as her dazzling smile filled the auditorium. Teri glowed—absolutely glowed. Just like an angel in the great forever.

BOOK FIVE

● ● ● ● ●

Island
● ● ● ● ● Dreamer

To my kindred spirit, Donna Hendrix,
whose rich, fragrant friendship over the years
has opened up to me
the mystery of "God-things."

Acknowledgments

I affectionately appreciate the contributions of Juliette Montague Cooke, who sailed from New England in the 1840s to be a missionary to the Hawaiians on the island of Oahu. Her diary, which I read while writing this book, changed my heart and how I told this story. I can't wait to meet her in heaven.

Mahalo to Mark, Claire, Joe, Maureen, Bud, Lola, Mark, Nancy, and all our brothers and sisters at Kumulani Chapel, Lahaina, Maui, for your *aloha* and *kokua* at a time we needed it most.

1

What's So Funny?

"I'm really going to miss you, Todd. I hope you have a good time." Christy Miller flipped her nutmeg-brown hair behind her ear and pressed the phone closer with her shoulder, waiting for his reply.

Todd laughed. "Hey, we're both going to have a good time."

Christy switched the phone to her other ear and crossed her long legs. "Yeah, I guess I'll have a good time with Paula when she gets here. But I wish I was going to Maui with you and Uncle Bob. How long do you think you'll be gone?"

"Two or three weeks," Todd answered in his easygoing manner. "Depends on how long it takes us to paint and do all the repairs on Bob's two condos. So, when does your friend get here?"

"She's coming tomorrow. If you stay in Maui longer than two weeks, you won't even get to meet her." Christy released a heavy sigh. "I guess I thought all along that you'd be here when she came, and we could go places together. Only now, you're going to Maui, and Paula and I will be stuck here in Escondido!"

Todd chuckled. "Like I said, we'll all have a good summer. You'll see."

He paused, and Christy wished just this once he would say something tender and meaningful like "I'll miss you" or "I wish you were coming." She fingered the gold ID bracelet he had given her and waited.

"Hey, I have to get my stuff together. Your uncle's going to be here in about twenty minutes."

"Okay, well, I know you'll have a great time." Christy switched from her moping tone to a teasing voice. "And I know better than to ask you to write me. But maybe you could send me one little postcard of a waterfall or something tropical to help me feel even more depressed that I'm not there with you."

He laughed again. For such a wonderful guy, Todd could also be a brat. What did he think was so funny?

"I'll see you, Chris. Aloha!" *Click.*

That's how abruptly he often ended his phone conversations. As usual, Christy kept holding the phone to her ear, hearing the dial tone and dreaming about what it would be like if Todd ever talked to her on the phone the way Rick did.

She considered Rick only a friend, yet when he called a few weeks ago to tell her about his upcoming trip to Europe, he had said things like, "When I look into the blue Danube, I'll be remembering your blue-green killer eyes."

At the time all Christy could think was, *Oh brother!* Yet if Todd ever said something like that, she'd absolutely melt.

Placing the receiver back in its cradle, Christy hopped down from her perch on the kitchen counter and tugged open the refrigerator door in search of breakfast.

Mom walked through the kitchen, lugging a laundry basket bulging with dirty clothes. "Christy! I didn't realize you were up already."

"We're out of milk," Christy mumbled. "Mom, how come Dad works for a dairy, yet we're always running out of milk?"

"We had half a gallon in there last night. Your brother must have used it up this morning. There are banana muffins in the basket on the counter and orange juice in the freezer."

Mom paused and rested the basket on the counter. "Oh, did you call Todd yet? He and Bob are leaving for Maui this morning, you know."

Christy peered over the top of the open refrigerator door at her round-faced mother, standing a few feet away. Christy heard suppressed laughter in Mom's voice, and one look at her big grin proved it. Her own mother thought there was something funny about Todd going away for several weeks.

It wasn't funny! Christy was going to miss him terribly, even though they lived too far away to see each other more than once a week during the summer.

"Yes, I called him." Her words came out chopped, and her actions were swift as she closed the refrigerator door.

"I just wondered," Mom said in a motherly way before stepping down into the garage to start the laundry.

"Oh, you're up." Christy's dad, a large man with reddish hair and strong hands, entered the kitchen and poured himself a cup of coffee. "Why don't you get dressed, and I'll take you driving?"

"Driving?"

"Yeah, driving."

"Today?" Christy felt like someone had just put ice cubes down her back.

"We don't have to go." Dad opened the refrigerator and looked around, shuffling jars on the top shelf. "Where's the milk?"

"It's all gone," Christy answered, her thoughts still processing the paralyzing idea of driving today.

"We're out of milk?"

"I guess so. That's what Mom said."

Dad made a pinched face as he sipped his coffee black. "Come on, let's go driving. We can pick up some milk on the way back."

"Okay." She did an exceptional job of sounding like she really wanted to go.

"Can you be ready in ten minutes?"

"Sure. I'll go get dressed."

"Margaret?" Dad called to Mom in the garage. "Why is it I work for a dairy, but we're always running out of milk?"

Why is it I really want my driver's license, but I'm always running out of courage to practice driving? Christy asked her reflection in the bathroom mirror. *Why do I freak out like this? I'm going to be sixteen in only...* She quickly counted *...in five days. Five days! I've got to get over this fear, or I'll never get my license!*

Soaking a washcloth, she held it on her face and then bit into the wet terry cloth, chomping down hard. *This is ridiculous! Everyone I know has a license. They all did it. What am I so afraid of?*

Twenty minutes later, sitting in the church parking lot in the driver's seat of their parked car with Dad next to her, Christy knew exactly what she was afraid of. She was afraid of the car.

That was it. The power a car put at her command was scary. The possibility of misusing that power and getting hurt, or worse, hurting someone else—that's what she was afraid of.

"Dad..." Christy began but then didn't know what to say.

"Ready?" Dad cinched his seat belt and checked to make sure it was secure.

"Do you ever think about how fast, I mean, how a car could..."

Dad looked intently at her, his eyebrows pushed together, waiting for her to finish her thought.

"Never mind. I just feel a little nervous."

"Don't. If you let yourself get nervous, you'll be a nervous driver." Dad squared his shoulders and looked straight ahead. "Start the car, Christy."

She responded right away, swallowing her anxious thoughts and taking a quick peek at Dad out of the corner of her eye. How was she supposed to relax when her dad had braced his arm against the door and planted his feet on the floorboard, looking as is he were about ready to take off in a rocket for Mars?

"Ten and two," Dad said.

"Ten and two?"

"Hands on the steering wheel at the ten- and two o'clock positions. Release the parking brake."

Christy followed his orders and tried to calm her heart, which had begun marching much faster than her brain.

"Okay. Put 'er in drive."

As she slipped the gearshift to D, Christy slowly pressed on the gas pedal. The car inched across the vacant parking lot like a reluctant caterpillar. She made it to the other side of the lot without going more than seven miles per hour and promptly pushed on the brake. The car faced the back fence at a complete stop, and Christy glanced at her dad, awaiting his approval and further instructions.

He sat there with his chin tucked down to his chest and looked at her without turning his head. "That was very nice—if you only plan to drive through car washes the rest of your life."

Christy let out a loud bubble of laughter. Dad was right! It did feel like they'd just driven through a car wash. As she laughed, she felt more relaxed.

Dad relaxed too and looked behind them. "Put 'er in reverse, and let's see you drive as you would on a city street."

Still smiling, Christy popped the gear to "R" and looked back over her right shoulder. She pushed the gas pedal, but nothing happened.

"Give 'er some gas," Dad said, still looking straight ahead.

So she did. She put her right foot down hard, and the car lurched backward at a startling speed. Her hands jerked the wheel first to the right, then to the left.

Dad hollered, "Hit the brakes!"

So she did.

Bam! The bumper hit the cement base of a parking lot light pole, jerking their heads back then forward.

"Put it in park. Turn off the engine," Dad barked and reached to turn off the ignition himself before ejecting from the passenger seat and running to the back of the car.

Christy sat completely still. Her lower lip began to tremble, and she felt the hot tears rushing to her eyes. She didn't dare turn around. She couldn't move.

"Come here, Christy."

She blinked and forced her frozen arm to open the door and her wobbly legs to carry her to the back of the car. Dad pointed to the bumper.

"Could've been worse. I can pound it out. Best thing for you is to get right back in the saddle."

She couldn't believe Dad was acting so calmly! She had been sure the impact had crushed the entire back end of the car. How could such a sickeningly huge thud cause so little damage?

Her face must have mirrored all her terrified feelings, because Dad slipped his arm around her shoulders. "Don't worry about it."

A few tears tumbled down her face. She pressed against Dad's chest and in a small, shaky voice said, "I'm really sorry. I just didn't...I mean, I was...I, I don't know."

From where her ear was pressed against Dad's chest, Christy heard a rumbling sound. She looked up at him, and he let out a roar of laughter. He kept laughing, and she smiled frantically, trying to figure out what was so funny.

"Look around," he invited.

She looked and saw nothing. No cars in the parking lot. No people. Only several parking lot lights planted strategically across the large lot. "I don't see anything."

"Exactly," Dad said, smiling broadly. "What are the chances, in such a huge space, that you'd find something to run into?" He chuckled again.

For the third time that day, Christy felt a squeeze in her stomach, knowing that she was the only one who didn't see what was so funny.

"I didn't mean to do it," she said defensively. "You said to give it gas."

"No, Christy," Dad said, the laughter evaporating, "don't blame me, and don't blame yourself either. That's why they're called accidents. Come on." He headed back to the passenger side of the car. "Let's give it another try."

They went through the same seat-belting motions as before. Dad looked quite serious again. When Christy put the car in drive, she noticed Dad's right foot automatically hit the floorboard as if he were going for his invisible brakes.

Christy looked straight ahead. "Can I just ask you one little question?"

"Yes?" Dad faced forward, right arm braced against the door and left hand on his seat belt.

Christy playfully leaned forward, gripping the steering wheel like a race car driver, and said with a giggle, "You sure your life insurance is paid up, Dad?"

"Now, don't get silly. Driving is serious business."

She could see the smile he suppressed, so she added in her best Disneyland ride attendant voice, "Please keep hands and arms inside the moving vehicle at all times, and remember there is no flash photography."

Then smooth as can be, she began her driving exercises around the parking lot.

"Let's hope there are no flashes of any kind," Dad said in a low voice. "Pay attention to what you're doing now. Turn right up here, and go down to the end."

Greatly relieved and feeling more relaxed than before, Christy did what she considered to be a very good job of navigating the parking lot, and she told her mother so when they got home. She left out the part about the bumper, and thankfully, Dad was still outside so he couldn't fill in any of the missing details.

Christy flopped into the well-used recliner and hung her legs over the armrest, waiting for Mom's encouraging comments.

"That's good, dear," Mom said, folding clothes and stacking them in neat piles on the couch. "Don't be disappointed, though, if you're not fully ready or able to get your license exactly on your birthday."

"I will be. Besides, it's a big deal here. I mean, maybe it wasn't back in Wisconsin when you were growing up, but everyone I know in California who is sixteen has a license. I'd be embarrassed if I didn't."

Mom placed a folded T-shirt on Christy's pile of clean laundry and tossed her a mound of bath towels, still warm from the dryer, which Christy snuggled into like a kitten in a feather bed.

"Those are for you to fold, not make a nest out of," Mom said. "All I'm saying is you shouldn't try to take the test until you're completely ready."

Christy dropped the first folded towel to the floor beside the recliner. "Mom, do you think Uncle Bob really meant it when he said he'd pay for my insurance the first year?"

"Certainly. You do remember the condition though. You must pass your test the first time you take it. He was very firm about that. Which is why I'm saying don't take the test until you're absolutely certain you'll pass. Oh, I almost forgot."

Mom handed Christy a letter that had been underneath

the mound of laundry. "This came for you today."

Christy folded the last towel and took the letter from her mom. She didn't recognize the handwriting. The letter, written on a single piece of notebook paper, read:

Dear Christy,

I've thought about what you said, and I think you're right. I'll tell you more about my decision when I see

That was all. The last sentence wasn't finished, and the letter wasn't signed.

"Who's this from?" Christy asked, scanning it again before trying to decipher the smeared postmark on the envelope.

Who wrote this? What did I say? And what kind of decision did somebody make based on something I said? This is strange!

Mom hadn't heard her. She stood by the screen door, a load of folded clothes in her arms, looking at Dad, who was bent over the back of the car in the driveway.

Christy decided to check the handwriting against some of Paula's old letters and started down the hall to her bedroom.

"Christy, what is your father doing to the car? He has a hammer in his hand. Christy?"

Christy quickly slipped into her bedroom and quietly closed the door.

2

Do You Want to Know a Secret?

"This family sure doesn't know how to keep secrets," Christy complained to her mother the next morning in the car.

"Why do you say that?" Mom changed into the fast lane on the freeway and glanced at her watch.

"When Aunt Marti called this morning, she knew all about what happened in the church parking lot yesterday."

"That's 'cuz I told her," David piped up from the backseat.

"Why?" Christy turned around and scolded her nine-year-old brother. "You don't have to always tell everybody everything."

David, a compact version of their dad, had a silly smile on his face. His funny look was exaggerated by his glasses sliding down his nose.

He ignored her by returning his attention to the miniature cars on the seat beside him. Rolling one of the cars along the vinyl seat, he spoke in tiny cartoon voices. "Look out! There's a telephone pole up ahead! Don't worry, it's over a mile away. Doesn't matter! Christy's driving! Oh no! Aaaaayyee! Crash! Bang! Boom!"

Christy didn't do him the honor of turning around. She calmly said, "Mom, make him stop."

"David, don't make fun of your sister."

"I'm not, Mom. I saw this on a cartoon once. Really!"

"David!"

"Oh, all right. Can you put on some music? When are we going to get there? Are we going to stop and get something to eat?"

"We've still got another hour before we get to the airport," Mom said, checking her watch again. "And no, we're not going to stop to get something to eat. You can wait until after we pick up Paula."

"Are we going to stay overnight at Aunt Marti's?" he asked.

"No, we'll probably just stay for lunch and then come home."

"How come I have to go to the airport with you? It's boring!"

"Because last night you begged to go," Mom answered. "Or did you forget?"

"I wish I'd stayed home." David folded his arms and leaned against the door.

"You're not the only one," Christy muttered under her breath.

"Christy!" Mom snapped. "Listen, you two, I want you both to try harder to be kind to each other, especially when we go..." She stopped, and they both waited for the rest of her scolding.

"Well, especially when we go places together like this. Just try harder, all right?"

Neither of them answered, and Mom shot quick, serious glances at them. "All right?"

"Okay," came from the backseat.

"All right," Christy said with a sigh.

They did pretty well the rest of the drive into Los Angeles International Airport. The only disagreement they had came when Mom tried to hurry and David wanted to get a drink of water.

"Come on, David!" Christy yelled. "We don't have time!"

Mom had already scooted ahead of them into the flurry of people. As Christy took David by the arm, she could barely see which way Mom was going.

"Stay with me, David! It's too easy for a little kid like you to get lost in the mob."

He wiggled his arm free but stayed right by her side until they reached Mom, who was talking to somebody in the waiting area. Christy stepped up behind Mom. Since she was several inches taller than her mother, she could see over her shoulder, but she wasn't ready for what she saw.

"Paula?"

The Wisconsin farm girl with the baby-doll face and big, round blue eyes jumped up and shrieked, colliding with David as she wrapped her arms around Christy in an exuberant hug.

"I'm here! I'm here!" she announced to Christy and everyone in the waiting area.

Paula looped her big bag purse over her shoulder and breathlessly, dramatically said, "I was freaking out, you guys! I guess my plane came in early. About ten minutes early, they said. And I got off, and I didn't know anybody, and oh man, I was really worried, and I just sat down and tried to be really calm and everything, and then your mom walked up, and I almost started crying, and then I saw you, and it was like it hit me that I was really here!"

Christy laughed at her friend's enthusiastic commentary. Paula had been like that ever since Christy could remember. She seemed "more" Paula than the Paula Christy had grown up with and hadn't seen for almost a year.

"You cut your hair!" Christy exclaimed.

Paula fingered the side of her very short hair. "I had to! You got yours cut when you came here last summer, and so I thought I should get the California look before I got here, but..."

Paula seemed to notice Christy for the first time. "You're growing yours out! I can't believe it's past your shoulders already! Last time I saw you it was short!"

Then her round cheeks turned a spicy shade of pink, and in a panic she said, "Oh no! Is everybody growing their hair out this year? Am I the only one with short hair? Oh no!"

"Paula!" Christy laughed and spoke softly, hoping Paula would take the hint and lower her voice too. "You look great! This is California. You can wear your hair any way you want. Don't worry. Relax!"

Mom suggested they pick up the luggage, and Paula kept chattering. Christy watched her and thought how really good Paula did look.

She always had been a little cutie, with her long blond hair and innocent, little girl looks. Now, except for the same big baby-doll eyes, Paula looked more like a young woman than a little girl. Her figure had turned out to be much better proportioned than Christy thought her own was, and the sophisticated hairstyle and obvious makeup made Paula look much older than her fifteen years.

It felt strange walking beside Paula, listening to her ramble on, oblivious to how loud she was and how people were turning to look at her. Christy thought of how the year they'd been apart had changed both of them and how she'd waited so long to see Paula again. Now that she was here, well, for some reason Christy felt squeamish.

"You know what I mean?" Paula said, snapping Christy back into the present.

"Oh, yeah, uh-huh." *Whatever you just said.*

"I mean, who knows when I'm going to get back here again, so while I'm here I want to see and do everything we can, and I've been saving up my money so you won't have to pay for me for anything, and maybe I can help pay for gas and stuff when we go places."

Mom calmly turned and spoke solid words to Paula, which made Christy listen carefully. "We will all have a good time, Paula. Just keep in mind that you may get to see some things you didn't expect to see and you may not get to see some things you'd hoped to."

"Oh, I know. My mom said the same thing. I'll be fine whatever we do, really. I don't want to be a bother or anything."

"You're not a bother," Mom said as they stood at the crowded luggage carousel. "We're glad you're here."

"Oh! Look! There are my bags already. That big, ugly brown one and the two little ones next to it."

"Looks like you brought enough stuff to stay a month!" Christy teased as the girls stepped back and let Mom and David capture the moving targets.

"Oh, don't I wish! I had a hard enough time coming for two weeks because we have this big family reunion I have to go to right when I get back. I'm going to have the best tan of anyone there too!"

Christy laughed at Paula's innocent comments. She sounded like such a playful little girl, yet everything in her blue eyes told Christy that Paula had become very serious about her goals.

And she had a lot of goals!

The two girls shared the backseat during the hour and a half drive to Bob and Marti's. Paula went on about how her friend Melissa had gotten her a job at Dairy Queen and how she had saved all her money for the past seven months. She had more than three hundred dollars left, and that was after buying some new clothes and paying for half of her airfare.

"I have to buy a new bathing suit before we go to the beach. I'd just die if I had to wear my old one and people started to laugh at me like they did at you last summer."

"They didn't really laugh at me," Christy said defensively.

"Yes, they did. When you wrote me, you said they made fun of your green-bean bathing suit!"

"Is that right, Christy?" Mom looked in the rearview mirror. "You never told me that."

It was one of those embarrassing moments Christy didn't want to repeat, especially to her mother.

"Thanks for reminding me, Paula!" Christy said, with enough sarcasm that she hoped no one could tell how much it really bothered her.

"I'm only saying that I learn from your experiences, Christy. So I wouldn't let my mom buy me a new bathing

suit before I came to California because I wanted to buy one
here, like you did."

"Is that why Marti bought you all those clothes last summer?" Mom asked.

"Well…" Christy had long struggled with the way her
aunt so freely gave to her and yet also tried to control
through the giving. "You know how Aunt Marti is, Mom.
She likes things to be her way, and she's very generous." *I
hope that came out okay. The last thing I want is for Paula to misquote me to
my aunt!*

"I can't wait to meet your sister, Mrs. Miller." Paula
leaned forward in the seat. "I've heard so much about Aunt
Marti that I just know I'm going to like her. I can't wait to
see their house. I've never known anyone who lived in a
house right on the beach, and at Newport Beach too!
Christy, you are so lucky! Is it very far from here? Where are
we?"

"We're almost there," Christy's mom said and then
asked Paula about how her mom and dad and all her family
were. That filled the twenty minutes it took to arrive at Bob
and Marti's.

"There's never any parking here during the summer,"
Mom said with a sigh and then remembered, "Bob's in
Maui, so I'll park in his usual spot in the driveway."

"Your uncle is in Maui? That's in Hawaii, isn't it? What
am I saying? Of course it's in Hawaii…isn't it?"

"Yeah." David spoke up for the first time in an hour.
"And Todd's there, too! I wish I could've gone with them."

Mom pulled into the driveway and said to David with an
unusually perky smile, "Watch what you wish for, son. You
just might get it."

"Huh?" David said.

Mom turned off the ignition and was the first one out of the car, followed by Paula. Christy had to admit that watching Paula experience the aura of the California beach lifestyle really was fun. Paula approached everything with a fresh excitement and delight.

"Look at this house! Is it gorgeous or what? I can't believe this house! Is that your aunt at the front door?"

Aunt Marti, a slim, sophisticated woman who only slightly resembled Christy's mother, stepped out onto the front steps, which were decorated with painted clay pots brimming with bright summer flowers. The blooms spilled over the sides and down the front walkway.

"So, this must be Paula!" Marti greeted them. "Welcome to California, darling. How was your flight?"

Marti gave each of them her usual feathery kiss on the cheek without smudging her lipstick or ruffling her short, dark hair.

"You always smell like flowers," David said when he got his kiss.

"Why, thank you, David," Marti said.

Before she could invite them inside, David turned to Mom. "You always smell like spaghetti sauce."

"Like spaghetti sauce!" A quick ocean breeze caught a curly bunch of Mom's short, dark hair and scattered it across her forehead. "What made you think of spaghetti sauce?"

Christy thought Mom looked a little hurt to be the "spaghetti sauce" next to her sister, who was the "flowers," even if Mom had grown used to such comparisons over the years.

"It's 'cuz Marti smells more like a garden, and you smell more like a kitchen."

"David, that is so rude!" Christy stopped his analogy, feeling bad for Mom. In a low voice between her teeth, she said, "I can't believe you said that!"

"Why?" David looked surprised. "I love spaghetti. It's just different from flowers, that's all."

Marti took the peculiar moment in her clever grasp and concluded, "I believe we have both been given a genuine compliment. They say the way to a man's heart is through his stomach! Now come in, everyone, please."

They filed past Marti into the plush, modern-decor house. Paula took in everything as if this were a famous museum and responded with what Christy considered to be overly exaggerated oohs and ahhs. Paula's exclamations continued into every room as Christy gave her the grand tour.

"Lunch is all ready and waiting in the kitchen," Marti called up the stairs. Christy was showing Paula the guest room that had been her bedroom while she stayed with her aunt and uncle last summer. "I thought we'd be informal, so I picked up a few things at the deli."

Marti's "few things" turned out to be a full tray of various sliced meats, cheeses, relishes, four kinds of bread, and a choice of three salads. David set to work immediately and built a sandwich so big that Mom warned him he wouldn't be able to eat it all. And he couldn't.

"Can I go out on the beach?" David asked.

"Actually…" Marti placed her diet soft drink down and looked at David with a serious expression. "I need to talk over something with you before you leave the table."

Christy thought something might be wrong, but when

she looked at Mom, she was wearing that perky little smile again. As soon as she noticed Christy looking at her, Mom tried to put on a serious expression, but it didn't work.

"As you know," Marti began, "Bob is gone for several weeks and has left me all alone here."

Her dramatics reminded Christy of Paula's flair for animation. "It's really become more than I can bear, so I've come to a decision."

David jumped up and spouted, "You want us to come stay here with you!"

Paula gasped and entered in with the same enthusiasm. "Oh! Really? You'd let us all stay here with you? What a dream come true! I've always wanted to stay at a beach house!"

"No, no, no." Marti held up her hand and regained the floor. "I am not inviting you to stay here."

"Oh," said Paula.

"Oh." David sat back down.

Christy felt the same way inside, but she kept her reaction to herself.

"I'm not going to be here, so you can't stay with me here," Marti said. "But I would like you to stay with me on Maui!" This time she jumped up and opened her arms, waiting for the congratulatory hugs. Instead of trampling her, the three kids sat frozen in their seats, waiting for the punch line to what seemed like a joke.

"Didn't they hear me, Margaret?" Marti asked her sister.

Mom smiled and tried the direct approach. "Bob and Marti have invited us all to go to Maui. We leave in two days."

Paula screamed. She screamed so loud that Christy put her fingers in her ears and let her mind replay Mom's words one more time. "...*go to Maui. We leave in two days.*"

Marti received her awaited hugs from a screeching, jumping Paula and David. As soon as Christy let herself believe the announcement, she joined in the frolic.

When the noise died down, Paula said, "You guys! This is just like winning on a TV game show or something! My mom is never going to believe this!"

"Your mom already knows," Christy's mom said. "I called and talked it over with her before you came out here."

"How long did you know, Mom?" Christy asked, feeling her heart steady itself from a wild sprint back to a jog.

"Oh, I don't know. A week or two. It was awfully hard keeping it a secret!"

"Does Dad know?" David asked.

"Yes, and that's something I haven't told you yet. Dad can't arrange to get off at the dairy, so he's not coming with us."

"He deserves a vacation more than any of us," Christy said.

"I know," Mom agreed.

Marti jumped in. "He said he'd come with us next time, and he even joked with Bob that the only reason we wanted him to go was to put him to work painting. Bob assured him that's why he took Todd along."

Todd! He must have known all along, because he kept saying we'd have a good time. No wonder he was laughing at me. That turkey!

This wasn't the first time Christy's aunt had arranged a special, extravagant surprise. It wasn't that Christy had grown accustomed to such treatment and no longer fully appreciated the special treats. She did. But the news of going to Maui didn't shock her the way it totally unnerved Paula.

"I can't believe this! Can you believe this? I can't believe this!" Paula grabbed Christy and hugged her, squealing right in her ear. Then pulling herself out to arm's length, a horrified look came over Paula's face. "Oh no. Oh no!"

"What is it?" Marti reached over to pat Paula on the shoulder. "What's wrong?"

Paula turned around and moaned, "I won't have time to get a new bathing suit!"

Then Marti did something Christy had only seen a few times before. Marti laughed out loud, a real back-on-the-farm kind of laugh. "I should've known! You young girls are all alike! What do you think, Margaret? Why don't we take the rest of the afternoon and go shopping?"

"I guess we could do that."

"Aw, do we have to?" David griped. "Can't I just stay here on the beach?"

"In a few days you'll be on one of the most beautiful beaches in the world. Today, we shall go shopping!" Whenever Marti made declarations like that, David had learned better than to try to cross her. The girls were the first ones in the backseat of Marti's new black car, which had more room than her old Mercedes and softer upholstery than Christy had ever felt.

David wadded himself up by the left door, and when Marti started down the street, he played with the electric windows until Mom told him to stop. Paula began to talk the minute she slid into the backseat and didn't stop until they got to South Coast Plaza.

Marti took the car around to valet parking, and Paula asked in amazement, "You mean you can hop out right here in front of the store and somebody parks your car for you way down there and you don't have to walk or anything? That's so cool. This is so unbelievable! Yesterday I was making cones at the Dairy Queen, and today I'm shopping in California for my trip to Maui!"

She shrieked again and clutched Christy's arm. "When are you going to get excited about this trip and show some enthusiasm?"

"I am excited, Paula. It's just that you're expressing enough of it for both of us."

"If the way you're acting now is your idea of enthusiasm, then it's no wonder you didn't make cheerleading!"

What a blow! Christy stopped walking, and Paula turned around and playfully said, "Aw, come on, Christy! Lighten up! I was just kidding!"

Why would Paula say such a thing? She knows I made the team but turned down the spot so another girl could take it. Why would Paula twist it like that and make me look bad?

Mom, Marti, and David were walking ahead of them, but Christy felt sure they must have heard. It was hard not to hear Paula when she was cranked up.

Christy could feel a headache beginning to streak across her forehead. She wished she was taking a nap instead of participating in Marti's shopping parade.

Watching Paula's exuberance over the variety of bathing suits to choose from only made the situation worse. "Which one should I get, Christy?" Paula held up a neon green bikini on a hanger and modeled the same style in hot pink in the spacious dressing room.

"I don't care. Either one," Christy answered from her slouched position on the dressing room chair.

"Oh, well you're a lot of help! Where's your aunt? I should ask her."

"She's still looking at stuff for my mom."

"I guess I'll get the green. I've never owned anything this bright in my life. I think I'll look more tan, don't you?"

"Yeah."

Paula took her eyes off her reflection and examined Christy. "Are you all right? You've been a total blob since we started shopping."

"I have a headache, and I feel kind of yucky."

"Why didn't you say so?" Paula sprang into action and dug into the bottom of her huge purse. "Do you want real aspirin or acetaminophen?" She pulled out a travel-size bottle of each.

"Look at you, Little Miss Organized!" Christy teased. "I'll take either. Just one. And I need some water. I'll be right back."

Christy took the tablet and headed for where she'd seen a drinking fountain, glad for the excuse to get out of the dressing room. She knew it was a stupid little thing and it shouldn't bother her, but the whole time she was watching Paula pick out a bathing suit, she felt waves of jealousy over Paula's figure.

To tall, lanky Christy, Paula seemed to have the perfect body. She was just the right medium height and well-proportioned, with a much larger bust than Christy's. Paula seemed proud of her figure too, judging by the way she didn't hesitate to try on skimpy little bathing suits and model them without embarrassment.

I would never even try on that neon bathing suit! Christy thought as she sipped the cold water and swallowed the pill. *I'd never look as good as Paula does in a suit like that, but also Mom would never let me out of the house with so little on.*

By the time Christy returned to the bathing suit department, Paula had paid for the swimsuit and stood waiting for her by the register with the bag in her hand.

"Did you get the green one?" Christy asked, trying to hide her jealousy.

"Nope. Changed my mind. I got the pink one. Now I want to find some of those really cool sunglasses like I saw in a magazine. Do you think they have sunglasses here?"

"I think we'd better find my mom first," Christy suggested. "We can ask Marti about the sunglasses. She'd know where to find them."

"Aren't you going to get anything?" Paula asked.

"I don't know. Maybe. I can't really think of what I need."

"Forget what you need. Get what you want! I bet your aunt would buy anything you wanted if you just hinted you liked it."

"Yeah," Christy agreed, "she would."

What Christy didn't add was that she'd tried that route with her aunt before, and it hadn't produced the kind of satisfaction she'd expected. Almost all of Aunt Marti's gifts came with a string attached, and Christy had concluded that being content with what she had was more freeing than having lots of things and feeling like Marti's marionette.

"Girls!" Marti called. "Over here! Margie's getting a new bathing suit and cover-up. Did you two find anything?"

"Paula got a bathing suit too," Christy offered.

Marti looked at the bag in Paula's hand and with a slightly offended tone said, "You paid for it yourself?"

"Well, yeah," Paula answered, confused at Marti's reaction. "I planned on buying a suit once I got here, and I had the money all saved up and everything. It was even on sale!"

Marti handed her credit card to the clerk at the cash register, and in a voice that sounded like a cooing dove, she said to Paula, "You tell me how much it was, and I'll give you the cash back. I wanted to get the swimsuit for you as my little Welcome-to-California gift."

Paula's eyes stretched wide open, resembling two bright blue marbles. Christy thought she looked like a character in a storybook right after being sprinkled with fairy dust and told all her dreams were about to come true.

I didn't look that way last summer...did I?

They shopped another three hours, with David continually complaining until Marti bought him a frozen yogurt sundae in a waffle cone. Mom warned him that he wouldn't be able to finish it, and he didn't.

Paula spotted the sunglasses she wanted in a store window, and Marti swiftly bought them for her, as well as a matching pair for Christy. Christy didn't even really like them. They were expensive, and she knew she should be appreciative to her aunt for the gift, so she said thank you. But she refused to gush the way Paula did.

When the valet brought the car around, Marti suggested they go somewhere for dinner. Mom declined, saying she was anxious to get on the road since they still had another hour and a half drive back home to Escondido.

"Thank you soooooo much." Paula gave Marti a hug as

they parted in her driveway. "I love the sunglasses and the bathing suit and everything you got me. Thank you!"

"Thanks," Mom said, giving her sister a hug. "I guess we'll see you at six o'clock on Tuesday morning when we pick you up."

"Right," Marti said efficiently. "Six at the latest, because the plane flies out at eight-thirty. Why don't you take the leftover lunch meat home for dinner? I won't eat it before we leave, and it's a waste to throw it out."

Mom followed Marti inside for the leftover deli tray, Christy and Paula transferred the shopping bags from Marti's car to Mom's car, and David claimed the front seat, where he lined up his tiny cars on the dashboard.

"You sure didn't get much," Paula commented once the bags were all in the car. "How's your headache?"

"It's gone. Thanks."

"Can you believe we're going to Hawaii? I still can't believe it! And Todd is there! I can't wait to meet him! I noticed your bracelet while we were shopping. That must be the one he gave you on New Year's Eve, right? And didn't he give it to you somewhere right around here, in the street? You'll have to show me the intersection on the way home. I thought that was so romantic when you wrote and told me all about him jumping out of the car and giving you the bracelet and kissing you and everything!"

"Ewwww!" David exclaimed. "You and Todd kissed? That's gross!"

Oh good, Paula! Great. Thanks a lot. I'm so glad you feel free to make my private life public! Why did I ever tell you all those personal things?

Christy's expression mirrored her feelings, and Paula instantly got quiet while making a face that said "Oops!"

Then she giggled a tiny secret giggle like she and Christy had many times in the past. But this time the last thing Christy felt like doing was giggling.

All the way home Christy pretended to be asleep, her head resting on the window. Paula didn't slow down a bit. She talked about the farm where Christy grew up and about the new owners while Mom kept her going with questions about a variety of people who lived in their small community.

Christy filtered it out and tried to figure out why she was feeling bothered by everything. This was Paula, her best friend ever since she could remember. They were going to Maui to spend a week with Todd.

Maybe she hadn't gotten enough sleep the night before. Whatever it was, she didn't like being so grumpy, and she decided to lighten up and try to act carefree like Paula.

Come on, Christy! She tried out Paula's favorite phrase while mentally lecturing herself. *You're too uptight. Try to be perky like Paula. Paula's excited. You be excited too. Paula's cute. You try being cute too.*

With her eyes still closed and her head resting against the window, Christy pressed her lips together and forced them up into a puffy-cheeked, cutesy grin. She pictured herself opening her eyes, round and dreamy like Paula's. Instead of seeing herself looking sweet and darling like Paula, the only image that came to her was Miss Piggy tilting her head and getting mushy over Kermit the Frog.

The picture struck Christy as so silly that it actually chased away her foggy-headed feeling. The rest of the way home all she had to do was think, *Oh, Kermie, Kermie!* and a fresh little giggle bubbled up inside.

3

If Only Katie Could Fit in My Suitcase

How odd it was, then, that when they got to Christy's house, Christy perked up and started being bubbly, while Paula took one look at their small rented house and said, "This is where you live?" Then Paula became the moody one or tired one or whatever her problem was.

Dad suggested they order pizza, since it was late. Then Mom wouldn't have to cook.

"Fine with me," Mom said. "Marti sent the rest of her deli tray home, so it looks as though you can snack on left-overs for at least the first few days we're gone."

Dad didn't seem to mind that they were all going without him. He listened to their exciting plans for Maui and said he'd go next time. He just had too much work at the Hollandale Dairy to be able to take off right now.

In a way she couldn't explain, Christy admired her dad, watching him be happy for them without acting left out. She also knew that Hawaii was not her dad's idea of the perfect vacation spot. He preferred a quiet lake and a fishing pole. They'd had many such camping vacations while she was growing up.

What she saw in her dad now was comforting.

Something inside her said, *Even though Dad isn't a Hawaiian-vacation kind of person, he doesn't try to stop us from going.*

David ate three pieces of pizza, leaving all the green peppers on his plate. Paula barely nibbled on one piece before saying she felt tired.

"I'll bet you are," Dad said. "It's half-past midnight where you come from. I put the roll-away in Christy's room for you. It's a tight squeeze, so don't try to open the door all the way."

Christy showed Paula where the towels were in the bathroom. At her friend's request, she came up with an extra pillow for her and then got ready for bed while Paula occupied the bathroom.

When Paula returned to Christy's room, she found Christy lying on her bed, reading her Bible.

"What are you reading?"

"My Bible."

"You're kidding. Do you do that all the time now?" Paula tossed her dirty clothes in the corner of the bedroom.

"Well, I try to every day—even if it's only a little bit."

Paula responded with an "Oh." Then she slipped into her roll-away bed, fluffed up the pillows, and turned her back to Christy.

A few minutes later, Christy heard a huge yawn followed by, "Are you going to turn out the light pretty soon? Not to be rude or anything, but I'm really, really tired."

"Oh, sure." Christy obliged, closing her Bible and snapping off the light. "Sweet dreams, Paula. Dream about Maui—the golden beaches, the summer sun, the clear blue water...Paula?"

The only sound coming from Paula was the deep breathing of a sound sleep.

Christy stretched out under the covers, folding her hands behind her head and facing the dark bedroom ceiling. Then in a whisper, with her lips moving but no sound emerging, Christy prayed.

"Lord, I have to tell her about You, but I don't know how. I've told her in letters, and last summer I told her how I gave my life to You and promised You my whole heart.

"But she doesn't understand. I feel as though we're so different now, Paula and I. There's so little between us that's the same, and before we were like twin sisters.

"I think that's why I was so bummed out today. I wanted to be close to her like I used to be, but we've both changed too much.

"She needs to become a Christian, like me, and then we can be close again. I'm going to try everything I can to show her she needs to give her life to You.

"Oh, and Lord, thanks for working out everything so that we could go to Maui. Please be with Todd right now and keep him safe. Good night, Lord."

Before she could add "amen," Christy drifted off into a beach-and-surf island dream.

The July morning sun hit Christy's window at 6:20 and flooded the room with light through her thin, lacy white curtains. Christy had adapted all summer by pulling the covers over her head and hovering between the real world and dreamland for at least another hour.

Paula, however, wasn't the hovering type. She greeted the early morning sun by opening the bedroom window and unpacking her suitcase, singing softly to herself.

"What are you doing?" Christy asked the early bird.

"You're awake? Good! Why don't you get up and give

me your opinion on which clothes I should take to Hawaii and which ones I should leave here. Remember, your aunt said we should try to take only one suitcase each. I have too much stuff, so I have to decide what I really need and what I don't. Is it always hot in Hawaii? Or should I take jeans and sweatshirts?"

Christy pulled the covers over her head and mumbled, "I can't believe you're up! Do you know what time it is?"

"In Wisconsin it's almost ten o'clock. I'd be getting ready for work right now if I were home, but I'm not! I'm in California, and tomorrow we're going to Maui."

Christy rolled over and pulled back the covers from her eyes. "You mean that wasn't just an exotic dream I had last night? We really are going to Hawaii?"

Paula laughed and tossed a pillow at her. "I know! I still can't believe it either. This is going to be the absolute best summer of my whole life! But wait a minute."

Paula plopped herself down next to Christy's legs at the end of her bed. "You haven't told me anything at all about Todd since I've been here. I thought you'd be going on about him nonstop like you do in your letters."

Christy propped herself up on her elbow. "I haven't exactly had a chance to tell you much. I mean, I'm not exactly into telling my whole life story in front of my little brother, like some people I know!"

She flung back the pillow at Paula. Paula caught it, hugged it to her middle, and giggled. "Sorry about that! It's probably good for David to realize that people, you know, kiss and stuff. He's old enough to figure all that out, isn't he?"

"I don't think so. Besides, Todd is like a big brother or

a cousin to David. Sometimes I think he spends more time with Todd than I do!"

"So, tell me everything. I've been dying to hear. Are you in love?"

Christy laughed.

"Come on!" Paula urged. "How far have you guys gone?"

"What?"

"You know. How far have you gone? Like kissing and everything."

"Well, he's kissed me about five times."

"And?"

"And what?"

"What else?" Paula nudged Christy's feet with her elbow.

"That's all. There is nothing else."

Paula stared at Christy a second and then, as if convinced she was telling the truth, pulled back and said, "Then something's wrong."

"What do you mean?"

"Think about it, Christy! You guys have known each other for more than a year, and you've pretty much been going together the whole time, right?"

"We're not exactly going together."

"You're not going out with anyone else, are you?"

"Of course not! Paula, you know I'm not really allowed to date until I'm sixteen."

"I'll bet you anything Todd is going out with someone else."

Christy gave Paula a slightly disgusted look and tried to figure out what she could be getting at.

"You don't see it, do you? Christy! How could you be
so blind? When a guy likes you, he does more than just kiss
you, and more than five times in a year! If Todd really, truly
loved you, he'd be much more, you know, aggressive. That's
how you can tell if a guy really likes you—by how hard he
comes after you. He's probably got another girlfriend in
Newport Beach, and you're just like the backup, girl-next-
door, good friend kind of girlfriend."

Christy knew Paula was wrong, but she didn't feel quite
awake enough to try to prove it. She'd heard these kinds of
accusations from another friend months ago. The other
girl's words had awakened a fear and anxiety in Christy over
Todd. She'd since become more secure in her relationship
with him, even if their relationship didn't fit anyone else's
idea of "normal."

"You know," Paula adjusted her position at the end of
the bed, "I'm pretty surprised. All along I thought you guys
were a whole lot more serious, and you just weren't writing
it in your letters in case your mom or my mom read them."

"Paula, wait until you meet Todd. He's not like any
other guy. He would never try to push our relationship into
anything more than what it is. Physically or otherwise.
That's just the kind of guy he is."

"There is no such guy!" Paula declared. "No eighteen-
year-old guy who is as good-looking and wonderful as you
say he is is going to limit himself to only one girl. I still say
he has another girlfriend he hasn't told you about."

Christy shook her head. "Wait until you meet him,
Paula. You'll see. He's a Christian. He really loves the
Lord."

As soon as Christy mentioned the Lord, Paula ended

the conversation by heading for the bathroom to get ready for the day. Christy tried to snuggle back down and get some more sleep.

Too late. Her brain was functioning at full speed, sorting through everything Paula said and throwing out most of it.

It did occur to Christy, though, that Paula had drilled her for details about her boyfriend, yet Paula hadn't volunteered one word about any of the guys she'd mentioned in her letters over the past year.

When Paula returned to the bedroom, Christy asked, "You didn't tell me if you have a boyfriend or not. What happened to that one guy? I forgot his name. Wasn't he Melissa's brother?"

"Him?" Paula looked surprised Christy would ask. "No, he's long gone. I don't have a boyfriend. I wanted to come to California available for all the surfers I thought you were going to introduce me to." She looked cute and playful when she added, "Now I guess I'll have to settle for a Hawaiian surfer."

Christy's mom appeared in the hallway and stuck her head into the girls' room. "I thought I heard you girls up. Ready for some breakfast?"

That stopped the talk about guys until that afternoon, when Christy's redheaded friend, Katie, came over. Paula and Christy were in Christy's room packing when they suddenly heard a cheery voice say, "Okay, tell me David is great at making up fairy tales, and I'll save myself a couple bucks."

"Katie! Hi!" Christy said. "This is Paula. Paula, this is Katie."

"Hi."

"Hi."

"So, what did my brother do this time?"

Katie leaned against the door, her green eyes flashing from Paula back to Christy. "Dear David gave me some fairy tale about you guys going to Maui tomorrow. When I told him I didn't believe him, he made me agree that if he was telling the truth I'd have to buy him an ice cream cone. So tell me he's a confused little kid living in a fantasy world."

"He is," Christy said quickly. "But he's also telling the truth. It's one of my aunt's little surprises. We leave tomorrow morning."

From the hallway they could hear David chanting, "I told you so! I told you so!"

"I can't believe it! Do you guys realize how lucky you are?"

"I know!" Paula jumped in and rattled off the details to a straight-faced Katie, who had lowered herself onto a corner of the roll-away bed and sat still, taking in the whole story.

Christy felt awkward. She thought about how much it must hurt Katie that Paula had suddenly shown up and taken her place as Christy's closest friend. And now they were preparing to be whisked away to paradise and leave Katie behind.

Christy felt especially uncomfortable because last fall Marti had taken her and two other girls to Palm Springs, and Katie couldn't go along because of her obligations as school mascot. The trip had turned into a disaster, and Christy now rarely even saw the girls she'd invited along on that adventure. But she'd promised Katie after the Palm Springs trip that she'd invite her along on the next trip Marti set up, no matter where they were going.

And now here the whole Hawaii trip had been planned

to include Paula, and Katie hadn't even been told they were going. Christy knew Katie would understand later when she got a chance to explain everything in private. She couldn't attempt to explain things now without offending Paula, especially if it came out sounding like Christy would rather have taken Katie than her.

"That's pretty incredible," Katie exclaimed when Paula finished the exciting account. "I hope you guys have a good time. I sure wish I was going with you!"

Now Christy felt even worse. Those were the same things she'd said to Todd the morning he left. But she didn't have any secrets up her sleeve like Todd had.

For one instant Christy considered asking her mom if she could call Aunt Marti and see if Katie could somehow come too. She threw the idea out when a mental picture of Mom's face appeared. Mom would never let her ask such an expensive favor, and besides, she'd vowed long ago to never again beg her aunt for anything.

"I came over to see if you both wanted to come spend the night while Paula was here, but it looks like your social calendar is filling up too fast for me." Katie said it good-naturedly, and Christy admired her for it.

"We're only going to be gone a week," Christy suggested. "Maybe we could get together when we get back, before Paula goes home."

"Sure," Katie agreed. "Bring back some grass skirts, and we'll have an all-night hula contest."

They all laughed, and then Katie graciously offered to help them pack. She pitched in with a sweet attitude.

Katie, you amaze me. If I were you, I'd be on my way home, crying by now. You are the kind of friend I want to be.

"What do you think?" Paula asked Katie. "Is it always hot there, or should I take some sweatshirts?"

"I guess I'd take one sweatshirt, just in case."

"Then which one? I brought three. They're all university ones. Whenever I wear them, people come up and ask if I go there, like to Michigan State or whatever. So what do you think is the coolest university to be identified with in Hawaii?" Paula laid out her three sweatshirts.

"Which one is the farthest away," Katie suggested. "You know, it makes you look like you came a long way to see the islands."

"I did come a long way," Paula returned.

"Then wear the Wisconsin one and be true to your home state."

"But the colors in the Pennsylvania one match more of my clothes." Paula eyed the three displayed sweatshirts.

"All I know," Christy said, folding a pair of shorts, "is you'd better decide, Paula. We are leaving in the morning!"

"Taking your tennis shoes, Christy?" Katie asked, bringing over a pair from the closet.

"I guess so. Are you, Paula?"

"We'd better, in case we go jogging. Jogging is a great way to meet guys, you know."

"I'll remember that." Katie laughed at Paula's serious advice. She placed Christy's tennis shoes in the bottom of her suitcase and offered her own advice. "I always put my shoes and Bible in the bottom since they're the heaviest things."

"Good idea," Christy said, fitting her cloth-covered Bible in next to her shoes as though she were putting together a puzzle.

"You know," Katie said, her fair-skinned face becoming sober, "I think it's really a God-thing that you get to go to Maui."

"A 'God-thing'?" Paula asked with a laugh. "What's that?"

Katie remained serious, which didn't happen too often. "It's when something happens in your life, and you look at it and can't explain how or why it happened, but you know there's a reason for it. You know that God is doing something in your life, and it changes you. There's no other way to explain it except to see it as a God-thing."

"We know why this happened, though," Paula quickly responded. "It's because Christy's aunt invited us to go with her."

"Yeah, but think about it. How many people do you know who get invited to Hawaii, all expenses paid?" Katie asked. "Don't you think it's a God-thing, Christy? I think God's going to do something in both of your lives while you're over there."

Christy wasn't sure what a God-thing was supposed to be, but she appreciated Katie's encouraging words. They were like a blessing from someone who could have felt hurt or left out.

A little bit later, when Paula went to the kitchen for something to drink, Katie continued her thought. "Don't you think it's a God-thing, Christy? I mean, I know how long you've been waiting for Paula to come visit, and I know how you've been praying that she'd become a Christian. If you ask me, this whole trip is set up so you and Todd can witness to Paula. Isn't that kind of how you became a Christian last summer? From hearing about the Lord from Todd and another girl?"

"Sort of. Her name was Tracy. But it wasn't so much what they said; it was more who they were. Todd and Tracy both had something I didn't, and that's what got me the most."

"But didn't they both witness to you together? I thought that's what you told me one time when you showed me your Bible. Didn't they both give you your Bible?"

"Yeah, but I don't know. It wasn't like they told me about the Lord, and I said, 'Okay, sure I'd like to give my life to Christ.' It was more like they kept telling me in dif-ferent ways that I needed the Lord. I kind of ignored them—at first. Then later everything they'd been saying, along with some other stuff that had happened, hit me really hard. I knew I had to make a decision."

Katie's green eyes were serious as she said, "You know what I think? I think you shouldn't get discouraged if Paula doesn't hear you and Todd or understand right away when you talk about Jesus. You've got to give it time."

"I know, I know." Christy couldn't explain it, but she felt irritated by Katie's advice. Realizing she must sound rude, she added, "Just pray for us, okay?"

"I will," Katie said. "I promise. And I still think this trip is a God-thing."

After Katie left, Paula made fun of the way she had called their trip a God-thing. "Don't you get freaked out around people who talk about God as if He were, you know, a Spirit watching over you or something?"

"Well, He kind of is, Paula," Christy began, hoping for a chance to explain. "I think what Katie meant—"

Paula cut her off. "Oh, you don't have to defend her, Christy. I like Katie. I think she's really nice. I'm just saying she seemed great until she got all mystical on us."

Just then Mom poked her head into the room. "You girls all packed? I hope you managed to get it all into one suitcase each."

"Just about." Christy surveyed her neatly packed suitcase. "All I need to do is put in my cosmetic bag in the morning."

Mom stepped closer to examine their packing job. A hot pink string hung out of the side of Paula's packed but not yet closed suitcase. Mom tugged on the string until the rest of the bikini top popped out.

"Oh my!" was all Mom said. She kept holding it up as if she were trying to figure out what to do with it. "Is this yours, Paula?"

"Yes," Paula answered politely and without expressing any of the embarrassment Christy felt.

"Is this the swimsuit you bought yesterday?"

"Yeah." Paula plucked the small top from Mrs. Miller's hand and crammed it back into her suitcase, making sure all the strings were tucked in this time.

"Paula," Mom began diplomatically, "I'm not sure your mother would approve of that suit."

Look out, Paula! Here it comes!

Christy struggled with her feelings for both sides. If she could get up the nerve or had the right kind of figure, she'd probably want to wear a hot pink bikini too. Still, she knew her mom was about to appeal for the side of modesty, and she agreed with that side too.

"Oh, don't worry, Mrs. Miller. I only bought this one to sunbathe in. I have my old one-piece for swimming. I bought this one because, I mean, what's the point of going to Hawaii if you can't come home really tan?"

Mom seemed satisfied with Paula's reason and only gave her a warning. "I'd like you to make sure you have a T-shirt or cover-up along so you can slip it on in case you're sunbathing and the guys show up."

Paula smiled her agreement, and Mom let it go at that. She urged the girls to get to bed early since they'd be leaving at four in the morning for the airport. Christy couldn't help but think that if she ever tried to bring home a bikini, her mom and dad would forbid her to ever wear it—for sunbathing or anything. Paula had gotten off easy.

Paula fell asleep quickly again that night, while Christy kept finding little things to finish up or stick into her suitcase, which she did in the dim light from the hallway so as not to disturb Paula. One of the things Christy came across as she cleaned off her desk was the mysterious letter she'd received a few days ago. She stuck it in her purse, intending to ask Paula the next morning if she'd written it. And what did the part "I thought about what you said" mean?

Christy glanced around her room in the faint light and felt pleased that she was leaving everything basically neat. She liked having things where she could find them.

The only thing left to clear away was the mound of dirty clothes the two girls had been tossing into the corner for the last two days. Christy scooped it up and carried it down to the washing machine in the garage.

As she dumped it on top of the washing machine, she saw Paula's one-piece bathing suit wadded up and tucked in with the other dirty clothes. Christy tried to figure out why Paula would put her bathing suit in the wash, especially after telling Mom she planned to wear it while swimming instead of her new bikini.

She must have accidentally tossed it in the corner when she was sorting out her clothes. Or maybe Paula was trying to hide the suit and leave it at Christy's so when she got to Maui she'd have no choice but to wear the bikini the whole time?

Christy leaned against the cold washing machine and thought about how the Paula she grew up with would never do something deceptive like that. Trouble was, Paula had changed. Christy wasn't sure who this new Paula was or what she might be capable of.

4

Flight 272 Is Now Boarding

"Here today, gone to Maui!" David said for about the fifteenth time as Mom drove the car along the freeway. It was almost six o'clock, and they'd be late picking up Marti. That would make Marti mad, and if they missed their flight, that would make everyone mad.

"All right, David," Mom snapped. "That's the last time I want to hear you say that. Understand?"

He nodded and wisely kept quiet. Mom didn't get ruffled often, but when she did, look out.

Christy exercised the same prudence and kept her mouth shut, feeling the tension Mom displayed as she clutched the steering wheel tightly and drove close to the car in front of them. They'd left home when it was still dark, but now the day was wide awake, and the freeway was crowded with vacationers and commuters.

"Come on, come on," Mom muttered to the motor home in front of them. "Either speed up or move it over, buddy."

Christy had rarely heard her mom talk to other motorists, and she thought it was kind of funny.

"My mom does that all the time too. Talks to cars, I mean," Paula told Christy in the backseat, where they sat with a big duffel bag between them. "It cracks me up. She really gets upset at tractors on the road. I just pass them, but my mom follows them for miles. It's so funny."

"You have your license already?" Christy asked.

"No, just my permit. But I drive all the time anyway. Everyone does."

"What about the insurance? What if you got in an accident?"

"I don't know."

"You're kidding!" Christy looked at bright-eyed Paula. "Insurance is a big deal here. Nobody can drive without insurance, and it's super expensive. My Uncle Bob said he'd pay my insurance for the first year if I passed my driver's test the first time I tried."

David turned around and announced, "And she needs insurance! She already had an accident!"

"You did? What happened?" Paula quizzed her.

Christy gave her brother a dirty look before explaining the parking lot incident in a matter-of-fact way, hoping it would come across as no big deal.

Paula giggled. "That must've been embarrassing! Did anyone see you do it?"

"No, just my dad."

"So, did you get your license yet?"

"I haven't taken the test yet. My birthday's not until..." Christy's eyes grew big and bright. "I can't believe it! I almost forgot all about my birthday!"

"Hey," Paula added, "it's tomorrow, isn't it? With all the Hawaii stuff, I almost forgot too. Can you believe it? You're going to spend your sixteenth birthday in Hawaii. Is that like a dream, or what?"

"You may end up spending your sixteenth birthday in this car if that motor home doesn't move it!" Mom sputtered.

Christy and Paula turned and made giggly faces at each other, laughing at Mom's anxiety attack. A few minutes later, they spotted the reason for the clogged freeway—a stalled truck had closed off the center lane, and traffic had been routed around on both sides.

Once they made it past the holdup, the freeway cleared, but the tension kept building until they reached Marti's. Then the fireworks really began. Christy and Paula watched as the two women acted like teenage sisters, squabbling over why Mom was fifteen minutes late, which car they should take, and why they couldn't have been more organized.

The group ended up in Mom's car, with David in the backseat, his seat belt tightly holding both him and the duffel bag, and Marti in the front seat with a suitcase under her feet.

"This is precisely why I requested you each fit your things into one suitcase apiece," Marti scolded. "This day is certainly starting out wrong; I've never left so late for a flight in my life!"

"We hit a lot of traffic, and there was a stalled truck," Mom explained, still gripping the steering wheel tightly as she maneuvered back onto the freeway.

"We might be able to bypass some of the traffic," Marti suggested, "if we get on the 405. See the sign there? Stay in this lane."

Mom followed the directions while Marti continued to make plans. "Okay, now if we do miss our flight, which I certainly hope we don't, then we'll find out when the next flight leaves and switch to that."

As it turned out, they didn't need Marti's alternative. They made it to the airport, checked their luggage, received their seat assignments, and ended up with half an hour before they could even board the plane. Mom gave in to David's pleas for a pack of gum, and the two of them scurried off to the nearest shop, leaving a somewhat subdued Marti sitting in the waiting area with the girls.

"We should've gone with them," Paula suggested after Mom and David were out of view. "I don't have any gum, and my ears always bother me on airplanes."

"Paula," Christy pointed out, "you've only been on one airplane in your whole life, and that was a few days ago coming out here."

"I know. And I chewed gum the whole time. Marti, would it be okay if we went to get some gum?"

"I suppose. If you hurry. I'll stay here with the carry-ons. Don't forget, we board in less than half an hour."

"Would you like us to bring you anything?" Paula asked sweetly.

"No thanks, dear. Just hurry!"

Paula and Christy briskly nudged their way through a throng of people lined up at the check-in desk. Christy suggested they make a quick stop at the bathroom too since Marti had said the flight would take five hours.

"First some gum," Paula directed. "And I saw a magazine I wanted to get while we were running past all those shops on the way in."

Suddenly, Paula stopped. "I don't believe it!" she squealed under her breath, or as under her breath as Paula was capable of squealing. Then plunging her hand deep into her huge shoulder bag, she rummaged around until she pulled out a pair of glasses, which she quickly slipped on.

"When did you start to wear glasses?" Christy asked.

"That's him! Over there...see him? That's the guy from that TV show—what's that show? You know, there are these two guys and—"

Grabbing Christy by the arm, Paula yanked her past the bathroom area and into another section of the terminal. "Come on! He's going this way! Did you see him? What's his name, Christy? I can't remember his name!"

"Paula!" Christy yanked her arm back and yelled at her friend. "Paula!"

Paula turned, looking dazed but still heading toward the movie star. "What? What? Come on!"

Christy hustled to keep up with her. "I don't see who you're even talking about! Come on, Paula! What are you doing?"

"I'm going to get my first movie star's autograph! Come on!"

They blitzed past a large tour group and ended up in a section of the airport that had two wings to choose from.

"This one." Paula grabbed Christy by the arm again. "I saw him go this way."

"Do you even know who we're chasing?"

"I can't think of his name. He's on that show, you know..." Paula stopped short. "Where did he go? I don't see him!"

"Paula, I mean it! We have to go back right now! I didn't see anybody who looked famous. This is stupid!" Christy brimmed with anger and exasperation but kept her words brief. "We have to go back right now!"

She abruptly turned and marched away from Paula.

"Okay, okay, I'm coming." Paula caught up. "I know I saw him, though. What's his name? This is going to drive me crazy! He's really cute and popular, and he's on that show…"

"Most movie stars are cute and popular and on shows!" Christy picked up her pace, scolding Paula over her shoulder. "I can't believe you! We could've gotten lost or missed our plane over this phantom movie star!"

"Wait, Christy." Paula slipped her glasses back into the bag and grabbed Christy's arm again, which she jerked away. "I want to go in here and get some gum."

"We don't have time!"

"Yes, we do. Your aunt was just pressuring everybody. We have like an hour until the plane takes off."

"Half an hour," Christy corrected.

"Half an hour till we board; then it takes another half hour until the plane even takes off. We have plenty of time."

Paula entered the small souvenir shop and took her time browsing through the magazines before selecting one. She picked up a pack of gum and held it up for Christy to see. "You like this kind?"

"I don't care. Anything. Let's go!"

Paula slipped her purchases into her bag, and the two girls stepped back into the main terminal area and looked around. Neither of them moved. Nothing looked familiar.

"We go this way," Paula said, regaining her self-assurance.

"Are you sure? I thought our gate was over there."

A cloud of uncertainty came over Paula, casting a puzzled shadow on her expression and revealing her growing feelings of terror.

The noise and constant hubbub from the throngs of

people rushing past them made Christy feel dizzy.

"Let's ask somebody," Paula said breathlessly, scanning the bustling crowd, apparently looking for a stranger who appeared approachable and trustworthy.

"We can't just start talking to some stranger!"

"Then what are we going to do?" Paula dug her finger-nails into Christy's arm, sounding as panicked as she looked. "What are we going to do? We're lost!"

"Let go!" Christy said. "Where's one of those monitors that shows all the flights and their times?"

"Over there!" Paula pointed to one on the wall behind them. "What flight are we on? What airline? Do you know? I don't even know what airline we're on!"

"It was United, wasn't it?" Christy asked as they scram-bled closer to the monitor for a better view.

"There!" Paula said, pointing. "Honolulu! There's a flight in half an hour to Honolulu. That's us, isn't it? Honolulu is in Hawaii, isn't it? Of course it is. Isn't it?" Her voice rose and became squeakier.

"Yes! Yes! Yes!" Christy's irritation overtook her fear. "But what's the one listed above it? How do you say that— Ka-hu-lu-i?" Christy asked. "I think that's the airport we're going to because that one leaves at the time we were supposed to, and it has a Hawaiian name."

"How do you know it's a Hawaiian name? Honolulu— now that's a Hawaiian name. Kahului could be some place in Bora Bora, or worse, it could be a flight to the Antarctic! We can't go jumping on the first flight we find that has a Hawaiian-sounding name! I think we should go to Gate 87, where the flight to Honolulu is. Everyone knows Honolulu is in Hawaii."

Just then the Kahului line began to blink, and instead of a time being listed, the words "Now Boarding" flashed across the screen.

"Now boarding, Paula! I know that's our flight! I know it! And they're leaving right now. Come on! Gate 57. Where's Gate 57?"

The girls took off, sprinting down the nearest wing of the terminal, then realized it was the wrong one and ran the other way, following signs and bumping into people. Both of them were starting to cry. Panting and blinking wildly, they suddenly recognized the wing they'd started from.

"This is it! I'm sure of it," Christy said. The girls dashed to the waiting area, which previously had been crowded with people. It was empty now, except for Christy's mother, who had her back to them. She stood next to the ticket counter, talking to the flight attendant and using sharp hand motions.

"Mom!" Christy yelled from twenty yards back, not caring who heard her. "Mom!"

"Mrs. Miller!" Paula screeched.

Mom spun around, and instead of welcoming them with a relieved embrace, she planted both fists on her hips. Her face, stern as stone, told Christy everything she didn't want to know.

"We missed the plane, girls," Mom stated. "We missed the plane! Where have you been?"

Christy scrambled to regain her composure and respond as maturely as possible. Before she could say a word, Paula let her emotions rip. With wild sobs, she clung to Mom's arm and went on hysterically about trying to get away from some strange man and getting lost and being afraid the man was going to kidnap them and a whole bunch of other unintelligible garble.

Mom instantly changed her approach and tried to calm Paula down before she drew a crowd.

"Excuse me," the flight attendant said, leaning over the counter and looking much sweeter and more concerned than she had when Mom had been talking with her a few minutes ago. "Are you girls okay?"

Christy nodded.

Paula could have won an Oscar for her reaction. She curled in her lower lip, opened her eyes wide, and let more inky, mascara-stained tears zigzag down her baby face.

Then softly, to Christy's mom, the uniformed woman said, "We did experience an abduction of an eight-year-old girl at the airport last Thursday. Perhaps I should call security."

"No!" Paula said quickly. "I mean, it would take too long. We already missed our flight, and it would take too long to answer all the questions and everything."

"We're okay," Christy added. "Nothing really happened. We got lost. That's all." No one seemed to believe Christy's mild account.

"Let me check on something." The woman lifted the phone and held it in place with her shoulder while typing something on her computer keyboard.

"Mrs. Miller," she said in a professional tone, "why don't you and your daughters have a seat. I'll let you know what I can find out here."

The three of them moved over to the seats in the waiting area, and Mom pulled out some tissues from her purse for the girls. "You sure you're all right?"

They both nodded and blew their noses. "Mom, I'm really sorry. We got lost, and—"

"It's okay, honey. Marti and David boarded the flight, and I had you paged. I also tried to get us on another flight, but they're all booked. Right before you came up, the gal was telling me that the best we could get would be three seats on a flight leaving tomorrow night."

"Tomorrow night!" Paula wailed and began to cry all over again.

"That's my birthday!" Christy bleated, joining Paula in another round of tears.

Just then a security guard drove up in a tan motorized cart. "Mrs. Miller? Would you like to get in? I'll drive you to the gate."

Mom looked questioningly at him. The woman at the desk then slipped out from her spot behind the computer and placed a tender hand on Paula's shoulder. "I've cleared three seats for you on another carrier. You'll have to change planes in Honolulu and take Aloha Airlines Flight 210 into Kahului."

She handed Mom some tickets and pointed to the handwritten information at the top of the packet. "Make sure you give them this code number when you check in on both flights. It's very important that you show them this number."

She turned and smiled sympathetically at the girls. "You two look out for each other on your vacation now, okay?"

Before any of them fully realized what had happened, they were seated on the cart and whisked away through the crowds to the other side of the terminal. Mom showed the tickets and the special code number, and they were immediately ushered onto a waiting plane and given three seats in first class.

People looked at them, and the flight attendants treated them like royalty. In a few minutes, they had their seat belts on, and the plane was taxiing down the runway. The roar of the engines matched the roar of emotions revving up inside Christy.

She leaned over and whispered to Paula, who was watching the smoggy world miniaturize below, "Why do you think they treated us like that?"

"It must've been because of the abduction thing. They thought we had been chased by a kidnapper."

"But Paula, that's not what happened at all! They thought that because you made it sound that way."

"Well, I was scared!"

"I was too! But you shouldn't have lied."

"I didn't really lie, Christy." Paula looked offended.

Christy clenched her teeth and gave Paula a serious look.

Paula broke into a big smile and breathed a lighthearted laugh. "Relax, will you? You should see yourself right now! You look like that old prune-faced lady who used to work at the post office. What was her name?"

Christy was not pleased with the comparison. The prune-faced lady at the post office, a lady whose glares had frightened her as a child, was not a person she wanted to remember and definitely not a person she ever wanted to resemble.

"Besides, I don't much remember what I said." Paula reached for her headphones and began to untangle the cord. "Everything turned out fine, so I think it's best if we just don't say any more about it, okay?"

"It isn't right, Paula. It's deceitful."

"Why? Nobody was hurt, and we didn't get in trouble. Actually, it turned out great. If we hadn't been crying and frightened and everything, they certainly wouldn't have given us all the special treatment. They never would have put us on this flight, and we wouldn't have left until tomorrow night. Think about it, Christy. Would you like to spend your birthday at an airport or on the beach?"

"On the beach, of course, but—"

"Then give it a rest!" Paula interrupted, confidently reclining the plush, first-class seat and popping her headphones into place. "Face it, Christy. This is what your friend Katie would call a God-thing."

Aloha!

Five hours in an airplane is long enough for anyone to "give it a rest." Christy pretty much decided to put the whole morning ordeal behind her. She couldn't convince herself, like Paula had, that the "happy" ending to their run through the airport was a God-thing. But she certainly didn't want the rest of the trip to turn into one big, ongoing emotional battle with Paula.

So Christy decided right before they landed in Honolulu that she'd have to do everything she could to show Paula the difference between right and wrong, truth and lies. After all, she was a Christian and Paula wasn't.

The first thing Christy noticed when they got off the plane was how sweet the air smelled. It was midday when they arrived, and the air felt warm and balmy. She'd expected that from the movies she'd seen and from her idea of what tropical weather felt like.

But the flower scent dancing in the air was unexpected. The wonderful fragrance came from young Polynesian women dressed in tropical attire, their arms looped with fragrant leis, who greeted certain travelers as they exited.

Following the many signs, the girls trotted after Mom,

who led them directly to the Aloha Airlines booth and presented the flight transfer papers she'd been issued in Los
Angeles. They were ushered within minutes onto a nearly full
plane and were barely in their seats before the plane took off.

Mom twisted around in her seat to talk to Christy.
"That was a tight connection! Marti and David flew directly
to Maui. We're only about an hour behind them. Maybe a
little less."

"Look how clear the water is," Paula remarked as they
soared over the Pacific Ocean. "You can almost see to the
bottom."

"Alissa used to live here," Christy said, "and she told me
the water is really warm."

"Who's Alissa?"

During their quick island-hop to Maui, Christy told
Paula about the gorgeous girl Christy had met on Newport
Beach last summer. Christy had thought Alissa had a lot
going for her, but she had gotten involved with a bunch of
guys, one of whom was Todd's best friend, Shawn.

"You mean Shawn, the one who died last summer in the
surfing accident?" Paula asked.

"Yes."

"Wasn't he on drugs or something?"

"It's a long story, but yeah, he'd been smoking dope."

"And this guy was Todd's best friend?"

Christy nodded. "Anyway, Shawn and Alissa were
together for a while during the summer, if you know what I
mean."

Christy spoke softly, not sure how much of this her
mom might overhear. Paula leaned closer, waiting for
Christy to finish the story.

"Well, Alissa got pregnant, and she had a baby girl last spring. She named her Shawna Christy because of, well, you know, because Shawn was the father, and Christy because we were kind of friends."

"And she kept the baby?"

"Last I heard she was going to try to raise it on her own."

"If that ever happened to me, I'd give the baby up for adoption," Paula said matter-of-factly. "Wouldn't you?"

"I don't plan to ever be in that situation!"

"Nobody ever plans to be in that situation, Christy. It just happens."

Christy lowered her voice even more, though inside she felt like raising it. "It's not going to *just happen* to me. I'm not going to bed with a guy until our wedding night. I won't have to worry about it just happening."

"I used to think that too," Paula said wistfully, looking out the window. Then she turned to face Christy, and with a mist rolling over her ocean-blue eyes, she spoke softly. "I'm the only virgin I know, Christy. Except for you."

"Oh, come on."

"I'm serious. Of all the girls I hang around with, I'm the only one. Do you know what a freak they think I am? If I don't get a boyfriend during this trip..." Her voice trailed off, and she turned her gaze back out the plane window, ending the discussion.

Christy leaned back into the seat and let Paula's words sink in. She couldn't believe Paula had changed so much that she now couldn't wait to give away her virginity so she'd fit in with her friends. Christy had become close to a group of Christian girls during the past school year, and all of them seemed to be trying as hard to keep their virginity as Paula and her friends were trying to give theirs away.

More than anything else that had happened on this trip so far, the last few sentences from Paula hit Christy like a gust of wind, strong enough to bend her opinion of her lifelong friend. She didn't want to see Paula turn out like Alissa.

The pilot's calm voice came over the loudspeaker, announcing their arrival. "We are now beginning our descent into Kahului Airport. The time is 1:20, and the temperature is a balmy 86 degrees. We hope you enjoy your stay on the Valley Isle, and *mahalo* for flying Aloha Airlines. *Aloha*."

Paula and Christy grabbed their purses.

"That was sure a quick flight! My hair is a mess!" Paula gasped.

"Mine too! Do you have a mirror?"

"Here, help yourself." Paula opened her purse and offered its contents to Christy.

The two girls quickly combed their hair in an effort to be presentable.

The plane made a smooth landing, and soon the passengers were standing, excitedly squishing into the aisle and moving like cattle toward the front exit. The flight attendant, wearing a flowered muumuu and a gardenia behind her ear, smiled and said her Hawaiian thank-you of mahalo to each passenger.

The herd of passengers kept Christy, Paula, and Mom boxed in as they moved through a long passageway into the terminal. Christy's gaze swooped back and forth, looking for Todd. She felt almost panicky with anticipation.

Todd! Where are you?

"Stay together now, girls," Mom instructed. "Keep an eye out for Bob. Marti said she'd tell him to wait at the airport for us."

You look for Bob; I'm looking for Todd!

They stepped expectantly through the automatic doors. The only official island greeter was a warm trade wind that gusted on them, destroying their hairdos.

Oh, great! So much for fixing my hair!

"Aloha!" said a warm voice behind Christy. "You made it!"

It was Uncle Bob, heaping flower leis on them, all delivered with kisses and much commotion. Christy looked behind Bob, then to the side of Mom, then over Paula's head.

Didn't Todd come to meet us? Where is he? Suddenly, Christy's gaze stopped.

Tall, tan, and smiling, Todd leaned against a post, hanging back from all the frenzy. He calmly held out to her a fragrant white-flowered lei. His boyish grin and outstretched arms invited Christy to join him.

With three shy steps, Christy left the circle of Bob's joyful greetings and entered another circle, a circle that held only her and Todd. He moved closer, calmly smiling, and placed the lei over her head.

After the traditional Hawaiian kiss on the cheek, she heard his golden voice say, "Aloha, Kilikina!"

What a dream! Christy thought, fixing her gaze on his brilliant silver-blue eyes. *What did he call me? Kilikina! What does that mean? Oh, Todd! I wish I could say all the things I'm feeling right now.*

"And there's Todd!" Mom said, bursting into their

bubble, releasing the dreamers and bringing all the commotion with her.

Todd immediately responded by taking the next white-flowered lei off his arm and placing it around Mom's neck with the same gesture of an aloha kiss.

"This is beautiful! Thank you, Todd. Oh, and Todd, this is Paula. Paula, this is Todd."

What Christy saw in that moment terrified her.

Paula absolutely froze in place. She wasn't even blinking. Obviously, all Paula saw was Todd—totally Todd. Nothing else existed in her world at that moment. She wasn't smiling; she wasn't breathing. She was fixed on Todd.

Her words from the plane came rushing over Christy like a wild gale. "If I don't get a boyfriend during this trip..."

Not Todd, Paula. No way! Stop looking at him like that!

Bob broke the spell. "So, you caught the next flight with no problem." He said it in his usual carefree, good-natured manner.

Bob looked like he belonged on an island, with his flower-print shirt and shorts, and flip-flops. Todd had on the same sort of "native" attire. They looked like they'd been on Maui all their lives, not just a few days.

Todd casually slipped a lei over Paula's head and brushed her cheek with an aloha kiss.

Paula responded by enthusiastically throwing her arms around Todd's neck and returning the kiss to his right cheek.

That does it, Paula! Stay away. Don't you dare touch him again!

"It's really quite a story," Mom said with a laugh.

They began walking toward the parking lot, and Paula

slid in right next to Todd, looking up at him like a dreamy-eyed Miss Piggy gushing over Kermit.

This time the Piggy-Kermie image did not initiate a giggle inside Christy. Instead, every possessive, jealous response Christy had within her sprang into action.

She grabbed Todd's arm and said coyly, "So this is why you said we'd have such a good time! You knew I was coming all along, didn't you? How could you keep this a secret, Todd?"

Paula followed Christy's example by clutching Todd's other arm and declaring in her most exuberant manner, "You've got to teach me how to surf, Todd! Promise me you'll teach me! Okay? Promise? I just have to learn how to surf. That's like my ultimate, all-time dream!"

Poor Todd, Christy thought. *Without warning, you've been pounced on by two Miss Piggys. It's up to you, Kermit the Todd. Which one of us is it going to be?*

Bob interrupted before Todd had a chance to respond to either of the "Piggys." "Marti and David went ahead in the van with all the luggage. The five of us are going to squeeze into the other car we rented. It's only about a forty-five-minute drive to the condo."

"We don't mind!" Paula said pertly. "We just can't believe we're finally here! And these flowers!" Paula used her free hand to lift the two leis to breathe in their fragrance.

"What are these?" she asked Todd. "I love them!"

"Plumeria. The big white and pink ones are plumeria, and the little white ones are tuberose."

"Oh, I love them! They smell so...so...exotic!" Paula went on, still clinging to Todd.

"You told me about the plumeria before," Christy said, slightly tugging on his arm, hoping for Todd's full attention. "Weren't these the kind of flowers you could smell on the way to school when you lived here?"

"Yeah." Todd turned his head to look completely at Christy. "You remember me telling you that?"

Yes, Todd, oh yes! I remember everything you tell me. Ignore her; look at me! I'm the one who's been listening to you for more than a year. Don't let Paula come between us.

Bob stopped in front of a red Jeep. "Tight squeeze. What do you think? Will you three be okay in the back?"

Paula broke into one of her squealing sessions and scrambled into the backseat. "A Jeep! I've always wanted to ride in a Jeep! And a red one too! I'm not kidding! This is like one of my all-time biggest dreams! Can you believe this? Come on, you guys, let's hit it!"

She stood up in the middle of the backseat and held on to the roll bar, acting like she was in some kind of dune buggy race. The wild wind had totally destroyed their hair when they came out of the terminal, and now Paula's short ends stuck up even more dramatically.

Bob helped Mom into the front seat, and Paula positioned herself snugly in the middle of the backseat. Christy stood her ground in the parking lot, fuming that Paula would try to pull off this seating maneuver, guaranteeing she'd sit next to Todd.

Todd began to climb into the backseat when Uncle Bob said, "You know, it's just a suggestion, but you kids might consider letting the person with the longest legs sit in the middle. Like I said, it's a tight squeeze, and long legs can fall asleep back there awfully quick."

Paula slid to the side behind the driver's seat. "You win, Todd! You have the longest legs." Then she patted the seat, indicating right where he should sit.

Todd obliged. Christy made a less-than-graceful entrance and wondered how Paula managed to "gazelle" her way in so easily.

Bob was right. It was a tight squeeze, and Christy, being the last one in, found she had only enough room to sit on one hip, with her long legs crossed and tangled together. Mom fortunately was able to scoot her seat forward, allowing Christy a few more inches of wiggle space.

Paula chattered on, holding Todd's attention while Bob put the Jeep in gear and hummed through the parking lot, down the narrow streets, past the airport, and out of town.

The adventure of riding in the Jeep in the warm air thrilled Christy until they were out of town. Then Bob picked up speed and zipped past the sugarcane fields. Christy's hair whipped her face mercilessly. It became impossible to hear anyone talking, except Paula, who had no difficulty yelling her sentences of excitement.

She asked Todd what everything was as they passed it, and he was gracious enough to answer once for Paula, then lean forward and give the same explanation to Mom and Christy. He pointed out the pineapple fields, an old sugarcane mill, and the cloud-covered top of Haleakala, a ten-thousand-foot volcanic crater.

When they could see the ocean, he pointed out the neighboring islands of Molokini and Kahoolawe and then the pineapple island, Lanai, when it came into view.

They entered a short tunnel dug through the black volcanic rock, and for one wonderful moment the wind couldn't tease Christy's hair. She pulled all the tiny strands out of her eyes and mouth. Paula, of course, didn't have that problem with her new short haircut.

The ride was annoying but not terrible. Being in the Jeep and next to Todd was a wonderful feeling in itself. Christy felt relieved, though, when they stopped at a red light in the first real town they came to and Bob said, "Our condo is about ten miles up the road. You guys going to make it?"

"Sure!" Paula answered for all of them.

Todd leaned over and told Christy, "This is Lahaina."

"Is this where you lived?" she asked.

"Yeah, when I was a kid. It's a great old town. A lot of history. One hundred and fifty years ago the whalers and sailors used to spend their winters here. But before the Westerners came, when it was unspoiled, the Hawaiian royalty lived here—surfed here too."

"Really?" Christy asked. "Have you ever surfed in the same spot?"

Todd nodded. "My friend Kimo and I used to go there after school, and all the older guys would make fun of us because Kimo used a long board that belonged to his dad. Funky old wooden thing. Then one day this guy came to the beach and offered Kimo big bucks for the board to put it on display in some museum."

"I bet the older guys stopped laughing then!" Christy said.

The light turned green, and they were on the move again, the wind scattering Todd's answer. The wind, however, did not scatter his expression. He looked directly at her and smiled a real, honest Todd smile that showed his

dimple. He'd been resting both his arms across the backseat
for some time, but now he put his right hand on her shoulder and gave it a squeeze.

Christy returned the warm smile, wishing she could
completely relax and disconnect all her jealous, competitive
feelings. She felt self-conscious about how her windblown
hair must look. She also was uncomfortably aware that when
Todd squeezed her shoulder, as romantic as that was, his
arm crushed all the beautiful flowers on the back part of her
lei.

*Come on, Christy! Lighten up! You're in Maui. Why are you worried
about squished flowers and messed-up hair? He just squeezed your shoulder,
not Paula's. He's glad you're here!*

Paula didn't appear to feel self-conscious about anything as she eagerly pointed and said, "That's more
sugarcane, right?"

Todd nodded and talked directly to Paula, pointing out
something on her side of the Jeep. Bob kept driving past
condominium complexes until they finally pulled into an
underground parking lot and parked the Jeep next to a light
blue minivan.

The squeals of delight and excitement started all over
again as they tumbled into the elevator and joked about
their windswept hair. Even Todd's short sandy-blond hair
looked ruffled.

Bob's two condos, located on the sixth floor, both had
their front doors open, and the balmy sounds of Hawaiian
music floated from one of the stereos.

"You made it!" Marti said when they converged on her.
She looked startled. "We've only been here a few minutes, it
seems. David went down to the pool, and I was about to call

all the airlines to see which flight you were coming in on."

It took her only a minute to regain her composure before starting in on room assignments. Christy and Paula were given the guest bedroom to share, and Mom had the master bedroom in that same unit. Todd and David shared the guest bedroom in the condo next door, and Bob and Marti, of course, had the master bedroom.

"Point me toward my luggage," Paula said. "I want to change and hit the beach!"

Marti pointed, and Paula called over her shoulder, "Oh, Mr. Surf Instructor? Are you ready for my first lesson?"

"The big kahuna surf instructor," Bob intercepted, "is on wallpaper duty this afternoon, I'm afraid. You girls go on down to the pool. It should only take us another two or three hours to get the wallpaper up in the bathroom."

"Yeah," Todd said good-naturedly, "two or three Hawaiian hours."

"What's that?" Christy asked.

"You'll find out. People around here are on 'island time.' Two or three hours Hawaiian time usually turns out to be half a day mainland time." With a smile to Christy, he added, "The big kahuna boss says I can have tomorrow off if I work real hard today. You want to see what we've done so far?"

Christy followed Todd around the condo, admiring the freshly painted walls and listening patiently to him explain how tricky it had been to peel off the three layers of wallpaper in the hallway. Todd obviously took real pride in his work, and that was fun for her to see.

When he went back to work with Bob, Christy stepped

into the living room. She could hear Paula's laughter bubbling up from the pool below, where she and David had begun a splash war. Mom and Marti stood on the front balcony, or lanai, as Marti called it, looking past Paula and David in the pool and admiring the turquoise-blue Pacific.

Christy joined them, breathing in the moist tropical air and noticing the perfectly clear blue sky. Everything looked exactly as she thought Hawaii would—tall palm trees swaying in the breeze, caramel-colored sand kissed endlessly by gentle white-laced waves, lounge chairs around a sparkling swimming pool, and Paula swimming in her new hot pink bikini.

Paula swimming in her new hot pink bikini!

Christy's first instinct was a "sisterly" one—she'd tattle. "Mom," she began very determinedly, "I need to talk to you about a few things."

"Yes?" Mom looked surprised, probably because Christy usually didn't come across so forcefully.

"Would you like me to leave?" Marti asked.

"No, it's something you both need to know. It's about Paula."

Mom and Marti gave Christy their full attention.

"First of all, I found her one-piece bathing suit in the dirty clothes last night. I put it in my suitcase because I didn't know if she forgot it or if maybe she was trying not to bring it."

"But I paid for her new one." Marti looked over the edge of the lanai. "She's wearing the new one, so what's the problem?"

Christy looked to Mom for backup.

Mom explained that she'd talked to Paula about wearing

the one-piece for swimming, especially around the guys. "I think her mother would want her to dress a little more modestly than the pink bathing suit."

Marti laughed and looked at Mom as if she couldn't believe her own sister could be so prudish. "Around the guys? For goodness sake! That's David down there swimming with her. David barely knows the difference between boys and girls yet. Certainly she doesn't need to wear a one-piece for David's sake!"

Mom didn't answer.

Christy tried to reason with her aunt. "It doesn't matter if it's David or...or...Kermit the Frog! The point is, she said she'd wear the one-piece when she went swimming, and then she left it at my house. I think she did it on purpose, because she didn't even miss it when she got here and changed to go swimming. She just put on the pink one, and now she's swimming in it."

Marti gave Christy another look that made her feel like a miserable little snitch. "She looks perfectly modest to me. I think you're being childish, Christina. Could it be that you're jealous of Paula's lovely figure?"

Christy ignored the question and kept going, realizing she wouldn't get anywhere with Marti on the bathing suit issue and not at all desiring to be openly compared with Paula in any area.

"Never mind the bathing suit, then. The main thing I wanted to talk to you both about was what happened at the airport. We weren't exactly chased by anyone. Paula thought she saw some movie star, and we started to follow him and got lost. It was all our fault."

Christy felt better for telling what really happened.

What confused her were Mom's and Marti's responses.

Mom shrugged her shoulders. "I don't know what to say, Christy. Everything worked out. I actually think the problem was Marti letting you go on your own in the first place."

"They were only going to get gum," Marti snapped back at Mom. "I believed they were old enough and responsible enough to do that!"

"At an airport, Martha? Didn't you think it would be slightly risky and that they might get lost?" Mom looked mad—not with Christy, but with her sister.

"If you hadn't been so late getting us to the airport, none of this would've happened! We would've had plenty of time. So don't try to blame me that you were late!"

A strange, choking pause followed. Mom retreated, putting up her hands in silent surrender. Christy wondered how many times over the years her mom had been the one to back down from her determined sister.

"Christy," Marti said in a sugary controlled voice, "it would appear to me that you're experiencing some sort of sisterly jealousy here with Paula. This is to be expected. After all, you two grew up together. You've been apart for a long time, and now it would be easy for you to be critical of her for many things just because she's different from you. But that's not fair to Paula, now is it?"

Are you talking about Paula and me or you and my mother? Christy gave a slight nod, which she knew Marti was waiting for.

"Now." Marti put her shoulders back and stuck out her chin. "We are in paradise, and I suggest we all put the past behind us and concentrate on having a wonderful week together."

With a wide smile and an air of confidence that made Christy wince, Marti turned to Mom. "Margaret? Why don't we get ourselves something to drink? A diet soda? Christy, you really should go down to the pool and have some fun."

Christy watched as her mother dutifully followed Marti into the kitchen, leaving her alone on the lanai. Her wad of angry thoughts stuck to the inside of her stomach like a pack of chewed bubble gum.

You don't understand! This is serious! Paula is telling lies and getting away with it. She wants a boyfriend—my boyfriend—and she'll do anything to go home with a "victory" to tell her friends about.

"Aren't you going to join the others at the pool, Christy?" Marti called out in her silvery voice from the kitchen.

Everything inside Christy wanted to shout back, "No! Stop trying to run my life!" She held her tongue and her composure and walked past her mom and aunt without looking at them. Then stepping out the door and retreating into the condo next door, where her things were, Christy flopped onto the couch.

I'm going to show Paula that she can't play any of her cutesy games around me! Maybe she can get away with it with everyone else, but I see right through her. And Todd will too!

Jumping up, Christy went straight to her suitcase and yanked out Paula's "forgotten" one-piece bathing suit. She laid it out in the middle of Paula's bed.

6

"Sweet" Sixteen?

"Where did this come from?" Paula asked in an accusing tone, pointing at her old bathing suit on her bed. She and Christy had just come back from several hours down at the pool.

"Oh, I found it back at my house," Christy answered in her most innocent voice. "I thought maybe you'd forgotten it, so I brought it along for you. Now you'll have a bathing suit to swim in since you said you were only going to sun-bathe in the bikini."

Paula didn't answer with words, but her face said plenty. She was fuming.

The rest of the evening, Paula ignored Christy and did her best to amuse and entertain everyone else, especially Todd.

Bob took all of them to dinner at a seafood restaurant that was within walking distance. The air felt as balmy as it had when they arrived in the afternoon. A sweet breeze was blowing that puffed up the short sleeves of Christy's white T-shirt. Todd was in front of the group with David, and Christy was stuck in the back with Uncle Bob. Paula ended up in the middle between Mom and Marti, talking and laughing loud enough for all of them to hear.

At the restaurant, Mom, Bob, and Marti sat at one table, and Todd, Christy, Paula, and David sat at the table next to them.

"Order whatever you want, kids," Bob said over his shoulder.

"I want either macaroni and cheese or a hamburger."

"David, this is a seafood restaurant. You should order fish like everybody else," Christy said.

"I'm not having fish," Paula announced. "I hate fish!"

"You might like the fish here," Todd said, looking over his menu. "They have a great variety, and it's all fresh. You want to try some opakapaka? Or how about some hapu'upu'u?"

"No, thank you! I have a rule about not eating anything I can't pronounce!" Paula smiled cutely and snapped her menu closed. "I'm having the New York steak, medium rare, so there."

"How about you, Christy?" Todd asked.

He was sitting next to her, and she'd accidentally bumped his knee twice already. Now that he was looking at her, she could feel herself blushing. Or was the heat on her cheeks coming from a tiny bit of sunburn?

"What was that first one you said?"

"Opakapaka." Then leaning closer he said, "Don't tell Paula, but it's snapper, and hapu'upu'u is bass."

He smiled, and Christy smiled back. Not being much of a fish-eater normally, even after hearing their names in English, she wasn't sure if she knew the difference between how snapper and bass tasted.

"Have you decided?" The waiter suddenly stood before

them. Christy needed more time, but everyone else was ready. She hated these moments when she had to make a quick decision, especially when she barely even knew what she was deciding between.

David ordered a hamburger, Paula ordered steak, and Todd ordered something called mahimahi broiled with pineapple rings. Now it was up to her.

"I guess I'll have the New York steak also. Medium well, please."

"See?" Paula said. "You knew I was right all along, didn't you, Christy? Never order something you can't pronounce."

Paula's words hit Christy like a stinging slap. Here was yet another area in which Paula seemed to say, "I'm right, and you're wrong."

Todd's comment didn't help much either. "I can see you three aren't exactly ready to live adventurously. I'll have to teach you how to hang loose and live *'da kine* island-style."

"I can be adventurous, Todd, really!" Paula said. "You'll just have to teach me how."

Todd isn't going to teach you a thing if I can help it! You stay away from him, Paula!

"I'm not sure you can teach anyone to be adventurous. Either you are or you aren't. I don't think it's a learned thing," Todd said, looking serious. "And living 'da kine island-style is, well, it's something you just do. You can't teach somebody how to relax."

"Why do you say that 'da...what is it?" David asked.

"'Da kine," Todd told him. "It's the pidgin way for saying, 'the kind,' and in Hawaii they use it to mean, well...just about anything."

"What's pidgin?" David asked.

"Slang. You know, like an easygoing way of talking. I think pidgin is a combination of all the languages that came to Hawaii. It's the way all my friends and I talked when I was growing up here. Not in school. Just with each other when we were hanging out."

"Like your own secret code?" David asked.

"It's more than that. When you talk pidgin and understand it, it's a way to show other locals that you live here and you're not some *malihini,* some tourist, just passing through."

The waiter appeared with four carefully balanced platters on his arm. Christy's steak turned out to be much more than medium well. Burnt would be more like it. She ate about six bites and gave up when her jaw started to hurt from all the tough chewing.

Todd's fish looked really good. It was a large serving of tender white fish with pineapple rings on top. Christy wished she'd ordered the same.

Next time I'm going to learn from what Todd does. If Paula can have a rule about not ordering anything she can't pronounce, then I can have a rule too. Whatever it says over the restaurant's door, that's what I'll order. If it says steak house, *I'll order steak. But if it says* seafood, *from now on I'll order fish!*

David wanted dessert, but Mom said no since he hadn't finished all his hamburger. Christy didn't want anything but a nice, soft bed. It had been a full day, and they were all too exhausted to even watch TV after they walked back to the condo.

Without saying much to each other, Christy and Paula both soon floated off to sleep, lulled by the endless rocking of the ocean right outside their window.

It seemed to Christy she'd only been asleep for an hour when she slowly opened her eyes and surveyed the surroundings of the bedroom in the brightness of the morning light. It took her a moment to realize it was morning already, and this wasn't part of the sweet dream she'd been in all night.

This was a real dream. A waking dream with a real ocean outside her open window and calm morning breezes tiptoeing across her face.

We're in Hawaii, and today is...hey! Today's my birthday! "Paula," she whispered to the lump of sheets on the bed across the room, "Paula, wake up!"

Paula wasn't in the bed, and she wasn't in the bathroom either. Tumbling into a pair of shorts and a T-shirt, Christy quietly checked in Mom's room. Empty too.

"They must all be next door," she decided while washing her face and doing a few twists with the mascara wand on her eyelashes. She smiled at herself in the mirror. "Maybe it's like a surprise birthday breakfast."

That thought prompted her to plug in her curling iron and pick out a nicer top. She chose a red one. Rick once said he liked her in red.

Rick! I can't believe I thought of Rick. I'm in Hawaii with Todd on my birthday. What am I doing thinking about Rick?

Then she remembered why. For months and months, Rick, a tall, good-looking, popular guy from her school, had promised that when she was officially old enough to date, he would take her out. He even told her once that he'd never forget her birthday, July 27, because he'd marked it on his calendar.

Christy set to work curling her hair, reminiscing about

the numerous up and down times she'd had with Rick during the school year. She'd never quite figured out if she liked him or not. How convenient, as it turned out, that he'd gone to Europe with his family, and she'd gone to Maui. Now the long anticipated and promised birthday date would never take place.

In a way, she felt relieved. Rick, who had just graduated, would go away to college in the fall, and she'd be only an elusive high school memory to him. She could pack away her complex bundle of feelings toward him. It was a nice solution to their nothing-more-than-friends relationship.

Putting the curling iron down with a bump, Christy looked in the mirror. She tried to look at herself the same way she'd often looked at Rick. Every time she had, he'd called her "Killer Eyes."

Then with her chin forward and her voice soft and clear, she said, "Okay, Christy Miller, try explaining this one. If Rick means nothing to you and you say he never really has, then why is it that on your sixteenth birthday, of all the things you could be thinking of, your first thought is of Rick Doyle? He is far away, and he should be far away from your thoughts today. I'm sure he's not thinking of you. You're here with Todd, remember? Now go next door and act like you're sweet sixteen, and let Todd, not Rick, make this a birthday to always remember."

After three crisp little knocks on Bob and Marti's door, Christy tried the knob. When she found the door open, she bounced in with a vibrant "Good morning, everyone!"

Silence. She felt like Goldilocks.

With a much softer voice, she said, "Hello? You guys up yet?"

Oh, how fun! What if they're hiding around the corner, waiting to pop out and surprise me!

Just then the bedroom doorknob turned, and Christy braced herself for the surprise. She was surprised, all right.

Bob, dressed in his pajamas and robe, emerged, yawning like a Papa Bear, so wide that his eyes remained only slits on his groggy face.

"Oh, Christy!" He looked startled to see her. "I didn't see you there. Good morning." He yawned again. "What got you up so early?"

She followed him into the kitchen. "I thought, I mean, it's, well... Paula and Mom were gone, so I thought they were over here."

Bob measured the coffee beans into the grinder, and with a push of a button, the wonderful aroma of ground Kona coffee surrounded them. "Nope. I heard the boys leave more than an hour ago. My guess is Todd went surfing as he has every morning since we got here. I don't know where the rest of them are."

Christy pulled up a stool at the kitchen counter and tried to figure it out. She also tried not to let her hurt feelings show while Bob propped open the front door to let the morning sun and wonderful breeze dance around the room.

"Beautiful day," Bob said, breathing in the morning freshness. "Couldn't ask for a more perfect day."

"Yeah, if you're a weatherman," Christy said under her breath.

Bob turned to look at her. "You hungry?"

"No thanks. I don't feel like eating."

"You want a cup of coffee?"

"No." Then something inside Christy made her change her mind. "Well, yeah, maybe I will. Do you have cream and sugar?"

He handed her everything, and Christy prepared her first cup of coffee. She loved how coffee smelled but never drank it because previous sips had proved to be so bitter. The cream and sugar would change that. At sixteen years old, it was time to have her first cup of coffee.

The first taste was awful. She added more cream. That didn't help, so she put in more sugar. By the time she finished her concoction, it tasted like warm hummingbird nectar, and she could force herself to swallow only a few sips.

Bob sliced open a papaya, scooping out the black pearl-like seeds and squeezing a lime over it. Then he spooned out the orange portion and popped it in his mouth.

"So, tell me," he said. "I haven't heard yet. Did you pass your driver's test?"

"I haven't taken it yet."

"I thought you were going to take it on your birthday?"

Christy felt like sobbing out, "*Today* is my birthday!"

But before she had a chance, Todd and Paula charged through the open door, laughing and looking like they'd just shared the kind of birthday morning Christy should have been having.

Todd wore a wet bathing suit, and Paula had on her pink bikini with a beach towel wrapped around her waist. Her wet hair gave away that she'd been in the water with Todd. David followed right behind, also wet.

At least David was with them. Knowing that helped, but it didn't diffuse Christy's hurt and anger.

"Christy," Paula gushed, "you should've seen me! I almost got up on the board. A few more tries, and I would've had it. We'll have to try again tomorrow, or maybe later today. You should've come. It was so fun! I love the ocean, and you were right, Christy. The water is really warm."

"I would've loved to come," Christy said flatly, trying to hold back an ocean full of churning emotions.

"I tried to wake you." Paula fluffed her hair with her fingers, unaware she was sprinkling little flecks of sand and saltwater across Christy's face. "You just rolled over and told me to leave you alone, so I did. Face it, Christy. You're a night person. You need to switch over and become a morning person like Todd and me, at least while we're here!" Paula smiled brightly at Todd.

He smiled back and then poured himself a cup of coffee before saying, "She's really good, Christy. You should've seen her. She's got a natural sense of balance."

And I'm a klutz. Go ahead and say it, Todd. You could barely get me to balance on a body board last summer. I definitely don't have a natural sense of balance. Go ahead! Tell everyone how uncoordinated I am and how graceful Paula is!

"We came back because the guys were starving," Paula explained. "Todd said he'd take us snorkeling to a place where we can actually feed the fish. He said they like frozen peas. Isn't that wild?" She continued on with a glowing expression that infuriated Christy. "I'm up for the adventure. Are you?"

Then Christy remembered Todd's comments from the restaurant the night before about her and Paula not being adventurous. Now she could see Paula's game. Paula was trying to prove to Todd she already was adventurous, and Christy was a prissy little cream puff.

"I'm so excited! This is going to be so much fun! Todd said he knows a place where we can rent masks and snorkels. We'll get one for you if you want to go snorkeling too, Christy. Do you? Do you want to come with us?"

"No, I don't want to go on a snorkeling adventure!" Christy spouted loudly and sarcastically. "I'd rather stay here all by myself and spend my birthday alone in my room!"

Everyone became silent and stared at her.

The intensity, the embarrassment, the anger of the moment, pushed Christy out of her chair, swiftly through the open door, and into her condo.

"Christy?" Mom called out as Christy ran past her and into her room.

"Christy?" Mom followed and stood next to the bed where Christy had thrown herself down face first. "What happened? I went for a walk along the beach, and when I came back, you were gone. What's wrong?"

"Me!" Christy sobbed. "I'm wrong. Everything about me is wrong. Why am I such a jerk?"

Mom sat on the bed and placed a loving hand on Christy's back. "This isn't like you, honey. What happened?"

Christy didn't answer.

"Is it something with Paula?" Mom ventured.

"Which Paula?" Christy asked between sniffs. "The one I used to know or the new, improved Adventure Woman who has Todd wrapped around her little finger?"

"So that's it," Mom said, removing her hand. "Listen,

Christy. It's never worth losing a best friend over a guy. And it's silly for you to be jealous of Paula. Actually, I'm kind of surprised. I've always been proud of the nice, healthy relationship you have with Todd."

"Well, what if Todd wants a 'nice, healthy relationship' with Paula instead of me?"

"He might. And that's okay," Mom said calmly.

Christy turned to face her. "No, it's not! You don't understand. Paula wants a boyfriend really bad, and she's setting a trap for Todd."

"Christy, I think you're exaggerating."

"I'm not, Mom. You don't understand." Christy scrambled her thoughts together, trying to figure out how to explain everything she knew to Mom.

It wouldn't matter, though. It hadn't mattered when she told her about the bathing suit or chasing the movie star at the airport. Christy could tell by the kind smile smeared across Mom's face that, regardless of what she said now, it wouldn't matter.

"Let me give you some advice my mother gave me when I was a little bit older than you." Mom paused, then precisely formed her words. "If it is meant for you and Todd to be together, then nothing or no one will be able to break you up. If you're not meant to be together, then nothing you try will keep you together."

Christy rolled Mom's words over in her mind before asking, "Did Grandma say that about you and Dad when you two were dating?"

"No, actually, it was when I was crying over a boy I liked very much. His name was Chuck Clawson."

"What happened to him?" Christy propped herself up

on her elbow, intrigued because Mom seldom shared this kind of story.

"Well, as it turned out, he married my best friend, Pat."

"Oh, great!" Christy flopped back onto her pillow. "You're supposed to cheer me up, Mother."

Mom looked as if she had expected Christy to be enthusiastic about her story. "Don't you see? God had someone better for me, and that was your father. I didn't know that at the time because I hadn't met your father. All I knew was how much I liked Chuck and how much I wanted him to like me."

Releasing a deep sigh, Christy said, "It's hard, Mom. It's really hard."

"Yes, it is hard. So don't make it any harder, okay?"

After a moment Christy pulled herself up. "Okay, I'll try. I guess I'd better go apologize to everyone."

"I'll go with you. I want to see if Bob has any more coffee. I can smell it from here."

"I want to apologize to everybody," Christy announced to the group, which was seated around the patio table, feasting on scrambled eggs and toast. "I didn't mean to act like that."

"Don't worry about it!" Paula moved her chair closer to Todd to make room for Christy. "If everybody forgot my birthday, I would've thrown a bigger fit than that!"

"Happy birthday, Christy." Bob kissed her on the cheek. "Have a seat, and let's try to start this beautiful morning all over again. It'll be a happy birthday, I promise. Ready for some eggs?"

"Sure. They look great." Christy pulled up a chair and listened as they discussed their plans for the day.

More than once Todd caught Christy's eye and looked like he was trying to ask her something or tell her something. She wasn't sure which. Even though it perplexed her, it made her feel closer to him and gave her hope that he really wanted to continue his "nice, healthy relationship" with her and not start something with Paula.

She didn't have a chance to talk to him alone until later that afternoon. All seven of them piled into the van and went snorkeling at a beach Todd called Black Rock, named for the lava flow of black rock that protruded out into the water.

Black Rock was high enough and the water deep enough that many high-diving tourists followed the supposed old Hawaiian custom of jumping from the rock into the warm water below. Todd jumped three or four times for their cameras and tried to convince David to go off with him. But once David climbed to the top of the rock and found it looked too scary to jump, he took the rocky trail back to the beach.

Christy loved snorkeling. She released handfuls of bright green peas into the water, then watched the fish swim quickly to gobble them up. The colors of the fish amazed her.

Later she stretched out on an air mattress, floating on the calm water above the fish. Todd suddenly popped his head out of the water right by her raft.

"Did you see those little yellow ones?" He lifted his mask up to his forehead.

"I like the ones with the blue and yellow. They look almost iridescent underwater," Christy said.

Todd agreed and then, in his usual right-to-the-point

manner, said, "What was going on this morning?"

"What do you mean?"

"You made it sound like you were upset about your birthday, but something else was bothering you."

"No, nothing was."

"Christy," Todd rested his arms on the raft's side, "you're a bad liar. Your eyes give you away."

She leaned her head back and closed her eyes, her face lifted toward the sun. "I was just tired, that's all."

"Oh, right!" Todd said, and the next thing Christy knew, he had tipped the raft and dumped her into the water.

She came up laughing and splashing as Todd tried to get on the raft.

"Oh, no you don't!" She tried her best to flip him over but didn't succeed.

They both laughed and splashed each other, and then Christy dove under the raft and tried pulling it out from under him. Todd reached under and grabbed her wrist, pulling her up out of the water.

"Okay, okay, we'll share." Todd slipped into the water up to his waist, resting his elbows on the raft. Christy did the same on the other side of the raft.

Todd didn't use any words. He spoke only with his eyes. Christy knew what he was asking, and she knew she couldn't lie.

"Okay, Paula's bothering me. She's changed so much since we were friends back in Wisconsin."

"So have you."

"Yeah, but I changed for the good when I became a Christian last summer. I know that sounds egotistical, and I don't mean that I'm perfect now or anything."

Todd smiled.

Christy could guess what he was thinking. "I guess I proved that this morning, didn't I?"

"None of us are perfect, Christy."

"Right, but the thing about Paula is she's not even trying to live morally or anything. I wish she'd become a Christian. I'm worried she'll turn out like Alissa."

"Turn out like Alissa? Alissa's not done yet."

"What do you mean?"

"Well, Shawn, for instance. Now, he's done. He doesn't have any more choices or any more chances. He's dead."

It sounded so blunt. Christy winced inwardly and waited for Todd to continue.

"You know, I prayed for Shawn every day for more than a year. As far as I know, he died without ever surrendering to Christ. And now—" Todd looked away as he spoke—"he's done. They have a word for it in Hawaiian: *pau*."

"Pow?" Christy repeated.

"Yeah, pau. Means 'finished,' 'complete,' 'no more chances.' Shawn is pau. But Alissa's not. And neither is Paula."

Christy fluttered her legs in the warm ocean water and felt the sun pounding on her back. She thought she understood what Todd was saying.

"I've been praying for Alissa," Todd continued, "every day."

"And you think that's what I should be doing with Paula? Praying for her?"

Todd nodded, his smile returning. "And love her for who she is, not for who you want her to be."

"That's hard to do, Todd. I want her to become a Christian so badly."

"That's good. I want her to become a Christian too. You know, it's really God's kindness that leads us to repentance, not His judgment. We have to start praying, Kilikina."

Christy recognized that name as the same one Todd had used at the airport. "What does that word mean?"

"Kilikina? That's your name in Hawaiian. Actually, it's Hawaiian for 'Christina.' 'Christy' would be *Kiliki*."

The word sounded like a wild bird call with the syllables rolling off Todd's tongue. Christy loved the way he said it. "Say it again."

"Kilikina."

"How did you know it?"

Todd looked down, almost as if he was embarrassed to give her his answer. Without looking up he said, "When I was in the third grade here, there was a *haole* girl—"

Christy interrupted. "What's a how-lee?"

"A white person. You know, blond, fair-skinned, blue-eyed. Someone who's obviously not Polynesian. Only four of us haoles were in my third-grade class—me, two other guys, and then this girl named Christina."

Todd looked at Christy and smiled a third-grader kind of smile. "I had an awful crush on her. The teacher called us all by our Hawaiian names in class, and Kilikina was the first name I learned."

Todd looked cute, the sun lighting up his hair, elbows propped up on the raft, confessing his first crush to her.

"What's your name in Hawaiian?" Christy asked.

He hesitated, then smiled and said, "*Koka*."

"Koka?"

"Yeah. I hated it because all the kids called me Koka Cola."

Christy laughed and noticed someone on the shore waving to them. "Is that my uncle?"

Todd looked across the bright glare on the water. "Looks like he wants us to come up. Come on. I'll give you a ride."

Their time together ended too soon for Christy. Every time she talked to Todd she felt like she learned something new about him, and they became closer to each other as a result.

When she slid all the way onto the raft and stretched out on her stomach, she took in a sweeping view of the clear sparkling lagoon, the curving shoreline dotted with tourists, and behind the hotels, the smooth green West Maui Mountains wearing their afternoon halo of baby's breath clouds.

I will always remember this day…forever. I never would have guessed I'd spend my sixteenth birthday on a tropical island with Todd. Somebody pinch me; I must be dreaming!

She didn't need to be pinched. At that very moment, Todd toppled the raft, and the dousing proved to be sufficient evidence that she was awake. They splashed each other some more before Christy resumed her position on top of the raft, then holding on tightly, she called, "Take me to shore, mister, and no more funny stuff!"

He looked like a sea turtle, sticking his neck out of the water at intervals while tugboating her raft back to shore. Christy laughed aloud with glee, wondering how she could have been so angry this morning or why she ever felt Paula could possibly come between her and Todd.

"Marti and your mom already headed for the car," Bob told them when they arrived back at the beach towels, breathless and sparkling with saltwater. "David's over there by the tide pools, trying to catch a fish, and Paula is about twenty yards down the beach, talking to some guys. We need to get going."

"What are we doing for dinner?" Christy asked.

"That's our little surprise," Bob said with a wink. "Why don't you go find Paula? Todd, you get David, okay?"

Christy jogged off down the beach and found Paula sitting on a grass mat next to two guys. By the looks of things, they enjoyed her entertaining conversation. Paula introduced them as Jackson and Jonathan, two members of a band called Teralon.

"We need to get going," Christy said politely. "It was nice to meet you both."

"We're going to a luau tonight." Then Paula immediately pressed her hand over her mouth, her baby-doll eyes opening wide, and cutely added, "Oops. You didn't hear that, Christy."

"You're in trouble now, Paula," one of the guys teased from behind his dark sunglasses.

"I'd better go." She rose to her feet. "Maybe I'll see you guys again."

"You never know," the other guy said as Christy and Paula walked away. "If not here, then hopefully in heaven!"

"Were they Christians?" Christy looked back over her shoulder and returned their friendly wave.

"Slightly!" Paula said. "Of all the guys on the beach, I have to pick two Jesus freaks to talk to. They really were

sweet, but all they wanted to talk about was 'the Lord.'"
Paula shook her head. "First Todd this morning with all his
bits of spiritual wisdom and now these guys. What's going
on here?"

Christy broke into a wide grin, using all her self-control to keep from laughing aloud.

Paula saw the grin, though. "What?"

Christy didn't say a word. She didn't have to. Paula
came to the same conclusion Christy had and voiced it with
an air of disgust.

"Oh, don't you dare try to tell me meeting those guys
was one of your little God-things!"

"Okay, Paula." Christy kept grinning. "I won't tell
you."

7

Come On, Christy, Show Us How to Hula!

"Go ahead," Todd encouraged. "Try some poi. You put two fingers in like this."

He stuck his fingers in the small wooden calabash bowl in the center of the table and quickly drew the sticky gray substance to his lips.

"It looks too gooey," Paula said, making a face. "What does it taste like?"

Todd licked his lips and stuck his fingers back in the bowl. "Like, um, like poi. That's it! It tastes like poi. Come on, Christy. The birthday girl can't go to a luau and not eat poi."

Christy bravely dipped a finger in and drew it to her lips. "What is this stuff, anyway?"

"The old Hawaiians ate it. It comes from the root of the taro plant. They pound it to make it mushy like this."

Christy touched the tip of her tongue with the poi, which had the color and consistency of wallpaper paste. Paula, sitting directly across from her, watched her reaction.

"It doesn't really have a taste." Christy turned to Todd, who sat next to her. "Did you eat this stuff all the time you lived here?"

"I've had my share. You get enough down there, Bob?"

Bob, Marti, Mom, and David all reached for their bowl of poi at the same time. Marti was the first to say, "Here, Todd. You can have the rest of ours."

They all laughed, and the merry mood continued through the luau. Christy decided to be adventurous and try a few things she didn't normally eat, like mangoes in the fruit salad and shredded pork wrapped up in ti leaves, which Todd called *laulaus*.

Paula, not demonstrating an adventurous spirit, barely ate a thing besides the white rice. Part of Paula's problem was her sunburn.

All day at the beach Christy had obediently smeared her skin with sunscreen, but Paula refused, saying she tanned easily and never burned. Even Marti's warnings bounced off Paula, who seemed determined to soak up as much Hawaiian sun as possible, parading her white flesh up and down the beach in her pink bikini.

When they dressed for the luau, Christy had covered herself with aloe vera gel, and now in the coolness of the setting sun, she was only a tiny bit sunburned on her back. Paula's flaming red face proved she'd gotten too much sun. Even her lips and eyelids had swollen. She was hurting, even though she'd convinced all of them on the way to the luau that her stomach felt a little pink, but that was all.

Todd looked incredibly good in his blue-flowered Hawaiian shirt. Like an island boy. With his tan face, sun-streaked blond hair, and screaming silver-blue eyes, Todd had never looked better.

Christy wasn't the only one who noticed how good Todd looked. Paula had once again locked her gaze on him, and all during dinner, every time Christy looked up, she felt something was going on between the two of them.

By the time the show began and the Polynesian dancers appeared on stage in their ceremonial costumes, Christy had convinced herself that whatever game Paula was playing, Christy could play it too.

They applauded the talented hula dancers, and when David's favorite, the fire dancer, jumped onto the stage, Christy moved her chair closer to Todd for a better view. She slightly moved her arm so that she brushed up against the sleeve of Todd's shirt. She couldn't tell if he noticed or not. He seemed completely caught up in the show.

The show's host came to the microphone and asked for the crowd to "put your hands together" for the fire dancer one more time. Then he asked if there were any birthdays or anniversaries in the group.

David pointed at Christy, whistling loudly. She shrank down in her seat and prayed they wouldn't make her stand up or anything. To her relief, all they did was ask the group to sing "Happy Birthday" to the six birthday people. It was kind of fun being sung to, as long as she didn't have to stand. That would have been too embarrassing.

"You got off easy." Todd leaned closer to her. "I thought they were going to call you up on stage."

He barely finished speaking before several guys, dressed only in cloths around their waists and wreaths of thin green leaves around their heads, came running through the audience to select their dance partners. One of the brown-skinned dancers appeared at their table and beckoned to Christy, holding out his hand as the drums on the stage beat their commands, "Come, come, come, come…"

Christy resisted, sinking into her chair, shaking her

head. She could feel her pulse begin to beat time with the drums.

"Go on, Christy," Paula urged. "Go with him!"

"No, you go, Paula. Take her!" Christy pointed across the table. *Now's your chance to be as adventurous as you want, Paula!*

"Take both *wahines!*" Todd shouted to the dancer. "Make both girls go."

The dancer stood firm, one arm stretched out to Christy and the other arm now pointing to Paula. In a voice much larger than himself, he spoke. "Both wahines come!"

And so they did.

The drums changed into Tahitian dance music the minute Christy and Paula stepped onto the stage. They joined the seven other "victims," and in front of more than a hundred people, Christy swayed and wiggled and stamped her feet, feeling silly and embarrassed.

The flowered lei around her neck swished back and forth across her favorite flowered sundress, and she couldn't tell at all if she looked cute or ridiculous. By the time she'd come up with some kind of pattern for her feet to follow, she had the feeling she looked more like a cheerleader in slow motion than a fluid-moving hula dancer.

Paula was into the dance, wiggling her hips so her white shorts swished back and forth. She locked her blue-eyed gaze on her native dance partner, who by now had turned his back on Christy, totally ignoring her and having fun showing off with Paula.

The drums came to an abrupt halt, and the dancer slipped his arm around Paula's waist and said something Christy couldn't hear. She wasn't about to stick around on stage to see if anyone had any secret messages for her.

Quickly making her way down the stage steps, she was aware some people she passed had video cameras. They might have actually taped her embarrassing moment on stage.

Good thing I didn't do anything really embarrassing. I could have ended up on that TV show as one of "America's funniest."

Before she managed to get back in her seat, the girl dancers had spread out in the audience. It didn't surprise Christy to see that Todd was one of their first selections. He slid past Christy, shrugging his shoulders and obediently following the wahine in the grass skirt.

David laughed at Christy when she sat down, but Bob, Mom, and Marti had sweet things to say. They repeated the same bits of praise to Paula when she returned to her seat.

Now it was Todd's turn. The drums began slowly, and the dancers swished their grass skirts back and forth, inviting the guys to follow their motions. Since Todd had proved to be so familiar with Hawaiian ways, Christy sat back, waiting for him to wow the audience with his expert hula dancing.

To her surprise and everyone else's humor, Todd turned out to be a total hula klutz.

"Guys just can't move their hips like that," Paula said in between bursts of laughter. "Look at him! He's the star of the show."

Of the eight or nine men they'd called up on stage, Todd stood out as the worst dancer. A large man in the front row balanced his video camera on his shoulder and taped the whole thing. The funniest part was that Todd seemed to be sincerely trying to hula and didn't realize how hilarious he looked with his arms in the air and hips doing a sort of offbeat wiggle.

Before the music ended, all the hula-dancer girls formed a circle with Todd in the middle. They danced around him so all Christy could clearly see were his arms waving in the air.

"I'd try to hide that kind of dancing too." Bob chuckled. "A surfer he is; a dancer he's not."

Bob teased Todd when he sat down by patting him on the shoulder. "We all have our strengths and weaknesses, son. Stick to surfing!"

Christy laughed along with the rest of them, yet she wondered if their teasing hurt Todd's feelings. If it did, he didn't show it. He even made some jokes about himself as they left the luau and began a leisurely stroll along the winding Kaanapali Beach walkway.

Christy made sure she was positioned right by Todd's side while they walked, wondering if she should clutch his arm the way she had at the airport or wait to see if he'd reach for her hand. At the luau Todd had divided his attention equally between Christy and Paula. Now, with the ocean singing its eternal song only a few yards to their left and the velvet sky sprinkled with diamonds high above them, Christy felt hopelessly romantic.

It's my birthday, Todd. It's my sixteenth birthday, and here we are, walking along the beach in Maui. You have to hold my hand or pay some kind of special attention to me. You have to!

"Todd," Paula chirped loudly, "wait up!"

She left the clump of Bob, Marti, Mom, and David and scooted up to Todd's other side, freely clutching his arm and holding it with both hands.

"We should make a deal. You teach me to surf, and I'll teach you to dance. Wouldn't that be fun?"

Christy's mind whirled through a split-second debate on how she could respond to this situation. She could grab Todd's other arm, she could fall back with the grown-ups to test Todd and see if he came back for her, or she could turn into a cat-woman and scratch Paula's eyes out.

Before she could choose the best option, Marti nosed into their threesome and stated, "Paula, I've been wanting a chance to talk with you, and this is the perfect opportunity."

Marti abruptly linked her arm through Paula's and pulled her away from Todd, positioning herself and Paula several feet in front of Todd and Christy.

All right, Aunt Marti! I take back every mean thing I ever thought about you. You really are on my side!

"I've been meaning to tell you, Paula dear, that with a few simple pointers, I believe you could lose some of your Midwest flavor and take on a more West Coast style. First, let's evaluate the way you walk…" and on Marti went, conducting her unique style of charm school with a rather willing Paula.

Christy thought of a whole string of things to say to Todd as the gentle evening breeze caressed her shoulders, awakening the sweet fragrance in her plumeria and tuberose lei. But she couldn't get herself to jump in and start talking because she kept hoping Todd would slip his arm around her or take her hand.

When he didn't, she struggled miserably over how she could encourage him, even though Mom, Bob, and David were right behind them, watching. She was capable of being forward like Paula. She could easily slip her arm through Todd's and say, "Isn't it a gorgeous night? What a perfect setting for my birthday! Isn't it romantic, Todd?"

Okay, Christy, she coached herself, *go ahead. Make a move. Paula would if she were you.*

"You know..." Todd sliced through the silence between them and leaned close so the others couldn't hear what he said. "That's one of the things I like most about you, Christy. You don't play games or try to be flirty like a lot of other girls."

She swallowed hard, feeling caught.

If only you knew, Todd! One more minute, and I would have been playing "Miss Piggy."

"It's not that I don't think about it," Christy said, shocked that the honest words tumbled out before she could stop them.

"Really?" Todd looked at her curiously. "What do girls think about? I mean, why do they do that to a guy?"

Christy didn't allow herself to hesitate. If she did, she might not say any of the things she truly felt or thought—things she often wanted to talk over with Todd but usually chickened out on before she said them.

"I guess we're looking for some attention, some way to find out what the guy is thinking or how he feels about us."

"That's all backward," Todd stated. "I think the guy should be the initiator and the girl should be the responder. Not the other way around."

"But you don't know what it's like to be the girl and to have to wait and wait and wait for the guy to initiate something. When he doesn't, you feel he's not interested in you."

"So girls think that the level of a guy's interest is based on how much he touches her?" Todd sounded surprised, and his voice rose a bit.

Christy wondered if everyone else could overhear their

conversation. She was saying so many things to Todd she had longed to tell him that she continued but spoke softly.

"I agree that a girl should let the guy be the leader, but I also think sometimes the guy can be a little more, well, gentle and caring by, you know, holding her hand or other little expressions of how he feels without it being a big deal." Christy looked up at Todd, and in the dim light she could see an amazed expression on his face, as if he'd never considered that point of view before.

"Does that make sense? What I'm trying to say is that if a guy holds a girl's hand or something like that, it lets the girl know he likes her. That's all. It doesn't mean he's trying to, you know, make out with her or anything. It just means she's special to him."

"Interesting. It's different for guys," Todd said. "For a guy it's like—"

He didn't get to finish his sentence, which frustrated Christy, because Bob interrupted them. He directed them to stop at Whalers Village and find a seat on the patio at Leilani's Restaurant.

David helped Todd push two of the round tables together under the light of a gas tiki torch and pull up seven chairs. David then made a beeline for the seat next to Todd. Then, before Christy could get around to the other side, Paula grabbed the chair on Todd's other side. Feeling as though she'd been cut off from one of the best conversations she'd ever had with Todd, Christy dropped into a chair next to Marti.

"Oh, Christy," Marti scolded, "that certainly is not the way a young lady takes her seat! I thought I'd taught you better than that."

Fortunately, the waitress stepped up to their table, and Christy didn't have to answer.

"We'll have seven Naughty Hula pies," Bob ordered for them all. "And how many coffees?"

"Bob," Marti interjected, "I only want a little bite of yours, and perhaps the girls would like to split one. The slices are gigantic, and they're awfully rich."

"Not the birthday girl!" Bob flashed a warm smile at a pouting Christy. "Tonight she gets whatever she wants."

If that was true, I'd get Todd all to myself, and I'd hold his hand tightly, and I'd find a way to tell him how I feel about him. If I could wish for anything on my birthday, that would be it.

They all ordered their own slice of pie, except Marti. Then they laughed at their optimism when the huge slices of macadamia-nut ice-cream pie, covered with hot fudge and whipped cream, arrived at their table.

"I tried to warn you," Marti said. "Now you know why they call it Naughty Hula pie. Can you even begin to guess how many calories are in this monstrous piece?"

"Let's sing to the birthday girl and let her enjoy her pie without the guilt," Bob suggested. "Go ahead, honey. Make a wish."

Christy closed her eyes. She knew exactly what to wish for.

On the drive to the condo, Christy felt overly full, yet not willing to tell her aunt she had been right about the size of the pie. She told herself she'd wasted her birthday wish on something that would never come true. Todd wasn't even sitting by her in the van. He sat by David on the back bench seat, with Paula close on his other side.

"You have something in your hair, Todd," Paula said. Christy turned slightly in her middle seat so she could see what game Paula was up to now. Paula began to comb her long fingernails through the side of Todd's hair, leaning close in the dark car to find the something in his hair.

"Did you get it?" Todd asked.

"I'm not sure. It's kind of dark in here." She kept grooming his short, sun-lightened mane. "You really have nice hair."

Let go of him, Paula! Stop your stupid little games. Todd hates your games anyway. You're not going to score any points with him this way.

"That feels good," Todd said. "Little more to the left."

He leaned his head closer to her, so she could keep scratching.

"Eww! I think you still have sand in your hair!" Paula squealed.

"Probably. I need fingernails like yours to get it out, I guess."

That's just great, Todd. Now who's playing games?

Christy curled her hands into two fists in her lap. The cat-woman image reentered her mind. Would anyone try to stop her if she sprang from her seat and used her claws on Paula at this very moment?

But they were home.

Bob parked the van, and the sand-scratching ritual in the backseat came to an end.

Scrunched together in the elevator, Christy shot angry darts at Todd. Being mad at Paula was one thing. She expected Paula to play all her games to win Todd's attention, regardless of this being Christy's birthday. But why, oh, why would Todd say he didn't like it when Paula played those games and he liked Christy because she didn't play them, and then give in to Paula whenever she came on to him?

Didn't he see what he was doing when he accepted her attention? Didn't he understand how that made Christy feel?

"I'm going to bed," David announced when the elevator deposited them on the sixth floor. "I don't feel very well."

"We have a few presents for Christy. Can you wait until after she opens them?"

"No," David groaned, holding his stomach, "I'm too full to sit up. I just want to go to bed."

David went right to his room, while the others gathered on Bob and Marti's lanai to admire the stars. While everyone chatted, Christy stared into the vast ocean before her.

She had to admit, the night was beautiful. She didn't want to ruin what was left of her birthday with such a bitter attitude.

I'm sorry, Father God. She sent her heartfelt prayer on a sudden breeze that rustled the huge palm tree growing beside the lanai. *Please help me not to be so jealous but to act the way You want me to.*

Then she remembered. Today, or more accurately tomorrow, was her spiritual birthday. One year ago she had given her heart to the Lord.

I'm not exactly acting like one of Your daughters, am I, God? I'm sorry.

"You going to join us, Christy?" Marti called from the lanai table. "We have some presents here, and they all have your name on them."

Christy took a breath and allowed a smile to replace her scowl. As demurely as possible, she sat in the seat next to her aunt, secretly pleased with her delicate descent.

The night wasn't over yet. A few dreams could still come true.

8

Mystery Call from the Blue Grotto

"Open my present first," Paula urged, sitting, of course, right next to Todd. "It was actually my mom's idea. I hope you like it."

Even in the dim light on the lanai, Paula looked horribly sunburned.

"Did you use anything for your sunburn yet?" Marti asked. "You really got too much sun today, Paula. You can get sick from sunburn, you know. Your lips will swell and blister, and your skin will peel. You did use sunscreen today, didn't you?"

Paula avoided answering by focusing on Christy, who had opened the small box from Paula and lifted out a picture in a heart-shaped silver frame. Christy held it closer in the dim light to see better.

"It's us," Paula said. "My mom took it on our first day of kindergarten."

Christy held it up to the light and smiled at the two little faces, pressed cheek to cheek. Both had a front tooth missing.

Christy couldn't explain it, but all of a sudden she felt like crying. The picture delighted her. It warmed her from

the inside out. It brought an ocean full of childhood memories and dreams. It made her feel closer to Paula than she
had felt their whole trip. She couldn't be angry with that
little cherub beside her in the picture.

"I love it, Paula. Thank you." Christy reached over to
give her a cheek-to-cheek hug.

"Owww!" Paula responded the instant Christy touched
her.

"Oh, I'm sorry. It's your sunburn, huh?"

Instantly, the surge of closeness receded. An invisible
shield went up between them again.

Mom and Marti admired the picture and handed it to
Todd for his examination.

A smile spread across his face, and he teased, "Which is
which?"

"Can't you tell?" Christy asked. "I'm the one on the
right."

Todd kept looking at the picture and smiling.

Mom handed Christy her gift in a shopping bag and
apologized for not being organized enough to have brought
along a box and wrapping paper. It was a big, multicolored
beach bag.

Christy really liked it, which was good since she and
Mom usually didn't have similar tastes.

"Here," Todd pulled a cardboard tube out from under
his chair. "I'm not one for wrapping paper either."

Popping the plastic end off the tube, Christy pulled out
a rolled-up picture of a gorgeous waterfall surrounded by
tropical foliage. An old bridge stretched across the top of
the waterfall.

"This is pretty. Thanks." It was a pretty picture, but it

wasn't exactly a personal, romantic kind of gift like the gold ID bracelet Todd had given her for Christmas. He had had the word *Forever* engraved on it. Christy had grown familiar with its light touch on her wrist and all the hope and promise for their relationship it carried.

"You said to send you a postcard of a waterfall," Todd said in his teasing way. "And that's a waterfall that, well…" He looked like he wanted to explain something about the waterfall, but it was too deeply personal. "Well, I like it a lot."

Christy smiled her thanks, unsure of his unspoken message, and rolled the picture back up. Gently, she eased it into the tube.

"One more gift, Christy," Marti said with a song in her voice.

Christy felt even worse at the thought that she might now receive an expensive gift. "You've already given me my birthday present, bringing me here and taking us to the luau and everything! I really couldn't accept anything else."

Bob handed her an envelope, and she felt a bit relieved, thinking it might be a card with twenty dollars or something that would be easy to accept.

It was a card, all right. "Happy Sweet Sixteen," the front proclaimed. Fortunately, no money was inside. Only an odd-shaped piece of paper that floated to her lap. Christy held it up and then looked at her aunt and uncle and asked, "What's this?"

"Can't you tell?" Marti bubbled. "It's a clue. Try to guess."

"It's a picture of a car."

"A car!" Paula spit out the words as if they disgusted

her. "I'm so sure, Christy! You're so spoiled, and you don't even know it."

"Hold on now," Bob said calmly. "It's not a brand-new car."

"Remember my old car?" Marti asked.

Christy gulped, "The convertible Mercedes?"

Paula turned away and looked out at the ocean.

"We traded it in," Bob explained. "Well, sort of traded it in. The bottom line is, after you get your license, you and your dad will go with me to the dealer and trade in your parents' car as well. We'll use the credit from their car and the Mercedes to do a little wheeling and dealing. Hopefully, we can manage to come up with a car for you and one for your mom and dad as well."

"I can't believe this! Thank you." Christy hugged Bob and Marti and then Mom.

Her stomach had begun to do flip-flops the moment Bob said "when you get your license," and now she felt that strange sensation of horror and expectation. So much depended on her taking the test when she got home and passing it the first time.

Just then the phone rang inside the condo.

"Who could that be?" Marti asked. "After all, your father already called this morning."

"Want me to get it?" Christy offered, since she was the only one standing.

"Sure," Bob said.

Christy lifted the receiver on the third ring. "Hello?"

A loud crackling and clicking came across the line.

"Hello?" she said louder. "Hello?"

A woman spoke in what sounded like Spanish or Italian,

and then the phone clicked and a surprisingly clear male voice came on the line. "Yes, hello. I'm trying to reach Christy Miller."

"This is Christy." Her heart pounded, echoing in her ears. *This is strange! Who could be calling me?*

"Christy! Do you know who this is?" There was a delay and a little bit of an echo on what seemed to be a cell phone, which made it even more difficult to identify the deep, vaguely familiar voice.

"Ah, ahh…" She didn't know what to say.

Obviously, this person knew her, knew she was in Maui, and somehow had gotten the phone number. Suddenly, she remembered the mysterious, unsigned letter she had stuck in her purse. Could this be the person who wrote the letter?

The voice laughed on the other end of the line, and she knew she had heard that laugh before. But where? When? Who was this?

"I'll give you a clue. You owe me something, which you promised to give me on July 27. Well, where I'm calling from, it's already July 28, but I'm calling to tell you that just because you're in Maui, you can't forget your promise. You still owe me."

The strong voice had taken on a Mafia-type accent, and Christy felt a little frightened, even though she knew it had to be someone playing a trick on her.

"I intend to collect on what you owe me before the summer's over, got it?"

"Well, um…" Christy tried hard to sound light and playful, but she was in a fog over what this masked voice was talking about. "Just exactly what is it I owe you?"

The voice laughed, not deep and mysterious but freely, in its natural range. Then switching back to Mafia style, he said, "A date, Killer Eyes. You owe me a birthday date."

Christy burst out in wild, relieved, delighted laughter, causing everyone on the lanai to stop talking and look inside the condo at her. She pulled the phone cord around the corner, into the kitchen to be out of their view.

"Rick! I can't believe you're calling me!"

"You really didn't know it was me?" he asked in his usual self-confident tone.

"No, I couldn't figure it out at all! Where are you? I thought you were in Europe."

"I am. I'm on the island of Capri."

"Where's that?"

"Off the coast of Italy. We took a hydrofoil over from Naples yesterday. We're going to Rome later this afternoon and then up to Florence and Venice."

"I can't believe this. How'd you get my number?"

"I called your house yesterday. Your dad told me you were in Maui, and he gave me your number. It was easy. You didn't think I'd forget your birthday, did you?"

"But Rick, this is going to cost you a fortune!"

"About the same as dinner and a movie in Escondido," he teased. "We'll compare prices when I take you out in August. If we plan it just right, there should be about a week before I leave for college, and we'll celebrate your birthday then. You pick the day."

"Okay." She knew she should keep talking, but her mind went blank. She felt her cheeks burning and heart pounding over Rick calling her all the way from Europe. He hadn't forgotten her birthday. She never expected this.

"I thought of you yesterday," Rick said in a low, rich voice. "We went to the Blue Grotto. You ever heard of it?"

"No."

Her no echoed in her ear before Rick continued. "We got in this little boat, kind of a cross between a rowboat and a gondola. The guy paddled us into this place like a cave, and we had to scrunch down on the bottom of the boat because the opening was so low. Inside, the water is the most unusual color of blue. The sun reflects into the cave somehow. I don't remember what does it, but the whole inside looks blue from the sunlight and the reflection off the water onto the rocks."

"Sounds pretty," Christy said.

"Not just pretty. Incredible. Awesome. Outrageous. It was killer, Christy. Just like your eyes. I felt like the whole cave was filled with Christy."

Christy let the romance of his words sink in.

"That's where I would've taken you for your birthday if I could've picked anywhere in the whole world, Christina. I would've taken you to the Blue Grotto on the island of Capri."

There was a pause, during which Christy felt certain the sound of her heart pounding in her ears had exploded through the phone and burst in on Rick on the other side of the world.

His voice switched back to teasing. "We'll have to check out all the Italian restaurants in Southern California and see if there's a Blue Grotto restaurant somewhere. If there is, that's where we'll go in August."

Christy laughed. "Okay. Sounds like fun."

"It will be," Rick said confidently. "You try to have a

happy birthday there without me, okay? I know it'll be hard, but try."

"Okay. Thanks for calling."

"Did you think for one minute I wouldn't call? That shows how little you know me, Christy. We'll work on improving that in a few weeks. Until then, ciao!"

"Bye, Rick."

She stood perfectly still for a moment before hanging up the phone.

How bizarre! Why would he call me and say all those sweet, sweet things? I never would have expected that from Rick. Never. Maybe I don't really know him, like he said.

Christy started toward the lanai, not sure of how to answer when they all asked who was on the phone. What an unexpected birthday evening! First the car from Bob and Marti, then Rick's call.

Fortunately, no one asked about her call right away. They were involved in an argument, and when Christy entered, Marti appeared to have won.

"Do like I said, Paula. Take a lukewarm bath, and put the aloe vera gel all over your sunburn. Do it now, or you're going to be much worse in the morning. Go on!"

Paula slowly stood, showing clearly that every movement caused her pain.

"You want some help?" Christy offered.

"Doing what?" Paula snapped. "Running my bath water? I think I can handle that myself."

"I just thought—"

Bob cut Christy off. "You holler if you need anything, Paula."

Mom rose. "I was going back to our condo anyway. I'll go with you, Paula."

"Whatever you do, don't touch me anywhere!" Paula warned as the two of them exited, followed by Marti.

"I'll get her some extra aloe gel in case the tube in her bathroom is low." Marti set off, Christy thought, to make sure her instructions were followed thoroughly.

"Well," Bob pushed himself up from the chair, "I'm ready to call it a day. Can I get you two anything? Something to drink?"

"No thanks."

Just that fast, Christy and Todd were alone on the lanai. Bob had turned on the news on the TV behind the sliding glass door and stood in front of it rather than sitting down.

Todd stood and moved his chair over so he would be next to Christy.

They sat silently for a few minutes, gazing at the ocean and the sky full of stars. The moon sprinkled light on the wave crests. Christy thought it looked like a giant bottle of silver glitter had spilled from the deep heavens and all the tiny flecks were now stuck to the waves with frothy, white Elmer's glue.

Thoughts of Rick evaporated; dreams of Todd soared.

This is so beautiful! What a perfect night, and how romantic to be here with Todd. I love the way he moved his chair over to be next to me. This is exactly what I wished for! I wonder what he's thinking?

"How's Rick?"

"Rick?" Christy echoed.

Todd kept looking straight ahead into the night. "That was Rick, wasn't it?"

"Yes, but how did you know?"

Todd turned and gave her a look that said, *We guys know these things, okay?*

"He's fine, I guess. He's in Italy."

"Italy?"

"His family is on vacation there." *Is Todd jealous of Rick the way I'm jealous of Paula?*

Todd kept looking out at the ocean, his jaw pressed forward as it did when he was deep in thought or about to say something profound.

Christy waited.

Todd remained silent.

Then Christy did something rather bold for her. She knew Bob was still in the living room, watching TV behind them, but this was her birthday—her sweet sixteen—and this was her wish, to be alone with Todd. She slipped her hand through Todd's arm, which rested on the chair.

Todd immediately responded by reaching for her hand and meshing their fingers together. Christy felt relieved. Calmed. Full of birthday wishes. She hoped that her reaching out to him like this would assure him there was really nothing going on between her and Rick. At least, she didn't think anything was going on between her and Rick.

Todd stroked Christy's *Forever* bracelet with his thumb, watching the ocean and studying the darkness without saying anything. Christy thought of about fifty different things to say but kept silent too. She knew she didn't have to apologize for Rick calling, and she didn't have to define her feelings for anybody.

She wished she could find words from her heart that would tell Todd how she felt about him. Every time she had tried to explain it in the past, she had gotten all goofed up and felt silly. She could write her feelings for him accurately and had many times in her diary. But she didn't know how to say what she felt. Maybe Todd didn't either.

"See Molokai over there?" Todd broke the silence with a quiet yet direct voice.

Christy knew two islands were visible from the condo, Lanai and Molokai. If she remembered correctly, Molokai was to their right.

"Yes." She followed Todd's gaze to the right.

"It's less than nine miles away. See those two lights?"

Christy noticed for the first time that on the dark, sparsely populated island two lights twinkled like stars, right next to each other on the shoreline. "Yes?"

"From here we can't tell what they are," Todd said. "Just two lights that look about the same." He sighed deeply. "I guess the only way to tell which one you want to end up at is to get close enough to see clearly what each of them is. Then you can make a wise decision between the two. It's hard to decide this far away."

Like a secret decoder wheel, Christy's thoughts spun furiously, trying to figure out Todd's message.

This has to do with Rick. Todd must think he and Rick are like the two lights. What did he say? I have to get close enough to make a wise decision.

Christy moved a little closer to Todd, and he responded by holding her hand a little tighter. Her thoughts came tumbling together, and she quickly lined them up to give Todd a clear response.

She'd tell him she agreed and thought this time in Maui would be perfect for them to get to know each other better than ever and to get closer and closer to each other. If he would make some kind of gesture or some kind of statement to Paula, then she would know he wasn't interested in her games and he only wanted to spend time with Christy. Then all their difficulties would be cleared up.

Before she could tell him all that, he let go of her hand, sprang from his seat, and with a look of little-boy excitement he said, "That's what I'll do! I'll just keep going, and I'll ask God to show me which one to choose. It'll get clearer the closer I get!"

He looked pleased, but Christy felt confused. She had thought the hidden message of the island lights was directed at her, when Todd really must have been thinking about a decision he was trying to make. But what decision?

"I'm turning in for the night," Bob called out to them, switching off the TV.

"I'm right behind you," Todd said.

He took one more glance over his shoulder at the lights and then offered a hand to Christy. She took it and wanted to pull him back to the chair so they could keep talking and living out her birthday wish. But Todd pulled her up to a standing position, and she could see more clearly in the soft light how pleased he was with his "lights on the island" analogy.

"Man, I'm glad we saw those two lights. It really clears things up for me. Hey! Don't forget your presents." Todd picked up the straw beach bag Mom had given her so she could fill it with the other gifts. "I'll see you in the morning."

After Christy gathered her things, Todd disappeared into the room he shared with David. She walked back to the next door condo with a sunken heart.

Why was our magical time cut off so suddenly? It was like my birthday wish only came half true.

Paula and Mom were already asleep, so she quietly got ready for bed. While brushing her teeth, she remembered the conversation she'd had with herself in the mirror that morning.

What's my problem? This has been an incredible birthday! The best I've ever had. How come I'm never happy with what I get? I got my wish, to be with Todd. I got a promise of a car and a surprise call from Rick. I just spent my sixteenth birthday in Hawaii, so why am I feeling so discontented?

She lay awake a long time that night, sorting out everything. What was Todd deciding? Were the two lights her and another girl? It couldn't be Paula, could it? And why did he ask her about Rick? Would Todd object if she told him she was going out with Rick in August?

As far as Christy could see, all along she and Todd were free to go out with other people. Todd had taken another girl named Jasmine to dinner the night of his senior prom. Christy hadn't ever really gone on a formal date with Todd, like out to dinner, since her parents didn't allow her to date. Now that she was sixteen, finally she could date.

But what if Todd wanted to date only her? Then she couldn't go out with Rick—or could she?

Todd would never ask her to go out with only him.

What if Rick wanted her to date only him? Then she couldn't go out with Todd anymore.

The more she thought, the more complicated it all became. She decided her life was actually easier when she was younger, because she didn't have to make all these decisions. She never did like making decisions!

In the darkness of her room, Christy felt her *Forever* bracelet and remembered the warm feeling she felt when

Todd had held her hand and stroked the bracelet. That opened another string of questions.

Did that bracelet already mean they were going together?

Christy turned on her side and pulled the sheet up to her chin. What if her mom was right and some other guy was out there for her that she hadn't even met yet?

An idea came to Christy, and she responded to it immediately. She jumped out of bed and tiptoed into the bathroom with her purse. Closing the door softly, she turned on the light. She scrounged through her purse, looking for a piece of paper.

The first thing she found was the mysterious letter she'd never asked Paula about. Could it have been from Rick? No, he would have said something when he called her tonight. Besides, it looked like a girl's handwriting. Christy left it on the bathroom counter so she would remember to ask Paula in the morning.

Then she pulled out her notepad. Christy had intended to write out her feelings, the way she often did in her diary. But now, sitting on the floor with her back against the bathroom wall, listening to the never-ending surf outside the bathroom window, she had a different idea.

She hesitated, chewing on the eraser and curling and uncurling her toes. Then she released her insecurities and let what she felt deep in her heart appear on paper.

Dear Future Husband,

I turned sixteen today, and I know it may seem weird writing this to you now, but this letter is sort of my way of making a promise to you in writing.

Maybe I already know you, or maybe we haven't met yet. Either way, I want to save myself for you. I want my whole self, my heart and body and everything, to be a present I'll give you on our wedding day.

I don't care how long it takes or how hard it gets, but I promise you I won't let anybody else "unwrap" me so that on our wedding night I'll be the kind of gift you'll be happy to receive.

I know I have a lot of years ahead of me before we get married, whoever you are. That's why I want to make this promise now, so that no matter who I go out with, I'll always think of myself as a present I want to give to you alone one day.

I also promise to start praying for you, wherever you are, whoever you are, that God will be preparing you for me and that you'll save all of yourself for me too.

I already love you.

Your future wife,

Christina Juliet Miller

9

Mosquito Nets and Prayers

"I tried to tell you!" Christy snapped back as Paula complained about her sunburn the next day. "You should've used sunscreen like everyone told you. Have you seen your lips? They look like they bubbled up overnight."

"So, are you Little Miss Perfect?" Paula sat on the edge of the bed, holding a damp washcloth on her chest and letting her words fly fast and furious. "You can't tell me you've never been sunburned in your life! You know what your problem is, Christy? You think you're so right about everything.

"You weren't like this before you got your Christianity, or whatever you call it. You used to be fun to be around. Now you're just a spoiled little brat who goes around condemning everyone because that person isn't perfect, like you."

"I do not!"

"Yes, you do. You and your perfect little dream world. Who else writes letters to her future husband?" Her voice turned into a whine. "I'm saving my body for you, honey. It's a perfect gift for you alone!"

Christy sprang from her bed and rescued her notepad,

which she had left on the bathroom counter and Paula had obviously found this morning.

Wagging the notepad in front of Paula, she warned, "That was really rude, Paula! Stop being such a big snoop, and leave my stuff alone."

"Hey, hey!" Mom broke up the confrontation. "What's going on here?"

Neither of them spoke. Their eyes flashed the remainder of their angry messages back and forth where Mom couldn't see.

Mom looked first at Christy, then at Paula, and with a calm, motherly voice said, "I suppose this was bound to happen. You two always were more like sisters than friends. Why don't you each try giving the other some space this morning, okay?"

"Fine with me," Paula said firmly.

Mom took a good look at Paula. "You must stay out of the sun today. You overdid it yesterday, and you'll make yourself sick. Now you two settle your differences, and give each other some space."

Mom folded her arms and waited for them to respond.

"Sorry," Christy offered meekly.

"Sorry." Paula mumbled the expected word like a young schoolgirl.

Satisfied, Mom walked away. Christy held up the notepad to Paula and whispered between her teeth, "Stay out of my stuff."

"Don't leave your stuff lying around."

Christy grabbed her clothes and marched off to the bathroom to change. As soon as she soundly shut the door, the accusations came at her for being such a horrible

Christian and a poor example of a best friend. She was supposed to be witnessing to Paula, not alienating her!

The guilt feelings hung on her all day. She went swimming in the pool and then in the ocean with David until about noon. Then without interrupting Paula, who had set up her own little camp on the couch, where she spent the day watching TV, Christy showered and changed and joined Mom and Marti for lunch in Lahaina.

They meandered through shop after shop along Front Street and ended up at an open-air restaurant, where they ate salads at a table right by the water.

Mom and Marti chattered about all the boats they could see in Lahaina Harbor. Then they started in about some uncle Christy didn't even know who had had his gallbladder removed.

Christy tuned them out and watched the dozens of tiny crabs skittering across the rocks below them. The afternoon was kind of dreamy and the setting like something from a movie.

While shopping Christy had enjoyed the brightly colored tropical birds they had seen pacing up and down their perches like a pirate's first mate. And she loved the plumeria trees down by the little public library. They filled the hot afternoon air with a heavy, sweet fragrance.

However, it didn't matter how charming the town was or how exotic the afternoon air smelled. She felt miserable.

"It seems like a cruel joke," she whispered to the uncaring crabs over the railing, "to be here with Todd and Paula—two people I consider my friends—and to feel so lonely. I know Todd had to paint today, and he didn't go surfing this morning, so I wasn't able to spend any time with him. But I want to find out what he was talking about last night. What was he trying to decide?

"As far as Paula goes, I wish she'd never come. I wish she'd stayed in Wisconsin, and we could let our childhood memories be the way we think of each other. We've both changed too much to try to be friends now. I wish Katie had come instead of Paula."

"Ready for some more shopping?" Marti asked, breaking into Christy's grumbling monologue.

"I guess so."

"Don't you need to get a few more gifts for your friends?" Marti prompted.

"Yeah, I'd like to find something to take back to Katie."

"It's too bad Paula couldn't have come shopping with us," Marti said, counting out the dollar bills she planned to leave as a tip.

"She needed a day to catch her breath," Mom said. "What with the jet lag, time change, and horrible sunburn, I think she needed a day of complete rest."

"Whatever you find for Katie, why don't you get the same thing for Paula?" Marti suggested.

Christy didn't want to. She didn't want to do Paula any favors. After all, Paula hadn't done any for her.

She ended up buying a white shell bracelet for Paula at the very first shop they stopped in. Actually, Marti bought it. She picked it out too. To keep Marti happy, Christy agreed that Katie wasn't a bracelet kind of person, but Paula would probably be thrilled with it. So Marti bought it, and Christy hoped that would be the end of that.

A few shops later, Christy found a University of Hawaii T-shirt for Katie. Marti insisted on buying three of them so

Paula, Katie, and Christy could all match. Christy agreed as long as she could pick out three different colors, which she did, reserving the light blue one for herself.

For fun, she also bought a grass hula skirt to take back to Katie.

With hands full of shopping bags, they headed back to where they'd parked the van. They passed an old, two-story white house with green trim and a sign in front that said, "Missionary Home of the Rev. Dwight Baldwin, 1834, Museum Open Daily."

"Could we go in there?" Christy asked.

"It's only an old house turned into a museum," Marti said. "Missionaries built it when they first came here. I don't think you'd find it very interesting, Christy."

"Yes, I would. It looks like a neat house. I'd like to go on the tour."

"So would I," Mom said.

For some reason, Marti looked annoyed.

"Go ahead. You have to pay for the tour; it's not free." The way she said it, Christy thought it must be a huge fee. "I'll wait here on the bench."

Mom and Christy paid their admission fee of a few dollars.

You are so funny, Aunt Marti. You left more money than this on the table for a tip!

The inside of the house looked very American, not tropical at all. There were wooden floors, four-poster beds, blue and white china on the large wooden table, and handmade patchwork quilts on the beds.

The tour began in the bedroom, where Christy noticed the large mosquito net over the bed. The tour guide explained that the missionaries were not popular with the sailors who harbored here every winter because they discouraged the sailors' immoral lifestyle.

"It's said that no mosquitoes were on the islands," the guide stated, "until some sailors tried to get back at the missionaries by dumping a barrel of brackish water into the canal that used to run behind the missionaries' homes. The barrel came over on a ship from Mexico and was teeming with mosquito larvae. Hence, mosquitoes made their home on the islands."

One of the women in their little tour group snorted. "What a foolish thing to do!"

The guide went on. "The missionaries were fired on as well but survived the attack. Mind you, this was not the Hawaiian natives attacking them, but their fellow Americans."

"How did they respond?" someone in the group asked. "Did they retaliate?"

The guide smiled as if she'd been asked that question before. "You must keep in mind, these were God-fearing New England Christians. They stood their ground on what they believed to be right, morally and biblically. It's been said their only retaliation was to pray for their enemies."

During the rest of the tour, Christy only took in parts of the guide's sentences. She had become absorbed with the thought that as God-fearing Christians the missionaries prayed for their enemies.

Todd said he prayed every day for Alissa, and he had told Christy she should pray for Paula. Even though she had agreed with Todd and thought it was a good idea, she hadn't prayed for Paula once since then. Not that Paula was truly an enemy. She was a friend, just like the American sailors should have been friends with the American missionaries, but their moral standards separated them. In a way, Christy had felt that separation from Paula over her choice of bathing suits and her goal to lose her virginity.

When they rejoined Marti and strolled back to the car, Christy imagined Lahaina's streets alive with crusty, drunken sailors hurling insults at a pious missionary woman in her long-sleeved dress with her bonnet tipped down, praying for them as she passed by.

All Christy could think about was how much she wanted to talk to Todd about all this, to get his perspective on how to pray. It was one thing for him to tell her she should pray for her friend and another thing to teach her how.

When they arrived at the huge, shady banyan tree, Marti insisted they cross the street and enter Lahaina's Wharf Cinema Center. She led them to the lower level, marching like a woman who knew right where she was going. Apparently she did, because they entered a shop labeled "TCBY"—The Country's Best Yogurt.

Marti briskly announced, "This is the only frozen yogurt I'll eat. Their white chocolate mousse is absolutely divine. Order what you like. I'm paying."

Christy ordered a small chocolate from the friendly dark-haired guy behind the counter.

"Would you like a topping?" he asked, his white smile peeking out from under his mustache. "The macadamia nuts are really 'ono on the chocolate yogurt."

"'Ono?" Christy asked.

"The best." He lifted the ladle, ready to scoop the nuts onto her yogurt.

Christy hated nuts. She had always hated nuts. She used to suck the coating off Peanut M&M's and throw the peanuts away. At this very moment, though, Christy felt adventuresome. "Sure, go ahead. I'll try the macadamia nuts."

The guy was right. The macadamia nuts were 'ono! As she scraped the last spoonful out of her cup, she felt proud of herself for trying something new. Todd would be proud of her.

Back at the condo, Christy found Paula napping and Todd still painting, so she joined David on the couch at Bob and Marti's condo and watched the end of some cartoon. Within minutes she dozed off and was awakened almost an hour later by Marti, who suggested they all go for an evening stroll on the beach.

Christy shook herself awake and, with a string of yawns, found her flip-flops and joined Marti, Mom, and David by the front door. Todd, freshly showered and in clean shorts and a T-shirt, stepped out of the kitchen as Christy was smoothing down her hair.

He gave Christy a smile. "Looks like you had a good nap."

She could have taken his comment as an insult to her appearance but decided not to take offense. "I was really wiped out."

"Bob is going to stay and clean up," Marti said, "and Paula said she'd rather not go this time, so we're all set."

Todd walked next to Christy to the elevator. As she began to wake up, all her afternoon thoughts came back to her, and she was anxious to talk them through with Todd. Even though it was a little thing, she couldn't wait to tell him she had eaten nuts on her yogurt.

"I think I'll stay behind," Todd suddenly announced as the elevator door opened and they all filed in. "I'll check on Paula and help Bob finish up."

With that, the door sealed, and the elevator lowered them to the ground level.

"If Todd's not going, then I don't want to go," David stated. "I'm going back up."

"You don't need to go back, David," Mom said. "Stay with us. Help me find some shells."

"I don't want to go!" David whined. "Can't I go back up, please?"

"Of course you can," Marti answered for Mom.

The elevator stopped at the bottom floor, where Mom, Marti, and Christy exited and David shot back up to the sixth floor. Christy could feel Mom watching her, trying to read her feelings, but Christy kept them hidden.

It was impossible, though, for her to enjoy the sunset or the way the warm sand slipped between her toes knowing that Paula and Todd were alone together. It seemed like a very long walk. Mom and Marti contentedly collected tiny shells, and Christy followed them along, bending occasionally to snatch a shell and drop it into her shorts pocket without even looking at it.

When Marti stopped by the condo pool on the way back and began to talk to some people, Christy went up to the condo. Bob was washing out paintbrushes.

"Hi," she said, hiding her anxiety and distrust. "Where is everybody?"

"I sent Todd across the street for pizza. Paula may have gone with him. David's in the shower." He added with a grin, "But then, you weren't really worried about David, were you?"

Christy smiled and went back to her room to check her appearance in the mirror. A little more makeup, a few more brushes to make her hair fuller, a squirt of perfume. There. If Todd was trying to make a decision between the two of them, she would do her best to make it an easy choice.

"Pizza's here!" Christy heard Mom call, and she stepped out of her room to find everyone gathered on their lanai to eat.

Paula, apparently revived from the day's rest, had turned back into her bubbly, fun-loving self and was sitting on the arm of Todd's chair, gingerly biting into a slice of pizza.

Christy plopped a slice of pizza on a paper plate and took the only spot left, the lounge chair. She felt as if she were separated from the rest of them by an invisible screen. Lively conversation hummed around the table, but no one directly addressed her.

How can I sit here with my family and friends and feel hopelessly lonely?

Todd excused himself as soon as he had downed three large slices of pizza. "See you all in the morning."

Bob looked at his watch. "Nine o'clock already! No wonder I'm so tired. Todd, why don't you take tomorrow off? We pretty well finished up the painting today. I can do the rest myself tomorrow."

Todd stood by the sliding screen door. "Cool. Might be a good day to go to Hana. Good night, everyone."

How can you do that, Todd? How can you go a whole day without saying more than one sentence to me?

Todd had spent the whole day around Paula. Was it part

of his decision-making process? Maybe he had planned to spend all that time with her to get closer to her so he could decide who he liked more.

The rest of Christy's pizza went uneaten.

"Where's Hana?" Mom asked.

Bob explained that Hana was a small community on the other side of the island and that Todd had mentioned that his dad had taken him camping there years ago.

"Sounds like a fun trip for the kids," Marti suggested. "They can take the Jeep, and Margaret and I can get some more shopping in."

"Settled," Bob stated, eyeing the last piece of pizza. "Anybody want another piece?"

Christy excused herself and went to bed, choosing the agony of loneliness over the chance of another confrontation with Paula. She knew she should read her Bible and pray before she went to sleep, but she didn't want anyone to think she was awake. She lay still for a long time, with her face to the wall. When she did fall asleep, she dreamed about the lonely life of the virtuous missionary woman in Lahaina long ago.

10

Which Way to the Waterfalls?

The next morning Paula acted as if no tension had ever existed between the two of them. She complimented Christy on her hair as they shared the bathroom and asked Christy to put some aloe vera gel on her back.

The raging red of Paula's skin two days ago had toned down to a tender pink, and her shoulders had begun to peel.

"I should've listened to you," Paula admitted. "I've never been sunburned like this before."

"Well, I have to admit that when I went to California last summer Marti kept telling me to use sunscreen, and I didn't. I got burned too. I even spent a day on the couch, just like you did. Only I moaned a lot more, and the only thing I did all day was sip ice water."

Paula laughed. "Why didn't you tell me!"

"I don't know. You were so set on getting a tan. Some things I guess people have to figure out for themselves."

"Christy, that's exactly what I've been wanting to tell you." Paula met Christy's gaze in the bathroom mirror. "You should know me well enough to know that I'm the kind of person who likes to figure things out for herself. I mean, you might be right about the sunscreen and maybe about some other things. But I have to figure them out for myself. That's just the way I am."

"I know. I'm that way too," Christy said.

"No, you don't understand," Paula said. "What I mean is, do us both a favor and stop bugging me about becoming religious."

"Becoming religious!"

Paula's tone heightened. "You haven't stopping bugging me since last summer. First in all your letters, and now that we're together, you're so self-righteous about everything. I still can't believe you brought my old bathing suit along! You have such a perfect little standard for living. That's fine for you. And you could even be right about God and everything. But I have to figure it out myself."

Christy blinked but didn't respond.

Paula looked down and pulled her mascara from her cosmetic bag, untwisting the top and jamming the wand in and out. "I've wanted to say that ever since I got here, and I'm glad I finally did, especially since we're going to be together all day."

She began to apply her mascara, and Christy could see Paula's hand was shaking.

"So, if it's okay with you, let's go back to being friends the way we've always been and let me figure out my life and make my own mistakes."

Silence hung between them for a moment. Then Christy broke the stalemate by swishing out of the bathroom and into the bedroom. She began to toss things into the straw beach bag Mom had given her.

I'm just trying to help you, Paula, and you don't even see it. We're so different now! Things that are important to me mean nothing to you. How can I let you live your life when I see you about to make some major mistakes?

With deliberate steps, Christy marched to the linen closet and yanked out a couple of beach towels. Hugging the towels, she closed her eyes, took a deep breath, and tried to exhale all her frustrations.

"She's not pau." Todd's words from earlier came back to Christy. *"You should be praying for her."*

Just as she was about to piece together a prayer for Paula, David and Todd bounded through the open door. With ice chest in hand and the Jeep keys between his teeth, Todd jerked his head toward the door, motioning Christy to come.

Paula appeared, bright and smiling, and Christy decided she wouldn't let anything ruin this day. Even when Paula snatched the front seat of the Jeep and settled in, smiling at Todd, Christy made a deliberate effort not to let it get to her.

The four of them sailed down the road with the wind in their hair. It was impossible to hear anyone speak until they came into Lahaina and Todd took a right toward the center of town.

"You want to see the first church the missionaries built here?" Todd asked. "I used to walk past it every day on my way home from school."

"I thought we were going to the waterfalls," David griped.

"Yeah," Paula agreed as Todd drove slowly through a small intersection and into a part of town with lots of old wood houses lining the narrow street.

"I'd like to see it," Christy said firmly.

"There's the church right there." Todd stopped the Jeep under some tall palm trees next to a low stone wall. A sign in front said Waine'e Church.

"This actually isn't the original one. The first one blew down, and they rebuilt it. Then I think it blew down or burned down again. The missionaries never gave up though. They kept rebuilding the church. This one stayed because they built it the right way, facing the mountains. That way when the Kona winds came, all they had to do was open the front and back doors and let the wild wind blow right through, out to the ocean. Pretty good thinking, huh?"

Paula gave a yawn.

Todd smiled and started up the engine. He looked at Christy over his shoulder. "I studied all this when I was growing up here. I forget not everybody is as interested in the early missionaries as I am."

"I am!" Christy said, eagerly leaning forward. "My mom and I toured the missionary house."

"The Baldwin House on Front Street?"

"Yes. I really liked it." Christy felt an air of satisfaction, knowing she had one up on Paula.

"The very first missionary was Reverend Richardson." Todd pointed to the graveyard next to the church as he slowly pulled out onto the road. "He's buried right there. An amazing man. They say he single-handedly stopped the epidemic of smallpox from wiping out Lahaina, and he wasn't even a doctor."

"Wow," Christy said, enjoying Todd's full attention.

"Is this going to turn into a historical tour?" Paula

interjected. "Or are we going to the waterfalls?"

"Yeah!" David protested.

"Okay, okay," Todd said as the Jeep connected with the main highway and they sped on toward the other side of the island.

Christy sat back satisfied knowing that she and Todd could talk more about the missionaries later, just the two of them, an interest Paula didn't share.

She felt something more than a shared interest with Todd in the missionaries. She couldn't explain why, but she felt awed and thrilled when she thought about men and women who loved God so much that they didn't give up, even when their church blew down. She had admired their perseverance when she toured the Baldwin House.

A little ways past the airport, they slowed to go down what appeared to be the main street of a funky-looking little town. Just before they reached the town, Todd shouted, "Right up here is the wind-surfing capital of the world. You guys want to stop and watch?"

"No!" David answered. "Not unless we can go swimming there."

Todd smiled over his shoulder. "Okay, David. We'll get you to a waterfall. Hang on. It's going to be a long, winding road."

During the next few miles, the road became narrower and narrower. Around every bend and curve, they met another bend and curve.

Christy thought it all looked like she imagined old Hawaii to have been—waterfalls were tucked behind valleys that were carpeted with huge ferns; bright flowers literally grew out of the rocks; exotic birds sang in the overhanging trees; and every now and then simple little tin-roofed houses built on stilts appeared.

Because the Jeep was open, everything seemed close up. Christy felt that if she were quick enough, she could pick flowers and ferns as they passed them.

The scenery stayed like that for mile after winding mile. On they traveled, bump after bump, curve after curve, sliding through tight spots in the road. Twice they had to stop and back up so an oncoming car could get by. Christy figured they must have driven for more than three hours already.

"Can't they do something about improving this road?" Paula exclaimed after a swift curve brought her dangerously close to the jagged volcanic rock wall on her side of the Jeep.

"Actually they have," Todd said. "When my dad and I used to come out here camping, it was much worse."

"Worse!" Paula squeaked. "How could it be worse?"

"Parts of it weren't paved. It was gravel and dirt and very muddy when it rained."

"They sure don't make it very appealing for a tourist to come all the way out here," Paula said.

Todd smiled and nodded. "I think that's the idea. The locals like it unchanged. I don't blame them. Hana is a unique place."

"Are we almost there yet?" David asked for what seemed like the fiftieth time.

"Almost."

About fifteen minutes later, the Jeep hit smooth pavement and wider road. They knew they were in Hana by the community of small houses that suddenly appeared on the hillside.

Christy spotted an old white church with a tall steeple and smiled to see that the undaunted missionaries had found their way to remote Hana more than a century ago. Across the road from the church lay a huge fenced pasture with a carpet of emerald grass running all the way to steep cliffs. The cliffs dropped into the bright turquoise ocean. The blending of colors struck her as incredibly beautiful.

A dozen or so horses nibbled on the rich green grass, their shiny coats looking silkier in the tropical sun than that of any horse she had ever seen.

She felt twinges of homesickness for the farm she had grown up on in Wisconsin. But Wisconsin grass never turned this dazzling shade of green, and horses back on the farm were merely black or brown, not silky ebony, amber, and caramel like these.

"Where are the waterfalls?" David whined.

Instead of answering, Todd swung the Jeep into a tiny old-fashioned gas station and filled the tank.

David whined the whole time. "I'm hungry. When are we going to eat? How much farther is it? Can't we get out here?"

"David, stop it! You sound like a big baby," Paula scolded. "We shouldn't have let you come with us."

Before Todd got back in, he roughed up David's already wind-snarled hair. "Think you can hang in there another half hour, dude?"

"A half hour!" David squawked.

"I thought we were almost there," Paula moaned. "You didn't tell us it would take all day to get there! I thought you said it was about seventy miles."

"It is," Todd explained. "Something like that. But you

may have noticed that we haven't been driving very fast."

"Then let's get going," Paula ordered. "It seems like the middle of the afternoon, and we're not even there yet. We're barely going to have any time left before we have to turn around and go back."

"Oh no," David groaned. "Do we have to take the same road back?"

"Unless you want to go the long way back on the dirt road," Todd said, hopping into the front seat and bringing the engine to a roar. "Come on, you guys, where's your sense of adventure?"

"Yahoo!" Christy shouted spontaneously as Todd made the tires peel out on the road.

Christy loved this. She really, truly did. If this was what he meant the other day about being adventurous, then maybe she really was after all.

"Oh, one thing I should tell you," Todd called over his shoulder as they drove under a huge plumeria tree, which filled the air with its rich fragrance, "the road to the falls is ten times worse than the road we just came over."

11

The Bridge

"This road should be condemned!" Paula shrieked. "How much farther is it?"

"Not much. Relax, Paula. This is the real Hawaii," Todd said.

"I'd rather be back at the condo," Paula muttered, crossing her arms.

"I like it," Christy called out. They were driving slowly, and the wind had subsided, so her voice traveled clearly.

She laughed at her own exuberance and then let loose all her pent-up feelings. "Look at this, you guys! It's beautiful. I don't care how long it takes to get there. Look! Have you ever seen flowers growing out of a rock before?" With a daring grab, she snatched a tiny purple flower. She sniffed the fragrance and told them all, "I could live here the rest of my life."

Todd glanced at Christy over his shoulder, and she could see his dimple when he smiled. "I knew you'd like it here."

He slowed the Jeep to creep over another one of the many bridges they had crossed. But this bridge was longer, and people were standing at its edge, looking over the side.

"This is it, guys!" Todd announced. "The parking lot is

down the road, and then we walk to the falls."

"Finally." Then with a quick look around, David said, "That's all there is? No waterslides or anything?"

"Sorry, dude. It's all natural, the way God made it."

From her side of the Jeep, all Christy could see was black rock lining a round pool that flowed into the ocean.

All of a sudden Paula shrieked, and Todd slammed on the brakes.

"He's going to jump!" Paula screamed. "Somebody stop him!"

Too late. A man in fluorescent green trunks sprang from the edge of the old stone bridge and jumped into the water below.

"Oh. There's water down there!" Paula said in a flash of discovery. "I didn't know he was diving into the water!"

"Whoa!" David exclaimed. "Did you see that, Todd? Have you ever done that? Have you ever jumped off that bridge?"

"Not yet."

After they parked, they hiked the long grassy trail down to the lower pools. Then they waded through the chilly water over slippery rocks until they came to a gravel spot by a large pool, where they put down their belongings. Paula laid out her towel and began to sunbathe. David yanked off his T-shirt and glasses in one motion and jumped into the pool.

"Anybody want to go exploring?" Todd asked.

"Not me," Paula said without looking up. "I got enough Indiana Jones trailblazing on the ride here."

"I do!" Christy followed Todd over the rocks and into the refreshing water.

Todd motioned to a big black rock and excitedly said, "Here. This is the one. Sit right here. What do you see?"

"It's beautiful," Christy said. "So tropical. I love it!"

What she didn't tell him was that she also loved having him all to herself.

"Take your time." He placed his foot on the rock next to where she sat. His soggy tennis shoe dripped water on her leg. "Take it all in and tell me if you see it."

Slowly, she scanned the tall black sides of the canyon, covered with foliage hanging down in long vines. She counted three large pools that each flowed into a waterfall, then on into the next pool. A fourth pool stumbled over precarious chunks of black lava before giving itself over completely to the hungry ocean, which sent wave after wave to lap up the fresh mountain spring water.

"You mean the colors?" she asked Todd. "The blues are so blue, and the plants are an indescribable shade of green I've never seen before."

"No, no, up there," Todd pointed.

Christy studied the huge volcanic mountain dressed in the ruffled green gown of wild foliage that flowed down to the canyon where they sat. Then she saw it. It took a minute to place where she had seen that exact scene before. Finally, she remembered.

"The bridge! It's the bridge on the poster you gave me. This must be the exact spot they took the picture from."

Todd smiled and nodded, looking pleased that she had figured it out. "I found that poster the first day Bob and I were here. In the grocery store, of all places! I bought three. One for me, one for you, and one for my dad."

He wedged himself onto the rock next to Christy. "My

dad and I sat right here on this same rock when I was about ten years old."

"Really? That's why you remembered the bridge and bought the posters?"

"There's more to it. Remember the guy who jumped off the bridge when we were going across it?"

"It's the same bridge, right? The one we drove over?"

Todd nodded. "My dad jumped off the bridge a couple of times, and he wanted me to jump too. But I never could get up the nerve."

"Well, I don't blame you." Christy tried to sound encouraging. "It's a long way down! How far is it?"

"I don't know. Maybe sixty feet or more. And you have to land in a certain spot where it's deep enough, because lots of rocks are hidden underwater. Kimo came with us one time. He jumped. But I couldn't do it. I thought my dad would be disappointed in me, you know, that I wasn't a real man or something because I wouldn't jump."

"You were only ten years old."

"Kimo was ten too." Todd looked at Christy.

She turned away from the bridge and met his gaze. His eyes looked as blue as the sky. As blue as the ocean. As blue as the freshwater pool at her feet. It hit her in that moment, looking into his eyes, that there was so much she didn't know about Todd and so much she wanted to know.

"So what happened?" Christy asked, feeling a tiny bit nervous with Todd sitting so close and looking at her so intently. Yet at the same time she wished they could sit there all afternoon and talk and talk and talk.

"My dad brought me over to this rock, and we sat here just like this. He told me to look at the bridge and always remember it, because my life would be full of bridges. With every bridge would come a choice. Then he told me he admired me that I didn't jump just because Kimo did."

"Wait a minute," Christy interrupted. "He said he admired you for not jumping?"

"Yeah. He said, 'I don't care if you ever jump off that bridge. All that matters to me is that you make your own decision and follow through on it because it's your choice, not because someone influenced or persuaded you to do it,' or something like that."

Todd paused, and Christy could see that this moment meant as much to him as it did to her.

"Anyway, I've never forgotten that day and what my dad said. I think I became more of an individualist after that, making my choices because that's what I chose to do, not because someone cornered me into it."

Todd stood up, reached for Christy's hand, pulled her to her feet, and said, "Come on, I'll show you the trail up to the top."

Christy slipped on the first rock, then regained her balance and kept holding tightly to Todd's hand as he led the way up a narrow trail on the rocks. They wound their way under the jungle growth of huge leaves and trailing vines. The pools on their right side grew smaller and more distant the farther up they climbed.

Halfway up in a clearing, Todd stopped and called down to Paula. She lifted her head from her beach towel and looked all around. Not being able to determine where Todd's voice was coming from, she lay back down and closed her eyes to soak up some more sun.

Christy thought Paula probably couldn't see them

without her glasses, anyway. Knowing Paula, she probably left them back at the condo with the unused one-piece bathing suit.

David, who had joined some local boys in the shallow water, was busy watching his new friends catch prawns with their homemade metal cages.

Todd and Christy kept climbing until the trail met the road, and Christy realized they were at the top—at the bridge. A few cars passed slowly, and two older ladies stood at the side, cautiously holding onto the railing while snapping pictures of the pools and the ocean.

Todd led Christy along the bridge's edge, looking into the water far below. He stopped at what seemed to be his chosen spot, a few feet from the old ladies. He let go of Christy's hand.

She caught something in his expression and carefully said, "Todd?"

His silver-blue eyes locked on hers, and she knew he was going to do it. Todd was going to jump.

"You don't have to, you know," she fumbled. "Like your dad said, it has to be your decision, not a whim or a pressure thing."

Todd firmly grasped Christy by the shoulders and pulled her close as a car passed inches behind them. His eyes were swimming with the secret dreams of his heart, and she knew he spoke the truth before he even said the words.

"This is my decision. I'm not doing it for my dad or Kimo or anybody. This is for me." He broke into a wide grin. "In case I don't come up, the keys to the Jeep are in my backpack."

Then he enveloped Christy in his arms and kissed her

quickly and firmly, like a soldier giving his beloved one last kiss before going off to war.

Before she could respond, Todd released her and positioned himself on the stone railing of the bridge. He set his sights on the small area of deep water below. Without looking back, he bent his knees, and without a sound, Todd launched his six-foot frame into the thick tropical air.

12

Hana After It Rains

"*Ahhhhhhh!*" screamed one of the old women on the bridge's edge.

Her friend frantically waved her arms. "Someone save him! He jumped! A man jumped off the bridge!"

Christy, clawing her fingers into the stone railing as she leaned over as far as she dared, held her breath and waited for the splash.

Splash!

Then she counted and frantically scanned the water's surface, watching for Todd's sandy-blond head to pop up. *Three...four...five...six... Come on, Todd, How long are you going to stay down there? Seven...eight... There he is! There he is! He's okay! He did it!*

Christy reached over and touched the arm of the old woman, who was still screaming and waving her hands to the passing cars. Her friend had trotted down the road, hollering and trying to flag down a car.

"Look!" Christy pointed, trying to get the woman's attention. "He's okay! See him down there?"

Todd, treading water in the center of the pool, called out to Christy with hoots and hollers, waving wildly.

Christy stretched her arms over the edge so Todd could see her applauding him.

"Thelma!" the woman on the bridge called. "He's all right! Come see!"

Thelma bustled back to the edge and peered over. Todd waved at her with both arms.

"Oh, my heavens!" Thelma sighed. "That young man gave me quite a scare!" Then turning to Christy, she said, "Whatever possessed him to do that?"

"He wanted to," Christy said defensively. "He knew what he was doing. He's been here before...with his dad."

The women did not look impressed, nor did they join Christy in applauding him. Rather, they clutched their cameras, linked arms, and cautiously made their way off the bridge.

Christy heard one of them mutter, "These young people today..."

"Hey, Christy!" Todd yelled. "You coming in? The water feels great!"

"I think I'll take the trail down," she called to him. "I'll meet you down there."

"Sure you don't want to jump?"

Christy shook her head briskly, waved once more, then quickly made her way off the bridge and down the narrow trail. It was much harder going down alone, without Todd holding her hand. At one point she lost her footing and landed on her rear end. No one was around to see her, so her embarrassment quickly disappeared. She proceeded with greater caution.

Arriving at the trail's end, she stepped into the shallow water and gingerly placed her feet on the slippery rocks. She stopped to rest on the rock she and Todd had sat on earlier.

David stood only a few feet away, fishing with something tied to the end of a string.

"Hey, Christy! Where have you been? Some guy jumped off the bridge. Did you see him?" David asked.

"Yep, I saw him, all right. You know who it was?"

"Who?"

"Todd."

"No way!"

"Yes way, David. Ask him yourself."

"Where is he?"

"Hey!" Todd called out from the gravel spot where they had left their small ice chest and towels. "Anybody else want some lunch?"

Paula sat next to Todd on a towel. It seemed to Christy that Paula scooted closer when Christy approached.

"Hey, Todd!" David called out. "Did you really jump?"

Todd took a deep breath and let out a poof of air before saying, "Yeah, dude, I really jumped."

Christy thought he looked and sounded like he still didn't believe it himself.

"There's probably not much left," Paula said, poking her hand in the ice chest. "Your little brother got into it and started taking the meat out of the sandwiches to use for bait."

"I only opened one sandwich," David said defensively.

As usual, Uncle Bob had supplied a generous portion of everything, and they had plenty to eat. They all talked about Todd's jump while they ate.

Christy became so hot sitting in the sun that when she finished her sandwich, she stepped down the natural rock steps into the deep pool to cool off. At first, the water felt freezing cold against her sun-baked legs. It felt miserable to be half cold and half hot, so taking a deep breath, she stretched her arms in front of her and took the plunge.

"Brrrr!" she called to the others when she surfaced. "Verrrrrry refrrrrrrreshing!"

"You convinced me." Todd sprang to his feet and did a shallow dive off the side, coming up right next to Christy.

"You're right!" he said, blinking as he surfaced. "It's refreshing. Come on, Paula! It'll wake you up."

"No thanks."

"Come on," Todd urged. "You can't drive all this way to Kipahulu and not even go in the water!"

"I went in already."

"What? Up to your ankles?" Christy teased.

"If you won't come to the water, we'll have to bring the water to you!" Todd hoisted himself out of the pool and grasped Paula by the wrists.

She began to kick and scream, trying to pull away so Todd wouldn't throw her in. He, of course, overpowered her, and with a typically loud Paula screech, she landed in the pool with Todd right behind her.

They came up laughing and splashing water at each other. Christy fought hard to resist the urge to crawl out of the water and curl up on a rock by herself.

"Hey," Todd called out to them, "you ever been underneath a waterfall before?"

"I want to go!" David yelled from the shore and then jumped in to join them.

Todd motioned with his head toward the waterfall, and Christy swam after him along with the other two, telling herself this was too wonderful a place to sit alone feeling sorry for herself. The roaring noise and the carefree spray on her face made her feel more excited and nervous the closer they came to the waterfall.

"It's easier to go in this way," Todd directed. "Follow me."

They swam around to the side and pressed their backs against the rock until they could slide into a hollowed-out part of the wall. Slowly inching along, they found a ledge to sit on directly behind the waterfall with the rock overhang sheltering them like a thick black umbrella.

"This is incredible!" Christy said, her words echoing in the cavern. "Look how the water comes down like a thick sheet of glass and then shatters into a billion foaming bubbles when it hits the pool below."

"There's a much bigger waterfall about a mile and a half up the trail, and you can go behind that one too," Todd said, his deep voice resounding in the hollow.

"Let's go there," Christy suggested.

"He said it was more than a mile, Christy. You want to walk that far? I think we'd better start to drive back. What time is it?" Paula was shivering and not enjoying the novelty of sitting behind a waterfall at all.

"We probably should get going," Todd agreed. "If we stay too long, we'll have to drive that road in the dark."

"No, thank you!" Paula spouted. "I'm going back to dry off."

"Can't we stay a little longer?" David moaned. "I haven't caught anything yet."

They followed Todd out past the side of the waterfall, and Christy was amazed at how much easier it was to hear the farther they swam from the crashing falls. Swimming back, Todd agreed to help David try to catch his elusive pet prawn.

The girls dried off, and Paula fished for her camera in Christy's bag and began to snap a roll of pictures. Christy watched David and Todd hunt for the prawns, which looked like miniature lobsters about three to seven inches long.

The prawns hid themselves well under the rocks, but the lunch meat tied to the string on David's stick beckoned them to come out of hiding to try to snatch it. Todd and David caught two but lost them before they could lift the string out of the water and grab them.

David decided to stand very still in the water next to the rock and grab the critter before it had time to scamper away. It worked. He caught a big one.

Gleefully splashing his way over to Christy and Paula, David proudly showed off the prize in his fist.

"Get that pinchy thing away from me," Paula wailed. "It's gross!"

"He's my new pet," David announced. "Sydney the Shrimp."

"David, you can't keep that thing," Paula said.

"Sure I can. I'm going to keep it in the ice chest with some little rocks and water." David set about turning the empty ice chest into a new home for Sydney.

Paula looked thoroughly annoyed. "Todd, don't you think we'd better get going? When we first got here lots of other people were around, but now there's hardly anyone."

"Good. Not as much traffic." Todd reached for his towel and backpack and said, "You guys ready?"

Christy scrambled to get her things together and reluctantly slipped her feet back into her cold, soggy tennis shoes.

The four of them waded through the water and over the

slippery rocks. The late afternoon shadows darkened the water, making it difficult to find sure footing. David received the assignment of carrying the small plastic ice chest since he had turned it into a prawn playground.

The hike to the parking lot was uphill, and when Christy reached the Jeep, she felt tired and wasn't at all looking forward to the long ride home. She plopped her beach bag in the front seat, as if to say "Front Seat Reserved for Christy." Todd and Paula weren't behind them.

"What are they doing?" Christy asked David as he opened the ice chest to check on his treasure inside.

"Todd said it was some kind of fruit or something, and Paula wanted him to get it. Here. He told me to put his backpack in the car."

Christy shielded her eyes from the sun and watched as Todd climbed a tree at the far end of the grassy parking lot. It was too far away, and she was too tired to try to join Paula, who stood below the tree, pointing to the clumps of fruit.

When did they take off? And how come I didn't notice?

Christy decided their delay was to her advantage, and she settled herself in the front seat. She watched them in the rearview mirror.

Todd slid down the tree and handed Paula the fruit, but suddenly he hopped on one foot. Then he grabbed his other foot, and from all Christy could see, he either fell down or lay down. Paula tossed the fruit into the air and dropped to her knees by his side.

"David, what's going on down there?"

"Where?" David looked around as Christy undid her seat belt.

"I think Todd fell or something." She got out of her

seat, and when she saw Paula frantically running toward her, she broke into a run.

"What happened?"

"Backpack!" Paula shrieked. "Where's his backpack?"

She ran past Christy to the Jeep.

"David had it!" Christy started running toward the Jeep with Paula, and then on impulse turned and ran toward the tree, where Todd was still lying with his eyes closed.

"What happened? Are you all right?" She fell to her knees and grasped his arm.

Todd opened his eyes and hoarsely said, "Backpack."

"Paula's getting it." Christy glanced over her shoulder. "They're coming. Here they are."

She took his hand in hers and squeezed it.

Paula nearly flung the backpack at Christy's face. "Get it, Christy. He said it's in there. I can't do it!"

"What?" Christy yelped frantically. "What happened? What's in here?"

She tore the zipper open and dumped out the contents.

"A bee!" Paula shrieked. "He got stung, and he's allergic, and he said he'll go unconscious unless he gets a shot!"

Christy grabbed a long, yellow plastic container that tumbled out of the backpack.

"It must be this thing," she said, taking control of the situation. "Todd? Can you do this? Are you okay?"

"Look at his foot!" David shouted.

Todd's right foot had already swollen to twice its normal size.

"Oh, you guys! What are we going to do?" Paula broke into loud sobs. "Is he unconscious?"

"Chris," Todd said in a breathy voice, "do you have it?"

Christy popped open the plastic case and removed the hypodermic needle and syringe. "It's right here. What do I do with it, Todd?"

"Take off the cap and hand it to me."

"Oh, I can't look! I can't look! Needles always make me faint!" Paula turned away, still crying.

"Okay, Todd. Here it is. Can you see this okay? I'm putting it in your hand." Christy sounded much braver than she felt.

Todd opened his eyes and pulled himself up. Christy quickly moved behind him to prop him up. It felt as though he weighed a thousand pounds. She pressed her shoulder hard against his back to keep him sitting up and closed her eyes while he gave himself the injection.

I feel like I'm going to pass out. Don't do it, Christy. Take a deep breath.

When Todd's back pressed even more heavily against her shoulder, she slowly pulled away so he could lie down.

"Is he going to be okay?" David asked in a small, scared voice.

Todd licked his lips. Beads of perspiration dripped off his forehead. He drew in a deep breath and said in a low voice, "Give me another five minutes." He took a breath. "Then I'll be fine."

Paula stopped crying and turned to face the others, sniffing and drying her eyes. "He took off his shoes to climb the tree, and when he was coming down, this huge bee—it had to be as big as a moth—buzzed past my head. The next thing I knew he must've stepped on it or something, 'cuz he dropped like he'd been shot or something and told me to get his backpack."

"Sorry I scared you." Todd opened his eyes halfway. "I'm allergic to bee stings."

"Oh, no kidding!" David said, releasing the tension with his comical voice and face. "We all thought you were taking a nap!"

Todd's lips pressed together. "If I keep completely still, I stay conscious longer. It takes a little while for the injection to work. I'll be fine."

"Do you think you can walk?" Christy asked.

"Sure. I'll be fine."

"Christy!" Paula sounded panicked again. "A better question would be, can he drive?"

"Sure. I'll be fine." Todd raised himself up on his elbows, blinked his eyes a few times, and shook his head. "If you guys carry my stuff, I think I can make it to the car."

They took it slowly. Todd tried to hop on his left foot. A painful grimace distorted his face.

"I've got an idea," Christy said. "Paula, go around on his other side. Here, Todd. Put your arms around us. We'll be your crutches."

They made it to the Jeep, and Todd wedged his tender foot into place on the gas pedal. David raced to conquer the front seat, leaving Christy and Paula sentenced to share the back one.

At this point, Christy didn't care where she sat. She could tell by Todd's expression that even though he said he would be fine, he really wasn't. He tried hard to sound normal.

"Everybody in? Let's hit it!" He aggressively pressed his bare foot on the gas, and the Jeep sailed over the bumps in the parking lot and onto the narrow road. Right before the bridge, Todd swung into a small turnout. He looped his arms over the top of the steering wheel as if holding on to it for support and sucked in a deep breath.

"It hurts too much, huh?" Paula asked anxiously, leaning between the two front seats. "You can't drive, can you? What are we going to do? You guys, I think he's going to pass out!"

"I'm not going to pass out. I need to elevate my foot for a few more minutes. Maybe we should hang out here another half hour or so."

"But it's getting dark!" Paula said frantically. "We have to get over the really rough road while it's still light. Isn't that what you said?"

Todd stretched out his still red and swollen foot, propping it on the slim dashboard. "We've still got another few hours before the sun sets."

"Then why is it getting so dark?" Paula moaned.

"What's that?" David asked, looking up. "Hey, I think it's starting to rain!"

"Eeeeee!" Christy and Paula both wailed as a sudden attack of rain pellets hammered them.

"Didn't this Jeep come with a cover?" Christy asked, rummaging through her bag for her sweatshirt.

"Use your beach towels," Todd instructed, grabbing one off the floor board and draping it over David. "It'll probably last only a few minutes."

"Ahhhhh!" Paula cried. "I'm getting drenched!"

Christy pulled her towel over her head and hunched over so that the torrent of rain hit the middle of her back and flowed into puddles on the seat. She thought the whole situation was kind of adventurous and exciting, like a movie she had seen about a woman from New York who got lost in a Colombian jungle and had to hike through the rain and mud with her hero.

Then as instantly as it began, the warm rain turned off, and the not-so-happy adventurers peered out of their beach-towel tents.

"Look at me! I'm soaked!" Paula fussed. "Everything is soaked!"

Todd was especially wet, since he had given his towel to David and braved the gush with only his T-shirt. He roughed up his short hair, sending out a sprinkle of rain-drops. Pixie-like rays of returning sunlight danced through the jungle-growth overhead and teased their way into the Jeep, kissing Christy's damp bare legs with their warmth.

"It smells like, um, like a…" Christy tried to find the right word as she wrung out her towel over the edge of the Jeep. "It smells like…"

"Like Hana after it rains," Todd finished for her, taking in a deep breath. "Once you smell a tropical forest after the rain, you never forget it."

"It smells like mildew, you guys!" Paula was now stand-ing up, toweling down her legs, which turned out to be pointless because the towel was wetter than her legs. "We'd better get out of here before another bucket falls on us! Can you drive yet, Todd?"

One look at his foot gave them all the obvious answer. The swelling was not going down, and the redness seemed to be spreading. Todd didn't answer. They all remained silent, waiting for his conclusion.

Christy broke the silence. "I'll drive."

Todd turned and met her clear eyes and sincere smile.

"She can't drive!" David protested. "She doesn't know how. You'll get us all killed! Can't you drive, Paula?"

"I don't know how to drive a stick shift!" Paula spouted. "Besides, I can't see more than three feet in front of me without my glasses, and I didn't bring them."

"Christy," David warned, "you can't do it."

Todd kept looking at her. "You don't have to, you know."

Christy leaned forward, as if she were talking only to Todd, and said, "I want to. This is my decision. I'm not doing it for you or my dad or anybody else. I'm doing this for me."

A knowing smile lit up Todd's face. "This is your bridge, huh?"

"Yep," Christy answered bravely. "And I'm ready to jump."

"What are you guys talking about?" Paula asked.

Without answering, Christy scooted around the side of the Jeep and opened the door for Todd.

"Mind if I sit there, dude?" Todd said to David as he hopped around.

David climbed into the backseat, still protesting that Christy would crash the Jeep if Todd let her drive.

Paula started in too, about how they should try to call for help at a phone somewhere, wherever they might possibly find a phone in this remote spot, and maybe if they called 911, someone would send a helicopter to rescue them.

Todd positioned his foot on the dashboard and began to explain the gears to Christy.

"Hey," he suddenly said, turning to face the two complainers in the backseat, "could you guys cool it?"

They instantly hushed, and Christy listened carefully to Todd's instructions on operating a gearshift, remembering fairly clearly what they had practiced in driver's training.

The engine started on her first try, and Todd pressed down on the gearshift and popped it into reverse for her. "Let up slowly on the clutch, and don't worry about trying to go fast."

Flashing back to her day in the church parking lot with her dad, she giggled. "Don't worry. Slow is what I do best."

Swallowing her giggles and all her nervousness so they landed in her stomach like a big fizzing antacid tablet, she looked over her shoulder. Cautiously letting up on the clutch, Christy pressed slightly on the gas to back up onto the road. The Jeep slipped through the muddy gravel as it powered backward, and Christy slammed on the brakes.

Paula screamed, and David started to plead that they call 911.

Todd ignored them, and placing his hand on top of Christy's as she held the gearshift, he calmly said, "Good. Now this is first gear, right here. Go ahead and give it some gas."

She did, and the Jeep lurched forward, spinning mud and spraying all of them with reddish-black mud freckles.

"You've got it, Christy!" Todd praised over the sound of Paula's squawks. "Now put it into second gear, right here."

He moved her hand down and her *Forever* bracelet lightly tapped against the metal gearshift.

They rumbled over the bridge, and Todd squeezed her hand, rubbing the chain on the bracelet with his thumb. He didn't have to say a word. She knew he must be thinking the same thing she was thinking. This was their bridge.

Today they both had changed on this bridge. Todd, for jumping off it, and Christy, for driving over it. It would always be a forever moment for them.

Todd let go, and she placed both hands on the steering wheel in the ten and two positions.

"Should I keep it in second gear?" Christy asked as they bounced over the muddy road.

"Yeah, and don't try to go any faster. The curves come up quicker than you think."

Todd was right. The curves kept curving, and the bumps kept bumping. Christy's jaw began to send out shooting pains because she had clenched her teeth so long. With every breath, she drew in the fragrance that the tropical rain had scattered all around them, and even though she was nervous, she felt happier than she had ever felt before.

The shadows grew, and Christy squinted to see the road, which never seemed to stay in one place. It rose and fell and turned and in some places narrowed so that there was room for only one car. In other places, the passenger side dropped off hundreds of feet down a slide of angry, paralyzed lava that had been forced to stop there years ago by the strong hand of the cool ocean.

For nearly an hour, Christy used every bit of her courage and skill to conquer the Hana road. It was nearly dark when, without warning, the tires hit smooth, straight pavement. They all perked up, knowing they had reached Hana.

"Turn up that way." Todd pointed to a long driveway by a sign that said Hana Ranch Market. "If they're still open, we can get some supplies for the ride home."

"I'll take anything chocolate," Paula said. "I feel like I desperately need some chocolate now!"

Todd directed Christy where to turn and where to park, and as soon as she stopped, David and Paula jumped out of the Jeep and ran into the store like released prisoners.

Christy flopped against the back of her seat and let out a gigantic sigh of relief.

"You did it!" Todd straightened his cramped knee and stretched his greatly improved bee-stung foot. "You never stop surprising me, Christy." He said it firmly and softly while trying to get his stiff legs out the open door. Once he was up on his good leg, he said, "I'm going to call your uncle. I'll meet you inside."

Christy relaxed her tensed legs and repeated Todd's words: *You never stop surprising me, Christy.* From Todd, that was a compliment. Maybe he would never compare her eyes to the Blue Grotto. Maybe he would never take her to a fancy restaurant. But today they had shared an adventure, and Christy knew she would never be the same because of it.

Inside the small store, David turned to Christy. "I want to get this, Christy!"

He held up a T-shirt with a cartoon drawing of a frantic-looking character driving on a road filled with obstacles. Across the top were the words "I Survived the Road to Hana."

"Will you get it for me?" he asked.

Christy laughed. "Sure, David. I think we all should get one."

They all did and wore them home. The T-shirts were the first thing Marti made a fuss over when they stumbled into the condo at almost midnight—cold, tired, dirty, and hungry. All chattering at once, they told the details of their wild adventure.

"And you actually drove, Christy?" Mom looked shocked.

"Only the first hour back. When we stopped in Hana, when Todd called you guys, his foot was a lot better. So he drove the rest of the way. We were all wet from the rain, and it got so cold from the wind in that open Jeep!"

"I'll get some hot water going." Marti headed for the kitchen, nearly tripping over the ice chest they had brought in. "We've got hot chocolate here somewhere."

Suddenly, Marti shrieked, grabbed the broom, and began to pound the floor by the opened ice chest. They all ran into the kitchen just in time to see a lifeless Sydney squished on the floor.

"Aunt Marti," David wailed, "that was my shrimp!"

"Oh David, don't cry. You uncle will take you out tomorrow night and buy you a shrimp dinner, won't you, Bob?"

David broke into a bleating-calf cry and ran from the room.

"What did I say?" Marti asked.

They were too busy laughing to answer.

13

The "God-Thing"

The final few days of their vacation breezed by as refreshing and fragrant as the summer trade winds. They lounged by the pool, walked along the beach at sunset, shopped, and dined at fancy restaurants. Christy and Paula got along much better than at the trip's beginning.

Their last night in Hawaii, Bob took them all on a sunset-dinner sail on a catamaran. About twenty-five tourists like them took the cruise.

One of them was a university student from Denmark named Alex. Paula had set her sights on him the minute he came onboard, and within five minutes she had started up a conversation with him.

The two of them talked nonstop the entire trip. It seemed to Christy that Alex was captivated by Paula's Paula-ness.

After they had eaten, Christy left the group and, with rocking steps, made her way to the front of the catamaran. She sat on the webbed tarp spread across the boat's front.

The sun had just been devoured in three swift bites by the volcano that rose out of the center of the island of Molokai. All that was left was a halo of red-orange-yellow-pink fuzzy clouds that looked like a huge party napkin,

wiping the upturned lips of the greedy, sun-swallowing volcano. The ocean, so blue and clear and inviting, rocked her
gently with its never-ending lullaby.

Todd quietly joined her and stretched out on his stomach.

"Hey, look!" He pointed to Molokai. "There are the
two lights again."

"So, have you decided?" Christy asked, feeling a little
coy.

From the way the last few days had gone, Christy figured
he had evaluated her and Paula and had made Christy his
choice.

"No, I haven't," Todd answered slowly. "I still can't
decide if I should go to college in the fall or try to get in on
the pro surfing tour."

"That's what you're trying to decide?" Christy asked.

Todd looked surprised. "Yeah. What did you think?"

To avoid answering, she quickly asked, "You want to be
a pro surfer then?"

"No. I want to be a Bible translator." In the twilight, his
eyes looked as starry as the darkening sky above them. "My
dream is to go to some remote tropical island where the
natives have never heard the gospel. I want to live there,
learn their language, and translate the Bible into their
native tongue."

"You want to be a missionary?" Christy said the word
reverently, with the same sense of awe and admiration she
felt for the early missionaries to Hawaii.

"Yes." Todd said it like a true island dreamer. "I want to
be a missionary."

It all became clear to Christy. She understood Todd

better at this moment than ever before. Todd had the same never-stop-trying spirit the missionaries must have had when they kept rebuilding their church. Todd had the same God-fearing heart that prompted the Baldwins to pray for rather than retaliate against the sailors who infested their home and their island with mosquitoes.

As far as making his home in the jungle—yeah, that fit too. Last summer when they went to Disneyland, Todd's favorite attraction turned out to be the Swiss Family Robinson Tree House. Christy could see that Todd would make an outrageous jungle missionary.

"You know, when we were in Hana," Todd continued, "I started dreaming even more about being a missionary. Swimming in freshwater pools, living off the land, the smell of the air after it rains..."

"You'd better make sure you take along a lifetime supply of bee-sting antidote!" Christy warned.

Todd laughed. "Right! Don't leave home without it!"

He suddenly turned serious. "You did a great job that day, keeping cool in the emergency and everything. I might not have made it if you weren't there. And I never thanked you for driving the Jeep for me."

"That's okay, Todd. You know I did it as much for me as for you. I now have no fear of taking my driving test. If I can drive the Hana road, I can drive anywhere!"

Todd laughed along with her. "Good missionary training for you, Kilikina."

Then he caught himself, as if he had said something he hadn't meant to.

Christy remained silent, absorbing Todd's statement.

He called me by my Hawaiian name. He thinks I'd make a good missionary.

Todd thinks we'd make great missionaries together. He wants to marry me!

"Of course," Todd added quickly, "that's another bridge, isn't it? It has to be your own choice."

"Of course," Christy said, camouflaging all her heart-pounding feelings. "Like your choice between college and surfing." She pointed toward the two lights on Molokai. "The closer you get to that decision, the clearer your choice will become."

"This sure has been an intense week," Todd said. "It seems like God had a lot He wanted to teach us."

Christy flashed back to Katie's prediction about God doing something in her life during this trip. *Wait till Katie hears about all these God-things!*

They were nearly back to shore now, and as the catamaran gracefully whisked its way into Lahaina Harbor, Christy delighted in the sight of the old whaling ship anchored there, ablaze with tiny white lights up one side, all the way up its mast and down the other side. The old Pioneer Inn, standing firmly before them, belched loud music and raucous laughter from its open barroom doors.

Once again, Christy tried to imagine what Lahaina was like 150 years ago. She could picture the missionary ladies sitting on their front lanai at the Baldwin house only a block away, fanning away the mosquitoes in the warm summer-night air and praying for the sailors who had come into port that day.

That night Christy prayed for Paula. She prayed that night and every night until Paula left to go back to Wisconsin.

Things were different with Paula. Christy couldn't exactly say in what way, but ever since the trip to Hana, Paula had changed too. She hadn't become a Christian or even given any indication that she was interested. Still, she had mellowed in some way.

When Paula, Christy, and her dad arrived at the airport the morning of Paula's flight back to Wisconsin, they found out the flight had been delayed nearly an hour. To Christy's amazement, Paula handled the news calmly.

This is the first time I've been in an airport with Paula when she hasn't drawn attention to us!

Paula's outfit may have drawn a bit of attention, though. She had on her Hana Road T-shirt, the shell bracelet Marti had bought her, some dangling green gecko earrings, and a small backpack she had bought for herself that said *Maui No Ka Oi*. Todd had explained that it meant "Maui is the best."

With an hour to wait, the two girls automatically drifted over to the huge windows and watched the planes taxi down the runway.

"It's been a full two weeks," Christy began.

"It sure has! I can't wait to get home and see if Alex wrote me yet. None of my friends are going to believe I met a guy from Denmark! I feel like I have something none of them do."

Christy felt like being snippy and saying, "Yeah, you still have your virginity, which is something none of them can ever get back." Instead she said, "You have a lot that none of them have, Paula. And I don't just mean a boyfriend from Denmark."

"He's not my boyfriend, Christy. He's an international acquaintance." She sounded as if she had practiced that a few times in front of the mirror while trying to come up with the perfect title for Alex. "He is cute though, isn't he? He's so different from any of the guys at school—his accent and everything—and he was so nice to me. I still can't believe he called me the morning we left Maui."

"Guys should be nice to you, Paula. You're worthy of having the best guy in the whole world."

"You already have him," Paula said with a sincere but mischievous tone. "And you don't even appreciate him."

"Yes, I do!"

"No, you don't. He's the only boyfriend you've ever had, so you don't know how many creeps are out there. And he's so loyal to you, Christy! When I went surfing with him and when we went for pizza that one time, well, I don't think I should tell you this…"

"You'd better tell me!"

Paula adjusted her position and took off her sunglasses. "You're going to hate me, but I think you should hear this. When we went for pizza, I tried to, you know, come on to Todd and stuff. That day we went surfing, he didn't act interested in me, but I figured it was because David was there."

Christy felt anger rising within her. With tremendous effort, she pushed it down.

"So when we walked to the pizza place, I flirted a bit with him. But he still didn't respond or anything. Instead he gave me this really sweet big-brother talk about how girls shouldn't tease guys by coming on to them and by wearing, you know, skimpy clothes. And how a girl shouldn't let a guy tease her by touching her too much or saying a bunch of flattering things."

Paula kept looking down. "He told me I should hold out for a hero. He made me feel that I really deserved a prince and not just the first frog that came along. I want to find a guy who likes me for who I am and what I'm like on the inside, and not just for what he can get from me. I want to find a guy like Todd."

She looked up. "But don't worry! I'm not trying to take him away from you anymore. He's totally in love with you, Christy. When you're around, no other girl exists. Believe me. I tried!"

Christy didn't know if she should be thrilled or furious.

"I wanted to tell you before I left," Paula said. "I guess it's a good thing the plane was late so I had a chance to."

"Yeah, a good thing," Christy said softly.

A smile crept back into Paula's expression. "I know, I know. Katie would tell me it's not a 'good thing' the plane is late—it's a 'God-thing.'"

"Does that mean you're beginning to agree with Katie about God-things?"

"I have to admit, Katie did make sense the other night at our slumber party when she said it was a God-thing that Todd got stung and couldn't drive," Paula said.

"I don't know. That whole ordeal was pretty scary."

"Right, but like Katie said, look what happened. You had to drive the Hana Road, and as a result, when you took your driving test, you passed with flying colors! That never would have happened if Todd hadn't gotten stung."

"I don't know. I might still have passed my driving test, even if I hadn't driven in Maui."

"No, you wouldn't have. You would've been too scared. And you know what else? If I hadn't spent that time with Todd and if I hadn't seen the way he treats you and other girls, I wouldn't have gone back to setting high standards for myself. A lot of good things—oh, excuse me, a lot of God-things—happened on our trip, just as Katie said they would."

"Well, I'm still not positive I know exactly what a God-thing is, but I agree with you that our trip was good for both of us."

Christy smiled, but inside she felt completely serious. "Paula, there's something else I wanted to talk to you about. I know we had some rough times during our trip, and I know I really came down hard on you. But I was trying to get you to become a Christian."

Paula squirmed a little bit, so Christy got right to the point. "I still want that for you really badly, but what I know now is that it has to be your decision. It's your bridge, like when Todd jumped from it and when I drove across it in the Jeep. It has to be something you decide and commit to yourself, not something you get persuaded into. So I promise to let up on all the stuff I've been writing to you about and trying to push on you. I'm still going to be praying for you though."

"You can keep writing whatever you want. I don't mind. I like your letters. They're always really interesting. It's like I told you in Maui, you're probably right about God and everything. It's just that I'm the kind of person who has to figure things out for myself."

The two friends smiled their agreement, and then Christy started to cry tiny, salty tears. "I wish we could start this visit all over again and be as close at the beginning as we are to each other right now."

Paula also let a tear or two drip. "But then we wouldn't have learned all the stuff we did."

Christy nodded and brushed her tears off her cheeks. "I'm glad we keep trying, even though over the years our friendship kind of goes up and down."

"I'm glad we keep trying to rebuild it every time too," Paula agreed.

Christy pictured the church the missionaries had built in Lahaina. Todd said the church was destroyed more than once. Then the last time they rebuilt it, they learned from the past and faced the two doors so they could both open toward each other. That way, when the wild Kona winds came, they blew through the church rather than against it.

"I'm going to miss you, Paula," Christy said, picturing herself as one open door facing another open door. She knew the strong winds of heaven now had the freedom to blow through, rather than against, their friendship.

"I'm going to miss you too. I'll try to write more, I promise," Paula said. "And maybe I can come back out at Christmas or Easter, because the way I see it, you still owe me a trip to Disneyland."

They both laughed. A few minutes later, when the plane boarded, the two friends said good-bye with laughter, hugs, and tears.

It was a painful farewell for Christy, and she felt a sweet sadness all the way back to Bob and Marti's house.

Bob had returned from Maui, and he and Christy's dad had made plans to go car shopping after they took Paula to the airport. Marti met them at the door with a look that Christy had come to recognize. It said I know something you don't know.

"Christy dear," she said almost immediately, drawing her into the entryway. "You did bring a bathing suit with you, didn't you?"

"Yes."

"Splendid!" Marti clapped her hands together. "Then you don't need to go car shopping with the men. You can go lie out on the beach."

Christy knew something was up. She raced to the conclusion that Todd must have come back with Bob. He was probably out on the beach right now, where she had first met him last summer. Marti was trying to set it up so that Christy would be surprised when she went out on the beach and just "happened" to stumble into him.

Christy obediently scurried upstairs and slipped into her bathing suit. She pulled back the white eyelet curtains and checked out the beach to see if she could spot Todd's orange surfboard.

Nope. No sign of Todd or his board. She would play along with Marti's surprise and go down to the beach.

The beach was crowded, as Christy would have expected for a Saturday afternoon in August. She wove her way around several different clumps of people, not sure who she should be looking for. Then someone called her name.

It was a girl's voice. She looked all around and didn't see anyone she recognized.

"Christy!" It came from a girl sitting all by herself on a beach towel near the water. Christy moved toward her, certain she had never seen the girl before.

She had blond hair pulled back in a ponytail and wore a bikini that looked too tight for her pudgy stomach and thighs. The girl sat up straight and waved excitedly as Christy approached.

Who is she? How does she know me? I don't remember meeting anyone last summer who looks like her.

"Hello! You found me! Did your aunt keep it a surprise?"

As soon as she spoke, Christy recognized the unique accent. "Alissa?"

"Yes, hello! Did I surprise you?"

The girl-turned-young-woman, now stretched out on the beach towel, looked nothing like the tall, slim, blond-haired model who had slinked her way across the sand last summer.

Christy tossed down her towel and sat next to her friend. "I can't believe it! How are you? What are you doing here? Where's your…" She was about to say *baby* but felt she was getting too personal. "I mean, where are you staying?"

"So much has happened. I'm not surprised that you didn't recognize me. No one ever told me how much having a baby changes you both on the outside and the inside." Alissa looked a bit shy, an expression Christy had never seen on her before.

"My mom is doing so much better dealing with her alcoholism that we decided to come back and finish the vacation we never had last summer. We got here yesterday. We're staying for three weeks. I couldn't wait to see you and tell…" Alissa hesitated.

Christy was anxious to hear more, but she sat quietly, using only her eyes to say, "Go on."

"Last week I gave Shawna up for adoption."

"Alissa, you're kidding!"

"It was the hardest thing I've ever done. If it hadn't been for you, I probably wouldn't have gone through with it."

"Me?" Christy felt startled. "What—I mean, why?"

"Didn't you get my letter?"

"No! Wait!" Christy tried to remember the message on the mystery letter. Something about, "I thought about what you said…"

"Was it really short, and you didn't sign it?"

"Oh, did I forget to sign it? I had so much going on during this last month. You see, I'd thought about giving Shawna up for adoption a bunch of times, but everyone told me I'd be sorry. I kept feeling so sure I should because she really needed a mommy and a daddy. And then I got your letter, and I knew I had to do what was right, even if no one else agreed with me."

"What letter? What did I say?"

"It was right after you made cheerleading and you decided to give up your spot to the other girl because you knew it was the right thing to do. That took a lot of courage, Christy."

"Not really. At the time it didn't seem that hard because Teri deserved to be cheerleader. Deep down, I knew that's what God wanted me to do."

"Exactly!" Alissa agreed enthusiastically. "I found out about this couple, through an adoption agency, who wanted a baby so much. The wife had had four or five miscarriages and several operations and still couldn't have a baby. I knew they would love Shawna and be the kind of parents she deserved.

"Oh, and Christy, you should've seen them when I signed the papers and handed her over to them. They took her in their arms, and the first thing they did was pray. Aloud! In front of the lawyers and everybody! They thanked God for answering their prayers and for giving them the baby they'd been asking for for so many years. Can you believe it?"

"Wow!" Tears blurred Christy's vision. "I can't believe it. Do you still feel like you did the right thing?"

"Oh yes, definitely! I gave them a long letter I wrote Shawna, along with a copy of a letter Todd wrote me all about Shawn. When she's old enough to understand, they promised to give her the letters. She'll know that when I gave her up it was because I wanted what was best for her. She'll know how much I loved her. I know I did the right thing."

A silence came between them. It was a silence filled with awe.

"There's something else, Christy," Alissa said, her round face looking more like that of a little girl than that of the mother of an infant. "I don't know how to ask this."

"That's okay," Christy said, thinking nothing more could surprise her today. "Ask away. Anything."

"Okay. Well, I wanted to ask you how I could be like you and Todd. You know, the way you both are with God. I mean, I want God in my life and all those other things you and Todd both told me about in your letters. Only I don't know how to do it."

Christy felt her heart pounding wildly. "You mean you want to become a Christian?"

She couldn't believe that after two weeks of trying so hard to get Paula to turn her life over to the Lord, Alissa, of all people, had come to her.

"Yes, but I want to become a real Christian, like you and Todd and Frances, the lady at the Crisis Pregnancy Center. You guys all talk and act like you know Jesus personally. That's what I want."

"Then tell Him that," Christy said excitedly. "Tell Him everything you're feeling. He already knows, but tell Him you're sorry for all the wrong stuff you've done, and ask Him to forgive you. Then invite Him in, and give Him everything in your life. He really loves you, Alissa. But then, you probably already know that." Christy paused to take a breath, not sure if she had said any of the right things.

"Yes, I do know God loves me, that He loves everybody. But do you think…" Alissa hesitated. "Do you think God wants me?"

"Oh yes," Christy answered in a tight whisper. "Yes!" A huge lump had nearly closed off her throat. "If only you knew how much He wants you!"

"Well, I know I want Him."

"Then tell Him," Christy said, swallowing her rising emotions.

"Should I close my eyes?"

"I don't think it matters."

"I think I'll close them." Alissa closed her eyes, bowed her head, and folded her hands, like a little girl in Sunday school.

Christy did the same, wondering only for a moment if any of the people around them might notice them praying. Then she decided it didn't matter. This was too much of a miracle to worry about what others thought.

"Lord God, I don't really know what to say. You know how sorry I am for everything I've done in the past. I want to ask You to please forgive me. I don't want my life to be like that anymore. I want You to come in and change me. I want You to take over my life. Amen."

Their eyes met before they had lifted their heads all the way. Christy broke into a huge smile.

Reaching over, she hugged Alissa. "I'm so excited for you! Todd is going to go totally wacko when he finds out!

Did you know he's been praying for you for a whole year?"

Alissa blinked back a train of runaway tears and said lightheartedly, "Well, it worked! After I met you guys, I kept meeting more and more Christians. Things I couldn't explain started happening. I started to feel like there really was a God out there and that He wanted my attention."

"And what do you feel like now?" Christy asked.

"I feel like…like, I don't know, like a little kid—all fresh and silly. I feel like running into the ocean, screaming and dancing all the way."

"Then come on!" Christy hopped up like an ignited spark. "Let's do it!"

"All right." Alissa giggled, springing to her feet.

"One, two, three, go!" Christy shouted.

With bare feet thumping into the sand, they ran together, waving their arms, shrieking and laughing like schoolgirls on the first day of summer.

Alissa brazenly shouted to the wind and the waves and any people who happened to be close enough to hear, "Jesus loves me!" Then laughing wildly, impulsively, she shouted, "And I love Him!"

Exuberant and full of amazement at Alissa's transformation, Christy scooped up the cool ocean water with her open hands and joyfully sent the spray shimmering through the air, showering Alissa with its sparkling mist. Alissa immediately sent a splash back at Christy, giggling like the giddy, trembling new creation she was.

Standing on the edge of forever and laughing until the tears came, Christy tilted her head back, squinted at the brilliant sun, and said, "Now this, this is a God-thing!"

BOOK SIX

• • • • •

A Heart Full
• • • • • *of Hope*

To the youth group
at the First Evangelical Free Church of Reno:
May the Lord bless you and keep you.
The Lord make His face to shine upon you
and give you His peace.

1

Dazzling Dream Date

"Come on, Christy, try not to blink." Katie patiently held the mascara wand.

"I'm trying, Katie, but it's hard." Sixteen-year-old Christy Miller looked up at her red-haired friend and scrunched up her nose. "Why don't you let me do this part?"

"What would be the point of having me do your makeup for your big date if you end up doing everything yourself? Now hold still and look up." Katie carefully twirled the wand on the eyelashes lacing Christy's blue-green eyes.

"This feels weird, Katie."

"Hush. Look up. I mean it, Christy, don't move!" Katie finished the right eye and started on the left. "Good. Now don't blink. Let it dry."

Stepping back to examine her work, Katie smiled. "Perfect! Rick is definitely going to call you 'Killer Eyes' tonight."

Christy adjusted her five-foot-six-inch frame on the edge of her bed. For almost an hour she had patiently endured Katie's complete makeover, which included cucumber slices on her eyes while her nails were painted.

The cucumbers were Christy's idea—something she had read in a magazine. As the article promised, her eyes had felt cool and refreshed.

That was before Katie started with the eye shadow, eyeliner, cover stick, and mascara. Now her eyes felt a little thick.

"You don't think you used too much eyeliner?" Christy asked.

"Not at all. Take a look." Katie handed her the mirror.

"Oh no!" Christy laughed as she looked at her long nutmeg-colored hair, now filled with hot rollers. "I forgot about these brain fryers. Do you think my hair is sufficiently cooked? I mean, look at me, Katie! I look like some kind of space alien wired for communication with my home planet."

"Yes, my little Martian. Your hair is now a toasty golden brown and ready for a comb out. First tell me what you think of your makeup."

"I don't know. I've never worn this much before. It doesn't feel normal."

"Good!" Katie snatched back the mirror and grabbed a blush brush. "This is not a normal date, so you're not supposed to look normal." She swished the soft brush over Christy's cheeks. "There! Now let's start on your hair before the space shuttle makes contact and lands in your backyard."

"Very funny. You sure you know what you're doing?"

"Yes. Now hold still."

Christy could feel herself getting more and more nervous the closer she was to being ready. After being "buddies" with Rick for so long, Christy wasn't sure how it would feel being dressed up and eating dinner at a fancy restaurant with him tonight. Or what the ninety-minute drive from Escondido to Newport Beach would be like.

"You're not getting nervous now, are you?" Katie asked.

"Ouch!" Christy squeaked, pulling away from Katie's aggressive hair combing.

"Sorry, but I have to hurry. You only have half an hour until he gets here."

For five days Christy had avoided asking Katie her opinion of this date with Rick. Now, with the time melting away, so was Christy's courage. Knowing how opinionated Katie could be, Christy finally ventured the dangerous question: "Do you think I'm doing the right thing by going out with Rick?"

"You've been looking forward to it since he promised you this special date months ago—in a phone call from his vacation in Italy, I might add."

"I know, but do you think it will make things different between Todd and me?" Christy crossed and uncrossed her long legs beneath her bathrobe and listened to the swishing sound her nylons made.

"That depends," Katie said. "Todd knows you're going out with Rick, doesn't he?"

"No. Of course not."

Katie stopped combing. "I thought you said you talked to Todd yesterday, and he knew you were going to spend tonight at your aunt and uncle's in Newport Beach. Didn't you happen to mention to him that the reason you were going to be in Newport was because Rick was taking you to dinner there?"

"Well, no."

The two friends locked gazes. Katie's green eyes demanded an explanation.

"See, Todd called to ask me to a party at Tracy's house tonight, so I told him I couldn't go to the party. Then I told him I'd be at Bob and Marti's tomorrow, and he said he'd come by the house around noon. He didn't ask why I was going to be there, so I didn't tell him."

When Katie's expression didn't change, Christy continued. "What was I supposed to do? I couldn't cancel my date with Rick. He's going away to college next week. And why should I tell Todd about it?"

Katie went back to fixing Christy's hair.

"It's only a dinner, Katie! I don't have to ask Todd's permission. I'm sure it wouldn't matter to him at all. He's not the jealous type. You know that!"

"Hey, relax! You're going to mess up the perfect job I did on your makeup. I'm here, aren't I? Supporting you, helping you get ready. I'm on your side, Christy. I'm not saying anything against Todd or Rick. It's your choice. Close your eyes. I'm going to spray your hair."

Christy obliged, tilting her chin down so Katie could spritz her bangs. Mentally, she convinced herself that there was nothing wrong with being interested in two guys at the same time. How could she possibly cause problems with Todd by going out with Rick? Neither of the guys would know a thing about the other. She'd have a nice dinner with Rick tonight and then spend tomorrow afternoon with Todd. Simple.

The problem was Katie. She had never been a big fan of Rick. Even though she was being sweet and supportive, if she really spoke her mind, she would slash Rick into ribbons, saying he was a smooth talker, a show-off, and not the kind of guy Christy should be going out with—especially since Christy already had a guy like Todd in her life.

"Your dress!" Katie exclaimed. "We should have put it on before I did your hair. I know, try to step into it."

Katie pulled Christy's black dress off the hanger and unzipped it. It was a dress Christy had only worn twice because it made her look and feel too grown-up. She wasn't sure she was ready to dress like that. But it had been Katie's first choice for what Christy should wear tonight. Even Christy's mom had agreed it was the right dress for a formal dinner.

Katie held out the dress as Christy carefully stepped into it.

"Perfect." Katie zipped up the back. "Don't move a muscle, Cinderella. I'm searching for your glass slipper."

Christy laughed. "I think you're into all of this more than I am."

"I like all this frou-frou stuff. Just because I'm not the one being invited on dream dates to romantic restaurants doesn't mean I can't enjoy the part of the fairy godmother."

Katie hunted for Christy's black shoes in her closet while Christy examined her hair in the mirror.

"You're sure it's not too foofy?"

"What?" Katie asked. "Your hair or your dress?"

"Either. Both. I don't know. All of me. Are you sure I look all right?"

Katie joined Christy in looking at her reflection in the mirror above her antique dresser. "You look dazzling!"

"Dazzling?"

"Yeah, dazzling! This is how you should look. You're

not going for fast food with Todd. This is a real date."

Christy took a deep breath and smiled. "Okay, you're right. I'm relaxed. I'm going to have a great time. Everything is going to be wonderful."

"Not just wonderful," Katie said. "Dazzling!"

Ten minutes later, when tall, dark-haired Rick arrived and handed Christy a long-stemmed red rose, she began to believe that Katie could be right. This could be a dazzling evening.

Christy felt a little embarrassed when her mom and dad made them pose for pictures, but she would be glad she had them later. Mostly she wondered what Rick thought of her. Did she look all right? Did he like the dress? Her hair?

Rick, the all-around athlete, stretched his six-foot-two-inch frame with a serious expression as Christy's dad gave him strict instructions that Christy must be to Bob and Marti's house by eleven o'clock. Rick agreed, shook hands, and held the front door open for Christy.

Right before swishing out the door, Christy turned around and blew a tiny kiss off her index finger. The kiss flew down the hall to Katie, who was hiding in Christy's room with the door open a crack.

"You look beautiful." Rick opened the passenger door to his '68 Mustang.

Christy slid onto the upholstered seat. For one quick second she flashed back to how different this was from all the times she had hopped into Todd's battered Volkswagen van, Gus the Bus.

You're with Rick. Get Todd out of your head.

"You look really nice too," Christy said as Rick got into

the car. He had on black slacks, a crisp white shirt, and a black jacket.

"I especially like your tie," Christy added, reaching over and feeling the unique tie. In keeping with Rick's flashy side, it looked as if someone had thrown a handful of confetti at him and it had all stuck on his tie.

"You like that?" Rick said. "I got it in Italy. Thought it might add a festive touch to our evening, Killer Eyes." Then giving Christy a smile that said, "I've been looking forward to this date for a long time," Rick turned the key and roared down the quiet street.

Lifting her rose to draw in its rich fragrance, Christy thought, *No, this isn't a normal night. Katie, you were right. Tonight is going to be dazzling!*

2

When Rick Got on His Knees

"Here we are!" Rick announced an hour and a half later as he turned the car into the restaurant's driveway. The place looked like a charming old Italian villa. "I told you I'd find the best Italian restaurant in Southern California, and this is it—the Villa Nova." Rick pulled up behind a Cadillac and waited for the valet to park his car.

As Christy wondered if she should bring her rose with her, her car door opened, and the valet extended a hand to help her out. Without looking up, she grabbed her purse and the rose with one hand, and let the young man pull her to her feet by her other hand.

Instead of letting go of her, the valet suddenly wrapped his arms around her and, with a wild hug, roared, "Christy, I can't believe it! How are you doing?"

She vaguely recognized the voice, but since her face was now buried in the guy's shoulder, Christy was at a definite disadvantage. He pulled away. She looked up and saw his face and then viewed Rick's puzzled expression.

"Doug!" Christy caught her breath and smoothed down her hair. Todd's best friend was the last person she had expected to see this evening. "I'm so surprised! I haven't seen you in a long time."

"You look awesome, Christy. What's the occasion?" Doug asked, an exuberant smile lighting up his tanned face.

"Doug, I'd like you to meet Rick. Rick, this is Doug." Christy hoped the introductions would help her avoid having to give any explanations.

The guys shook hands good-naturedly, and Doug jumped right in. "This is so awesome that you're here tonight! We're having a party at Tracy's. You guys have to come. You remember how to get there, Christy?"

"Well, actually…" Christy fumbled for the right words, feeling a panic rising in her heart and pounding through her veins. This was the same party Todd had asked her to. She couldn't show up there with Rick.

Before she could get out any words, Rick answered for her. "Sure, we'll come. I've been wanting to meet some of these beach friends Christy talks about."

"Cool!" Doug said. "I'll see you there when I get off at nine-thirty."

Rick tossed Doug the keys to park his car. Doug jogged around to the driver's side. "Awesome Mustang!" Then before folding himself into the driver's seat, he leaned over the roof and said, "This is great, Christy! Everyone is going to be so surprised to see you."

"Yeah," Christy mumbled as Rick slipped his arm around her and led her into the restaurant. Everyone would be surprised, all right—especially Todd.

"So, who's that guy? Another one of your old boyfriends?" Rick asked.

"Doug? No, no, not at all! He's just a friend of..." Christy caught herself. "Tracy's. He's friends with Tracy. That's the girl who's having the party. They used to go out, but now they're just friends."

"And now he's looking for a new girlfriend," Rick said.

"I don't know. I don't think so." Christy could feel her heart still pounding as the hostess led them through the labyrinth of tables. Rick's questions weren't helping her calm down a bit.

"My guess is, he's looking for a new girlfriend, and you look pretty good to him."

The hostess stopped in front of a window table that looked out on Newport Bay. Rick pulled out a chair for Christy, and she seated herself. He pushed in her chair, leaned over, and whispered, "But you can tell Doug to give up, because you're already taken."

Christy gratefully accepted the menu held out to her. She opened it and hid her flaming red face behind its tall barricade.

I can't believe this is happening! What am I going to do? Why is Rick saying these things?

"What sounds good to you, Christy? You can't go wrong with any of the pasta dishes here, I've been told." Rick then rattled off a list of Italian names from the menu, complete with authentic accent. "Now this sounds good," he said, reading the name of another Italian dish. "What do you think?"

Christy shyly peered over the top of the menu and managed a weak smile and a nod. "Sure." Her voice came out cracked, so she cleared her throat and tried again. "That sounds good."

"Then that's what we'll have," Rick stated, snapping closed his menu.

What did I just order? It could have been squid brains for all I know! Everything is coming at me so fast. I want to go back to how things were in the car on the way here. I want to feel dazzling again.

Christy closed her menu and groped for the rose on her lap, automatically drawing it to her nose to sniff. Maybe its fragrance would bring back the magic.

Rick reached over, wrapped his hand around her wrist, and pulled the flower over to his side of the table. Taking a whiff, he smiled. "It's sweet, but not as sweet as you."

Christy felt charmed but not charmed enough to calm the frantic confusion raging inside. She wanted to move the conversation to a neutral subject. The view out the window, maybe. She turned her head and was about to make a comment on how pretty the summer evening light looked dancing on the water, but Rick had other ideas.

Still holding her wrist, he took his other hand and gently began to pick the lock on Christy's *Forever* ID bracelet. It was the bracelet Todd had given her last New Year's.

"What are you doing?" Christy asked, keeping her voice light.

Without looking up, Rick said smoothly, "You don't mind, do you?"

He'd already released the clasp and now held the gold bracelet in his fist. "Guys are funny. We like to know that when a girl goes out with us, she's not bringing along mementos from past relationships."

"It's not like that, Rick." How could she explain her relationship with Todd to Rick when she'd never been able to explain it to herself?

"Then what is it like?" Rick looked up, melting her with his gaze.

"Todd and I are good friends. We have been for a long time."

"But you're not going together, right?"

"Well, no."

"Todd goes out with other girls, right?"

"Well, yes, he has."

Rick took Christy's hand in his and held it firmly. "Then let me have a fair shot, okay? You don't mind not wearing that chain tonight while you're with me, do you?"

Rick laid the bracelet on the table and released Christy's hand. She knew the next move was hers. She knew what Rick wanted her to do.

Christy gingerly picked up the bracelet and slipped it into her purse. Looking up, she tried to echo the smile Rick beamed at her. Inside she felt overpowered, as if Rick had just burst into her heart and broken the lock on the treasure chest where she kept all her secret feelings. She didn't want him breaking in like that. But more important, she didn't want him to go away.

At that moment the waiter appeared, and the tension dispersed. Their water glasses were filled, and a basket of garlic bread was placed before them.

Christy eagerly began to nibble on the bread while she listened to Rick talk about his summer trip to Europe. As long as she kept chewing, she wouldn't have to answer. Rick seemed satisfied to keep talking as she smiled and nodded at the appropriate times. It gave her a chance to calm down and think.

By her third piece of bread, Christy had come to a conclusion. *I'm being far too immature and emotional about all this. I am having dinner with Rick. I want to be here. Why am I worrying about Todd? Nothing has changed between us just because I'm not wearing his bracelet. I'm going to have a good time tonight, and there's nothing wrong with that. There's no reason I should be upset.*

"Good bread, isn't it?" Rick asked.

Christy nodded and realized she had emptied the basket.

"I'll have them bring some more," Rick offered.

"Oh, no, really, that's okay," Christy said quickly. "I should save room for the dinner. It is good though."

Feeling calmed and ready to pay more attention to Rick, Christy hoped he wouldn't ask her any questions about what he had been talking about while she did her soul-searching. She had no idea what he had said. Maybe it would help if they moved to a new subject.

"Tell me about school," Christy said. "When do you leave, what classes are you taking, and all that."

Rick jumped right in with a full rundown of all his freshman courses at San Diego State.

"You realize, don't you, that even though I leave on Tuesday, I'm only going to be an hour away. That means I'll be back in Escondido every weekend."

"That's good," Christy said absentmindedly.

"I don't think you catch my drift here, Christy. I'll be home every weekend, and I plan to spend every weekend with you."

Christy didn't respond.

Her face must have given away her surprise, though, because Rick laughed. "Yes, Christy, I'm asking you to go out with me. You know, 'go together,' 'go steady.' Or like my brother says about his girlfriend, I want you to be my 'significant other.'"

Christy still didn't have a response for him.

"Why are you looking at me like that? Am I doing this the wrong way? Wait. I know." Rick scooted his chair back.

Then, stepping over to Christy's side of the table, he dropped to one knee, took her hands in his, and said in a gentle voice, "Christy, I've waited a long time to ask you this. I've never felt for another girl the way I feel for you. Will you go out with me?"

Christy felt as if her heart had stopped beating and the whole world had come to a standstill, waiting for her to answer him. All she could feel was Rick's firm grasp enveloping her shaking hands. All she could see were his soft brown eyes pleading with her to say yes.

"Yes," she suddenly squeaked, and the world began to move again.

The couple at the table next to them smiled and applauded softly. Rick confidently returned to his seat. Leaning across the table, he said, "I was hoping that's what you'd say."

What just happened? I thought this would be a simple dinner. A one-date thing, and now I just said I'd go out with him! How did that happen?

Just then their salads arrived, and once again Christy could keep her mouth full so she didn't have to talk. Rick enthusiastically told her his ideas for their future dates.

Christy smiled and nodded and halfway listened. She only halfway did everything for the next hour. She had gone numb.

After dinner, Rick ordered a dessert for them to share and coffee for both of them. Christy loaded her coffee with cream and sugar and then took about three sips. She poked at the elegant chocolate dessert with her fork, eating only one bite.

The numbness didn't leave Christy until they stood outside the restaurant waiting for the valet to bring the car. Sure enough, it was Doug who brought Rick's red Mustang around to the front.

"Perfect timing." Doug hopped out and handed the keys to Rick. "I get off in two minutes. You guys want to wait a second, and you can follow me over to Tracy's?"

Christy shriveled inside. *Oh, Doug, why did you have to bring that up? I was hoping Rick would have forgotten all about it.*

"Sounds good." Rick opened the door for Christy.

In a few minutes Doug's yellow truck swung around in front of them, and Doug motioned with his arm out the window for them to follow.

"You know," Christy said, drawing up all the strength and courage she could find, "we really don't have to go to this party. You won't know any of the people there, and it's not like they're expecting me or anything. Besides, I have to be at my aunt and uncle's in about an hour and a half, so we wouldn't have much time there, and—"

"Hey, it's okay," Rick interrupted, reaching over to give her a little pat on the leg. "I know what you're trying to say. Some guys get freaked out when they meet all their girlfriend's friends. It won't be like that with me. You'll see. I've waited a long time to be your boyfriend. I'll make you proud of me. I promise."

Christy's grip on the rose tightened when he called her his girlfriend. When he said he had waited a long time to be her boyfriend, her tensed finger found a small thorn toward the top of the rose.

Then, with a bump, Rick pulled into Tracy's driveway. Without warning, the thorn sliced into Christy's flesh.

3

The Luckiest Girl in the World

"Ouch!" Christy held up her finger. Just enough light shone on the cut for her to see a few drops of blood.

Rick turned off the car's engine. "You okay?" He pulled a tissue from a box under his seat, wrapped it around her finger, and examined the rose. "That's pretty cheap," he complained. "You'd think they'd know enough to cut off the thorns before they sell these things. Are you okay now?"

Without making any noise, Christy had been crying uncontrollably from the instant the thorn had pricked her. She couldn't stop the tears from streaming down her cheeks.

"Oh, you're crying," Rick said, as tenderly as if she were a small child. "Come here." He offered her another tissue with one hand and wrapped his other arm around her.

"I'm okay, really," Christy sniffed, pulling away so Doug wouldn't see them wrapped up together. "I'll go rinse it off in the bathroom."

Opening her own door and springing out, she hurried up the steps to Tracy's house. Christy glanced back and saw Doug standing by Rick's car, the two of them talking.

To her relief, Tracy's front door stood wide open.

Christy slipped in without anyone seeing her. She knew right where the bathroom was and disappeared inside, locking the door behind her. As if she had reached her own private refuge, she let more tears flow.

What am I going to do? What are we doing here? I've messed things up so badly that they'll never be straightened out. What does Rick think of me? What will Todd think?

A knock at the door made her jump. She ignored it, hoping the person would go away.

"Christy? Are you okay? It's Heather."

Christy hadn't seen Heather since last Christmas vacation. But she wasn't sure she wanted to see her or anyone until she had her feelings figured out.

"Christy? Will you let me in?" Heather knocked persistently.

Christy gave in and unlocked the door. Wispy, blond Heather burst in, pouncing on her with a warm hug. Christy quickly locked the door behind Heather.

"Doug said you were here!" Heather said in her breathless, excited way. "And who is that guy with him? Have you seen him? He's gorgeous! You're crying! What's wrong? And what's on your finger? What happened?"

Wiping away the tears, Christy explained, "It's really nothing. It was a thorn. I should have realized it was going to happen." Christy looked away and stared at the shower curtain, talking as if Heather weren't even there. "With the rose comes the thorn. I should have known. I thought I could have one without the other, but it doesn't work that way. Why did I think I could just go to dinner, and it wouldn't be a big deal?"

"What in the world are you talking about, Christy? Are

you totally freaking out on me here?" Heather tugged on Christy's sleeve. "Turn around and look in the mirror."

Christy looked and discovered that Katie's superb makeup job had dissolved into two rainbow rivers winding down her cheeks. At this moment she looked anything but the part of Rick's "Killer Eyes" girlfriend.

Heather giggled and handed her a washcloth. "You'd better wash that stuff off before it dries on permanently. Now explain to me how you got here. Todd said you couldn't come."

Plunging the washcloth under the running water, Christy said, "It's a bizarre story."

"Good, I like bizarre stories. Did you come with Doug?"

"No, I actually came with Rick, the other guy. We went out to dinner at the Villa Nova and just happened to see Doug."

"You mean you're on a date right now with that gorgeous guy? What's his name? Rick? Oh Christy, you have to be the luckiest girl alive!"

"Yeah," Christy said sarcastically. "I'm so lucky that I'm now going out with him."

"What?" Heather squealed, grabbing Christy by the elbow and squeezing it so hard that Christy dropped the washcloth. "When did this happen? Does Todd know?"

"No, of course not. Rick asked me tonight at dinner." Christy explained the whole situation as she washed her face and blotted it dry.

Heather listened to every word, wide-eyed and open-mouthed. "I was right. You're the luckiest girl in the world."

"I don't feel that way," Christy said with a sigh. "I feel like I'm in a huge mess."

"Why? Rick is a Christian, isn't he?"

"Yes, of course."

"Then what's the problem? Todd? Do you really think Todd would ever treat you the way Rick has—roses and dinner and saying he would wait until your parents would let you start dating? Think about it, Christy!"

"I don't know. I like Rick, but I've liked Todd for a long time."

Heather put her hands on her hips. "You are sixteen years old. A young woman. In some cultures, you could be married by now. You met Todd when you were fourteen, and you had a huge crush on him, am I right? A lot has changed since then. You've changed; Todd has changed. Face it, Christy. Todd is never going to be the kind of guy who takes a girl out to dinner. Don't let his blond, blue-eyed surfer looks fool you. He's not a normal guy. He wants to be a missionary, you know."

"I know."

"Todd is the kind of guy who'll probably never marry. He'll spend his life among the natives, sleeping in a hammock, eating bug larvae, and saving the souls of people in the jungle who have never seen a white man before. He'll probably win a Nobel Prize and die in some headhunter's stewpot."

"Heather!" Christy interrupted her dramatic friend with a laugh. "What is the point here?"

Heather looked Christy straight in the eye. "Don't you see? The point is, you want to go out with Rick. You want to be his girlfriend. Deep down, you've wanted it all along.

Otherwise, when he asked you, your heart would've said no, and you would've turned him down. You said yes to Rick because you want to be his girlfriend. Can you deny that?"

Christy took a deep breath. She thought about the way Rick had treated her so tenderly when she pricked her finger in the car. Todd never would have responded that way. Todd had never said the things to her that Rick said tonight. Rick wanted her to be his girlfriend, and yes, maybe deep down she liked the thought of him being her boyfriend.

"I don't know, Heather. You could be right."

"It's just hard because you probably feel bad about Todd finding out this way. That's not your fault. You didn't try to make it happen like this. Besides, I've known Todd a long time, and I hope I don't hurt your feelings when I say this, but Todd will probably get over you a lot quicker than you'll get over him. He's that way."

"You could be right."

They both were silent for a moment, and then Heather said, "Come on. Everyone's anxious to see you. Let's go join the party and let whatever is going to happen, happen."

Christy rummaged in her purse for her cosmetic bag and did a quick fix on her makeup. Then with Heather nudging her out the door, she walked slowly down the hallway.

When they entered the living room, Christy saw Rick but not Todd. Rick had wasted no time in becoming the center of attention in a circle of six girls.

"Look, you guys!" Heather broke Rick's spell on them. "Christy's here!"

"Hi!"

"How you doing, Christy?"

"You look great!"

Each girl had a warm greeting, but none of them moved from her spot. Turning back to Rick, they urged him to continue his story.

Rick looked up briefly, shrugged his shoulders, and gave Christy a wink.

"Come on," Heather said. "Tracy's in the kitchen. Let's go in there."

Yeah, and Todd's probably in there too. Am I ready to face him? What am I so nervous about? Everything Heather said made sense when she said it. Why don't I feel convinced now?

Tracy had her back to them, pulling out soft drink cans from the refrigerator. Turning around, she closed the door with her foot.

That's when Christy caught a glimpse of Todd, sitting in a kitchen chair, talking to Doug.

"Christy!" Tracy threw her arm around Christy's neck in a hug, almost knocking her in the head with a soda can. "Oh, I'm sorry!" She laughed. "I'm so glad you're here. Todd said you'd be at your aunt and uncle's tomorrow, but I didn't think you could come tonight."

Doug jumped into the conversation from his chair next to Todd. "Yeah, I told them how I found you and Rick going through the trash cans at my restaurant and how I felt sorry for you and brought you here."

"Very funny," said Heather. "Just because you guys don't know the meaning of taking a girl out for a nice dinner doesn't give you the right to make fun of those who do."

Christy suddenly remembered the last time she had been with these friends for a party. It was last New Year's, and she had worn this same black dress. Only that night she had come with Todd. And that was the night Todd had given her the bracelet. Right now, it all seemed like a lifetime ago.

She couldn't look at Todd. To make sure their eyes didn't meet, she kept looking down at her wound, pretending that her finger needed much more attention than it did.

Tracy followed her line of sight. "Do you want a Band-Aid for that? We have one right here." She pulled one out of a drawer.

I think I might need a Band-Aid for my heart. If I look at Todd, my heart will start bleeding all over the floor.

As soon as the Band-Aid was in place, Tracy handed Christy a soft drink. "Come in my room. I want to show you something."

Christy gladly turned her back on Todd and followed Heather and Tracy. Tracy shut the door, flipped on the light, and turned to Christy with huge eyes. "Where did you find him?"

"Rick?"

"That's Rick? The one you told me about from your school? I couldn't believe it when Doug said you guys were having dinner at the Villa Nova. And look at you. You're so dressed up! Tell me everything."

Christy began the story again for Tracy while Heather willingly filled in any missing details. Tracy listened carefully, and Heather concluded with the part about how Christy must have really wanted to be Rick's girlfriend or else she wouldn't have said yes when he asked her.

"Is that how you feel?" Tracy asked.

"I think so. Everything has happened so fast, I'm not sure what I feel."

"He seems like a really nice guy and a perfect gentleman," Tracy said. "I didn't realize you liked him this much though."

"It's weird. We were friends for so long because I wasn't old enough to date, so it never became anything more."

"Isn't that the best way for relationships to be?" Heather said. "Friends first, then boyfriend and girlfriend?"

"I guess. I've never been in this situation before."

"I think you're in the best situation possible. You're good friends, he's older than you, he's totally gorgeous, and he's a Christian too! What else could you ask for?"

When Heather said that, something melted inside of Christy. Heather was right. What more could she ask for? Why was she holding back? She should feel honored that Rick had picked her and waited so long to date her. It would be foolish to let her crush on Todd keep her from experiencing a real relationship with a guy who wanted to be her boyfriend and had already proved, more than once, how much he cared for her.

With her heart beginning to fill with excitement, Christy explained, "He's going to San Diego State, so we'll see each other only on weekends. He's got all these fun ideas of things for us to do. He said he started to make lists of ideas for dates more than six months ago, since he had to wait so long for me to be old enough to date."

"I ask you," Heather said with her eyes all sparkling, "what other guy on this planet would do that? He sounds like a dream come true. I'm glad you woke up quickly enough to realize it! And see how much better you feel about everything now that you've thought it through? You should have heard her in the bathroom, Tracy. Rambling

on about how roses have thorns. I thought she was going to
pass out on me!"

Christy laughed. "I wasn't used to the idea of having a
boyfriend, I guess. You know what I was thinking, don't
you? Rick is like the rose, but having to see Todd and everything was like the thorn."

Tracy's heart-shaped face took on a serious expression.
"You were right, Christy. That's exactly how going steady is.
It's a rose with a thorn, because when you break up, either
you get hurt or the other person gets hurt. There's no way
around it." Then she added thoughtfully, "Most of the
time, you both get hurt."

Heather cheerfully interrupted, "That's why I said you
shouldn't think it's a problem with Todd. I mean, how can
you break up when you two were never really going together?
It's not the same thing as what you've got with Rick."

Just then someone tapped softly on the door. "I hate to
break it up in there." Rick's voice came through the closed
door and filled Tracy's bedroom. "But I need to get my
girlfriend home."

"Girlfriend," Heather whispered, and the three of them
made gleeful faces and squeezed each others' arms.

"I'll be right there, Rick," Christy answered.

"You'll be at your aunt and uncle's tomorrow, right?"
Tracy asked.

Christy nodded, pushing away the thought that she was
supposed to meet Todd at noon tomorrow.

"Do you want to try to get together?"

"Sure. I'll be around, and I don't have anything else
going on." *Now that I've shown up here with Rick, I'm sure Todd won't be
calling me tomorrow.*

"I'll give you a call, then," Tracy promised and opened her bedroom door.

Rick stood in the hallway with his arms folded across his chest, comically looking up at the ceiling and whistling. "Oh, Christy, the invisible party girl."

"I'm sorry. We were just talking."

Rick took her by the hand and led the way to the front door. "Bye, everyone. Nice meeting you. We'll see you later!" he called out as they made their exit.

Doug surfaced from the kitchen, but Todd stayed behind. Something in the back of Christy's mind said, *See? If Todd really cared about me, he'd try to talk to me before I left. If he really wanted a relationship with me the way Rick does, he'd fight for me. But he's letting me go. He doesn't really care, and he'll never care for me the way Rick does.*

Doug shook hands with Rick. "Hey, we'll see you on campus next week. Christy, you didn't tell me your boyfriend was going to my school."

"You let me know if that other guy drops out of your apartment," Rick said. "I'd much rather live there than in the dorms."

"I will," Doug promised. "He has until Monday to turn in his money, and if he doesn't, he's out of there. It'd be great to have another Christian in our apartment."

This is too bizarre. It's like Rick is stepping in instantly to take Todd's place in my life, even by buddying up with Doug.

Rick waved to all the girls, then whisked Christy out the door and to the car. "Now tell me how to get to your aunt and uncle's."

Christy directed, and Rick drove the few blocks to the beachfront house.

"We only have a few more minutes before you have to go in," Rick said. "How about a quick walk on the beach?"

"You're sure we have time?"

"Positive. Come on!" Rick opened her door and, taking her hand, led her down the pavement to where the sand began.

They slipped off their shoes, and Rick put them on top of a concrete-block wall. "Remind me where I'm leaving these." He grabbed Christy's hand again and pulled her onto the sand.

"Come on!" He began to run, tugging Christy along beside him.

"Wait! Wait!" Christy cried out, coming to a halt next to a fire pit. "I'm getting sand in my nylons!"

Rick laughed as she tried to brush off the sand. Christy cautiously sat on the rim of a fire pit and wiggled her toes to get rid of the particles. She looked up at Rick then, noticing her surroundings, jumped up from the edge of the fire pit as if it had suddenly turned hot.

I can't believe it! Of all the fire pits on the beach, why did I stop by this one? I shouldn't be here with Rick. This is where Todd and I had breakfast on Christmas morning!

"Come on." Christy sprinted toward the water. "I'll race you!"

They ran through the sand together until they were a few yards from the water's edge. Rick, with a spurt of energy, sprinted ahead of her. Turning at the shoreline, he opened his arms and caught her.

"No fair," Christy said breathlessly. "The sand in my nylons slowed me down."

"So, what do you want? Best two out of three?"

The lacy edge of a wave crawled up and without warning grabbed their feet with its cold fingers.

Christy let out a tiny squeal of surprise and scampered up to higher ground.

"Look," Rick said, following her and pointing up to the sky, "it's a wishing moon."

Christy looked at the tiny sliver of bright alabaster. "A wishing moon?"

"Yeah," Rick said, "there's so little of it left you have to quickly make a wish on it before it completely disappears."

Christy smiled. "When my brother was little, he used to call that kind of moon 'God's fingernail' because it kind of looks like a fingernail when you bite it off. I remember the first time he saw it like that, and he said, 'Hey, God bit off His fingernail and left it in the sky.'"

Apparently not too amused by her story, Rick said, "Come on. Close your eyes and make a wish."

Christy played along, tilting her head toward the moon and closing her eyes. Before she could think of what to wish for, Rick kissed her.

She opened her eyes and saw Rick grinning.

"I got my wish!" he said.

"We'd better get back," Christy said quickly. Everything was going too fast again, and she wanted to retreat to the safety of her room at Bob and Marti's so she could think it all through.

"I'm sure we have more time." Rick reached over and held Christy. "Come here and tell me what you wished."

Christy nervously pulled away. "I don't want to be late. You know how strict my dad is. I really don't want to get in trouble."

"Okay, okay," Rick said, letting go. They turned to walk back, and he slipped his arm around her shoulders. "You cold?"

"Not really." The truth was, she was burning up. After running and being kissed like that and now meshing her feet through the sand with Rick's arm around her, how could she possibly be cold?

Christy wrapped her arm around Rick's middle. She had always felt tall and awkward because of her height. At this moment, with her arm around Rick and his strong arm around her, she felt petite and secure.

"How are you getting back to Escondido tomorrow?" Rick asked.

"My uncle is going to take me."

"You tell him to save his gas money. I'll come get you."

"But Rick, it's an hour-and-a-half drive."

"So?"

"You don't have to come back for me." Christy could feel his arm tighten around her shoulders, and she knew it was pointless to object.

"What time do you want me to come?"

"I don't know. What's convenient for you?"

"I'll be here at five o'clock," Rick said as they arrived at the pavement and he retrieved their shoes.

Christy noticed someone standing on the sidewalk by Rick's car, looking down the street. They walked a few feet closer, and she realized it was her uncle.

"Good evening," Bob said in his dry way as they met him at the car. "Nice night, isn't it?"

"It's not eleven yet, is it?" Christy asked, hiding her embarrassment that her uncle was outside looking for her.

Bob checked his watch. "11:27, to be exact. Will you be needing help with your luggage, ma'am?" He played the part of the hotel doorman perfectly, but Christy could tell she was in trouble.

Rick unlocked his car and handed Christy's overnight bag to Bob. With a friendly smile, Rick said, "Good evening, sir. I'm Rick Doyle."

"Oh, I'm sorry," Christy said quickly. "Rick, this is my Uncle Bob. Uncle Bob, this is Rick. But then, you probably figured that out already."

As she stumbled over her words, the two men shook hands, and Rick explained that he would be back to pick up Christy tomorrow.

"Well, I'll see you tomorrow night," Christy said, feeling unsure of how to say good-bye to Rick with her uncle standing there. She waved, and Rick waved back.

"Five o'clock," Rick echoed and then got into his car.

Christy followed her uncle to the front door, and even though she didn't try to think of Todd, she couldn't help being flooded with memories of when he had walked her to this front door. He had kissed her while they stood on this porch.

The minute Christy and her uncle stepped inside the house, petite, dark-haired Aunt Marti appeared, wagging her finger at Christy. "You'd better count your lucky stars that you have an uncle who covered for you tonight, Christina! Where were you? Your father called at 11:05 to make sure you were here, and we had no idea where you were!"

Christy felt sick to her stomach. "What did you tell him?"

Bob's calm voice overrode Marti's anxious scolding. "I'd seen you pull up a few minutes earlier, so I knew you were here. I figured you two were taking a little moonlight stroll. I was young once. I know these things."

"All I can say is, it's a good thing your father didn't ask to speak to you, or you would've been in real trouble!" Marti warned.

"I'm sorry," Christy said. "I wasn't wearing a watch, and Rick said we had enough time."

Bob and Marti exchanged a look that Christy didn't know how to interpret. Marti remained silent, and Bob picked up her bag and began to carry it up the stairs.

Over his shoulder, Bob said, "Guess you might as well decide now."

"Decide what?" Christy followed him up the stairs.

"Decide if you're going to believe everything that young man tells you."

4

Later, Christy

It didn't take Christy long to fall asleep that night. She wanted to put Rick's rose under her pillow but discovered she had left it in his car along with her purse. That didn't bother her, because she knew she'd see him tomorrow and they'd pick up where they had left off.

Even though she went to bed after midnight, she woke up at five-fifteen and couldn't go back to sleep. After rolling around for half an hour, she gave up and got out of bed. Drawing back the sheer ivory curtains, Christy looked out at the beach, feeling like a bird surveying the land from its lofty perch.

The deserted beach had always intrigued her with its vastness. She especially liked it in the early morning light, when a thin puff of fog floated in from the ocean, giving the sand a soft, hazy halo. Everything outside her window looked like a dream world, and this morning it beckoned her to come walk in its stillness.

Following her impulse, Christy slipped into her jeans and sweatshirt and tiptoed downstairs, out into the morning mist. The brisk dampness made her shiver, and she wished she had a jacket. To warm up, she began to jog, feeling the sand fill her tennis shoes.

She trotted along the firmer sand by the shoreline and thought of how fun it had been racing to the water's edge with Rick last night. Maybe they could go for another walk tonight. She wanted to feel his arm around her again and hear him say how much he liked her.

Yes, Rick definitely makes me feel things I've never felt before with any other guy. This must be what Heather was talking about—it's the difference between a crush and a real relationship.

Her lungs filled with damp air as she ran. Then a fit of coughing made her stop and sit for a moment in the sand. She had come quite a way down the beach and decided to catch her breath before jogging back. Hopefully, she would be able to sneak into the house unnoticed and go back to sleep for a few more hours.

Her mind and emotions didn't feel any more settled than when she awoke. At least the jogging had helped to tire her body some.

Christy was about to leave when she noticed another jogger coming toward her through the lifting fog. For the first time, she felt afraid of being alone on the beach. She realized it had been a foolish thing to take off on her own like that. She also realized that she would be more noticeable if she suddenly jumped up and started to run ahead of this person. With her heart beating rapidly, she decided to stay put and hoped the person wouldn't notice her.

Wrapping her arms around her drawn-up knees and keeping her gaze down, she thought, *Keep going, keep going, whoever you are. You can't see me. I'm invisible.*

The thumping of the jogger's feet approached. To her

terror, the foot-pounding stopped right in front of her. She knew the person was now standing still, examining her.

"Oh, Lord God, protect me!" she whispered under her breath.

The person slowly stepped closer and sat down beside her. She could hear heavy breathing.

Without looking up, and before a word was spoken, Christy knew the person sitting next to her was Todd. All her feelings crumbled like a sand castle does when the rising tide rushes in on it.

What is he doing here? Why is he out at six in the morning? Did he have trouble sleeping too? Is this a nightmare or a God-thing? I can't look at him. What am I going to say?

They sat silently for a long time as Christy listened to Todd's breathing slow to an easier pace. He didn't move. She didn't move. Her back began to hurt from being hunched and looking down for so long.

Worst of all was the way she shivered uncontrollably from the damp cold while everything inside her shouted, *Todd, can't you see that I'm cold? Why don't you put your arm around me?* But she knew he never would. She knew Todd well enough to know that he was probably praying right now and not thinking of how to make her feel more comfortable or secure.

Christy practiced a dozen opening lines in her mind. None of them made it to her lips. What could she possibly say? "I want to break up?" How, when they weren't really going together? She couldn't symbolically hand him the *Forever* bracelet and take off running down the beach, because she'd left it in her purse in Rick's car.

She could feel the thumping of another jogger coming

toward them and used the opportunity to lift her head and look at the passerby.

"Good morning," the older man called out to them. "Beautiful morning, isn't it?"

"Good morning," Todd yelled back, breaking the silence.

To her surprise, the instant she heard Todd's rich voice, something rumbled deep inside her, and she began to cry. She blinked and swallowed hard, but the tears kept coming. Struggling to find her voice, Christy whispered, "I'm sorry."

Suddenly, everything seemed to clear in her mind, and she prepared herself to say the truth that was on her heart. She had ignored it until this moment. Now was the time to speak it as openly as she felt it. She wanted to go back to the way things were with Todd. Last night had been a one-night date with Rick. She was not going to go steady with him. She was not his girlfriend. She would never go out with him again, ever. She only wanted to go out with Todd. She wanted to be Todd's girlfriend. She'd always wanted to be Todd's girlfriend.

"I...I know last night it looked like I was trying to be Rick's girlfriend or something, but that's not how it is. It was just a date. I'm not going with him. It doesn't change anything about the way I feel about you."

"I know," Todd said.

Christy caught a small breath and kept going, afraid that if she stopped she'd never say what was on her heart. "I don't know exactly how to say this, Todd. I've tried before, and I've never been able to find the right words." Christy took a long, deep breath. "I really, really like you. I care for

you in a way I've never cared for anyone else in my life. I..."
She wasn't ready to use the word *love*, yet there had to be
something stronger to say than *like*. She couldn't produce
such a word. "I really, really like you, Todd. I hope you can
understand what I'm saying." Christy felt as if she'd just
ripped her heart out of her chest and was holding it in her
hand, waiting for Todd to take it.

"I do understand what you're saying." Todd paused,
then spoke quick, deliberate words, as if he'd practiced
them all night. "But you've got two more years of high
school ahead of you, and you should feel free to date
whomever you want and not think you have to apologize to
me for it. It was selfish of me to think I could hold on to
you and wait for you to grow up."

His words hit her like a bucket of icy saltwater in the
face. All her vulnerable, transparent feelings of a few seconds ago flip-flopped to instant fury.

Wait for me to grow up? What does he think I am? A baby?

The tears changed too, into hot, angry pellets. Without
thinking, she blurted out, "Well, that's fine. I'll mail your
bracelet back to you then."

"No. It's yours to keep. Remember what I said when I
gave it to you? No matter what happens, we're going to be
friends forever. I meant it then, and I mean it now."

This is unbelievable! Christy thought, wiping her tears. *I pour
out my heart, and he tells me to grow up! And I can't even have the satisfaction
of breaking up, because he won't take the bracelet back.*

They sat in silence, with apparently nothing else to say.
Then in true bizarre, Todd-like fashion, he placed his cool
hand on Christy's forehead and said, "May I bless you?"

"Bless me?"

"Christy," he began, without waiting for her approval, "may the Lord bless you and keep you. May the Lord make His face to shine upon you and give you His peace. And may you always love Jesus first, above all else."

Bless me? Christy thought as Todd pulled his hand away. *Make His face shine on me and give me peace? I'm anything but peaceful right now! Todd, you spiritual geek, why don't you take me in your arms and tell me you love me and that you'll fight to get me back?*

Todd stood up.

What? That's it? I hand you my heart, you tell me to grow up, and then you give some kind of benediction to make it all right? Now you're going to go, just like that?

Todd wedged his feet in the sand and surveyed the waves with his arms folded across his broad chest. "I'm going to Oahu."

Christy sprang to her feet. "What?" It was one thing for him to give his "blessing" to her to date other guys, but news of his moving away filled her with a desperate sense of losing him forever.

"I've decided to hit the surfing circuit with Kimo, like he and I always talked about when we were kids. I called him last night, and there's room for me at his house on the North Shore. I'm leaving tomorrow."

"Tomorrow? Todd!" Christy's fearful, angry feelings ignited her words. "Why? What is going on here with you?"

"I'm going to U of H; registration is Monday."

"You mean the University of Hawaii? Why are you going there?"

"So I can get in a semester of school before the local surfing competition cranks up. That should keep my dad happy."

Keep your dad happy? What about me? I'm not happy you're leaving. And what about you? Do you really want to do this, or did you just decide last night when you saw me with Rick?

"Todd, what's going on? With you, with us? What's happening here?"

He turned to meet her tearful gaze. Those silver-blue eyes that had embraced Christy's a hundred times now held her at a distance as they clouded with a watery mist.

"We're changing, Christy. That's all. We're both changing."

Before she saw it coming, Todd's arms surrounded her in a fierce hug. Then he turned and forced his way across the sand.

"Todd!" she called out, but he kept moving away from her.

Run after him, Christy! Throw your arms around him. Talk him out of going to Oahu. This is your last chance! Do something!

Her mind barked its commands, and her emotions raced at a terrifying speed, yet her feet refused to move. Her throat closed up, and she stood frozen and speechless as Todd, with each step, moved away from her.

"Bye, Todd," she whispered into the thin morning air.

When he was several yards down the beach, Todd turned around, and wiping his eyes quickly with his forearm, he gave his usual chin-up gesture.

"Later, Christy," he called out, and the sound of his hoarse voice hung heavy in the air like a call from across a great chasm.

5

Holding Hands

Sleep, Christy told herself as she trudged through the sand back to Bob and Marti's house. *I need some sleep. Then I'll be able to think this whole thing through, and I'll know what to do.*

Her plan to slip back in bed backfired when she encountered her aunt and uncle seated at the breakfast table.

"Are you trying to give me gray hair, Christy?" Marti snapped. "First, you push your curfew last night, and then you're not even in our house six hours before you sneak out again! Where were you, and who were you with?"

Christy had never seen her aunt this furious. "I...I couldn't sleep so I went for a walk."

"Alone? Do you know how dangerous that is? What were you thinking, young lady?"

Bob stood up and put his hands on Christy's quivering shoulders. Looking into her tearful eyes, he calmly asked, "Are you okay?"

Christy couldn't decide if she should clench her teeth and turn into a rock or break down and sob all over her uncle. She ended up slipping by with a question. "Could you please excuse me? I need to use the bathroom."

She exited quickly and heard her aunt say, "That's it? You're going to let her go just like that?"

Christy locked the door to the bathroom adjacent to her bedroom. Curling up into a shivering ball in the corner, she cried until she had no tears left. Everything inside and outside ached. She forced herself to take a steamy shower and let the hot water massage away the pains.

When the tips of her fingers began to wrinkle, she shut off the water and wrapped her pink flesh in a thick terry cloth robe. Her bed had never felt so inviting before. Now, if only her aunt would leave her alone long enough so she could get some sleep. She rolled over on her side and curled up, falling into an exhausted sleep.

A persistent tapping on the bedroom door awoke her some time later.

"Yes?" she answered, trying to focus her eyes.

"Tracy's on the phone for you," Uncle Bob said through the closed door. "Do you want to talk to her?"

Christy propped herself up on her elbow. "Sure, I'll be there in a minute."

"I have the phone right here," Bob said. "You want me to bring it in?"

"Sure, thanks."

Bob stepped into her room and, before handing her the cordless phone, said softly, "You ready for me to bring up some breakfast?"

Christy smiled and nodded at her tenderhearted uncle. "Thanks."

He winked and disappeared, closing the door behind him.

"Tracy?"

"Hi. What did I just hear? You're getting treated to breakfast in bed? You never told me you had a personal slave."

"My uncle's like that, Tracy. You know him; he likes to baby me, and I let him. Believe me, this morning I need all the babying I can get."

"It's almost afternoon, I hope you know. And how rough could your morning be if you're still in bed?"

Christy explained her early morning encounter on the beach, carefully choosing her words, since Todd and Tracy were such close friends. For some reason it didn't sound as much like the end of the world as it had felt a few hours earlier.

"Todd called me an hour ago," Tracy said. "He didn't even tell me he saw you this morning."

See? Just like Heather said. I'm taking this much harder than Todd. He's already acting like nothing happened.

"But you know," Tracy continued, "he didn't seem completely himself. I mean, he acted all excited about going to Oahu, but I wasn't convinced he really felt that way. He'll probably get more into his adventure once it starts happening. He's definitely leaving tomorrow though. Did he tell you that?"

"Yes."

"I don't know why, but somehow I feel it's the best thing for him right now. And I don't think it's because of you and Rick. He's talked about going on the surfing tour ever since I've known him. I think it's the kind of thing a person has to do when the opportunity comes along. He needs to get it out of his system."

"I guess I should be glad for him that he has this chance," Christy said.

Tracy paused. "He told me he's glad you're going out with Rick."

Christy thought she had already cried all the tears her body had. Not so. A fresh reserve of them bubbled up. In a wild gush, she poured out her heart to her friend.

Bob knocked on the door just then and said, "I'll leave this tray out here. You can get it whenever you're ready."

Christy cupped her hand over the phone and weakly called out, "Thank you." Then she wiped her eyes and blew her nose. "Listen to me," she said to Tracy. "I'm a mess!"

"You have a lot going on and no time to think it all through. You're doing fine considering the circumstances."

"But I've completely ruined my relationship with Todd!"

"No, you haven't. Todd doesn't give up on any of his friends, ever. He'll never turn his back on you. Remember, it's not as if you broke up. Your friendship went into a different phase, that's all. You're changing, as he said. You're giving each other room to grow."

"How? How am I helping him grow? He's the one who told me to grow up."

"Don't you see though? If you hadn't come with Rick last night, Todd might never have been prompted to make that final decision to go on the surfing tour. The opportunity might have passed him by, and in a few years he would have regretted it."

"Tracy, I think you're saying all of this to make me feel better."

"Oh really? Well, how am I doing?"

"Not bad, I guess. You have me smiling at least. Hang on a second. I'm going to grab my breakfast from the hallway."

Christy brought the tray of fruit, orange juice, and a blueberry muffin back to her bed and snuggled under the sheets. She and Tracy talked for almost an hour, and by the time they hung up, Christy felt more settled about letting Todd go.

After all, he was part of her past, and now it was time to move on to a real relationship with a guy who thought she was wonderful. Obviously, Todd didn't see her that way or he would have tried to win her back from Rick. Todd cared more about surfing than he did about her.

Slipping into a pair of cutoff jeans and a sleeveless T-shirt, Christy ventured out on the back patio. Marti, wearing a stylish black and ivory sleeveless dress, sat in the shade of the table umbrella, going through a cookbook and affixing yellow sticky tabs to certain pages.

Pulling the lounge chair around so she faced Marti, she plunged right in. "I'm sorry about last night and this morning, Aunt Marti. You were right. It wasn't a very wise idea for me to take off by myself. I promise I won't do it again. I'm really sorry."

Marti let out a sigh. "I suppose it's all part of growing up, dear."

"Yeah," she said, half to her aunt, half to herself. "Growing up seems to be my problem today."

Not catching any deeper meaning in Christy's statement, Marti continued. "Your uncle and I have tried to be lenient whenever you've stayed with us. And until now, you've been quite dependable. I would hate to see you lose your privileges due to irresponsibility."

"I know; you're right."

"You know we trust Todd completely. He's become like

a son to Bob. But we don't know Rick, and although Bob said he seemed like a nice young man, you can't be too careful these days."

"Am I through getting yelled at?"

Marti looked offended. "I'm not yelling at you."

"I know, but you know what I mean. Because if you are, I'd like to ask you something." Christy shielded her eyes from the sun with her hand so she could see her aunt's reaction.

"You can come to me at anytime with any question. You know that. You've always known that. And you know I was not yelling at you."

"I know."

"So what's your question?"

"Do you think I'm old enough to go steady?"

"With Todd? Certainly." Marti answered without a speck of hesitation and returned to her cookbook.

"It'd be a little difficult to go steady with someone who's moving to Hawaii tomorrow."

"What?" Marti's reaction assured Christy that she now had her aunt's full attention.

It took more than twenty minutes to give Marti the details. When Christy finished, Marti said, "Why didn't you tell me all of this?"

"I did. Just now."

"This is a horrendous amount of decision-making for you to attempt on your own. You should have told me about Rick last night when you came in. And why didn't you tell us you were with Todd this morning on the beach? Christy, you must talk to someone about these things, and when your mother isn't around, you know you can always come to me."

"I know. I am. So what do you think? Am I old enough to go out with Rick?"

"Your mother will say no."

"I know. That's why I'm asking you." Christy could feel her legs getting sunburned and shifted to her side.

"I don't suppose you thought to put on some sunscreen?" Marti asked. "And are those the best shorts you have? You certainly can't wear those tonight when Rick comes to pick you up."

"I have a pair of jeans and a sweatshirt with me too," Christy said, knowing her aunt was not going to give her a straight answer to her question.

She also knew Marti was about to make an announcement of some sort. It seemed to be her way of taking control. She always lifted one of her eyebrows before making a declaration.

"And what about school clothes? What are you going to wear next week when school starts? I don't suppose you've gone shopping yet, have you?"

"No. The first few weeks are always hot, and everyone wears shorts."

Christy knew what was coming. She'd been shopping plenty of times with Marti. Even though she didn't always welcome her aunt's indulgences when it came to clothes, today Christy was delighted with the idea of buying something new to wear for Rick when he came to pick her up. She'd never felt that way with Todd, but then Todd had never noticed or commented on her outfits the way Rick did.

Christy's prediction was correct. A wild and generous shopping trip was in her immediate future. They had only two hours, which turned out to be all the time they needed since money was no object.

They arrived home with enough new clothes to last Christy the entire first semester. She felt excited at the thought of wearing a new outfit on every one of her upcoming dates with Rick.

At five o'clock, Christy heard the doorbell ring and quickly pulled on her new jeans. They were more in style than any of her other jeans. Pulling them up and zipping them, she felt like a model.

At Marti's suggestion, Christy had brushed her hair to one side and fastened it back with some new clips. She had never tried her hair this way before, and it made her feel even more like a model.

Galloping down the stairs, Christy anticipated seeing Rick standing in the entryway. He told her once that he liked her in red, so she specifically wore a new red shirt.

Instead of Rick, Alissa stood by the front door, chatting with Uncle Bob.

"Alissa!" Christy greeted her friend. "I didn't realize you were still here on vacation. And look at your hair! It's adorable!"

When Christy and Alissa met on the beach last summer, Alissa's long blond hair had been a point of envy for Christy and half a dozen other girls. Alissa's gorgeous mane was now cut short. She turned around so Christy could see how cropped it was in the back.

"You like it? It's the new me. Everything else about me has changed this summer; why not my hair?"

"You look great! I'm so glad to see you. Come on in." Christy led the way to the plush living room sofa. Before they could sit down, the doorbell rang again.

"I'll get it," Bob called out.

Christy knew it would be Rick this time. She felt eager to see him and even more eager to introduce him to Alissa.

Alissa had had a rough year. She had become pregnant and moved away, had a baby girl, and then gave her up for adoption about a month ago. Right after that she had returned to visit California with her mother. That's when she gave her heart to the Lord. Alissa had changed a lot. Christy wanted her to meet as many Christians as possible, including Rick.

"Hello, ladies," Rick said, stepping into the living room and eyeing Alissa.

When Christy made the introductions, Rick said, "You'll have to come down to Escondido sometime."

"It would have to be tomorrow," Alissa said. "We're going back to Boston next week."

"Why not come with us tonight?" Rick volunteered. "Your parents wouldn't mind if she stayed overnight, would they, Christy?"

"No, not at all. That really would be fun, Alissa. I was hoping to spend some more time with you before you left."

"Thanks, but I've already got something going on tonight. Doug called, and they're having some kind of surprise going-away party. That's why I stopped by. Doug told me you were here, and I thought we could go together."

"Going-away party?" Rick asked.

"It's for Todd. He's leaving tomorrow for Hawaii to go to school or surfing or something. Anyway, Doug is trying to throw a party together, and I told him if it was for Todd, I'd be there. Have you met Todd, Rick? He is the most incredible guy."

"Yeah, I've met Todd, all right. So he's leaving, huh?" Rick's grin looked a little too smug for Christy. At the same time, she felt relieved that Rick had heard about Todd this way. It would prove to Rick that she was completely available to be with him. If Rick believed Todd was a part of the past, maybe Christy could believe it too.

"Do you both want to go with me?" Alissa asked.

Rick looked like he was about to answer for them, the way he'd answered Doug last night, when Marti made a grand entrance.

"Actually," she said, "we have other plans. I'm sure you two girls will be able to get together in Escondido, don't you think, Christy?"

"Sure. I'll draw you a map to my house, Alissa. Come anytime tomorrow after church, like around one. Okay?" Christy excused herself to find a piece of paper.

Bob met her at the kitchen doorway with a pad of paper in his hand and a concerned look on his face. "You sure you want to let Todd go just like that? Marti told me about this morning on the beach. Are you sure you don't want to try to smooth things out? I could entertain Rick if you and Alissa want to go to Doug's."

"No, it would only make things worse. It's better this way. Really. Todd and I will always be friends. I'm dating Rick now, and I wouldn't want to be rude to him and put him off after he drove all the way up here." With each word, Christy further believed she was right.

"You're sure?"

"Yes, I'm sure. You'll like Rick once you get to know him. Really."

"Apparently your aunt is going to see to that. She's

made plans for the four of us to have dinner in Laguna Beach." Bob handed her the pad of paper, and Christy quickly drew the map.

"Thanks," she said.

"Don't thank me," Bob mumbled. "I'm not sure I'm doing you any favors."

After all the plans were settled and Alissa said good-bye, Marti turned to Rick. In her sweetest voice, she said, "I hope you don't mind my making dinner plans for us?"

"Not at all. It was actually very kind of you, Mrs.—"

"Oh, please, call me Marti."

Right then and there, Christy knew her aunt was smitten by Rick's charm. Now if only Bob would give his approval.

That was Christy's hidden goal during dinner. More than once she tried to get Rick onto a topic that sparked an interest in Bob. It proved to be quite a challenge, since Bob seemed to be taking her "breakup" with Todd personally.

The food at the quaint restaurant Marti had picked out on the Pacific Coast Highway was delicious. The atmosphere, with the beach only a few yards away, was delightful, and being with Rick was dreamy.

Marti did everything she could to keep the conversation light and cheery. Christy played along, even though she thought her aunt was acting like she and Christy were friends out on a double date on a summer night.

When Rick finished eating, he leaned back in his chair and rested his arm across the back of Christy's chair. As the four of them talked, Rick's warm hand rubbed the back of her neck. Christy loved feeling adored. This was what she'd always dreamed it would be like with a boyfriend.

"How about a stroll?" Marti suggested. "Most of the shops along here are still open. What do you think?"

"Sure. Sounds good to me." Rick stood and offered Christy his hand.

She felt so secure slipping her hand in his and feeling his strong fingers wrap around hers like a blanket. Rick held her hand firmly during their entire walk, and Christy loved it.

The only time he let go was in a pottery shop when he found a vase.

"Here," he said, carrying it to the cash register and fishing for his wallet, "you're going to need this."

She laughed at his impulsive manner and wondered what he meant. The vase was rather masculine-looking, with black streaks across a dark blue ceramic base. It looked handmade and earthy. She didn't particularly like it.

Rick's mysterious statement made sense when they returned to Bob and Marti's and loaded all her things into the back of Rick's car. On the front seat a bouquet of red roses awaited her.

"What are these for?" she asked shyly after Rick had started the car.

"For my girlfriend."

"They're beautiful," Christy said, nuzzling her nose into their velvet petals.

"Not nearly as beautiful as you. You look like my red rose tonight. Did I tell you how good you look? I like your hair like that. Not that you should wear it that way all the time, but tonight it looks good. Makes you look older."

"Does it make me look too much older? I mean, does it make me look like I'm trying to look older?" Christy asked, suddenly feeling self-conscious.

"Not at all," Rick said. "You look just right. I like it when a girl takes the time to make herself look good for her boyfriend. It shows she really cares about him, and she cares about what people will think of him when they see her with him. And the way you look, I'd never be embarrassed for people to see us together."

I know he meant that as a compliment, but somehow it didn't sound exactly right. Was he trying to warn me that I should always make sure I look good when we go out? It's a good thing Marti just made a major contribution to my wardrobe!

Rick reached over and took her hand. She felt close to him, warm and secure. She wanted that feeling to last all evening. She wanted him to hold her hand all the way home.

Driving with one hand, Rick put a CD in the player, and for an hour, mellow saxophone music rolled all around them. They didn't speak the whole time. They just held hands and let the music lull them. Christy closed her eyes and rested her head against the seat.

So this is what it feels like to have a boyfriend who adores me. I love it. I never knew it could feel this wonderful. Don't ever end, sweet night. Don't stop driving, Rick. Don't stop the music. Don't ever stop being my boyfriend.

Rick's car came to a stop, rousing Christy from her half-dream state.

"Where are we?" She looked around at the darkness outside the car window.

"Look out there." Rick pointed over the hood of the car. "The beautiful lights of downtown Escondido."

"I thought we were going to my house," Christy said, stretching the kink in her neck and trying to hide the nervous feelings creeping into her voice. "We really should get going."

"Is your neck sore? Here, turn around. I'll get the knot out."

Christy turned, and Rick's strong hands massaged her neck, then her shoulders. She felt herself beginning to relax beneath his touch. He leaned over and kissed her lightly on the neck, then again on the cheek. When he turned her face to kiss her on the lips, she pulled away and put up her hands in defense.

"Wait." It was all she could think to say. "Just wait."

Rick sat silently waiting, while she collected her thoughts. "What is it, Christy? What's wrong?" His voice sounded gentle and patient.

"This is coming at me too fast, that's all. I'm just not ready for this."

Rick let out a low chuckle. "Ready for what? I was only going to kiss you. Honest."

Christy remained on guard, with her back pressed against the passenger door, frantically trying to evaluate her colliding emotions.

"Hey," Rick said, "don't look so frightened. It's only me, remember? Your boyfriend. I'm not going to hurt you. Come here." He opened his arms and drew her to him in a gentle hug.

His hand stroked the back of her hair, and in her ear, he whispered, "You smell so good. You feel so good in my arms. Do you know how long I've waited to hold you like this?"

He tilted up her chin, and this time she let him kiss her. As soon as he did, the panic feeling in the pit of her stomach returned.

She pulled away, more slowly this time.

"I'm sorry, Rick. I'm not feeling well. My stomach kind of hurts, and well, I'm just not ready for all of this."

Rick pulled back and let out a huge puff of air. Folding his arms across his chest, he said, "It's that surfer guy, isn't it?"

"No." Christy shook her head and looked Rick in the eye. "Todd and I were never like this. I told you. He and I were very close friends. That's all. You're my first real boyfriend, and well, maybe I don't know how to act like the perfect girlfriend. But if you take it slow and give me a chance, I'm sure I'll get used to all these feelings rumbling around inside my stomach right now."

"So," Rick said with a slow grin returning to his face, "I make you sick to your stomach, do I?"

Christy let her smile return. "You know what I mean."

He reached over, grasped her hand, and squeezed it. All her fearful, overpowering feelings gave way to the more comfortable, warm, close feelings.

"Come on, Killer. I'll take you home."

6

Restrictions

several minutes later, when Rick and Christy pulled up in front of her house, Christy wondered what time it was and if her parents were still up. Rick carried her luggage and extra shopping bags to the front door, while all Christy carried was her purse, her bouquet, and her new vase.

The minute they stepped on the porch, the front door swung open, and Christy's dad stood behind the screen door looking like a grizzly bear. He didn't say a word, only opened the screen door and grabbed Christy's suitcase out of Rick's hand.

"Well, good night, Christy," Rick said quickly. "Good night, Mr. Miller." Then he vanished, leaving Christy to face her parents alone.

She stepped inside, her bouquet cradled in one arm, the ceramic vase in the other. "I'll put these in water," she said, feeling her mother's glare following her into the kitchen.

11:47 blazed out from the digital clock on the microwave.

It can't be that late! No wonder my parents are in a nuclear meltdown! I'm supposed to be home by ten o'clock except for special occasions. If I explain carefully, maybe they'll consider this a special occasion. Then again, maybe I'm in big trouble.

Haphazardly cramming the roses into the vase, Christy decided to leave them on the kitchen counter. Plopping them in the middle of the kitchen table would not add a festive touch.

With cautious steps, she returned to the living room and sat on the couch at the opposite end from her mother. This was not Bob and Marti's, where she could excuse herself and retreat to her room. She was about to receive the lecture of her life.

Mom went into the kitchen; Christy could hear her making coffee. Apparently, this was going to be a long night.

Alone in the living room with her dad, Christy broke the ice by asking, "Did Uncle Bob call to tell you Rick was bringing me home?"

"No. I called him several times." Dad's voice had a low growl to it that caused Christy's heart to beat faster. "I finally reached him at ten o'clock. He said you'd been out to dinner and that you left his house around nine-thirty. It is now almost midnight. Where have you been?"

"We stopped for a while and talked. Then Rick brought me home. We didn't stop for long."

"Just talked?" Dad's face was beginning to turn a shade of red that clashed with his red hair.

Mom stepped in just then and delivered a steaming cup of coffee to Dad. With a concerned look, Mom said, "Christina, we had absolutely no idea where you were. I had dinner prepared here for Bob and Marti, and when you didn't show up, and no one called us, and no one answered the phone there..." Mom choked up. "We thought the worst. Do you have any idea what you put your father and me through tonight?"

Christy lowered her head. "No. I'm sorry. I thought Bob called you."

"You should have called us," Dad said. "Just because you're old enough to date doesn't mean you can take off anytime you want with anybody you want! You still have to ask us before you go out or make arrangements to do things. Is that understood?"

"Yes."

Dad drew in a deep, steamy sip of coffee before coming down hard. "You want freedom. You want to drive the car whenever you want. You want to date whomever you want, and you want to wear whatever you want. If you want freedom, then you have to show your mother and me that you are responsible."

Christy glanced at her round-faced mother, who gave her a stern look and quietly went back to drinking her coffee.

"First, you drove the car to your babysitting job three days last week, and when your mother went to the grocery store today, she nearly ran out of gas. When you drive the car, you are responsible to fill it with gas."

"But that job ended last week," Christy reasoned. "I've already spent the little I made, and when school starts next week, I won't have any money for gas."

"Yes, you will. You're going to find a job. Your mother and I talked about it, and if you want to drive the car, you need to find a job that will provide you with at least enough for gas money each week.

"Second," he continued without leaving any space for Christy to protest, "you will have to have approval from your mother or me before you go on any more dates. You'll have to tell us where you are going; you must be home by ten o'clock, even on weekends; and we must approve of the boy you're going out with. Understand?"

"Yes," Christy answered, relieved that he hadn't taken away her privilege to date. She and Rick could be home by ten if they started out early enough. It really wouldn't change a thing.

"Next, where did you get that outfit? Those are not the kind of jeans I want my daughter wearing."

"But they're brand new. Marti just bought them for me today. They're in style, Dad."

"Fine. If everyone is wearing them, you'll have no trouble giving away yours. You are not wearing them. Is that clear?"

Christy nodded and looked down at her jeans, thinking of how a few hours earlier she had felt like a model in this trendy outfit. Now she felt ridiculous. It was one thing for Rick to notice her outfits and another for her dad to.

"Final point is, you're grounded for two weeks for your irresponsibility tonight."

"Norm?" Mom said softly. "I thought we decided on one week."

He tilted his coffee mug up for one last swig. "Any girl who comes home dressed like that needs two weeks' restriction."

Mom looked down at her coffee mug, which Christy knew meant her mom wouldn't press the issue anymore.

"We love you, Christy," Dad concluded. "You know

that. But we can't say we're real happy with the choices you seem to be making lately. We care about you too much to let you toss away your virtue so easily."

His last line, "toss away your virtue," haunted Christy through her long and fitful night of sleep.

What does he mean by virtue? Does he think I'm doing something wrong with Rick? Or that my clothes aren't modest enough? I'm totally conservative compared to my friends. He'd die if he saw some of their outfits! Just what is virtue, and how am I tossing it away?

The next day when Christy's family arrived home from church, Rick called to apologize for not meeting her at the service. He said his family had taken him out to brunch as a farewell before college. Christy quickly explained she was on restriction and needed to get off the phone.

"That stinks! What am I supposed to do for the next two weekends?" Rick grumbled. "I'm coming over. I'm going to talk your dad out of it."

"No, Rick, don't. You don't know my dad. You'll only make it worse."

"Christy?" Mom called from the kitchen. "I need your help with lunch."

"I have to go, Rick. I'm sorry. I'll talk to you later."

"When? If I can't call you or see you, how am I going to talk to you?"

"I don't know. I'm sorry. I need to hang up. We'll figure out something. It'll work out. You'll see."

"Yeah, I'll work it out. Don't you worry about anything, Christy. I'll work it out."

About ten minutes later, as they were sitting down to a lunch of tuna melts and coleslaw, Rick showed up at the front door. Since it was so hot, the front door was open, and they could all see him standing by the screen door.

"We're eating, Rick," Christy's dad said without getting up from the table. "Christy is on restriction, so she won't be able to see you for two weeks."

Christy felt like a five-year-old whose best friend had come over to play and was shooed away.

"That's what I'd like to talk to you about, sir. You see, I'm leaving for college on Tuesday, and I wondered if you'd reconsider and allow me to take Christy out tonight."

"No."

"Well, not 'out' exactly. I thought we'd spend the evening with my parents at my house. Would that be okay?"

"No."

Rick didn't know Christy's dad the way she did, or else he would have given up after the first no. The poor guy stood outside the screen door and tried at least five different approaches before saying with a sad puppy face, "Bye, Christy. Have a good first week of school."

She felt crushed, and furious with her dad. Sometimes he didn't seem to give a rip about anybody else's feelings. What had her mother ever seen in him, anyway?

Christy picked at her lunch, eating only the cheese and a tiny pinch of coleslaw. She was about to excuse herself when another car pulled up in front of the house, and a girl with short blond hair bounded up to the door.

Oh no! It's Alissa. I completely forgot she was coming today.

"Mom, it's Alissa. I invited her to come before I knew I was on restriction, and she drove all the way from Newport Beach. She's leaving for Boston this week, and this is the only chance I'll have to see her probably ever again!"

"Hello." Alissa tapped on the wooden frame of the screen door. "Is anyone home?"

"All right," Christy's dad said. "Let her in. But you're staying here. You're not going out anywhere."

Even though he sounded gruff, Christy could tell he really didn't mind Alissa coming to see her.

"Come in, come in," Dad said, getting up to open the screen door. "You must be the one who moved to Boston."

"Yes, I'm Alissa. It's nice to meet you, Mr. Miller." She looked pretty as usual, and she was losing some of the pudginess around her middle that had come with the pregnancy.

Christy stood up and introduced Alissa to Mom and Christy's little brother, David. Up to this point, David had been quiet, taking in all the afternoon's events.

Now he piped up. "How come Christy gets to have her girlfriends come over even though she's on restriction? That's not fair!"

Alissa looked sheepishly at Christy. "Did I come at a bad time?"

"No," Mom spoke up, "it's fine, really. You girls can go on back to Christy's room."

Christy automatically began to clear the table.

"That's okay. I'll get these," Mom said.

"That's not fair either!" David whined. "When it's my turn, I always have to do the dishes."

The girls retreated into Christy's room and closed the door. Christy flopped face first onto her bed. With her arms spread out, she hollered into the patchwork bedspread, "Aughhhhhhh!"

"Bad day?" Alissa ventured, gracefully alighting on the edge of the bed.

Christy talked nonstop for twenty minutes while Alissa patiently listened to her complicated dilemma with Todd and Rick and her parents and the restriction and having to find a job.

When Christy finally paused to catch her breath, Alissa smiled. "You don't know how blessed you are."

"Blessed?" It reminded her of Todd's "blessing," and right now that didn't help.

"Yes, you are blessed," Alissa said. "When my father died about a year and a half ago, I had no boundaries. I could do whatever I wanted. And I did. Who was going to stop me? My alcoholic mother? No one ever said, 'No, I won't let you do that. I care about you too much to let you hurt your future like that.' I wish I had then what you have now."

Christy instantly sobered. "I never thought of it that way."

"What are you going to do about Rick?"

"What do you mean?" Christy was more concerned about how she could get off restriction and how she was going to find a job. Rick seemed like the least of her worries. In two weeks, they could pick up where they had left off, and Christy had already imagined that they'd only appreciate each other more for the separation.

"Are you going to break up with him?" Alissa asked.

"Why would I want to break up with him?"

"Why are you going out with him?"

"Well, because we've been friends for a long time, and now that I can date, this is the next step in our relationship. Besides, this is what I've always wanted—a boyfriend. And Rick is a great guy. He really cares about me. I'd be crazy to break it off and give up all that for nothing."

"Christy," Alissa said gently, "I know exactly what you're saying about how good it feels to have a boyfriend and to be adored and desired and everything. But listen to me. It's not going to fill your heart."

"I'm not trying to fill my heart. I'm having a normal teenage dating relationship with a really great guy. That's all."

"Okay." Alissa readjusted her posture. "Then can I ask you to promise me something?"

"What?" Christy thought Alissa looked almost comical. She was so intense as she reached over and grasped Christy's right hand.

"Promise me you won't do any more than kissing—and I mean light kissing—with Rick or any other guy you go out with. Promise me that."

"Alissa, that's not even an issue. I don't plan to ever get really physical with any guy until I'm married."

"And last Friday afternoon you didn't plan on going steady with Rick, did you?"

"Well, no," Christy said.

"But you let Rick talk you into something you weren't ready for, and it sounds as though you felt pressured to say yes."

"Maybe a little pressure, but Alissa, going steady isn't the same as getting physically involved."

"It's the first step. And if you said yes to going steady when it was completely Rick's idea, you could give in to Rick's ideas on how far you guys go physically. You have to draw a line, Christy."

"I have good reason to feel so strongly about all this, and you know it," Alissa said. "My biggest concern for you is that you're looking for a guy to fill your heart—first Todd and now Rick. A guy will never be able to meet all your needs. You have to want God with all your heart, soul, strength, and mind. As long as there's somebody else there to fill your heart or mind, you won't really fall in love with Jesus the way you would if He was all you wanted."

Now Christy felt angry. *Why are you, of all people, lecturing me like this? Wasn't I the one who led you to the Lord only a month ago? How come you're instantly so spiritually mature?*

Instead of voicing her feelings, Christy forced a smile. "I can see you've sure been doing some soul-searching this past month."

"Actually, I've been reading. I finished the New Testament, and I'm starting on the Old Testament."

"You read the whole New Testament?"

"Sure, haven't you?"

"Yeah, well, I mean, parts of it. And parts of the Old Testament too."

When Alissa left two hours later, Christy hugged her and said, "Thanks for all the advice."

She meant it. Even though Alissa's directness was hard to take, Christy knew she spoke from her heart. But as Christy tried to make sense of the whole jumbled weekend, all she got for her efforts was a headache. When she slipped into bed that night, she hoped for a calm week to work through all her thoughts and feelings. Of course it would be calm, she reminded herself. She was on restriction.

7

One Hedgehog and
One Rabbit to Go

"Here it is, Christy!" Katie said, waving a newspaper
in her hand. Her red hair swung back and forth as she
marched over to the school lunch table where Christy had
just settled herself.

Katie plopped down across from Christy and thrust the
newspaper under her nose. "I hoped I'd find you here in
our old spot. How's your first day back treating you?"

"All right. What's with the paper?"

"I found a job for you. You said at church that your
parents were making you find a job, and here's the perfect
one. At the mall even."

Christy silently read the ad Katie had circled. Looking
up, she said, "At the pet store?"

"Yes! Don't you see? It says, 'Experience with animals.'
You did grow up on the kind of farm that had animals,
didn't you?"

"Most Wisconsin dairy farms come equipped with animals, yes," Christy answered.

"See? You're a natural! Call them after school. I bet
they'll hire you over the phone." Katie opened her sack

lunch, examined its contents, and said, "Did you get anything more exciting than peanut butter and jelly?"

"You can have my apple," Christy offered.

"No thanks. I don't touch food unless it's from one of my four basic food groups—sugars, fats, preservatives, and artificial flavorings."

Christy laughed and realized she hadn't smiled in several days. She hadn't heard from Rick since Sunday's standoff with her dad at the screen door. Being so far away from him made everything gloomy.

After running the pet shop idea past her mom, Christy called the number. The manager sounded young and in a hurry. He asked her to come in to fill out an application and then asked if she had reliable transportation and could work Friday nights. She said yes to both questions.

"Would it be possible for you to start this Friday?"

Remembering the restriction, she said, "I think so. I'll have to check and call you back."

"If you could come in around seven tonight, you could fill out the application and give me your answer then."

"Okay. Thanks." Christy hung up, and turning to Mom said, "I think they might hire me. I'm supposed to go there tonight at seven o'clock. Is that okay?"

"I suppose. We'll ask your father when he comes home. He's still quite serious about your restriction."

"I know, but he was serious about a job too. If I don't go in, they might hire somebody else."

Without much discussion, Christy's dad agreed to take her to the mall.

Before they walked into the pet store, he said,

"Remember to stand up straight, speak clearly, and pretend I'm not here."

The first two instructions she could follow easily enough, but pretending Dad wasn't there would be impossible.

This is so embarrassing, she thought as she stepped up to the counter. *Suppose they find out he's with me? They might not hire me.*

"May I help you?" asked a guy behind the counter. He looked as though he was in his late twenties and had a rugged, earthy appearance. He wore his thick black hair pulled back in a ponytail, which Christy was used to seeing on guys in California. But she was surprised that his ponytail was fastened with the type of plain green twist-tie usually found around celery stalks in the grocery store.

"I called this afternoon about the job, and Jon told me to come in and fill out an application."

"Oh, good. I'm Jon, and you're Christy, right?" He seemed surprised at her appearance. She knew it must be the dress. Mom insisted she wear a dress to make a favorable impression. Standing beside the mynah birds, Christy felt like someone applying for a job to serve tea, not sell kitty litter.

"You can come in the back and fill out the paperwork. Do you know your social security number?" Jon led her past the tropical fish tanks to a card table in the back room.

"No, I don't think so."

"That's all right, as long as you bring it with you on your first day." He left her alone at the table with a one-page questionnaire and a pen.

Christy nervously answered the questions, remembering how Mom told her to use her best printing. Aside from her name, address, age, and phone number, she couldn't fill out much, since the other blanks related to previous job experience. The paper looked awfully empty. Christy decided to write in *babysitting* and left it at that.

As soon as she emerged from the back room, she saw her dad, pretending to look at the tropical fish. Hoping he wouldn't act as if he knew her, Christy walked straight to the front counter, bravely handing Jon her application.

"Babysitting, huh?" Jon scanned the paper. "And you said you lived on a farm?"

"Yes. In Wisconsin. For fourteen years."

"And you're sixteen now, I see." He then put the application down on the counter and rang up a customer's purchase on the cash register.

Christy smiled politely at the older couple, who were buying a blue jewel-studded cat collar. The couple smiled back, accepted their bag from Jon, and left.

"So, you haven't had any experience on a cash register."

Still smiling, Christy shook her head.

"Doesn't really matter. You have to know how to read and push a few buttons. That's all. Computer does all the thinking." Jon turned the application over and wrote on the back as he verified, "You can work Fridays from four to nine, right? How about Saturdays, eleven to six?"

"Sure, that would be fine," Christy said.

"Great! I'll see you Friday at four o'clock. Oh, and you might be more comfortable wearing jeans to work. We don't tend to dress up much around here. The last girl who wore a flowered dress found the bunny rabbits nibbling on it. They thought she was a walking garden."

Christy smiled, said, "Okay, thanks," and left quickly to hide her embarrassment over her dress. Dad followed her out and acted proud of her. His affirmations helped make up for the insecurities she suddenly felt when she realized she had just been hired for her first job.

"What did I tell you?" Katie said the next day at school. "I knew the job was perfect for you. They don't get too many people with animal experience around here who are willing to work weekends for minimum wage."

"Oh, good! That makes me feel as if I'm the only one dumb enough to take this job," Christy said.

"I'm only kidding! You'll do great. It'll probably be a really fun job. I'll come see you, and you can sell me a dog bone or something. So when do you get off work?"

"At nine o'clock. Then I have to head straight home because of restriction," Christy said.

"Well," Katie sighed, "I hope you and Rick learn a lesson from all this. Now I guess we'll have to postpone our annual slumber party for two more weeks until your restriction is over."

"Where's it going to be?" Christy remembered the back-to-school slumber party of last year. That night the girls had toilet-papered Rick's house. Since she had been the new girl at school, she didn't have a clue who Rick was. That's how she first met him.

All the girls had left her hiding in the bushes, and when Rick came out to clean up the paper, Christy jumped out of the bushes and charged down the street with Rick running after her. The girls had returned in a motor home to pick her up, and Christy hopped into the vehicle before Rick had a chance to catch her.

"Hello." Katie waved her hand in front of Christy's eyes. "Where did you just go?"

"Oh, I was remembering the slumber party last year. That was a wild night!"

"It sure was." Katie joined in the memory.

"Remember how Rick kept asking you who I was?" Christy said.

"I remember. He's been chasing you for a whole year. He must be pretty pleased with himself for finally catching you."

"What's that supposed to mean?" Christy asked.

"Well, if you want my opinion, Rick is the ultimate competitor. Remember the awards assembly when he graduated? He won an award in almost every athletic category."

"So? He likes sports," Christy said.

"He likes a challenge. And you have been the ultimate challenge. You're about the only thing he didn't win while he was going to Kelley High."

"Oh, come on, Katie. You're exaggerating. Rick is a great guy, and I feel honored that he wants me to be his girlfriend."

Katie shook her head, and a smirk crossed her face.

"What?" Christy asked. "What are you thinking?"

The bell rang, its annoying blare ending lunch and their discussion.

Katie hopped up from the table. "You've changed, Christy. Six months ago you never would have said those words. But hey, we all change. It's okay. I'll see you after school—at your new job."

Katie hurried off in the direction of the gym, leaving Christy to ponder their conversation as she walked to class.

We all change. We do. So what if I changed my opinion about Rick? I'm not doing anything wrong. Why can't a girl have a little fun without all her friends and relatives trying to make her feel bad? They're not giving me a chance, and they're really not giving Rick a chance.

Katie kept her word and showed up at the pet store a few minutes after Christy started work. Christy was standing at the register, and Jon was explaining how to run it. Christy didn't want to get in trouble her first day for having friends come in and distract her, so she acted as though she didn't see Katie come in.

"Pardon me," Katie said, acting out the part of a non-chalant customer. "Where do you keep your dog bones?"

Christy tightly pressed her lips together to keep from laughing.

"Second aisle, toward the back," Jon answered routinely and then finished drilling Christy on the register functions.

She remembered almost everything Jon showed her and answered five of his six questions correctly.

Katie approached the counter with two dog bones in her hands. "Excuse me. We have a poodle, and I was wondering if you could tell me which one of these he would like best."

It took a tremendous amount of self-control for Christy not to blow the role-playing. Katie seemed to have no problem keeping a straight face.

"Which one would you recommend, Christy?" Jon asked, turning the scenario over to her.

She cleared her throat twice before answering, "Probably the larger one."

"Fine," Katie said brightly. "Then I'll take the smaller one." She pulled a five-dollar bill out of her pocket and handed it to Christy.

Christy looked to Jon, and he said, "Go ahead. Remember which button you press first?"

Christy remembered. She tried to ignore Katie and think through each step on the cash register. It worked. The drawer opened when it was supposed to, and the screen displayed the correct amount of change due, which she handed to Katie without looking her in the eye.

"You'll do fine up here, Christy," Jon said. "I'm going in the back. If you need me, press this button." Jon showed her a red button under the counter.

The instant he was out of view, Christy let her facial muscles relax and said, "You almost got me fired!"

Katie giggled. "You know what? I changed my mind. Could I exchange this dog bone?"

"Not a chance. I have no idea how to do returns. Go find yourself a dog and give him a treat," Christy teased.

"Speaking of dogs," Katie retorted mischievously, "what's happening with Rick?"

"Katie, that was low!" Christy could feel her resentful thoughts from their lunch conversation returning. Katie had no right to be so critical of Rick.

"You know I'm only kidding. Is he coming in to see you tonight?"

"I don't know. Probably. I wrote him and told him about the job and everything." She felt like adding, "What do you care?" But she noticed Jon coming back up to the front.

He stepped behind the counter and pulled out a clipboard with a stack of papers attached to it. Noticing Katie still standing there, he said, "Is there a problem here?"

I'll say! Christy felt like answering. *My closest friend is acting like anything but a friend.*

"Yes, I changed my mind," Katie said, falling back into her role-playing voice. "I don't think Poopsie will like this bone. I'd like my money back."

Jon calmly put down the clipboard. "Watch, Christy. This is how you do a return."

He went through a few simple steps, and when the drawer opened, he asked Christy to count out the money and hand it back to the customer.

"Thank you," Katie said, smiling at Jon. "Your sales-clerk here has been most helpful. I'll be sure to tell all my friends to shop here."

As soon as she walked out of the store, Jon said, "I hope her friends aren't like her."

Christy kept a straight face. After all, Katie deserved that comment.

"Come on back, and I'll show you how to clean the cages. Beverly!" Jon called to the other salesclerk, who was stocking fish food. "Will you cover the register?"

For the next half hour, Christy was tutored in the fine science of replacing shredded newspapers on the bottom of a wide variety of cages.

By the fifth cage, she thought, *Living on a farm didn't prepare me for this. Now, if I'd lived on Noah's ark, maybe.*

She then learned how to stock shelves, the right way to scoop up fish in a net, and which brand of dog food was on special. Jon didn't let up in his rapid training of every facet of the store, so Christy stopped him to ask questions. Twice she asked him to repeat his instructions because there were too many details to remember the first time through.

"Don't worry. You'll catch on," Jon said. "The last thing I need to show you is the snake."

Christy made a grim face. "As long as I don't have to touch it, I'll be fine."

Jon laughed at her squeamish response. "Walter wouldn't hurt a fly. A couple of rodents or a small rabbit, yes. But not a fly." He smiled at his own joke. "Walter's over here in this locked terrarium."

Christy stood back as Jon showed her how to lock and unlock the tank of the fifteen-foot python. She nodded every time he looked at her to make sure she was taking in all the instructions.

"I won't ever have to feed him though, will I?"

"Naw. I'm the only one who feeds him. I want you to keep an eye on this lock though. It's an old tank, and sometimes kids sneak back here and yank on the lock. They think it's funny to get Walter all excited."

Jon checked his watch. "Why don't you take a fifteen-minute break? When you come back, I have a dinner appointment."

Christy decided to spend her fifteen minutes out in the mall rather than at the card table in the back room. As soon as she stepped into the open space, she noticed how good the air smelled. Sniffing her T-shirt, she realized she had brought the heavy odor of the menagerie with her.

Maybe I should visit a department-store perfume counter and sample a few perfumes?

"Going somewhere without me?" a deep voice behind Christy asked.

She spun around and met Rick's overpowering hug.

"Hi. I'm so glad to see you!" She squeezed his middle then pulled back. "Better not get too close. I smell like a pet store."

"You smell fine," Rick said, leading her over to a bench. "What time do you get off?"

"Nine. I'm on a fifteen-minute break now. What's wrong? You look upset."

"Are you planning to work every Friday?"

"At first, yeah. That's the time they needed somebody. It might change later. Why?"

"Didn't you happen to think we might have plans for Friday nights?" Rick didn't try to conceal his anger. "There are plenty of places that need after-school help, Christy. You sure weren't thinking when you took this one. Now all our Friday nights are shot."

"Rick, I'm sorry. I had to find a job, and this one came up, and—"

"And I suppose it's the only one you applied for. Man! I can't believe you did this. I mean, don't you think it would've been considerate of you to at least talk this over with me?"

Christy couldn't answer. Now she was afraid to tell him she also worked until six o'clock on Saturdays.

Why didn't I think of this before? I can't believe he's so mad at me!

"You know, this is great. I come home for the weekend knowing that my girlfriend has been grounded because of some stupid thing about not calling to let her parents know I was driving her home. I can't talk to you all week, and your dad won't let up an inch. And now you're working every Friday night. That stinks, Christy! This is not the way to start off our relationship."

"I know," Christy whispered, feeling the tears bubbling up and spilling over onto her cheeks. "I'm sorry. I'll see if I can switch to another night."

"Why are you crying?" Rick slipped his arm around her and pulled her close. "Hey, it'll all work out. It took me by surprise, that's all. You'll be able to switch your hours or get another job or something."

He held her for a few minutes while she dried her tears.

"I'm sorry," Christy said, "but I probably should get back. I was only supposed to be gone fifteen minutes."

"You still have a few minutes," Rick said, stroking her hair. "I haven't had a chance to tell you how much I missed you this week. I thought about you every day."

"I missed you too. And I'm glad you're here." She smiled and wiped away one last tear. "Is my face okay?"

"Your face is great," he said, smiling broadly.

"You know what I mean. Did I smear my makeup?"

"A tiny bit, right here." Rick stroked his thumb under her left eye. "There, Killer Eyes. Now you're perfect."

"Far from it," Christy retorted.

"For me, you're perfect. Come on. I'll walk you back, and you can introduce me to all the animals. Except your manager. I've already met him."

"Jon is nice," Christy said defensively.

"I'm sure he is. If you like the zookeeper type. You don't, do you? I mean, he's not asking you out or anything?"

"Rick!" Christy playfully socked him in the arm as they entered the pet store.

"Just checking. Can't say I was too worried about competing with Tarzan, though."

Jon more than likely overheard Rick's last comment as they walked in because he gave Rick and Christy a scowl. Rick took off toward the back, where they kept the tropical fish. Christy stepped behind the counter, and Jon pointed at the clock on the wall behind him. "You left at five-thirty, Christy."

She looked up at the clock. It was now five minutes after six. "Is that clock right? I couldn't have been gone that long! It seemed like only a few minutes. I'm sorry. I won't let it happen again."

"Good. I'm taking your word on that. I'm late for an appointment. I won't be back until seven-thirty. Beverly is in the back; she can help out if you get stuck on anything."

"Sure. Thanks. And again, I'm really sorry about losing track of the time."

Jon lifted a hand in a slight wave over his shoulder as he rushed off. Christy felt relieved that Jon had been so understanding. She promised herself she'd never let herself be late again. That would be so unfair, especially when Jon had let it go this time.

A young boy with his mother passed Jon on his way out. They came right to the counter, and the boy said, "I want to buy a hedgehog, and it has to be a boy."

"We need some help," the mother said sweetly.

"Sure." Christy pushed the buzzer, which she hoped would produce Beverly. "We'll be with you in a moment."

Another boy now stood before her with a packaged aquarium filter in his hand. "Do you know if this comes with the charcoal, or do I have to buy that separately?"

"Um, I'm not sure. Does it say on the package?"

The boy scanned the package, and Christy rang the buzzer again. Down the aisle trotted Beverly. With her long black hair in a single braid down her back, and her wrists covered with beaded bracelets, Beverly looked like the kind of young woman who, if she had lived a hundred years ago, would have been a Pony Express rider.

Christy explained what each customer wanted, and Beverly said, "I'll take care of the register. You go on back and show them the hedgehogs. And no, the charcoal is separate. It's at the end of the far right aisle."

"The hedgehogs are back here," Christy said, trying to sound as if she knew what she was doing.

Maybe I'll be able to figure out which are the boys if I pick up a couple of them and check them out inconspicuously.

"I want that one," the boy said when they stopped in front of the cage with the African Pygmy hedgehogs.

"Does he roll up into a ball? I only want the kind that can roll up into a ball and eats bugs. I'm gonna name him Sonic. He'd better be a boy."

Christy and the mother exchanged knowing glances, and Christy said, "My little brother is ten. He's hedgehog crazy too."

She gingerly picked up the hedgehog, and its pointy spines pricked her hand. She tried to check the underside to see if it was a boy, but it instantly rolled up into a little ball. Putting the spiny creature down and pulling out another one, she tried to get it to open up so she could figure out if it was a boy or a girl.

"You have to get it to relax," Rick said, reaching for the hedgehog.

Christy didn't know how long he'd been standing there watching her.

"You can tell by the location of the belly button," Rick said as he soothingly coaxed it to open up. "The ones with the higher belly buttons are boys."

"You're kidding," Christy said. "I mean, yes. Right. Thanks."

"Yes, thank you," the mother said, smiling at Rick.

"You want this one," Rick said.

"Can you show us what we need to feed him, and how big of a tank we should buy?"

"No problem." Rick led the three of them around the store, collecting a tank and lid, food and water dishes, and wood shavings for bedding. "They like little tunnels to hide in. I think there're some plastic ones over here."

Christy caught Rick's proud glance as he pointed out the best kind of tunnels. He threw in a couple of pointers on feeding Sonic primarily cat food but throwing in an occasional mealworm or cricket as a tasty treat every now and then.

With their arms loaded, the mom and her son laid out their extensive purchases on the counter. Beverly's eyebrows arched slightly on her plain face, and she said, "I guess you figured out which one was a boy."

"I had a little help," Christy explained, sneaking a wink at Rick, who had retreated to the bird food section only a few feet away. He puffed out his chest jokingly and winked back.

Beverly returned to her inventory labeling in the back while Christy rang up the $205 hedgehog sale.

The woman handed Christy her check. "Won't my husband be surprised! I'm sure I'll hear about when he was a kid, and they fished their pets right out of the creek for free."

Rick strutted his way to the counter when the mom and son left. "Bring on the next customer. They can't resist, can they?"

Before Christy had a chance to swat at him for his joking arrogance, a man came up and said, "Can you answer some questions about the rabbits?"

"Sure," Rick said. "Let me help you." He followed the man back to the cages. Twenty minutes later, Christy rang up a $184 rabbit sale.

"You'd better leave before Jon comes back," Christy said, checking the clock and noticing it was nearly seven-thirty.

"Why? I'm making money for the guy. He should put me on the payroll!" Rick grinned. "Don't worry. I'll disappear. Actually, I ordered something, and I want to see if it's ready. I'll be back at nine o'clock to pick you up."

"I drove my car here," Christy said.

"You still need a bodyguard to walk you through the parking lot. I'll see you at nine." He waved and took off.

Not a minute too soon. Jon came in from the opposite direction only a few seconds later. "How did it go? Any problems?"

"No, not really," Christy said as Jon reached around and did a subtotal check on the cash register.

"This can't be right. It says you did more than four hundred dollars in sales while I was gone. What did you sell?"

"Just a hedgehog and a rabbit," Christy said with a smile, "and all the accessories they needed plus a month's food supply."

"Really?" Jon said. "How 'bout that. Guess I did the right thing hiring you. Keep up the good work!"

Number Eight on the List

"Come here, girlfriend," Rick said in the mall parking lot after he had walked Christy to her car. "I've waited all week to give you this."

He opened his arms and wrapped Christy in a warm hug. "Sorry about getting mad earlier. It won't be so bad spending a few Friday nights helping you sell out the store. And once you're off restriction, we can still take in a late movie."

Christy pulled back from his soft voice in her ear and decided to let him have all the bad news at one time. "Rick, even after I'm off restriction, I still have to be home by ten o'clock. And I didn't get a chance to talk to Jon about changing my hours. I'm also scheduled for eleven to six on Saturdays."

Rick released his hold and looked at her in disbelief. "You agreed to work Saturdays too? All day? What were you thinking, Christy?"

"I needed the job. I told you that."

"Fine, fine!" Rick held up his hands as though he didn't want to touch this topic any longer. "You go ahead and have your job and have your two weeks' restriction. That should give you enough time to figure out where I fit in your life. I've waited too long for us to be together to end up jumping all these hurdles you keep putting in my way."

"Rick..." Christy began, trying to reason with him, but he'd already stalked off, leaving her alone by her car.

She drove home, refusing to cry, and went right to bed. What a mess her life had turned into.

The next morning she showed up at work at ten-thirty, hoping her early arrival would help make up for the extended break the night before.

"Good morning, Jon," she said cheerfully. She had on some of the new clothes Marti had bought her—shorts and a flowered T-shirt. She had taken extra care with her hair and makeup, hoping Rick would come in to see her and that his anger would have evaporated.

"Check out the delivery that came in this morning." Jon motioned toward the back.

Christy found a large wire cage on the floor in the back room holding three adorable cocker spaniel puppies. She unlatched the door and reached for the one with the caramel-colored fur. He eagerly tried to lick her face while his flying tail beat the air like a high-speed wire whisk.

"You are the cutest little thing I've ever seen!" she said. "You look exactly like our old dog Taffy."

"You had a cocker?" Jon asked.

"When I was a kid. She was the sweetest dog. She used to run between the cows' legs when they were being milked. It's a miracle she never got kicked."

"These three are all males. They have their papers, and they should sell pretty fast. Why don't you get the front window ready for them?"

Christy went to work preparing the front window case for the puppies and scooting them into the display one by one. They drew a crowd right away, and Christy's favorite one sold before noon.

"You take good care of this puppy, okay?" Christy said to the little girl squirming with glee as her dad attached the collar and leash. "I had a puppy just like this when I was your age."

"What did you name him?" the girl asked, with a grin that revealed a gap where her two front teeth had been.

"Taffy, because our dog was this color too, and we thought she looked like taffy."

"Can we name our dog Taffy? Please, Daddy? Could we?"

"Whatever you want, Rachel." The dad smiled his approval. "He's all yours now."

"Come here, Taffy." She patted her open palms on her thighs. "Come here."

The cocker jumped up and licked her face before the dad tugged on the leash to get him down.

"He likes me, Daddy!" she squealed. "Taffy likes me. Come on, Taffy."

They made a cute procession—the little girl running ahead, patting her legs, and calling out "Taffy" as the dog scampered toward her, pulling the dad with him.

"Another satisfied customer, I see," Jon said, checking the register's subtotal. "Looks good," he noted, reading the figures. "Why don't you stay on the register until Beverly comes back from lunch, and then it'll be your turn to go."

It seemed the customers came in nonstop. All the business helped Christy keep her mind off Rick.

But during her lunch hour, the loneliness crept back. She went to the mall food court and stood in line to buy a corn dog and lemonade. While she ate, she kept looking around, hoping to see Rick. She saw some girls from school and a family from church, but no Rick.

The rest of the afternoon went by more slowly. When work ended at six, she felt tired and discouraged.

After dinner Mom reminded her it was her turn to do the dishes and fold the laundry. Christy completed her chores silently and with a sour attitude.

Finally, at eight o'clock she had time to herself. She rummaged around in her room for a packet of Victorian Rose bath powder and treated herself to a long, luxurious soak in the tub.

Life is so brutal, she thought, rubbing the animal smells off her tired arms. *Men are so strange. In some ways I wish my parents wouldn't have let me date until I turned seventeen. No, eighteen. My life was so much simpler before I could drive and date. It's terrible being allowed to do both at the same age. Only one more week of restriction, and then when Rick and I date again, hopefully things will be okay with us. We can start fresh. Everything can be dazzling again.*

The next week seemed gobbled up by the homework monster. Christy's junior year was definitely going to be harder than her sophomore year. Thursday night she stayed up until eleven reading for her literature class.

At last she crumpled into bed, thinking, *I wish Rick could have called this week—even though I don't know when I would have had the time to talk to him. I miss him so much. I hope he comes to work tomorrow night.*

By four o'clock Friday afternoon, the last thing Christy wanted to do was go to work. She felt exhausted and wished she could just take a nap. Having slept too late that morning, she hadn't had time to wash her hair and had pulled it back in a ponytail. Her white embroidered cotton shirt got a stain on it at lunch when she spilled some orange juice down the front. She wished she had time to go home and change.

Few customers came to the pet store, so Jon had Christy work in the back, marking prices on cans of cat food. She didn't mind, since she was able to sit on the floor while she worked. But it concerned her that she was hidden from view and wouldn't be able to spot Rick if he came by.

During her break, she sat out in front of the shop and ate a granola bar from the health food store next door. Rick never showed up.

Am I crazy, sitting around waiting for Rick like this? Katie was right. Six months ago, I never would have done this. What changed in me? Whatever it was, I'm not sure I like it. I don't think I've ever felt this lonely or depressed before in my life. I wonder if Rick misses me too, or if he's getting into college life and isn't even thinking about me.

The Saturday shift turned out to be a repeat of the previous Saturday—busy all day. Christy consoled herself by thinking that Rick probably hadn't come home from college that weekend since he knew she would still be on restriction. Tomorrow restriction would end, and then everything would change.

Monday afternoon Rick called about five minutes after she walked in the door from school.

"You're off restriction, right?" were his first words.

"Rick!" Christy headed straight for her bedroom and lowered her voice. "I've missed you so much!"

"I can take care of that. Do I have clearance from head-quarters to come over?"

"Now? Where are you?"

"About three blocks away. I tried to catch you at school, but I wasn't fast enough."

"Hang on a minute. I'll ask my mom if it's okay." Christy left the phone in her room and approached Mom cautiously. "Rick's on the phone. Would it be all right if he came over? I'm off restriction, and I don't have much homework. Could he even stay for dinner, maybe?"

"I suppose it would be all right. We're having spaghetti for dinner. Nothing fancy. Does he like spaghetti?"

"Rick loves Italian food. Thanks, Mom!" Christy felt as if she were flying as she raced back to her room to retrieve the phone. "Sure, Rick. My mom said that would be fine. And can you stay for dinner?"

"Probably not. I have a seven o'clock class tonight, so I'll have to leave by five-thirty to make it back in time. I'll be right over."

"I'll see you in a few minutes." She hung up and raced to her closet. She changed into her favorite pair of shorts and a clean T-shirt. It wasn't her nicest outfit, but it was definitely her most comfortable.

With lightning speed, she did a quick fix on her makeup and hair. *Rick, if I'd known you were coming, I would have spent a lot more time on my hair this morning. Look at me! I'm just thrown together. I look awful! Maybe I should change. These shorts are really old.*

"Christy," Mom called through the bathroom door, "Rick's here."

"I'll be right there." She decided to go as she was and grabbed some perfume from the basket on the counter, then stopped before giving herself a squirt. It was a new bottle of Midnight Gardenia. She used to wear it around

Todd, and he had said it reminded him of Hawaii. No, she definitely could not wear Midnight Gardenia with Rick. Scrounging in the bottom of her makeup bag, she found a tiny sample she had picked up some time ago at the mall. Snapping open the vial, Christy rubbed the heavy, musky fragrance onto her wrists. *Phew! What is this stuff? It's not me at all.*

Anxiously trying to dab it off with a tissue, Christy gave up. *I don't want to make Rick mad by having him wait too long. I'll have to go like this. My hair is a disaster!*

With her heart pounding but a wide smile on her face, Christy made her entrance into the living room. Rick rose from the couch when he saw her and gave one of his I-bet-you're-glad-to-see-me grins.

Did Christy notice a slight twinge of disappointment on his face? Was it because of what she had on? Her hair? She scolded herself for being so paranoid. "Would you like something to drink, Rick?"

"No, actually, I was planning on making a run to 7-Eleven. I already asked your mom, and she said it was fine for us to go as long as I had you back in time for dinner. Shall we?" He offered her his arm and escorted her to the car.

When they pulled into the 7-Eleven parking lot, Christy recognized eight guys out front who were sitting on the hoods of their cars. They were all on the football team and old buddies of Rick's.

Christy felt self-conscious and out of place as the casual introductions were made. The guys all started to joke and talk about things that made no sense to Christy. She was the only girl there.

After about five minutes, Rick pulled some money out

of his pocket and turned to Christy. "You want to go buy me a Big Gulp? Cherry Coke."

What else could she do? Christy took the money and stood in line to buy Rick's Cherry Coke. She felt funny about getting anything for herself, so she didn't. For another half hour they stood by the cars out front. Christy said a total of about seven words. Rick's friends treated her as if she were a nameless, personality-less devoted admirer of his. Last year at school she had avoided this group like the flu. Now she was stuck in the middle of them.

"We have to go," Rick suddenly announced, tossing his cup into the trash and making a perfect shot. "Two points," he said. "See you guys around."

"Bye," Christy said meekly and followed Rick to the car.

"How was your week?" Christy asked, anxious to turn the conversation in her direction after being ignored for so long. "How's school going?"

"Good."

"Do you like your classes and everything?" she ventured, hoping for a more detailed answer.

Rick turned a corner sharply, causing his wheels to squeal. "You sound like my mother, Christy."

"I'm sorry. I've been thinking about you all week and wondered how you were doing, that's all."

"I've been thinking about you too. That's why I came all the way up here this afternoon. I've missed you."

Turning another corner, Rick stopped by a park and shut off the engine. "Here we are. We're going to do number eight on my date list. Play on the swings at the park."

He jogged around, opened her door, and escorted her to the children's play area.

"Rick, this is crazy!" Christy noticed five or six children on the swings. "We can't take the swings away from those little kids."

"Hey, I'm not going to bully them. We'll wait our turn. Look. The merry-go-round is open. Come on, I'll give you a spin."

Those zany, dazzling feelings were beginning to return to Christy. She jumped on the merry-go-round, held on tight, and teased, "Don't go too fast."

"Don't worry. I'll go really slow. Slow as a snail."

Before he had finished his last word, Rick grabbed the metal bar and took off running a tight circle in the sand.

Christy laughed into the wind. "Not so fast!"

Three kids suddenly appeared. "Let us on!" they cried. "Stop. We want a ride."

Rick obliged, bringing the spinning merry-go-round to a halt. Christy took advantage of the opportunity to hop off while the little kids climbed on. She stepped back a few feet, brushing her hair out of her face, and admired Rick's playful nature with the screaming kids as he spun them around and around.

That's my boyfriend. Look at him. What a great guy, playing with the kids like that. Why is it I can feel both wonderful and terrible around him in such a short time? Does he have any idea how much control he has over my feelings?

Christy noticed that the swings were now empty. She positioned herself in the middle one, facing Rick. Slowly she swayed back and forth, watching him and listening to the happy sounds emerging from his spinning fan club.

The September afternoon was clear and sunny, still warm but with a soft breeze blowing in from the ocean,

424 ●●●●● Robin Jones Gunn

which was about fifteen miles west of them. Fall was tiptoeing in on ballet slippers, trying not to disturb the last few
days of summer. Even the air already smelled like autumn.

Rick left the merry-go-round and the band of dizzy
riders and walked toward Christy. With his hand clutching
his chest, he said, "That's my workout for the day."

"You're not done yet," Christy said playfully. "You still
have to push me in the swing. Remember? Number eight
on your list?"

Rick came around behind her and clutched the two
long chains in his strong arms. "Okay, baby. You asked for
it!" He drew her back like a human arrow in a bow and let
her go.

"Whoa!" she shrieked, holding on and feeling herself
take flight.

Rick's push turned gentle when her swing returned to
him. He pressed his hands against her back, and Christy
stretched her legs out in front of her, pointing her toes
toward the blue sky.

She felt silly and carefree. This is how she always imagined it would be to have a boyfriend, and this is how she
wanted it to always be with Rick. Feeling happy and having
fun like this was so much better than the gloom and depression she had battled all week when she wasn't with him.

"This is so much fun, Rick!" she called over her shoulder. "I haven't been on a swing for ages."

"Neither have I," Rick said, leaving his post and confis-
cating the vacant swing next to her. "Let's have a race."

They both pushed toward the sky, higher and higher,
laughing and shouting like kids. Christy's swing chain began
to tug and jerk each time she went up.

She slowed down and said, "Okay, okay, you win."

"As usual," Rick said, slowing to keep pace with her back-to-earth level. "I moved into the apartment with Doug and two other guys."

"Really? How's that working out?" Christy asked as they slowly swung back and forth and caught their breath.

"Okay. Beats the dorms any day. None of us knows how to cook, and we're pretty low on furniture. Other than that, it's fine."

Christy still didn't know how she felt about Rick slipping so easily into Doug's life and taking Todd's place in some ways.

"You haven't told me yet what you've decided," Rick said.

"About what?"

"About work. Have you changed your hours yet?"

Christy swallowed and hoped her answer would satisfy him. "I have to stay on Fridays for at least another month. There's another girl who said she'd work my Saturdays whenever I wanted, because she needs the extra money. I can't give up too many Saturdays, though, because I wouldn't be getting paid enough."

Rick stopped his swing and sat still, kicking the sand. "I had plans for us for this weekend. I guess it means more to me than it does to you for us to be together."

"I can get off this Saturday. What were your plans?" His pouting made her more irritated than nervous.

"Never mind."

"Rick, I'm doing the best I can! Give me a chance. I can get off Saturday, my restriction is over, and I'm as anxious as you are to spend time together. So, come on. Let's work it out."

"All right, let's try this. I wanted to fly kites at the beach, have Mexican food in Carlsbad, and then go to the movies. Think we can do all that, or do you have time limits on your dates?"

"No, of course not. It sounds great. I'll clear everything and let you know as soon as I find out, okay?"

"It's okay for me to start calling you?" Rick asked.

"Yes." Christy felt that everything was going to work out, and already she was eager to spend Saturday with Rick.

"One more race," Rick challenged, kicking off and pushing his swing into high gear.

Christy followed his lead, pointing her toes toward the sky and trying to swing high enough to keep up with her boyfriend.

9

Where's Walter?

After Rick dropped her off, Christy made a few phone calls and arranged to take off from work on Saturday. At dinner, she approached the plan carefully with her parents.

"I don't like the idea of your starting to take off work already," Dad said. "It's okay this time, but I don't think you should do it again except if you're sick or we have something planned as a family."

"It's okay with you, though, if Rick and I spend Saturday together? Going to the beach, dinner in Carlsbad, and to a movie?" Christy wanted to make sure no glitches existed in her weekend plans.

Her mom and dad exchanged glances. "As long as you're back by ten o'clock, it's okay. We're strict about curfew, though. One minute past ten, and you're back on restriction," Dad said.

Christy felt certain they could have an early dinner and find a movie that ended before ten. She couldn't wait to tell Rick everything was clear.

He called the next day after school, and when she told him, he sounded pleased. She felt great.

"I have a surprise for you," Rick said.

"Oh really? What?"

"You'll find out Saturday."

"Can I try to guess?" Christy asked.

"You can try, but it won't do you any good. You'll never guess. You might as well wait and be surprised."

They talked for more than an hour, and then it was time for dinner. Christy moaned when she realized it was her turn to do dishes again. She had let some of her homework from the previous night slide because of spending the afternoon with Rick at the park and being too tired to stay up much past nine. So tonight she had an abundance of reading to do.

It was nearly ten-thirty when Christy decided she couldn't keep her eyes open any longer. She still had four chapters to read and two pages of math. She gave up and went to sleep.

The next morning she felt awful. All day she seemed to be dragging.

At lunch Katie started in with her advice. "If you ask my opinion, you're coming down with something. You have that red look around the eyes."

Things had been tense between them for the past few days, and Katie's comments about how Christy looked didn't help much. Christy had learned to keep their conversations on neutral subjects, like school.

"That's from reading so much," she said. "And I didn't even come close to finishing it all last night. What is with all the homework this year?"

"They're getting us ready for college, didn't you know?" Katie bit into a candy bar. "Have you picked out your poem yet for literature class?"

"No. Have you?"

"I think so. They're all pretty hard to read aloud because of all the thees and thous. I mean, if we're supposed to stand up in front of the class and read one of these romantic masterpieces, you'd think they'd at least give us some written in English."

"They are in English, Katie. Victorian English. That's why they're from the Victorian poetry section, remember?" Christy didn't feel like eating much. This was one of the last warm Indian-summer days, and all she wanted to do was stretch out in the shade and sleep.

"Well, let me know what poem you pick, and tell me if it's easy," Katie said.

Christy stopped by the library on the way home and found a book with some of the suggested poems for class. She checked out the book, went right home, and took a nap. Mom woke her in time for dinner, which Christy ate little of.

"Are you feeling okay, Christy? Do you think you're coming down with something?" Mom placed her cool hand on Christy's forehead.

The hand on the forehead reminded her of something. What was it? *Todd.* Todd's blessing that early morning on the beach.

That tiny memory acted like a key, unlocking a treasure chest of thoughts and feelings. Christy fought to keep it all shut up inside.

"I'm okay," she told her mom. "Just tired out from too much homework, I think. I have a bunch more tonight too."

"I'll help you with the dishes," Mom offered.

They finished up by seven-fifteen, but just as Christy was ready to plunge into the homework pool, Rick called. She curled up with the phone on the end of her bed and let his soothing voice erase her earlier flashes of Todd.

"I miss you," Rick said. "I've been counting the days until Friday. You don't mind if I spend the evening at a certain pet store, do you?"

"As long as I don't get in trouble." Christy couldn't believe how energetic she began to feel as she talked to Rick.

"You know what I miss?" Rick asked. "I miss the smell of your hair."

"My hair? What does my hair smell like?"

"I don't know. It smells fresh, like lemons or something. And I miss the way your hand feels in mine—so soft and little."

Christy looked at her hands as he spoke his gentle words. She never had thought of them as little before. She noticed the nails were chipped on three of her fingers. She made a note to do her nails before Friday. Rick would notice.

He said a handful of sweet, heartwarming things he liked about Christy. When she hung up at nine, she felt like a princess who had just been thoroughly adored. She decided to put off her homework and work on her nails.

On Friday morning she was noticing a spot she had missed, when her literature teacher called out in class, "Christy Miller? Which poem have you selected to read in class next week?"

Christy grabbed the book she had checked out of the library. Quickly running her eyes down the list of Victorian poems, she stopped at one near the bottom of the page because it was written by someone who shared her first name.

"I'm going to read, 'Twice,' by Christina Rossetti." She hoped it was a short poem. Before she had a chance to look it up in the book, the bell rang.

"You didn't tell me you picked a poem," Katie said, joining Christy as they walked into the noisy hall.

"I didn't have one until a minute ago. I just picked it," she confessed. "Where did you find yours?"

"I went for one on the handout. The shortest one. Do you want to hear the first few lines? I have it right here. Tell me if this doesn't remind you of something." Katie held her paper up and read,

> I plucked pink blossoms from mine apple tree
>> And wore them all that evening in my hair:
> Then in due season when I went to see
>> I found no apples there.

Katie looked up at Christy, waiting for her response.

Christy shrugged her shoulders.

"Well?" Katie prodded. "Doesn't it make you think of something?"

"No. What's it supposed to make me think of?"

"Oh, nothing, I guess," Katie said, sticking the paper back in her folder. "Only it made me think of certain people who dance around with blossoms in their hair, not realizing there won't be any apples later."

"What are you trying to tell me?" Christy felt her anger begin to bubble up again. "This is about Rick, isn't it? You've been dying to give me your advice for weeks now.

Why don't you get it over with? What do you have against him?"

Katie's face turned red. "You want to know what I think? Good! I'll tell you. You're making a mammoth mistake going out with him. Rick is bad news. He's going to break your heart. Why couldn't you have gone out with him once and left it at that? Why did you have to break up with Todd and chain yourself to Rick?"

"Katie, it's not like that. I explained all this to you already. I didn't plan on things happening this way. They just happened!"

"Yeah, well, if the blossoms fit, wear them. But don't expect me to feel sorry for you when they die and you discover there are no apples left on your tree!" With a swish of her red hair, Katie turned and marched off to class.

What was that supposed to mean? What's her problem?

Two classes later, Katie stood waiting for Christy at her locker. "I'm sorry," Katie said. "Are you still speaking to me?"

Christy considered snubbing her for an instant but realized that this was her closest friend. She hated arguing with her.

"I just don't understand why you're so against Rick," Christy said, spinning through the combination on her lock. "You're not giving him a chance, and I don't think you're giving me a chance either."

"I know. You're right."

"You don't know Rick like I do. He's a perfect gentleman to me. I'm having a hard enough time with my parents putting me on restriction and trying to get used to a new job without my best friend yelling at me too."

"You're right, Christy. I told you before that I supported you, and I want to. It's just hard because now that you're working and have a boyfriend, you don't seem to have much time left for me."

"Then we'll have to plan on doing something together. I'm not trying to ignore you."

"I know. You have a lot going on. I understand that. We'll have to figure out a time for our slumber party."

"Sure!" Christy agreed, feeling as though things had cleared up between them. "We still have to have our slumber party. Maybe next weekend."

"Okay," Katie agreed. "Next weekend. Definitely next weekend."

As Christy drove to work after school, she thought, *My life is getting so complex. All of a sudden I have no time to do the things I used to.*

She pulled into a gas station and prepared to pump nearly half of her first paycheck into the tank of the car she shared with her mom.

Yes, she sighed as the sickening smell of gasoline filled her nostrils, *life is certainly complex.*

She arrived at work five minutes late and explained to Jon, "I had to buy gas. Have you noticed how expensive gas is lately?"

"Actually, prices are down a little," he said. "Oh, by the way, your boyfriend came by."

Christy stopped and looked at Jon. "My boyfriend?"

How does he know about Rick? He was here only one time. What did Rick do, come in and bully Jon by saying, "Stay away from her, Tarzan. She's mine"?

"Yeah, your boyfriend." Jon had a wry smile on his face, enjoying teasing her.

"Did he say anything?"

"No. He'll be back though. He went into the jewelry store."

Christy was surprised at Jon's perceptiveness. "You don't miss a thing, do you?" she said, feeling free to tease him back a little.

"Nope, not a thing. Do you want to hear what your best friend looks like? You know, the redhead with the poodle named Poopsie?"

Now Christy felt embarrassed. How did Jon notice all these things?

"And I knew you were from a farm when I saw your dad."

"I can't believe you! Do you have radar tracking skills or something?" Christy said, wondering how many other nonchalant things she had done in the store, assuming he wasn't watching.

"After you work here a while, you figure out different types of people. By the way, I have to leave early tonight, so Beverly is going to lock up. I know you're not working tomorrow, but I wanted to make sure you could stay a little after nine tonight in case Beverly needs help closing."

"Okay, that's fine," Christy said.

"Good. Here comes your boyfriend. I'm leaving you at the register. I don't mind if you talk to him, as long as you don't neglect any of the customers. And as long as you don't get into any lovers' quarrels. Tends to be bad for attracting walk-in business." Jon smiled at his own dry humor and took off for the back of the store.

"Hi," Rick said. Checking to make sure no one else was

around, he leaned over the counter and gave Christy a quick kiss on the cheek.

"Hi," Christy said, startled at his greeting.

"I have a surprise for you," Rick said. "But you don't get it until tomorrow. Think you can wait until then?"

"I guess. If I have to. Jon figured out that you were my boyfriend. He said he didn't mind if you hung out as long as it didn't keep me away from the customers."

"Oh, and did you happen to tell him what a wonderful salesperson I am?"

Christy giggled, remembering the night Rick sold the hedgehog and the rabbit. "No, but I'll be sure to mention it when the time is right. Why don't you find some poor unsuspecting person and sell him one of the tropical birds tonight? Those are expensive. Or I know, better yet, why don't you find a new home for Walter? Jon would love you forever."

"Who's Walter?" Rick asked.

"The snake back there. The huge, ugly, neglected one."

"And you're one of his biggest fans, I can tell," Rick teased. Then turning more serious, he said, "I won't be able to sell Walter for you tonight, babe. I'm going for pizza with some of the guys and then to the game. I only stopped by to tell you what time I'm picking you up in the morning."

Christy's heart sank. First she had to give up time with Katie because of her date with Rick, and now he was going to the football game while she worked.

Rick must have read the disappointment in her eyes because he said, "Hey, come on. We'll have all day together tomorrow, remember? I'm going to pick you up at eleven o'clock, so be ready and bring a jacket."

"Okay," she answered, trying to look more cheerful. "I'll be thinking about you all night though."

"You're not going to miss me a bit," Rick teased. "Not when you have Walter and Tarzan to keep you company." He checked again to see that no one was looking and gave her another quick kiss on the other cheek before jetting out the door.

Fortunately it turned out to be a busy evening, and Christy didn't have much time to feel sorry for herself.

Jon left at eight, and Christy had customers at the register right up to nine o'clock. None of them were big sales. Most were small things like fish food and dog bones. She couldn't figure out why on some days they had only a few customers, while on other days, like tonight, the store was packed with people.

At nine, Beverly took hold of the metal door that shut them off from the rest of the mall and pulled it halfway down. "We're closed!" she called to the three kids at the back of the store.

The kids scampered out, laughing and punching each other in the arms.

"A bunch of ten-year-old delinquents," Beverly muttered, closing the door the rest of the way. "Don't they have homes? Where are their parents?"

"Do you want me to do anything else?" Christy asked. "I ran a final total on the cash register and bundled all the checks."

"I can do the rest. Thanks."

Christy got her backpack and said good night.

"Before you go," Beverly called out, "could you check

all the cages? Make sure all the critters are bedded down for the night."

"Sure," Christy called back. She checked all the birds, rabbits, kittens, and puppies. They were all fine. She did a quick check on the fish, lizards, and turtles and was ready to tell Beverly everything was okay when she saw it.

Walter's cage was open, and Walter was gone.

"Bev-er-ly!" Christy yelled, scanning the floor. "Come here, quick!"

Christy ran for the back room and hopped up on a chair, which is where Beverly found her.

"It's Walter," Christy explained. "He's out of his cage."

"Oh no," Beverly groaned. "Now I know why those kids acted like they had some big joke when they left. We have to find him before he slips through the door and gets loose in the mall."

Christy grabbed a broom that was propped up against the wall and cautiously came down from her chair. "You go first."

Beverly stuck close beside her as they slowly made their way down each of the aisles.

"Here, Walter," Beverly called under her breath.

Christy couldn't tell if she was acting nervous or silly.

"Where would he go?" Christy asked.

"Just about anywhere. We probably should get on our hands and knees to look, because he likes tight, dark spots."

"Not me," Christy said. "There's no way I want to get on nose level with that monster."

Just then Walter shot out from under the bags of dog food and slithered under the cash register counter with a speed that surprised Christy.

She screamed, "Get him!" and held the broom over her head.

Beverly yelled, "Don't hit him. I'll try to corner him."

She bravely grabbed a trash can, dumped out its contents, and stepped behind the counter. "Here, Walter, Walter, Walter. Come here, boy."

They could hear a rustling noise like someone trying to open a bag of potato chips and squashing most of the contents in the attempt.

"Come on, Walter. We know you're here somewhere," Beverly said, her nervousness peeking through.

Christy cautiously moved back in case the villain decided to make a run for it in her direction. She scrambled on top of a stack of fifty-pound bags of dog food, using the broom as a support.

All went completely quiet. Too quiet. The only sound was the gurgling of the fish tanks at the back.

"Where is he?" Christy whispered.

"He's not on this side. Can you see anything on your side?"

Stretching her neck and leaning on her broom, Christy bent all the way forward to view the floor by the counter. It was too much strain for the bags of dog food, and the top bag began to slip. Christy tried to stop the landslide, but the broom bristles gave way to the sudden weight. She crashed to the floor, her arms and legs splayed in different directions, with chunks of dog food spilling from the torn bag and raining down her back.

"Are you all right?" Beverly ran over and grabbed Christy by the arm.

Christy groaned and opened her eyes. Then she froze.

Not more than two feet away lay the beast, as frozen as Christy was.

Beverly didn't see him. She continued her first aid survey. "Is anything broken? Can you move at all?"

Before Christy could breathe or even blink an eye, Walter turned and made a slithering getaway through the barred door and out into the mall. Beverly saw him make his escape.

"Oh no!" She jumped up and unlocked the door. "We have to get him!"

Christy, realizing her paralysis had come from fear, not broken vertebrae, pulled herself to her feet and numbly followed Beverly into the empty mall.

"Which way did he go?" Christy asked.

"This way. He's headed toward that big planter," Beverly said, running after him.

When they turned the corner, a security guard yelled out, "Halt right there!" He stood with his feet apart

"It's okay!" Beverly yelled. "We work here. At the pet store. One of our animals escaped, that's all!"

The guard joined them by the planter and asked, "What's loose? One of those frisky rabbits?"

"Not exactly," Beverly said, looking at Christy and then back at the security guard. "It was Walter."

"Walter?" the guard said.

"You know, our fifteen-foot python. Walter." Beverly cautiously peered into the foliage.

"A snake? You two girls let a snake get out? I'm calling for backup." The guard whipped out his walkie-talkie and began to issue commands. His commands included Beverly and Christy. "You young ladies step back. We have animal control coming."

"Make sure they don't hurt him. Jon has had Walter forever, and we'd be in big trouble if anything happened to him," Beverly said.

Several of the other employees who were closing up their shops noticed all the commotion and came out to see what was happening. Within ten minutes, the center of the mall was filled with people. Animal control arrived first, then the fire department with a paramedic backup unit, and a dozen curious onlookers.

After all that, Walter's capture turned out to be uneventful. An older man, dressed in padded gear, stepped into the planter, located Walter, and quickly extracted him with a long pole that had a sort of lasso on the end.

Wiggling his protest, the fifteen-foot runaway was marched back to his cage with a parade of followers. Beverly stayed behind to file a report with mall security, and Christy led the entourage to the pet store.

"Be careful," she warned, noticing the dog food still on the floor.

Walter was returned to his cage, the lock was secured, and for good measure, Christy placed a large bag of aquarium rocks over the top. Then she picked up the broom and went to work, sweeping up the dog food and trying to save as much as possible in a bucket.

Beverly returned, and the two young women laughed away the remainder of their tension.

"Should we tell Jon?" Beverly joked. "Or let him try to figure out why Walter suddenly has such a huge appetite?"

Christy laughed and glanced up at the clock. "Oh no! It's after ten o'clock! I have to call my parents."

Surely her parents would understand why she wasn't home by ten. They wouldn't put her on restriction for this, would they?

"Hello, Dad?"

"Where are you, Christy?"

"I'm still at work. You see, Walter was in the mall—"

"Walter?" Dad interrupted. "I thought you were going out with some guy named Rick."

Christy swallowed her laugh. "Dad, I can explain everything when I get home. I'm leaving right now."

She hung up and, laughing, told Beverly, "My dad thought Walter was my boyfriend!"

Beverly smiled back. "Maybe that's his way of telling you he thinks your boyfriend is a snake."

10

Wild Kites Dancing
in the Wind

Not only were her parents understanding about her getting home so late, but they also entered into the adventure. Mom scooped up bowls of ice cream, and the three of them sat around the kitchen table while Christy described every detail of the great snake escape.

She hadn't noticed it at the time of her tumble, but Mom pointed out a big bruise already blackening above her right elbow. Christy also guessed her knee was bruised from the way it was throbbing.

"Too bad you're not going to work tomorrow," Mom said. "Your boss might have more sympathy if he saw your bruises."

"Why aren't you working tomorrow?" Dad asked.

"I'm going to the beach with Rick to fly kites, remember? You said it was okay."

"Oh, right," Dad said. "I forgot. Flying kites, huh? Where does this guy come up with all these creative ideas?"

Christy explained about Rick's list and how he had wanted to ask her out for almost a year. It felt good telling Mom and Dad about this side of Rick. They couldn't help but think more highly of him for his persistence.

"Is this the same guy who called here on your birthday when you were in Hawaii and wanted your phone number?" Dad asked.

"Yes, that was Rick."

"Where was the kid calling from? Sounded like he was at the end of a long tunnel."

"He was in Italy."

"You mean he called you in Maui, all the way from Italy?" Dad's bushy red-brown eyebrows pushed up. "Maybe we've underestimated this guy."

The next morning Rick called at 11:10 to tell Christy he was running late. She had been ready since 10:30 and didn't feel like waiting around for him much longer.

"When do you think you'll be here?" she asked.

"As soon as I can. Some people dropped by. I can't leave yet, but I'll be over soon."

His "soon" turned out to be after one o'clock. Christy had cleaned her room while waiting, her stomach gurgling its nervous anticipation the whole time. When she heard the doorbell ring, she felt like jerking open the door and ripping into Rick for being so late.

Mom let Rick in, and when Christy joined them, she masked her angry feelings and smiled at him as if nothing were wrong.

"The weather has certainly taken a turn today," Mom said. "Do you still think it's a good idea to go to the beach? It looks like it might rain."

"This is the best time to fly kites," Rick answered, acting cool and confident. "I have a jacket in the car. Did you bring one, Christy?"

"No, I'll go get it."

How can he be so calm after making me wait for hours? I'd better relax or else I'm going to blow this whole day. He's here now, and that's all that matters.

She returned with a jacket and a smile, determined not to let anything ruin their time together. Her dad was now talking with Rick and her mom. Dad acted and sounded like maybe he was warming up to Rick.

"Do you two want something to eat?" Mom asked.

"I thought we'd pick up some sandwiches for lunch, and then I told Christy I'd take her to Felicidades for dinner. They have the best Mexican food in Carlsbad. Have you ever been there?"

"No," Mom answered, "we'll have to try it sometime."

Christy had to admit she felt proud of the way Rick was nice to her parents after they had been so strict about her dating. In her opinion, they had also been downright rude to Rick.

"Have a great time, and we'll see you when you get home," Mom added.

"At ten o'clock," Rick added.

"Or even before ten," Christy's dad said. He was smiling.

It made Christy think of something Dad said last night after their ice cream. He told her that if being a teenager sometimes seemed difficult for her and she felt her parents were too strict, she should remember that they had never before been parents of a teen who could drive and date. Dad said he thought some things were scarier for him than they were for her. It wasn't like he was experienced at all this and had the instant right answers.

As Rick and Christy got into the Mustang, David pedaled his bike to the side of the car. Before Rick could start the motor, David asked, "Where are you going? Can I go?"

Christy was used to David tagging along whenever she and Todd did things together since she wasn't technically old enough to date then. Having David along tended to keep it from being a date. Things were different now. She was on a date with her boyfriend and was about to say, "Sorry, David. Not this time," when Rick answered for her.

"In your dreams, dog breath! Get your own life!" He revved up the engine and screeched down the street.

Christy felt like scolding Rick and telling him he couldn't talk to her brother like that. She also wanted to let him have it for being so late. But she resisted the urge, not wanting to start off their special day with an argument.

Rick opened the conversation. "I should have stayed with you at the pet store last night instead of going to the football game. Vista High beat us again."

"Did you go out afterward or anything?" Christy asked.

"Yeah. The usual place, the usual gang. Not much has changed since last year. Oh, and Renee was all over me until I told her we were going out. She'll probably look you up on Monday." He added in a mumble, "And by then you'll have proof."

Renee and Christy had had major conflicts last spring at cheerleading tryouts, but this year their paths hadn't crossed much yet. Christy had to admit, hearing that Rick had called her his girlfriend in front of Renee felt satisfying.

"You like turkey?" Rick asked, parking in front of a sandwich shop and opening Christy's door for her.

446 ●●●●● Robin Jones Gunn

"I like you, don't I?" she teased, taking his hand and stepping out of the car.

"Oh, cute. Very cute," Rick said, squeezing her hand and pulling it until her arm was around his middle. He wrapped his arm around her waist. "So you think you're funny, huh?" And he proceeded to tickle her mercilessly.

The laughing spell made her glad to be with Rick. They had the rest of the day together, and she wanted to cherish every minute of it. She could forgive him for being so late. After all, he did call and tell her he was running late.

They ate their sandwiches in the car on the way to the beach. As they drove, the sky became more overcast. It definitely did not look like a good day to go to the beach.

Rick parked in a dirt clearing near a precarious cliff that dropped off to the sand below. They put on their jackets and carried their kites down a path to the practically deserted beach.

"This is pretty," Christy said, surveying the long, narrow stretch of sand. "It's so different from Newport Beach. I've never been here before."

"You think we have enough wind for the kites?" Rick fastened the string to the back of his.

The air felt thick and padded. A sliver of sun broke through the heavy clouds and struck the ocean like an iridescent javelin.

Rick handed Christy her kite. "Follow me. We're going to have to give these guys a running start."

Rick held his kite over his head and took off running down the beach. On the second try, his kite was airborne.

Christy followed Rick, and after six attempts, her kite

took off. She let the string reel itself all the way out until the kite was only a colorful little triangle against the gray cotton-ball ceiling.

"That's us," Rick said, looking up. "Two wild kites dancing in the wind."

For a long time they stood side by side, tugging on their strings and watching their kites whip and twist in the air. A few times their strings almost tangled together as the kites lunged toward each other and then pulled away.

"I don't think I've ever flown a kite before," Christy said, trying to link the present with some kind of memory from the past. "I probably did when I was little, but I don't remember. This is really fun."

"So, you think number four was a good choice for today?" Rick said with a grin, referring to his date list.

"A very good choice. Although my arms are starting to feel tired."

"Here," Rick offered, taking her string. "Find us a couple of good rocks, and we'll anchor these guys down."

Christy had plenty of rocks to choose from. She lugged the closest two over to Rick's feet, where he secured the kite strings in the sand.

"That ought to hold them. You want to go for a walk?" Rick offered Christy his hand, and they started down the endless beach.

Feeling secure with her hand in Rick's, Christy opened up more than she had all day and began to tell him about the adventure with Walter the night before.

"Boy, am I sorry I missed all the excitement!" Rick said. "Wish I would have stuck around."

"Me too."

Rick squeezed her hand. "It's been hard seeing you only once a week. I wish we could be together more. You don't have any idea what it means to me to be with you, Christy. I've waited so long to spend moments like this with you."

Rick stopped walking and looked at Christy with his warm brown eyes. "Sometimes I can't believe you're finally mine."

Then he wrapped his arms around her and kissed her.

Christy pulled away slightly, before he had a chance to kiss her again, hoping to catch her breath. As always, Rick came on too fast and too strong for her.

"Oh no, look!" She pointed over his shoulder. "Our kites are taking a dive into the water."

Down the beach, the wind had changed, and both kites were losing altitude rapidly. They took crazy, gyrating swoops toward the incoming surf.

"They're okay." Rick pulled Christy toward him.

"Come on," Christy urged, "we have to save them." She pulled away and started to run down the beach with Rick soon right beside her.

He's mad. I know it. He's mad that I pulled away. I'm still not used to him coming on to me like that. Does he really care about me, or is Katie and everyone else right? Is he going to use me until he's bored and then toss me away?

They reached the kites about the same time, but it was too late. The strings had become entangled, with both kites losing their momentum in the wind. Together they fell to earth at the edge of the shoreline, where the foamy waves rushed up to lick their paper wounds.

Christy examined the ruined bundle and wondered if they could be untangled and repaired. It didn't look too promising. They had crashed pretty hard.

"Well," Rick said lightheartedly, "so much for wild kites dancing in the wind." He gathered them up and wadded them into a crumpled ball.

An unexpected tear slid down Christy's cheek as she watched Rick toss the fragile kites into the metal trash can.

Tostada Surprise

After gathering their belongings and hiking back up the rocky hill, Christy enjoyed the warmth of Rick's car.

He didn't say much as they drove up the coast to Carlsbad. She wanted him to hold her hand and put on some soothing music, but he seemed deep in thought.

The moisture from the ocean mist had turned Rick's dark hair wavy and thick, making him look all the more rugged, like a mountain climber. She liked his hair this way and wondered if she should say something.

"We need to talk before we go to dinner," Rick said. "I want you to tell me everything you're feeling. There's too much that's going unsaid between us, and I want to clear everything up, okay?"

Christy nodded as he glanced at her. They parked in a paved area on a cliff overlooking the ocean. Rick turned off the engine of his Mustang and leaned against the window so he could face Christy.

She couldn't tell from his expression if he was angry or just serious.

"We've known each other about a year," Rick began. "From the first time I met you, I knew you weren't like a lot of other girls. I don't know how you did it, but you got inside my head, and I thought about you all the time. Somebody told me you already had a boyfriend, but then I took a chance and asked you to homecoming, remember?"

Christy smiled. "Yes. I was so embarrassed to have to tell you I couldn't date until I was sixteen—a whole nine months away."

"And do you remember what I told you that day?" Rick's voice matched his soft expression.

Christy felt her heart turn into a marshmallow as she looked into Rick's eyes. "You told me that for a girl like me, you could wait that long."

"I meant it, Christy." Rick reached over and took her hand. "I've waited a long time to have you as my girlfriend. And now every time I try to hold you or kiss you, you pull away. Do you realize that ever since that night when you toilet-papered my house and jumped out of the bushes—man, you sure scared me—you've been running away from me? Why? I'm not going to hurt you. I promise. I only want to be close to you."

He looked as if his heart had turned to marshmallow too. She had never realized Rick cared this deeply about her.

"I need to know why you won't let me hold you and kiss you. What's wrong with a guy showing his girlfriend how much he cares?"

How could Christy answer that? He made it sound so natural and innocent. How could she explain to him that she wanted to feel close to him too, but that his kissing overpowered her? How could he understand her promise to Alissa to do nothing more than light kissing with a guy?

"I want you to open up to me, Christy. Tell me what you're thinking," Rick pleaded, squeezing her hand.

Christy decided to try a question. "This may sound really stupid, Rick, but what is your standard? Do you know what I mean? How far would you go with a girl?"

Rick looked surprised. "What are you getting at, Christy? You think I'm trying to take advantage of you?"

"No, not really." Christy felt embarrassed trying to talk about this with Rick. "I guess I kind of have a standard of not doing anything more than light kissing. And today on the beach, the way I started to feel when you were kissing me was, well, it felt like more than light kissing."

Rick's smile spread across his face. "So I made you feel sick to your stomach again?"

Christy remembered how she had said that the night they parked at a place overlooking Escondido to admire the lights of city. It seemed to make Rick proud that he had such power over her.

"No, it's not that you make me sick to my stomach. I don't know how to explain it." Christy gathered courage to speak her mind. "You see, I love holding hands with you, and when you hug me, I feel warm and protected. Those things feel safe. The reason I keep pulling away, I guess, is because I don't want to go beyond that and get into a situation I can't get out of." The tangled kites came to her mind, but she decided to let her statement stand without adding the example.

"Okay." Rick readjusted his position and acted as if their heart-to-heart discussion had come to an end. "Then that's what we'll do. Hold hands, hug, and kiss lightly."

The way he said it sounded as if he was making fun of her.

Starting the car, he added with a grin, "For now, that is."

Christy didn't know if her openness had given her a victory or had merely postponed a defeat. At any rate she felt better, more settled and at ease with Rick, now that he knew where she drew the line and how she felt about things.

The Mexican restaurant was just beginning to seat guests for dinner. The hostess took them to a plush booth with high wooden backs covered in antique brocade fabric.

A man wearing an embroidered white shirt and a wide orange sash around the waist of his black pants brought them a basket of tortilla chips and filled their water glasses. *"Buenas noches,"* he said.

"Yeah, lots of nachos to you too." Rick scanned the menu. "You have to have the tostada."

"Oh, I do, do I? And who says I have to have a tostada?" Christy asked, her voice light and sassy.

"I do," Rick retorted, equally sassy. "Trust me. You want the tostada."

He slid to the edge of the booth. "I'll be right back. If the waiter comes, order me an iced tea and a number four combination."

Rick disappeared. The waiter appeared. Christy obediently ordered an iced tea and a number four for Rick. She hesitated, then gave in to Rick's directive and ordered a tostada and iced tea for herself.

Does this guy have power over me, or what?

Rick returned, all smiles. "You ordered the tostada, didn't you?"

"Yes, Your Majesty."

"What?" Rick looked startled that she would make such a comment. "You think I'm too demanding or something?"

Christy smiled. "Or something."

He shrugged and reached across the table to hold her hand. "Must be that magnetic force I seem to have over you."

He barely touched his fingers to her hand and made an electrical buzzing sound. "*Bzzzt! Bzzzt!* Oh no, we're making a magnetic connection!" Meshing his fingers through hers, he said, "I can't seem to break loose! Oh no!" He twisted and jerked their linked hands back and forth as if an electrical current had permanently bonded them.

"Stop it," Christy said, smiling at his antics but inwardly feeling crushed that she had opened up her heart to him in the car, and now he was making fun of her for explaining why she had pulled away from him.

Rick relaxed their hands. "Do you know you have the softest hands of any girl I've ever known?"

Rick used his free hand to dip a tortilla chip into the ceramic saucer of salsa and said, "So, what do you want to do tomorrow? You have any great ideas, or should we keep working our way down my list?"

"Would you like to come over for dinner after church?" Christy asked, reaching for a chip.

"I'm not going to church. Didn't I already tell you? My brother and I have a racquetball match at ten o'clock. I could be to your house by one-thirty, though."

It had been so long since Rick had been in church that Christy couldn't even remember the last time she had seen him there. It had to be sometime back in June, before he went to Europe. Each week it was a different excuse. She didn't want to sound like she was scolding him for not going to church anymore, so she said nothing and made a mental note to make sure he went with her next week.

The waiter approached their table with a steaming platter, which he placed in front of Rick. Then with a
particularly toothy grin, the waiter said, "Y señorita, your
tostada."

He set before her a plate heaped with a mountain of
shredded lettuce, capped with a snow peak of sour cream.
Something thick and silvery circled the lettuce just below the
sour cream, catching the light and glimmering at her.

"What's this?" She looked first at the waiter and then at
Rick.

They both grinned like schoolboys with frogs in their
pockets.

"Surprise!" Rick said, removing the silver ID bracelet
from the lettuce mountain. "Let me put it on you."

He wiped off the sour cream with his napkin and placed
the bracelet on Christy's right wrist, fastening the lock to
make certain it was secure.

The waiter left them alone, and Rick, still grinning,
said, "Do you like it?"

Christy looked at the wide silver bracelet now circling
the wrist where for so many months she had worn Todd's
bracelet. This one was thick and heavy. She held it toward
the light and read the inscription in fancy scroll. It said:
RICK.

"Now there's no doubt who your boyfriend is," Rick
said proudly. "You like it, don't you?"

"I'm just surprised, that's all. It's really nice. Thank
you."

"I knew you'd like it better than the other one. A more
than fair trade, I'd say." Rick picked up his fork and

attacked the huge platter of food before him.

That comment hit Christy hard. It didn't just make her angry; it made her furious. Why was Rick so competitive and jealous that he had to replace Todd's bracelet with a bigger and better one, with his own name in bold letters on it?

She moved her tostada mountain around on her plate but didn't eat much of it. Rick barely spoke at all but scarfed down his dinner, using the tortilla chips to scoop up his refried beans and rice.

Finally Christy concluded within herself that replacing the ID bracelet was a guy kind of thing. It apparently made Rick feel more macho, like he had marked his territory, and as he said, everyone would know that he was her boyfriend. Besides, being labeled as Rick's girlfriend wasn't a bad thing at all.

They left the restaurant hand in hand, the bracelet wedged between his hand and hers. It took only ten minutes to drive across the freeway to the Cinema Center, where Rick led her to the box office. Without asking her opinion, he bought two tickets for a movie that was starting in five minutes.

"Good timing, huh?" Rick asked as they stepped out of line and headed for the door to turn in their tickets.

Christy hung back, reading the sign over the ticket window.

"Come on," Rick called to her.

She hurried to catch up, but just before he handed the tickets to the guy at the door, she pulled Rick's arm, drawing him off to the side.

"Rick," she said quietly, "that movie is rated R."

"So? I'm eighteen."

"I'm not."

"You're with me. It doesn't matter. Nobody's going to ask you how old you are. Come on, we're going to miss the show."

"Rick," she said, letting her irritation show, "I can't watch that movie. I have an agreement with my parents that I won't go to R-rated movies."

"You're kidding." He laughed as if she were making a joke.

Christy stood her ground. "I'm serious, Rick."

People were watching their standoff.

"That does it!" Rick threw his hands up in the air. He turned on his heel and stalked toward the parking lot.

Humiliated, Christy followed him to the car, feeling like a puppy with its tail between its legs.

As soon as they reached his car, where there wasn't an audience, Rick started to yell at her. "Why didn't you tell me your little rule before we got here? Why did you have to wait until we were at the door and make me feel like dirt in front of all those people? You are so full of rules, Christy. You're driving me crazy! You can't date until you're sixteen, and then you have unrealistic curfews and get put on restriction for nothing. It's a major effort for you to even find the time to go out with me, and when you do, you have all these rules, as if I'm some kind of monster you have to keep caged up! And now you won't even go to a stupid movie because it violates your perfect standards."

Rick kicked a tire and turned his fierce eyes on Christy. "You're being a baby. That's what you're doing. I know you, Christy. I've watched you for more than a year, and I know you're not a wimp, but you're wimping out on me."

He folded his arms across his chest. "So you'd better decide if you're ready to grow up and experience a real dating relationship or else..."

Christy couldn't contain her fiery emotions any longer. "Or else what? You'll dump me and find some other girl who'll do whatever you want? Is that what you were going to say? Go ahead. Say it."

Rick backed down, breathing heavily through his nose. "That's not what I want, and you know it. I want to go out with you."

Christy's feelings were at an all-time high intensity, and she unleashed them. "You want to go out with me? Are you sure? You want me to be your girlfriend? Because if you do, then this is me! I have standards and rules and restrictions and everything else you just complained about. That is me, and if you want to date me, then you get the whole package, rules and all! I'm not going to change for you or any other guy."

Her whole body was shaking, but she mimicked his tough-guy stance by folding her arms and returning the hard look he had been giving her.

Rick unfolded his arms and stuck his hands in his pockets. He looked down at the pavement and shuffled some pebbles while he appeared to calm down.

Christy calmed down too. She had amazed herself with the words that had spewed out of her mouth, but she didn't regret one of them. For the first time ever with Rick, she felt like he was no longer in control.

"I was right," Rick said, looking at her sheepishly. "You're not a wimp. I shouldn't have blown up like that. I'm sorry."

"I'm sorry too," Christy said automatically. She wasn't sure why she said it because she really wasn't sorry for anything she said. She was sorry they had gone through such a scene though.

Rick opened up his arms, inviting Christy to receive his hug. She willingly stepped into his embrace.

As he held her tightly, he said, "I do want to date you, just the way you are. I don't ever want you to change. You are one of a kind, Killer, and that's the way I want you to stay. I can learn to make a few adjustments, and maybe you can make a few too."

They held each other long enough to feel calmed and restored. Christy lifted her head. "Do you still want to see a movie? There's one playing that's rated G."

"What, that animated one? Are you kidding?"

"No, I'm serious. Come on. It'll be fun," Christy urged.

Rick slowly gave in and walked back to the ticket booth with his arm around her shoulders. "I can see me telling my brother tomorrow on the racquetball court that I took my girlfriend to see a cartoon." Leaning down to speak to the girl in the ticket booth, he said, "Could we trade these two adult tickets for two tickets to the kiddie show?"

With the exchanged tickets in his hand, Rick led Christy to the door once more. Then, as if to make sure the guy collecting the tickets knew who was in control, Rick said, "I mean it, Christy. If I fall asleep in this one, you owe me a refund."

12

A Fair Trade?

Rick delivered Christy to her front door at five minutes to ten and stated for the fifth time that the movie was "sweet."

"I'll be over around one-thirty tomorrow," he said. "Or do you want me to call first?"

"Better call just to make sure it's okay for you to come for lunch. What do you want to do tomorrow?"

"I'll check the list," he said, grasping her by the shoulders and planting a hard, fast kiss on her lips. "You'd better get in there before the clock strikes ten and you turn into a pumpkin for another two weeks."

"Good night, Rick," she called as he jogged to his car. "See you tomorrow."

"Did you have a nice time?" Mom asked when Christy stepped inside.

"Yeah," she answered, not anxious to go into the details of the complicated day or to start answering questions about what the silver bracelet around her wrist meant. "I still have sand in my hair from the beach. I'm going to hop in the shower."

As Christy washed her hair, Rick's bracelet became tangled in it. She ended up yanking out a chunk of hair. Todd's bracelet had never done that.

Thinking of Todd's bracelet made her wonder where she had put it. The last time she saw it was when Rick took it off at the restaurant and she slipped it into her black purse.

After her shower, she pulled the purse out of her drawer and dumped its contents onto her bed. Lipstick, mascara, tissue, a quarter, and a pen. No bracelet. She felt around the inside of the fabric lining to see if it had caught there. Still no bracelet.

She went to the drawer where the purse had been and ran the palm of her hand inside the drawer in case it had fallen out of the purse. No bracelet.

She grabbed the Folgers coffee can off her dresser and emptied out the dried-up carnation petals from the first bouquet Todd had given her, remembering that she had buried the bracelet in there once before. It wasn't there.

What did I do with it? I put it in my purse. Then I left my purse in Rick's car, and he gave it back to me the next night. Could it have fallen out in his car?

Christy worked the purse's clasp back and forth. It was strong and couldn't have opened on its own.

She was beginning to panic. Scooping the dried carnations back into the coffee tin, she hurriedly returned it to its spot on her dresser.

The coffee tin collided with the blue pottery vase, knocking it off her dresser. Hitting the edge of her desk, the vase shattered into a dozen pieces on the floor.

Oh no! Not Rick's vase! How am I going to tell him I broke it?

She gathered up the shards of jagged pottery, wondering if she could glue them back together. The roses had died a week ago, and Christy had tossed them out, not even thinking of saving them the way she had Todd's carnations.

Todd, Rick, flowers, broken vases, lost bracelets—all like the pieces of broken pottery she tried to match up on the floor.

Christy gave up trying to piece the broken vase together and put it all in the trash can. She crawled under her covers and held her stuffed Winnie the Pooh bear that Todd had given her on her fifteenth birthday.

That was the night she had prepared herself for her very first kiss when Todd walked her to the door—only he didn't kiss her. He did kiss her the day he gave her the bouquet of carnations. She was leaving for the airport to go back to Wisconsin, and Todd had kissed her in the middle of the street in front of a whole bunch of people. His kiss had made her feel fresh and free, not like he was trying to "magnetize" her.

For more than an hour she lay with Pooh in her arms, thinking through all the comparisons and differences between Rick and Todd. For so long she had wanted Todd to be the kind of boyfriend Rick was being to her now. Yet Todd would never hold her or pressure her or say things to her the way Rick did.

Now she had what she had wanted for so long—a boyfriend, Rick. Rick adored her so much he even sat through a "kiddie" movie with her. He held her and kissed her and said things that made her feel beautiful. Rick had made a list of possible dates, he had brought her roses, and he had given her a bracelet.

Rick wanted her in his life. Todd had left her. Sure, things were bumpy with Rick, but they kept working at their relationship, and that's what really mattered. Things were getting better. Weren't they?

Even though her relationship with Todd was over, it still bothered her that she couldn't find his bracelet. She couldn't explain why, but that bracelet meant more to her than Rick's did. She had to find it.

Maybe it had fallen on the floor in Rick's car. Maybe Rick had it and just hadn't told her. She decided she would ask him tomorrow.

Christy's parents agreed that Rick could come for lunch, and Mom kept the meal warm in the oven, waiting for him to call.

He finally phoned at two o'clock, saying his racquetball game had run late. He suggested they go ahead and eat since he still had to shower and wouldn't be there for another forty-five minutes or so.

The family ate the dried-out chicken and cool mashed potatoes without much conversation. Dad retired to read the Sunday paper and take his customary snooze on the couch. Christy did the dishes and then went out front to wait for Rick. She didn't want him bounding up the steps and waking her dad.

She had Rick's bracelet in the pocket of her cutoff jeans. She hadn't worn it all day because she wasn't ready to answer the questions it would have raised at church or with her parents.

Christy waited patiently on the top step of the porch. Fall was definitely coming. The night-blooming jasmine that covered the trellis above her head had withered, and the vine was filled with hundreds of tiny brown squiggles where fragrant white flowers had once bloomed.

She could hear Rick's Mustang before she saw it turn the corner of her quiet street. She hurried down to the street to meet it.

"Hi," she said brightly through the open passenger window. "Who won?"

"Do you need to ask? I did, of course. My brother's ticked too. He's three years older than I am, and he hasn't been able to beat me at anything for the last six months."

"I can believe that," Christy said. "My dad's asleep, and I think my mom is sewing. Do you want me to see if we can go somewhere?"

"Sure. We'll go over to my house. Hey, where's my bracelet?"

"In my pocket. I'll be right back." She ran in the house, grabbed a sweatshirt, and asked Mom if she could go to Rick's.

"As long as you're back before six," Mom said. "And do you have any homework you need to finish this weekend?"

She had forgotten all about her mound of homework. "Some. I'll do it when I get back. Bye." She quickly scooted out before Mom had time to say anything else.

Once in the car with Rick, she tied her sweatshirt around her waist and, pulling the bracelet from her pocket, explained how it had become tangled in her hair the night before. A hair strand was still twisted around the clasp.

"Here," Rick said. "I'll put it back on you. You'll have to be more careful when you wash your hair."

Rick locked the clasp and then started the car. They had driven about three blocks toward the expensive side of town, where Rick lived, when Christy decided to ask Rick if he had come across Todd's bracelet.

"Rick, I wanted to ask you something," Christy said cautiously. The last thing she needed was for him to get mad because she was talking about Todd.

"Good." Rick pulled the car into a parking lot behind a complex of doctors' offices. "Because I wanted to ask you something too."

He turned off the car and reached his arms around her, then kissed her slowly and gently. Pulling back, he asked, "How was that for 'light kissing'? I'm getting better, aren't I?"

"Rick," Christy said, thinking she had better talk fast before her emotions clouded, "remember the night we went to that Italian restaurant?"

"You looked gorgeous. I loved you in that black dress."

"Rick, come on! Let me ask this and get it over with. That night you took off my gold ID bracelet, and I put it in my purse. I left my purse in your car. Then you gave it back to me the next night when you drove me home."

Rick leaned against his door. "Yeah, so what?" He sounded defensive.

"I wondered if you saw the bracelet after that. I thought it might have fallen out of my purse onto the floor or something. Have you seen it?"

"You don't need it anymore."

"But I don't like not knowing where it is. I'd feel awful if I lost it."

"Why?" Rick challenged. "Why do you even want to know where it is?"

"Because it's a valuable bracelet, and I don't like to go around misplacing valuable things."

"Calm down." Rick put his arms back around her. "You

don't need to get all upset about such a little thing." He spoke softly in her ear. "You're my girlfriend now. You don't need to worry about that jerk anymore. You have me."

Christy's anger flared. Todd was a lot of things, but he was not a jerk. True, she had called Todd names before in her mind, and *jerk* had been one of them. But that was different. She could call Todd a jerk, but Rick couldn't.

"Pretty good trade, don't you think? Me for Moondoggie. My bracelet for his."

Rick's last phrase played again in her mind like sour organ notes in a monster movie. *My bracelet for his.*

Grabbing his wide shoulders and looking him in the eye, she demanded, "Tell me the truth, Rick Doyle. Did you take my bracelet out of my purse?"

He put on an easygoing grin and said calmly, "Come on, Christy, relax. You didn't need that thing anymore. You have my bracelet now."

"You did! You took my bracelet! You had no right to do that. You can't just go into a girl's purse and take what isn't yours and keep it. How dare you! Where is it? I want it back right now!"

Rick looked shocked at her outburst. Then he opened fire on her. "You know what your problem is? You aren't mature enough to handle a real dating relationship! You want to keep all your childhood trinkets and let a perfect relationship go out the window."

"Where's my bracelet, Rick?" Her voice had changed to a low growl.

He stuck out his jaw and looked away from her.

"Where's my bracelet?"

"You're really making me angry, Christy."

She spoke her words with staccato force. "Where. Is. My. Bracelet?"

"I don't have it, all right?" He drew himself up straight in his seat and pointed his finger at her. "You decide right here, right now. Who's it going to be? Me or that surfer jerk? You decide right now, and that's it! Who's it going to be? Tell me!"

Christy had never seen him this angry, and it terrified her. She acted on impulse, opening her car door and taking off running.

"Fine! Go ahead and run. Only this time, Christy Miller, I'm not running after you!"

Hearing his car start, she ran between the buildings so he couldn't follow her down the sidewalk. She stopped at a bench in the deserted office complex and caught her breath. Once it sounded like his car was gone, she started to walk home.

I can't believe this is happening! Did I do the right thing by jumping out of the car? He's so mad he probably won't speak to me for a week. What if he calls? What will I say? I can't help it! I'm still mad he took Todd's bracelet.

When she reached the front of the office complex, there was Rick leaning against his parked car. "This is crazy. Why are we doing this? Come on, get in the car. Let's talk this through." Rick's voice was calm and persuasive.

Christy stood still, staring at her shoes. She didn't want to get in the car. She felt too shaken to let him smooth this one over.

Without looking up, she calmly restated her question. "Where's my bracelet, Rick?"

"You know," he said in a broken voice, "I thought I was

doing the best thing for us. I really did." He sounded like he was about to cry.

Christy battled with whether she should keep her distance or go to his side and comfort him. She stayed several feet away but spoke softly. "What did you do, Rick?"

"I didn't want anything to come between us. I had no idea that bracelet meant so much to you. I took it to the jewelry store and traded it for the one I gave you."

"You traded it?" Christy said in a whisper. Then with firm, angry words she said, "You had no right to do that."

"I know. I realize that now. At the time I thought it was the best thing for our relationship. I'm sorry."

She couldn't tell if he was truly sorry or only sorry the trade had backfired on him.

"You don't have to compete with everybody in the world, Rick. You don't have to be jealous of Todd. He's thousands of miles away."

"No, he's not. He's still in your head. I can tell. He's competition. He always has been."

"I can't believe this! Rick, I'm dating you, not Todd. Can't you see how much I've wanted to be with you?"

"What is it about him? Why is he still so important to you? Did he write you love poems or make big promises about your future?"

Christy couldn't help but laugh. "No. Todd has never written me a letter or note of any kind. And he is about the most noncommittal person I've ever known."

"Then what's the deal with him? What makes you so drawn to him?"

Christy had to think about it. Rick was right; some kind

of bond existed between her and Todd. How could she explain it?

"I think it's the Lord," Christy said finally. "I think what makes Todd unique is that he prays with me and—"

"We can pray. Is that what you want?"

Christy realized that during the entire time she had known Rick and had been dating him, they had never prayed or even talked about the Lord or spiritual things. "Yeah, I'd like it a lot if we prayed together. But it's not just that. It's…"

In trying to find the words to explain Todd's uniqueness, she remembered how Todd would look when he talked about God. It was a contented, vulnerable, strong-as-a-rock look. That was it. Todd loved Jesus more than anything. How could she explain that to Rick?

"Come here." Rick held out his right hand. "Do you want to try praying with me?"

Christy placed her hands in his. Rick bowed his head and closed his eyes. "Our almighty heavenly Father, we come to You asking for strength and direction in our relationship. Please grant us Your blessing and help us to work through all our problems. Amen."

He lifted his head and looked at her like a little kid waiting for approval. It wasn't anything at all like the way Todd prayed. Nothing about Rick was like Todd. She suddenly realized nothing ever would be. Rick was Rick. Did she really want to be his girlfriend?

"Do you want to go over to my house now? We can pretend all of this never happened and start over," Rick said.

"Actually…" Christy forced herself to finish her sentence before she chickened out. "I think we should break up."

Rick looked at her as if she had told a bad joke. "But we just prayed. And I told you I was sorry about the bracelet. Why would you want to break up?"

"Because I don't think I'm ready to be your girlfriend. I don't think I'm ready to be anybody's girlfriend. I want to go back to being your friend. We got along so much better when we were friends."

Rick ran his fingers through his hair and looked frantic. "I don't get it. I'm trying to do everything right. I've never, ever tried this hard with any girl before. What am I doing wrong?"

"It's not you. It's me. You've said it a couple of times: I'm not ready to have a serious dating relationship. I'd like to slow everything down. It seems like you went from being my buddy to my boyfriend overnight, and that's too fast for me. I think it would be better if we built up our relationship slowly."

"We have been building it up slowly," Rick said. "Or did you forget the nine months I waited to date you?"

"That's exactly it though. I thought you were waiting to date me, not possess me. I'm not ready to go steady—with anybody. I need time for myself, and I want to spend time with my girlfriends without feeling that I have to ask your permission."

Christy thought of other things she wanted to say, but Rick looked so wounded she decided to stop there. He obviously got the point. It surprised her how calm and peaceful she felt for someone who had just broken up with her boyfriend, especially since none of this had been planned or decided ahead of time.

"You know," Rick said, drawing himself up to his full

height and looking down on Christy, "I have a lot of pressures on me with starting college and all. I think we should slow things down and give each other a chance to catch up with everything in our lives. I don't know when I'll be back up here for the weekend. Thanksgiving, probably not before. I'll give you a call then. Maybe we can get together and go somewhere just to talk. The time will give us a chance to reevaluate our relationship."

Christy thought it was kind of funny to watch Rick take control of the situation, speaking smooth words like the closing lines of a movie. The way he restated everything, it sounded like he was the one breaking up with her.

"I'll look forward to your call."

Rick looked at her as though she were patronizing him.

"No really, I will! We still have a whole list of dates that you thought up, remember? And I'd like to go on them with you. We can take them one at a time instead of trying to do them all in one week."

Christy tried to sound as light and positive as she could because her emotions were catching up with her prior burst of logic, and she felt a major storm brewing inside.

"I think you should have the bracelet back. I'm always going to be your friend, Rick. But I can't be your girlfriend right now. Could you help me take it off?"

Rick picked the clasp with his thumb and held the bracelet in his fist. "I'm holding on to this," he said tenderly, "because I still think it belongs on your wrist. One day I want to put it back there."

His last statement felt like a clap of thunder, releasing the storm inside Christy. She lowered her head as tears fell on the pavement.

"Can I give my friend a hug?" Rick asked.

Christy nodded without looking up.

He wrapped his big arms around her and hugged her good-bye.

13

Twice

Monday morning Christy wanted to stay in bed and skip school. She hadn't touched her homework all weekend, and she was emotionally exhausted. How could she convince Mom that she was sick and needed to stay home?

Her mother saw right through Christy's scheme and gave her twenty minutes to get dressed and out the door.

Christy threw on a sweater and jeans and pulled back her hair in a braid. This was definitely not going to be one of her more glamorous days.

She slid through the first two classes, begging extended time on one of her homework assignments. In third period she wasn't so fortunate.

"Today, class," her literature teacher began, "we shall start our readings of the Victorian poems you've selected. Our first reader will be Christy Miller."

"I left my book in my locker," Christy answered, hoping she could get off the hook.

"That's half a grade off. Take a hall pass to get your book, and let's see if you can manage a passing grade. While Christy gets her book, does anyone else have to retrieve a book from his or her locker?"

When Christy returned to class, another girl was reading her selection, tripping over the *thees* and *thous*.

Christy had barely found the right page when the
teacher called on her to stand and read. She wished she
would have at least looked the poem over before having to
read it in front of the class—especially on a day when she
looked and felt so yucky.

"'Twice,' by Christina Rossetti," Christy began and then
read,

I took my heart in my hand
   (O my love, O my love),
I said: Let me fall or stand,
   Let me live or die,
But this once hear me speak—
   (O my love, O my love)—
Yet a woman's words are weak;
   You should speak, not I.
You took my heart in your hand
   With a friendly smile,
With a critical eye you scanned,
   Then set it down,
And said: It is still unripe,
   Better wait a while;
Wait while the skylarks pipe,
   Till the corn grows brown.
As you set it down it broke—
   Broke, but I did not wince;
I smiled at the speech you spoke,
   At your judgment that I heard:
But I have not often smiled
   Since then, nor questioned since,

Nor cared for corn-flowers wild,
    Nor sung with the singing bird.
I take my heart in my hand,
    O my God, O my God,
My broken heart in my hand:
    Thou hast seen, judge Thou.
My hope was written on sand,
    O my God, O my God;
Now let Thy judgment stand—
    Yea, judge me now.
This condemned of a man,
    This marred one heedless day,
This heart take Thou to scan
    Both within and without:
Refine with fire its gold,
    Purge Thou its dross away—
Yea hold it in Thy hold,
    Whence none can pluck it out.
I take my heart in my hand—
    I shall not die, but live—
Before Thy face I stand;
    I, for Thou callest such:
All that I have I bring,
    All that I am I give,
Smile Thou and I shall sing,
    But shall not question much.

At about the fourth line of her reading, Christy had
realized how similar this poem was to all that she had been
through with Todd and Rick during the last month. She had
chosen the poem from the list because it was written by a
Christina. But now she knew it wasn't an accident. Katie
would call this a God-thing.

With a heartfelt interest in the poem, Christy read with tearful intensity, as though she had practiced the reading all weekend. And in a way, maybe she had.

When she finished, her teacher stood up and, clasping her hands together, said, "Now that is an exceptional reading! Thank you, Christy, thank you!"

When the bell rang and the students herded through the hall, Katie caught up to Christy. "When did you have time to practice your reading? I thought you were with Rick all weekend."

"I didn't practice. I lived it." As generally as possible, Christy gave Katie a quick rundown on the weekend.

"So you can be happy that I'm no longer going out with Rick since you never did like us being together."

"That wasn't it," Katie protested. "I didn't want him breaking your heart, that's all. I'm glad you broke up with him instead of the other way around. I will admit that. I just didn't want to see you hurt."

"Then close your eyes," Christy said, "because I'm hurt."

After school she called her mom and asked if she could go to the mall to pick up her paycheck, since she hadn't worked Saturday. Even though Christy did want her paycheck, she had another reason for going. She entered the mall and headed straight for the jewelry store.

"May I help you?" asked an older balding man behind the counter.

"I hope so," Christy said. "A week or so ago, a guy named Rick Doyle came in here and traded in a small gold ID bracelet. He bought a silver one instead. I was wondering if, by any chance, you still have the gold bracelet."

"Let me check." The man disappeared into the back of the shop.

When he returned, he had a long, thin box in his hand. Opening up the velvet-lined case, he held the bracelet for her to see. "Is this it?"

Christy's heart jumped, as if she'd spotted an old friend in a crowd. "Yes, that's it. I can't believe you still have it! May I have it back? I mean, I'd like to buy it back."

"I'm sure we can arrange that," the man said, checking the tag now attached to the chain. "That will be $145.50, plus tax."

"A hundred and forty-five dollars? That can't be right!"

"This is a valuable bracelet, miss."

"You're telling me," she mumbled.

"Apparently, it was handmade. We've checked all our manufacturers' catalogs, and this is not a standard issue. That doubles the price. Plus it's 24-karat gold, not the usual 14-karat. It's one of a kind."

Christy tried to respond as graciously as possible. "I know it is, sir. You see, that is my bracelet. The guy I mentioned earlier stole it out of my purse and brought it to you without my knowing about it. He gave me a silver one to replace it, but it's just not the same."

"I see," the man said. "And have you reported this theft to the proper authorities? We do have a procedure we can follow for this sort of thing if you haven't already pressed charges."

Christy had to admit that for one minute it was tempting to press charges against Rick. "No, I haven't reported it, and I don't think I want to. I'd simply like my bracelet back."

"Did you bring in the silver one to exchange?"

"No, I don't have that one."

"How would you like to pay for this, then? Cash, check, or charge?" The man looked as if he knew she had none of them to offer.

"I'd like to pay cash, but I don't have enough yet," Christy explained.

"I see." The man snapped the case shut on the bracelet.

"I work across the mall at the pet store, and I get paid every Saturday. Could I put some money down on the bracelet today and then every week pay what I can until it's all paid for?" Christy tried to look as sincere as possible so the man would see she meant business.

"We could do a layaway for you. We would need 10 percent today, and you could continue to make payments until it's paid off."

"Okay," Christy agreed, mentally calculating what 10 percent would be. "I'll go cash my check and be right back."

"Fine. I'll hold the bracelet for you."

The rest of the week dragged by slowly, silently. The phone didn't ring, her parents asked few questions, and Christy spent each afternoon and evening buried in homework.

Her heart and mind continually battled over Rick.

Why did I ever break up with him? We could have worked it out. Every couple has problems. Why did I push him away? Am I just running from him again, or did I really do the right thing?

Of course I did the right thing! Our relationship was headed down the wrong road, and the farther I would have walked down that road with Rick, the longer and harder it would have been to get back.

But back to what? Todd?

This is all a cruel joke. Here I am, finally old enough to date, and the only two guys I ever cared about I've pushed right out of my life.

The biggest blow came on Wednesday when Renee, the cheerleader Rick had mentioned over the weekend, came marching up to Christy at lunch. She had two of her friends with her.

Tapping Christy on the shoulder, she said, "So, let's see your proof."

"What are you talking about?" Christy asked.

"Yeah," Katie jumped in to defend Christy.

"I want to see your proof. Rick said you two were going out, and I told him I'd believe it when I saw it. He told me to find you this week, and you'd have evidence."

Katie interrupted, apparently trying to protect Christy. "It's not any of your business who Christy is going out with."

"You're not going out with him, are you?" Renee taunted. "Rick has been after you for so long that he's having hallucinations that he's going out with you. Why don't you tell Rick to wake up and start dating someone who's more his style—like me."

"Rick is free to date whoever he wants," Christy said quietly.

"So you're not going out with him, are you?" Renee turned to the girls with her. "See? I told you guys. I knew it all along."

"Well, for your information—" Katie began.

"Katie." Christy tried to stop her, but it was no use.

"Christy and Rick were together. The evidence was a very expensive bracelet he gave her on one of their many dates out to dinner at expensive restaurants." Katie picked up steam. "But Christy gave it back to him and broke up with him because she saw right through that egotistical jerk!"

Oh Katie, I wish you would've kept your mouth shut.

Renee looked at Christy in disbelief. "You mean you had him? You had Rick Doyle in the palm of your hand, and you let him go?"

"It was a mutual decision," Christy said softly.

A smug looked crossed Renee's face. "You don't have to explain it to me. You'll get over him. And hey, if you're going to wait until you're sixteen to lose your virginity, it might as well be with a guy like Rick...even if he did dump you once he got what he wanted."

Christy and Katie both shot up from the picnic table like twin rockets and faced Renee.

"I did not lose my virginity," Christy said, her words flaming hot.

"Not that it's any of your business," Katie said.

Renee laughed at them. "You mean you didn't do it with Rick? I can't believe you're such a loser! What is your problem, Christy?"

"You're the one with the problem, Renee," Katie popped off.

Then Christy said firmly, "The way I see it, Renee, you're the loser. You see, I can become like you anytime, not that I want to. But you can never become a virgin again like me."

Christy thought Renee was going to slap her, but she spun around and marched off.

Katie and Christy sat back down and exchanged looks that said, "Can you believe what just happened?" Christy felt yucky inside. She was normally a private person, yet during the past few days she'd yelled at Rick in a parking lot, and now she'd blasted Renee in public. This was not the way Christy wanted to handle her relationships.

Katie kept muttering about Renee and how she acted like the world revolved around her. Christy closed her eyes and wished all this confronting and criticizing would just go away.

It took several days before all the uncomfortable feelings started to go away. By the week's end, it turned out to be a good thing that Christy had to work Friday and Saturday. The routine of the pet store helped keep her preoccupied and made her feel more emotionally stable.

The store was busy all day Saturday. Christy sold twenty-five tropical fish to one man who said he had a six-foot aquarium at home. On her break, Christy cashed her check and went to the jewelry store to make another payment on her bracelet. The check had been very small since she hadn't worked the previous Saturday.

"I only have twenty-one dollars to put toward my bracelet this week," Christy explained to the salesman. "I'll have the usual amount next week. I hope it's okay."

"Yes, it's fine. I checked with Jon, and he told me you're a dependable employee."

Christy smiled her thanks. "So after this payment, how much more do I owe?"

The man scribbled on a piece of paper. "At this rate, you could have it paid for by Thanksgiving."

"Good," Christy said, remembering that Rick had said he would be home at Thanksgiving. Maybe, just maybe, Todd would be home for the holiday too. "I'd like to have it back on my wrist by then."

When work ended, Christy had to swing past the library to return her poetry book. The night before she had copied the poem "Twice" into her diary and thought again of how she had felt that morning on the beach when she offered her heart to Todd and he set it down, telling her it was not yet "ripe."

I wonder what she was like, the Christina who wrote that poem? I wonder who the guy was who broke her heart? It's weird to think she lived more than a hundred years ago yet the same things she felt are what I'm feeling now.

Christy was a few blocks from the library when she noticed she was driving right by the park Rick had taken her to. It was after six o'clock, and the playground was empty. On impulse, she pulled into the parking lot, parked the car, and made her way through the sand to the empty swings.

At first she sat in a swing, just rocking back and forth slowly, etching circles in the sand with her tennis shoes.

A gentle autumn breeze rustled the trees, sending a flurry of dancing leaves into the air. Several of them fluttered down to Christy's feet. The once-green leaves had changed to a smear of oranges, yellows, and reds.

"We're changing, that's all. We're both changing." Todd's words from that morning on the beach came back to her as she picked up one of the leaves and examined it more closely.

The tree isn't dead; it's just changing. There will be new growth in the spring. Maybe that's how it'll be for Todd and me.

Christy let the leaf go. A puff of wind caught it and carried it spinning through the air until it landed on the grass.

"Father," she prayed in a whisper, "You know how much thinking I've been doing this past week. I keep coming to the same conclusion. I need to fall in love with You. I need to be content with just You as my first love. I'm not ready for a steady relationship with any guy until I'm first secure in my love for You.

"I want to love You with all my heart, soul, strength, and mind. I want to be more in love with You than I've ever been in love with anyone or anything. What did that poem say? 'All that I have I bring. All that I am I give. Smile Thou, and I shall sing but shall not question much.'"

As she prayed, Christy was slowly pumping her legs out and back. Without realizing it, she had gained altitude and was swinging pretty high. When the swing went forward, she hit a spot where the evening sun sliced through the trees and shot a beam of golden light on her face.

Up and back, up and back. Each time she swung forward, the sun shone on her face.

"The Lord make His face to shine upon you..." Those were Todd's words—his blessing.

In an amazing way, it was coming true. Christy felt as if the Lord's face was shining on her. And now that she thought about it, God had given her His peace.

What was that last part of Todd's blessing? Something about loving the Lord above all else.

For the first time all week, a smile found its way to Christy's lips. She pushed herself higher and higher in the swing until she felt the exhilarating rush of the wind through her hair. Then pointing her toes out straight and leaning back in the soaring swing, Christy sang out a spontaneous love song to the Lord of forever as her heart filled with hope.

Can't get enough of ROBIN JONES GUNN!

Christy Miller
COLLECTION

● ● ● ● ● ● **VOLUME 1**

Book 1: Summer Promise
Fourteen-year-old Christy Miller has the dream summer ahead of her in sun-kissed California , staying with her aunt and uncle at their beachfront home. Aunt Marti loves to shop, and those surfers are cute—especially Todd. Christy promised her parents she wouldn't do anything she'd regret later, and some of her beach friends are a little wild. But Todd and his "God-Lover" friends are giving Christy a new image of all things eternal. Can this summer live up to its promise?

Book 2: A Whisper and a Wish
Christy's family has moved to California just in time for her sophomore year of high school. But they're not in Newport Beach, where she spent the summer. Instead they're an hour and a half away and Christy has to start all over making friends. Despite an embarrassing escapade at a slumber party, things are going pretty well...until some midnight fun leads to a trip to the police station. Does God really hear every whisper? Does He know our every wish? Then why is it so hard to know who your friends really are?

Book 3: Yours Forever
Christy is back at Aunt Marti and Uncle Bob's house on the beach for the entire week between Christmas and New Year's...and Todd is in town, too! The cute surfer completely captured Christy's heart last summer, and she's eager to spend every possible minute with him. But soon Christy and her aunt are barely speaking, and it seems like all her friends are mad at her, too—including Todd! Is he hers or isn't he? And why would God let things get so tangled?

Available Now
ISBN: 978-1-59052-584-5

www.ChristyMillerAndFriends.com

Christy Miller

COLLECTION

●●●●●● VOLUME 3

Book 7: True Friends

When Christy finds herself on a ski slope in Lake Tahoe in the arms of a handsome ski instructor, she is suddenly pulled into the "in" crowd, while Katie is left out. And when Katie discovers some of the kids are up to no good, she expects Christy to help expose them rather than support her newfound friends. Can Christy and Katie patch up their damaged friendship?

Book 8: Starry Night

When Christy's ex-boyfriend, Rick, seems interested in Katie, Christy and Katie's relationship changes. Then an old friendship takes on new meaning, and Christy wonders why she never before saw Doug as the prince he is. All of these relationships collide, leaving Christy wondering what is happening. Will she end up counting stars with Rick or Doug?

Book 9: Seventeen Wishes

Working as a camp counselor is not how Christy envisioned spending her summer. Before long, she is up to her ears with kids who won't obey her, camp rules to remember, and an embarrassing incident that makes her the camp joke. Then a moonlight canoe cruise with a handsome counselor leads Christy to make some decisions about her future and trust that God knows what's best for her. What will she be wishing as she blows out the candles on her birthday cake?

Available Now
ISBN 978-1-59052-586-9

Christy Miller
COLLECTION

●●●●●● VOLUME 4

Book 10: A Time to Cherish
Juggling the stress of not having enough time with Todd, trying to understand Katie's relationship with Michael, and making Doug happy forces Christy to evaluate what's most important to her. Can Christy find a way to keep her friendship with Katie even though they're not in agreement on much anymore?

Book 11: Sweet Dreams
Christy is relieved her senior year is over. She and Katie have made up, and Christy's dreams of growing closer to Todd are coming true. Suddenly, Christy finds herself having to make what might be the most difficult decision of her life—one that could end every sweet dream she ever possessed. Will Christy find the strength to do what she knows is right?

Book 12: A Promise Is Forever
On a European mission trip with her friends, Christy can just see herself traveling across different countries and talking to new friends, like Sierra Jensen. But when tensions among the group set in, memories of Todd constantly swim in Christy's mind. Then she's sent to Spain alone while her friends travel elsewhere. Will Christy face her fears of the future? And can she truly trust that God has great things planned for her even when all seems lost?

Available Now
ISBN: 978-1-59052-587-6

THE GLENBROOKE SERIES

by Robin Jones Gunn

COME TO GLENBROOKE...

A QUIET PLACE WHERE SOULS ARE REFRESHED

SECRETS *Glenbrooke Series #1*

Beginning her new life in a small Oregon town, high school English teacher Jessica Morgan tries desperately to hide the details of her past.

978-1-59052-240-0

WHISPERS *Glenbrooke Series #2*

Teri went to Maui hoping to start a relationship with one special man. But romance becomes much more complicated when she finds herself pursued by three.

978-1-59052-192-2

ECHOES *Glenbrooke Series #3*

Lauren Phillips "connects" on the Internet with a man known only as "K.C." Is she willing to risk everything...including another broken heart?

978-1-59052-193-9

SUNSETS *Glenbrooke Series #4*

Alissa loves her new job as a Pasadena travel agent. Will an abrupt meeting with a stranger in an espresso shop leave her feeling that all men are like the one she's been hurt by recently?

978-1-59052-238-7

CLOUDS *Glenbrooke Series #5*

After Shelly Graham and her old boyfriend cross paths in Germany, both must face the truth about their feelings.

978-1-59052-230-1

WATERFALLS *Glenbrooke Series #6*

Meri thinks she's finally met the man of her dreams...until she finds out he's movie star Jacob Wilde, promptly puts her foot in her mouth, and ruins everything.

978-1-59052-231-8

WOODLANDS *Glenbrooke Series #7*

Leah Hudson has the gift of giving, but questions her own motives, and God's purposes, when she meets a man she prays will love her just for herself.

978-1-59052-237-0

WILDFLOWERS *Glenbrooke Series #8*

Gena Ahrens has invested lots of time and money in renovating the Wallflower Restaurant. Now her heart needs the same attention.

978-1-59052-239-4

Don't Miss the Next Chapter in Christy Miller's Unforgettable Life!

Follow Christy and Todd through the struggles, lessons, and changes that life in college will bring. Concentrating on her studies, Christy spends a year abroad in Europe and returns to campus at Rancho Corona University. Will Todd be waiting for her? CHRISTY AND TODD: THE COLLEGE YEARS follows Christy into her next chapter as she makes decisions about life and love.

CHRISTY AND TODD: THE COLLEGE YEARS by Robin Jones Gunn

Until Tomorrow • As You Wish • I Promise

The Sierra Jensen Collection
Excerpt from book 1—
Only You, Sierra

Sierra Jensen gazed out the train window at the cold, wet English countryside. In an hour she and her friends would be back at Carnforth Hall with the other ministry teams that had spent the past week in various European countries. Endless pastures, frosted with winter's ice, flashed past her window. Sierra sighed.

"What are you thinking?" Katie asked, uncurling from her comfy position on the train seat next to Sierra. Even though Katie was two years older than Sierra and they had met only two weeks ago, they had become close during the week they had just spent together in Belfast, Northern Ireland.

"About going back to the States." Sierra smiled her wide, easy smile at Katie, but she was really looking past her. Across the aisle from them, their team leader, Doug, was sitting next to his girlfriend, Tracy.

Katie folded her arms and settled back against the upholstered seat. "I'm not ready to go home yet. I'd like to come back. Maybe next summer."

Sierra noticed Tracy tilt her heart-shaped faced toward Doug's, giving him a delicate smile that, by the look on his face, melted him to the core.

Katie looked over her shoulder to see what had distracted Sierra. Turning back to Sierra, Katie leaned forward and whispered, "Don't they just make you sick?"

"Katie," Sierra said in a hushed voice. "I thought you

guys were all best friends. Why would it make you sick to see those two together?"

"It's just… well, look at them! They're totally in love."

"I know." Sierra cast another glance at the couple, now talking softly and looking deeply into each other's eyes. "I can't imagine ever being in Tracy's place and having a guy look at me like that."

"Are you kidding?" Katie's bright green eyes did a quick head-to-toe scan of Sierra. "Have you ever looked in a mirror, girl? First, you have the hair going for you. You have great hair! Wild, blond, curly. Very exotic."

"Haven't you noticed?" Sierra tugged at a curly loop of her long hair. "Straight, sleek hair happens to be in right now."

"Oh sure, this week. Wait a few days. Everyone will be running out for perms so they can look just like you. And your smile happens to be award-winning. Fantastic clothes. And I don't ever want to hear you complain about your body."

"What body? I'm shaped like a tomboy."

"Better to be shaped like a tomboy than a fullback."

"You're not shaped like a fullback," Sierra protested.

"Okay, a halfback."

"You're both beautiful," Stephen, the German guy on their team, inserted into the conversation. He was sitting directly across from them and had appeared to be sleeping.

Sierra blushed. He was the oldest one of their group, and his beard added to his older appearance.

"Why do women find it a sport to criticize themselves to their friends?" Stephen leaned forward. "You both are gorgeous young women on the outside and fantastically beautiful here—" he patted his heart— "where it really counts."

"Then you tell us why all the guys aren't falling at our feet."

"Is that what you want, Katie?" In an uncharacteristic move, Stephen tumbled to the floor and bowed at their feet.

Sierra burst out laughing.

"Get out of here!" Katie said. "You're making this a joke, and I'm serious."

Stephen returned to his seat, a satisfied little grin across his usually serious face.

"You're a guy. Tell us what you're attracted to in a girl," Katie said.

Stephen glanced at Tracy, then back at Sierra and Katie. "Well," he began, but it was too late. His unspoken message seemed clear.

Katie threw her hands up in the air. "I knew it! You don't have to say anything. You men are all alike! You all *say* it's the personality and what's on the inside that counts. But the truth is, your first choice every time is the Tracy type— the sweet, helpful, cute ones. Admit it! There's little hope in this world for the few individualists like Sierra and me."

"On the contrary. You're both very attractive. To the right man, you will be a treasure. You just need to wait on God."

"I know, I know," Katie said. "And until then, we have our own little club, don't we, Sierra?"

She and Katie had formed the Pals Only Club at the beginning of their trip. She slapped Katie a high five and said, "P.O. forever!"

"That's right," Katie said. "We may have lost Tracy, but it's you, me, and Christy from here on out."

"You women do not need a little club," Stephen said. "Perhaps a caveman with a big club might be helpful..."

Instead of laughing at his joke, the girls gave Stephen a tandem groan and twisted their expressions into unappreciative scowls. He folded his arms against his chest, closed his eyes, and pretended to go back to sleep. But a crooked grin was on his lips.

"Come on," Katie said. "Let's get something to drink."

Sierra followed her down the rocking aisle that led to the back of the train car. They passed through the sliding doors and headed for the compact snack bar at the end of next car. After buying Cokes, they stood to the side by the closed windows.

"Guys like Stephen really bug me," Katie said. "First they're all sweet and full of compliment, and then they make stupid jokes. You never know if they're serious about all the nice stuff or not. Enough talk about guys. Let's talk about something else."

"It'll be great to see all the other teams tonight and hear about everything that happened to them."

"Yeah." Katie agreed. "I can't wait to hear about Christy's week in Spain."

"I still can't believe they pulled her off our team at the last minute and sent her all the way to Spain after the rest of the Spanish team had already left. I don't think I could have done what she did, traveling all by herself for two days and then joining up with a team of people she barely knew."

"It's like I kept saying," Katie said, making a muscle-man pose, "she is Missionary Woman."

Sierra smiled. "I felt as if I was just getting closer to her, and then they shipped her off on a moment's notice. It must have been even harder for you to see her leave like that, since you guys have been best friends for so long."

"I'm sure it was a God-thing." Katie finished her drink and tossed her can into the trash can.

Sierra thought about how much had happened during their week of ministry at the church in Belfast. Sierra and Katie had worked with the children, had performed in a drama group, had gone out street witnessing, had prayed with teenagers when they said they wanted to give their lives God, and had visited some elderly women of the church who treated them to tea and cakes. It had been a life-changing experience for Sierra, and she was glad Katie had buddied up with her.

"You know," Katie said as they headed back to their seats, "I'm sure God had a reason for taking Christy off our team. If nothing else, it let me get to know you, and I'm really glad for that."

"I am too," said Sierra. "I'm just starting to feel depressed now that it's almost over."

"Not so fast! We have two more days before we have to leave," Katie pointed out.

"Next stop is ours," Stephen said when they reached their seats.

Sierra fought off the sadness that crept in when she realized the next time she boarded a train in England it would be to go home. Something caught in her throat every time she thought about returning to the States.

She hadn't been able to talk about it to Katie or anyone else. Maybe she should. Whenever she mentioned her situation, it had been with her usually cheerful, adventuresome spirit. No one knew that deep down she was nervous, knowing that everything in her life was going to be different when she returned home.

About the Author

Just like Christy, Robin Jones Gunn was born in Wisconsin and lived on a dairy farm. Her father was a school teacher and moved his family to southern California when Robin was five years old. She grew up in Orange County with one older sister and one younger brother. The three Jones kids graduated from Santa Ana High School and spent their summers on the beach with a bunch of wonderful "God-lover" friends. Robin didn't meet her "Todd" until after she'd gone to Biola University for two years and had an unforgettable season in Europe, which included transporting Bibles to underground churches in the former Soviet Union and attending Capernwray Bible School in Austria.

As her passion for ministering to teenagers grew, Robin assisted more with the youth group at her church. It was on a bike ride for middle schoolers that Robin met Ross. After they married, they spent the next two decades working together in youth ministry. God blessed them with a son and then a daughter. When her children were young, Robin would rise at 3 a.m. when the house was quiet, make a pot of tea, and write pages and pages about Christy and Todd. She then read those pages to the girls in the youth group, and they gave her advice on what needed to be changed. It took two years and ten rejections before *Summer Promise* was accepted for publication. Since its release in 1988, *Summer Promise* along with the rest of the Christy Miller and Sierra Jensen series have sold over 2.3 million copies and can be found in a dozen translations all over the world.

Now that her children are grown and Robin's husband has a new career as a counselor, Robin continues to travel and tell stories about best friends and God-lovers. Her popular Glenbrooke series tracks the love stories of some of Christy Miller's friends. Her books *Gentle Passages* and *The Fine China Plate* are dearly appreciated by mothers everywhere. Robin's bestselling Sisterchicks novels hatched a whole trend of lighthearted books about friendship and midlife adventures. Who knows what stories she'll write next?

You are warmly invited to visit Robin's websites at: www.robingunn.com and www.sisterchicks.com. And to all the Peculiar Treasures everywhere, Robin sends you an invisible Philippians 1:7 coconut and says, "I hold you in my heart."